A Soul Forgotten

A Soul Saga

Raquel Gabrielle

Dark Storm LLC

ISBN: 978-1-958970-06-5

eBook ISBN: 978-1-958970-05-8

Also By Raquel Gabrielle

A Soul Saga Novel:
A Hollow Soul
A Soul Forgotten
A Soul Remembered (Coming Soon)

There are many paths in life and you may not understand that path till further down it, but there is a reason for the chaos.

Chapter 1

"I HAVE TO GO back! I have to find answers at that house." Startling myself as the silent room engulfs me. I get up to pace the length near my bed. "It is where they lived. It has to hold something." These walls are driving me crazy. I look around the posh room I have stayed in for the past week with little movement. Blaise is still missing; Shade is still out there, and I am no closer to finding them or doing anything other than train.

My foot catches on the blanket spilling over the side of the bed. Feeling my face it is warm, I stomp back to the door after kicking it further under the bed. "I'm healed now... I promised Quintan and Natasha I wouldn't run off again." I mumble under my breath as I switch back away from the door.

Sweat runs down my brow as I move back and forth across the room in quick succession. "I'm just going to go find them and talk with them." I shrug, moving toward the doorway, my mind made up.

The doorknob feels hot under my touch, my grip tightens, and I feel the metal soften and bend. Twisting the knob quickly, I open it before it is fully melts. Blowing on my palm, I try to cool the heat pooling out of my hand.

"Lexi?" Trill, the oldest fire sister, says groggily as if waking up from a deep sleep.

"I'm sorry. I didn't mean to call on you. I'm still trying to get the hang of this. Go back to sleep," I whisper.

I have two fire spirits with me and still do not know how to properly call them or their power.

"Natasha said you should try meditation to help calm the chaos," Trill whispers softly as if she were trying to keep it down for her other sister.

"You would think I would have something down after all this reading and training I have been doing." I peek out of my room to see if anyone is nearby. "Shade took not only my magic with him; he took my only source of protection. Now I am under house arrest because everyone is afraid to kill, upset, or trigger the savior or destroyer!" Clenching my fists tightly at my side. "They don't even know which one I am yet."

"They mean well. Margaret was the same way with us. She wanted to protect my sisters and me, but eventually, she let us make our own decisions. That is why we are here with you," Trill says, trying to cheer me up.

"Aren't you worried about your littlest sister? We don't know where Shade has taken her." I chew on my thumbnail as I pace the room.

"Taz, though she is young, she is the strongest of us all. She will be fine; she would not go with someone if they were truly evil." Her flame body rises out of my thumb in front of my face.

I come to a standstill and jerk my thumb away from my face. Her flame licks my face but does not burn or feel hot to the touch. She walks across my fingers as I move them to keep up with her steps.

"Would you know if Taz is in any trouble?"

"We can sense her and know that she is well. That is all we can tell, especially from this distance."

"You can feel her? Like a direction?" I ask.

Trill nods her head and skips around on the back of my hand.

"I have to tell the others. Perhaps with that knowledge, we can at least work on tracking Shade down." Cupping Trill in my other hand, keeping her safe with my quick movements, I race down the hallway.

Trill yawns and giggles to herself. "I am going to go rest some more. Those meetings they are in are always boring and, as Tina says all the time, we must be ready for action. Tina is so excited to go adventuring." Her voice fades as she melts back into my skin.

"Tina? Oh, yes, that's the middle sister." I glance at the walls as I pass pictures of Margaret and Robert. Some are them together; others are with other people. I pass them quickly, moving on to the library. That is where Quintan usually resides. It is the biggest room where they usually hold the meetings for the council.

The double doors are closed when I come up to them. I hear indistinct murmurs and a discussion going on inside. I lay my ear against the hard wooden doors, trying to listen to what is being discussed.

"How far along is her training? Can we trust her?" An elderly voice calls out. Murmurs follow each of them, talking over the next. The words were hard to make out from this distance.

I test the doorknob and find it unlocked. Pressing against the door, I slowly ease it open and peek my head around the door.

Quintan looks around, his eyes wide with shock as he sees me. "It's... Come in. Come in," he reiterates with a more confident voice.

Everyone in the room turns to look at me. Quintan is no longer the center of attention. All eyes land on me. I come around the door and let it close behind me. I rub my palms on the sides of my thighs as I walk closer to the group surrounding Quintan.

"Is this her?" The same elderly woman from before speaks up.

Quintan grunts as he moves forward, meeting me at the edge of the circle, his breathing choppy. "Yes, yes. This is Alexia." His thick fingers envelop my thin shoulder, bringing me into the circle with him.

Whispers erupt from multiple people in the crowd. I scan them counting eleven different people plus Quintan and me. I lean into Quintan, relying on him for the first time, unsure of this group and my place in it. These were not people I knew of. I didn't see Natasha or Margaret, let alone Zeek or Robert.

"Calm down! If you have questions, we will try to answer them. Otherwise, it is business as usual," he utters roughly, giving each person around the room intense eye contact.

I look up at his hulking form and am amazed at how he moves them and keeps them in line. I am glad I had him as an advisor, even if I didn't fully trust him. He had a way with people that I just didn't.

A dark-tanned woman comes forward, pulling all eyes to her. "How do you expect us to follow some long-lost princess when she has no clue what we do or have gone through? She doesn't even know how to use her powers." She brings the group back to the issue at hand.

Several nods and agreements wanting to know the same answers. A younger man comes forward. "What if she isn't fit to lead?"

"Does she even want to?" Another asks.

I look at both people before my eyes travel back to Quintan. My mouth opens, but no words come out. Quintan motions me forward, wanting me to talk to these people. Forcing me into speaking, I felt very uncomfortable. I could feel they already knew I did not have answers for them. My eyes slide left and right around the group, searching for what to say.

"Do you even know your own history, or even ours?" Another in the crowd interrupts before I can speak. Soon many voices are adding to the multitude of questions being thrown out.

I back up, bumping into Quintan's stomach, but he holds me there, not budging. I would have to turn and run or go through the crowd he brought me to the center of.

A sharp whistle pierces the crowd and causes them all to settle down and halt their excruciating questions. A tall man who wears a cowboy hat is the one who whistles for everyone's attention. "Let the little filly speak," he says.

My cheeks heat as all eyes fall on me once again, all deadly quiet, looking at me with questioning eyes and some tinged with hatred. Quintan squeezes my shoulder, urging me forward, away from him.

I try to picture what my parents would say if they were in my position. "I may..." My voice breaks. Coughing to clear my throat, I continue. "I may not know much about this world, but if you give me a chance to learn what I must. I think I can do everything to the standard you wish. I have some plans to help me get up to speed, and others are helping me gain that footing as well."

The woman with a hard, stern face speaks up again, her voice laced with age and grit. "Why does it have to be you? Why not have one of us take over to run things? Most of us have been running things while you were gone, anyway. We have years of practice."

Staring at Quintan, I flounder with what I should say. He picks up, answering the question. "We have gone over that before, and that is why the council was formed because neither side can trust if only one person is appointed. You, along with everyone else, know whoever in charge would have ulterior motives for their own side. The council helps keep things balanced." His gaze and body move away from me.

The woman steps back as other heads bob, agreeing with what Quintan said. This group alone proves how much things have stayed the same after all these years. They still are separate and not thinking things through for everyone involved. Quintan did have a way of capturing and guiding the council.

"I am the one born of both worlds." I raise my hand, stopping the questions before they are voiced. "Yes, I know I was taken by the light side, but know just because they had me caged does not sway me to either side. I mostly do not remember those years. I also strongly believe in what my parents were trying to accomplish here."

Quintan smiles. "Don't worry. This council is not going anywhere. She will need our help and our knowledge to help with things."

I nod in acceptance. "I don't plan to change things immediately, but I want to work with each of you to better understand. So I can help." I didn't want them to think they could keep me out of the council forever, but I needed a way to gain their trust.

Another woman who looks a little older than me steps forward and claps her hands together. "Who's to say if one of us could not lead?" She shrugs her dainty shoulders. "I think the better question that most of us want to know is, do you want to lead us? Are you ready for what that would require from you?"

I bite my lip and look at the cowboy that came to my aid earlier. He takes his hat off his head as he comes forward. "Do you not want to lead us? To be in charge of things?" He asks.

"Honestly?" I give a heavy sigh. My eyes roam the ceiling, trying to think of the consequences of telling them the truth or not.

The elder lady busts in. "We would prefer it youngin, we don't have time for childish games."

"No, I don't really want to be your leader," I state calmly. "At least not how it is right now. Arguing every point I am trying to make. It does not sound fun. I don't want to fight against people who distrust me so much. People who use the excuse that I am new to all of this are just keeping you from realizing that you wouldn't trust me even if I had grown up in this world and had powers to rely on. You respected my parents and what they fought for, but I do not deserve that respect. Which I understand. That is not to say I don't want to learn and think I can't do the job."

Voices erupt around me, some happy, others outraged that the person they were looking to for answers has given them nothing to work with. People yell names at Quintan. He comes up beside me and holds a hand out in front of me, blocking the crowd from squeezing in.

"Your parents would be outraged if they heard that." The elder lady bites out.

"They are not here, are they?" My mouth pinches with anger as I focus on her. "You asked for my honest opinion!" My voice booms above the chatter that is still happening around the room. "I was never taught how to rule a kingdom or even raised to; I didn't know the etiquette that I should know when dealing with groups such as this. Leadership is not my strong suit. I came in here originally to talk to Quintan." Motioning to him. "To see if we can go look at my parent's old place to see if I can find something there that would help me connect to them in this world. It was that or go searching for Shade or Blaise, which they have turned me down at every turn." My eyes twitch as they fight not to glare directly at Quintan.

Quintan coughs in answer. "We are not keeping you here. You sound as if you are a prisoner."

"That is what it feels like. I understand you want me to wait to go over to the dark side to find Shade and Blaise, but why? Why are we waiting? Shade took my magic; I am not just going to get that back miraculously."

Some of the group gasps in astonishment.

"This is not the time or place for this conversation." Quintan hisses under his breath, hurrying back to me.

My eyes return to the group. "My way might be different, but perhaps that difference is good, and if given a chance, we can change things for the better. Isn't that what we all deserve, a chance?" I say proudly, bringing it back to the main point.

The cowboy smiles, liking what he hears. The young, strong-looking female gives a calculated grin but nods in acceptance. "Perhaps, darling, I could help you there with the dark side, that is." She laughs.

Quintan blusters. "But we are not ready. We wouldn't even know where to start."

Smiling, I bounce on the tips of my toes. "I have a thought about that. Trill, one of the fire sisters I carry with me." I explain, unsure if Quintan has brought them up to speed on what I can do. "She can feel her sister, Taz. Since Shade holds Taz, we can follow Trill's guidance to lead us to them."

Quintan steps in front of me, halting things. "Alexia, do you think this is the best time to discuss this right now?" He reiterates between clenched teeth. "These are the people designated as leaders. Charles over there." He points to the cowboy. "Is in charge of the animals around here. Most of who we have in attendance help us patrol the lands we hold or keep the others safe. Greta is the loudest and most resilient here." He motions to the older lady that has sat down after standing for so long. She waves, not afraid of being called out. "She is our herbalist and healer."

"And I am the most important person who will help you with the dark side." The young woman comes forward, extending her hand to me. "My name is Jazmin. I am a necromancer, among some other skills." She smirks.

I shake her hand, excited that she was on board with helping me and getting the ball rolling with Quintan. "Nice to meet you."

"I hope you don't let Quintan boss you around as he does us." She gives him a sly look.

He puts his hands on his hips. "What I do is for the safety of Alexia."

"Boring!" she says. "What I call it is stifling." She stretches as she sways around the room. Her long purple dress moves with her, making her look very hypnotic.

Covering my mouth, I hide a chuckle. "Jazmin is right. This place is making me crazy being stuck here. I know it's best for me since the last time didn't go so well, but I will be careful. If not to the dark side, at least let me go back to my parents' house. So, I can look through things. I'll even take Natasha with," I add.

"A child herself." Quintan grumbles. "Robert!" He yells out. "Come out here."

A moment goes by, and then I hear a sound behind a cubicle that was on the other side of the room. He stands up and takes his time getting over to our group. "I said I would sit in on these meetings, but unless it is an actual battle or fight, I don't care to be a part of it."

"Yes, yes." Quintan says. "Will you go with Natasha and Alexia to the old kingdom again and monitor them? Make sure they stay out of trouble this time? You are the head of security detail for this town. If not, please put someone competent in charge." He looks out the window. "Today is getting too late. I suggest getting a start first thing in the morning." His eyes flicker to mine. "Will this suffice until I can get with Jazmin and come up with a battle and travel plan?"

Robert gives a harrumph noise and moves back into his corner in answer. He keeps his eyes trained on the group, keeping them all in his peripheral and having the best vantage point on them. Though he opens his home to these people, he doesn't seem to trust them too much.

"Not always much of a talker, that one." Charles makes the excuse for Robert.

"Or he doesn't enjoy being told what to do as much as I do." I hear a low chuckle back from his corner. "That's okay, though." I turn back to Quintan. "Yes, that will do. I just need something to do. I am glad you understand that."

Quintan claps his hands together. "Well, it seems like everything is set. If there are no other questions, then Alexia, you should be off to get some rest or talk with Natasha about your plans for tomorrow." He turns back to the crowd, stops, and eases back. "Unless you would like to stay for the rest of this meeting?"

"Don't be cruel, Quintan. The poor woman has suffered enough." Jazmin whispers next to me behind her hand. "Leave now while you have an excuse to. We will be here for another handful of hours. Be glad you are not a part of these yet."

"You are incorrigible, Jazmin," Quintan says.

"Yes, it is one of my many charming traits and why I am so adored." She places a hand on her own cheek, gushing in excitement.

I hesitate, half expecting others to ask me questions or someone to say something demanding my time. "I think I will pass on this meeting. This was a good meet and greet, but I would be more of a hinderance than helpful until I have more time with each of you and learn more about this world." I walk slowly back towards the doors.

I wondered why Natasha was not a part of these meetings. She was my advisor as well. I would have to ask her about that. Though we were both young compared to some people here, we still deserve to have our voices heard.

Walking forward, I stop at the doors and turn the handle, opening it up just a sliver. "I have one last question before I go," I speak up.

Quintan nods and waits for me to ask my question.

"You all seem to know what I am and even what I can do. When will I learn the same information from each of you? I know many of you wear glamor here to some extent. I would like to know the true people that I am working with," I say. "I should not be the only one to be judged here, don't you think?"

"I like her," Jazmin croons. "We will meet later. I promise, perhaps, when you get back from your old kingdom. Then perhaps you can meet with Greta or Charles. Those crones won't know what hit them." She twiddles her fingers at them. "It will be nice not to be the only one to cause chaos here. These people need to wake up."

I give a wide smile and walk out, thumping the doors closed behind me. Though Jazmin is a wild card, she seemed like the best one to start with since she was being so friendly.

I find Natasha in her room. "Hiding out from Zeek still?" I knock as I come in, seeing her hunched over her desk, scribbling furiously over the pages.

She looks up. "No. I just didn't feel like being in Quintan's meeting."

"I was going to ask that. Why weren't you at Quintan's meeting?"

"There are better things to do than waste away in those things. They never make up their mind, and you just come out of them with more questions and nothing solved." She flicks the pen against her lips before scribbling something down in the notebook she was writing in.

"Yea, I met the group. I went to find you or him to see about doing something instead of being stuck here." I plop down on her bed, kicking my feet up, so I scoot further up, letting my feet hang over. "That was a doozy. Most of those people hate me for one reason or another."

She laughs. "They would hate you regardless of what you did. You can't make everyone happy. Might as well do what you want."

"Except when it goes against what you want."

"Duh, I am glad you are keeping up." She grins.

"So tomorrow morning, we will leave with Robert to check out my parent's old kingdom. I feel like there is something there that is calling to me. Some information I need to learn. It will give Quintan time to meet with Jazmin and whoever he needs to, to plan a trip to the dark side of this world and either find Shade or Blaise. Hopefully, both." I kick my feet in time with my nervous energy.

Her hand stops writing, and she turns slowly to me. "And where Robert goes, Zeek might be as well. Ugh."

"If you don't want to be around him, why do you stick around? Why not just leave?" I ask, unsure why she put up with the constant dodging when she could just go.

"I don't hate him. I just…" She sighs, places the pen in the book, and turns the chair towards me to better talk with me. "It's difficult for me to feel or express anything to do with love. I know what it can do to people. I would rather not deal with this at this point in time. Though I am mean and growl at him, I also like doing it."

"Wow." I lean back in amazement at all that she has shared.

"Fucked up, isn't it?" Her head falls forward, but I feel her eyes gaze up at me behind the curtain of hair that falls forward. She moves her blue hair out of her eyes, waiting.

"Not exactly." I think over things for a moment. "Maybe he just wants a friend. Have you talked to him about this?"

"You were there for that kiss." She shakes her head. "There was a lot more to that than a business transaction or friendship. He is not just wanting to be friends."

"You could always have fun and leave afterward."

"I guess." She rubs at her blue skin, fidgeting.

"But you don't really want to do that, do you?"

She shakes her head in answer.

"Let's, let that sink in for a moment. Maybe he won't even be there tomorrow. If he is, we can plan something else from there." I move forward on the bed. "I have some other questions from the meeting I just witnessed."

"A much easier subject. What kind of questions?"

"I know we have talked about glamor, but I want to understand it a bit more." I wave a hand in the air. "I know it is based on tradition, and most just find it easier to wear the glamor. But why not let it free once in a while?"

"Most are human looking in some way, so not all are wearing a cover. Others that are long-lived want to hide their true identity. We have some that are shifters, and they were always viewed as out of control if they let their animal free. We have embraced more acceptance toward other wild-looking creatures."

"But it is like they are lying to themselves."

"So?" she asks. "Don't humans do the very thing with makeup?" Natasha's eyes go dark in answer. "I only reveal my true self with people I am close to and trust." She gives a firm nod of her head.

"I think it should change."

"Okay, let me fire something back at you." She points at me. "You would have us in our true forms. Is that correct?" I nod in answer, but she knows very well that is what I meant. "Okay, to that effect, every person would have to show what kind of power they had. It would either be an all-out brawl because most do not take well to a visual threat. Another option is that some cannot change well, such as you. Would that separate you from the others because you do not have control yet? This could cause a worse separation than we are at already. Those are just a few thoughts you must remember when dealing with larger groups."

I swallow, trying to wet my dry mouth. "I could make this worse." My hands begin to shake. I run them instead through my loose, choppy hair. "I never thought that I could make things worse."

"A possibility is that you could be the destroyer of this world. But you could also save it, just like any other person." She gives a pointed look. "Start with small things. Work your way up from there."

"I did say I wanted to get to know each council member, starting with Jazmin."

"That is a good choice, and it is okay to talk about your thoughts and where you see this going, but be open to objections and really hear them. Give them the freedom to make their decisions. Perhaps you will get them questioning things and trying things you suggest, just by curiosity alone."

Rubbing at my hand, I shake my head. "This is going to be a lot harder than I am thinking, isn't it?"

"Now you understand why I feel it is better to run away." She gives a smile. "If it doesn't catch up with you, you don't have to answer to it. Or be responsible."

"That can be a lonely way, though."

Natasha's smile drops to a frown. "It can be." She looks back at what she was writing.

"Would you rather keep hiding and running, always wondering if those around you really like you for you, or would you rather know those around you are people you can count on when it comes down to it?" I jump up off the bed and walk over to Natasha. I lean down and hug her tight before she can say anything. "It is okay to feel and let people in, and not just me."

She stiffens in my arms but then melts into the hug and brings her arms around me. The pressure was light and stiff.

"There you go." I loosen my hold and withdraw from her.

She smacks my arm with the tips of her fingers. "Hey, you were contemplating coming over to my side not too long ago."

"Stop scaring me with all these people looking up to me, and maybe I won't try to run off." I think for a moment. "And allow me to feel useful and as if I am getting something done. So, I don't sneak off and go looking for trouble."

"What did you think of the group?"

I walk backward back to the bed and lean against it, relaxing. "I was only introduced to Charles, Greta, and Jazmin. He didn't really go into detail on many others. Said Charles was in charge of the animals? Did he mean actual animals or shifter animals?"

"He is in charge of all the animals, meaning he helps with the livestock, trains hunting dogs, and helps shifters learn how to fight with their animal forms and use them effectively," she answers.

"Quintan also said Greta was a healer and Jazmin was a necro... necro..."

"Necromancer."

"Yea, that thing."

"It is an animator of dead things; she also has this cool pet skull. You should ask her about some time."

"A pet skull!" I ask in astonishment. "Why would anyone want a skull to have as a pet? Is it haunted?"

Natasha gives a shrug but looks back at her writing and gets distracted.

"I meant to ask this a while ago when I was first brought here." I sink into the comforter. "Robert was there before he was actually there with me in the cell. He was ghostly white in appearance and in the shape of a fox, but had five tails, I think."

"He is a kitsune. It's why you may hear me call him nine tails every once in a while."

"A kitsune? He said he was projecting his form but was still a way away. He couldn't interact with things physically and could only communicate and see what was happening. I am pretty sure he also had less than nine tails."

"It's a moniker from your world, actually. It's a play on words and funny. He hates it, which is even more entertaining for me."

"I thought he would be a death dealer like Zeek since they are brothers."

"Brothers in arms, maybe? He works with Zeek on a lot of cases. Robert's skill set is very valuable and keeps Zeek at the top of his game. Which helps provide for his own family and this entire village."

"If you want, I can find Robert in the morning and see who is coming with us if it is just us three. I can see if we can take anyone else other than Zeek."

"No, don't bother. Robert would love to know a way to torment me, and if he knew it bothered me, he would ensure that Zeek was there no matter what." She gives sad eyes. "So please do not interfere."

"Okay, if, you're sure." I rise to my full height. "We should probably get some rest since he said we would be starting very early in the morning. I am thinking before the sun has even risen in the sky."

"It's a good couple of hours' ride by horse, so I understand if he wants to get there early to get back in plenty of time. That way, you also have enough time to look through rocks and rubble. What are you hoping to find out there?" I shrug. "We have all been through that place. It has to be picked over by now. If any dare to go there in the first place for fear of being attacked."

I rub my arm, missing Shade's fluttering that he used to do to let me know I wasn't alone. "I need a connection, something to know them by. I want something personal. I feel something tugging me that way more so than to Blaise or Shade, so you have to know how important this is to me."

"We do. We will go and see what we can find."

I nod, feeling at ease and better now that I am being heard. "Have a good night."

"Night."

I find myself wandering the halls, moving about them in no logical way as I work through thoughts spinning in my mind. Calming my mind down to get some sleep when I get back to my room.

Chapter 2

"UP AND AT-UM!" A voice booms into my ear.

I turn away from the loud voice and wiggle deeper into the blankets.

"You think I would tire of this?" She tears off the blankets. "But I don't."

"Why are you always up at a god-awful time?"

"Part of being Fae, remember?" Natasha grabs the pillow off my head. "I sleep in intervals. Four hours at a time. Knew this would be more difficult for you than it would be for me."

"Yea, yea." I wave her away. She walks out, letting me get myself together. A little while later, we walk down to the stables together.

"Hey, Robert," I mumble as we come closer.

"Nine tails," Natasha responds with too much cheer for how early it is.

He frowns in answer. Deciding to ignore her. "Let's get the horses moving. We will meet up with Jason halfway to your parent's kingdom."

I nod, not really paying attention, my eyes wanting to drop. It is a struggle to keep them open. "Who is Jason?"

"He helps me with running surveillance around this place and keeping the people safe around here."

Natasha whispers behind her hand, near my ear. "He's an actual dragon." She waggles her eyebrows. "A dragon shifter."

My eyes bug out, and I perk up. "He's a what? Those exist!"

"Natasha!" Robert berates.

"What? She would have asked eventually."

"To be fair, I would have." I raise a finger, letting him know she is right. "So he is like a dragon, dragon wings and all?"

Robert brings Gem and Lucky out of their stables, walking them out into the dewy morning air. "Yes, but he can transform into that of a man as well."

"How does that make good surveillance? You are either an enormous dragon, easily seen or just a human."

"He has a secret third form." Natasha whispers again and sticks her tongue out at Robert's retreating form. "He can turn into like a wisp of wind, little tendrils of mist." She walks slowly toward Roberts' retreating form.

"That sounds interesting. Will we see him in his dragon form?" I ask, following behind.

"If you're lucky." She laughs, twitching over to a stable to the left of the opening and where Robert is with Gem and Lucky.

Lucky's head pulls up to look at Natasha when she says his name, but he soon puts his head back down, nibbling at the grass after she doesn't look at him or call him again. I watch Natasha as she walks over to pat the nose of a blonde horse.

"Who do we have here?"

"This is Powder. She is such a good girl!" Natasha coos and pats the front of Powder's nose. She whinnies in answer. Natasha pulls open the barn door and takes her out. "This one is mine," she calls out.

"Did you have a horse stashed here? How did you know we would come here?"

She shakes her head. "No, no, no, silly, this isn't my horse. I haven't been to this section of woods before. Margaret told me about another of her horses that she recommended. She has a couple in here, and so does Robert. Though he likes that big brute, he calls a horse." She glares at Lucky, who ignores her.

I walk over to Gem, ready to get on the horse, hopefully, better this time. I crouch down and stretch before getting back in the saddle. Last time I felt the aches and pains for many days after traveling.

Robert holds the horse steady, waiting before mounting his own horse. He comes around to my side just in case I need his help. He holds the stirrup out as I kick up my leg and hop closer. I push off the ground with my shoe and yank myself up into the seat. My arms shake only a bit. The fighting and training have helped me gain muscle that I didn't have before.

"That was a lot better than last time." Robert pats Gem and crouches in front of her to get to Lucky.

This time we take a path toward the old kingdom instead of hiking and maneuvering around in the woods. The trek was much smoother, not sticking to the shadows. Robert sticks to guiding us forward, but every once in a while, he races ahead to check out things. He keeps his eyes alert. I lean against Gem's neck and doze on the trip there. Since there was a path, she needed only a little leading, so my eyes grow heavy, and I keep slipping off into dreamland.

I slept little last night between twisting, turning, and thinking about what I could find that no one else had. I couldn't connect with Blaise like I did last time. What if it was Tom who orchestrated everything with Blaise? What if Blaise wants nothing to do with me? What if we aren't actually mates? Aren't actually supposed to be together? A shiver runs up my spine as I think of that and cringe, trying to think of something else other than that thought.

Natasha looks chipper than usual, probably because Zeek was not around to pester her, so she felt like she could be at ease. I hope she will stick around; I need her. She is the only one that doesn't force me to be someone I'm not.

"There you are, Jason!" Robert calls out up ahead. "I knew you had to be somewhere close by."

I look around and don't see anyone. I look up, expecting to see a giant dragon, and there is none to be had. A breeze stirs the hairs that have come undone from my ponytail. I shriek as I feel something cold come across my arm.

Robert laughs. "You might want to switch forms." A man materializes halfway between Robert and me.

"This better?" He holds up his arms. He is in comfortable pants and a shirt that hugs his body. His clothes are dark. "This one is a bit jumpy," he says with a bit of a twang in his voice.

"You could have made some noise or not just materialized out of nothing." I gasp, trying to calm my racing heart.

Gem dances around on the trail as she feels my nervous energy.

"If I weren't sneaky and silent, I wouldn't be a very good guard, now, would I?" Jason gruffs in reply. "Though I can't get anything by that kitsune over here."

Robert smiles widely. I give a confused look. "Why could you sense him? How could you sense him?"

"Like Zeek, I see multiple plains of existence, which include his." He nods towards Jason. "Have you seen anything hanging around the old place?"

"Nah. They have vacated the place and haven't been back since." He kicks at the dirt on the path.

"Where're the others?"

"Around. They are running the perimeter and keeping me updated if anything is amiss."

"That's good. Well, on our way back, we will meet you part of the way to rest and meet with the others. It will be dark, and these ones will probably be starving by then."

"We have names!" Natasha snarks.

Robert rolls his eyes but motions to us all the same. "This one is Natasha; she will be a pain in the ass any chance she gets. This one is."

"Alexia," Jason finishes for Robert.

"Yep, that is correct." Robert nods.

"The whole town is a buzz about you. I wouldn't be surprised if other neighboring towns have also caught wind of the news. We don't get a lot of news out this way, let alone this. Your glorious return."

"You make me sound epic," I say.

"To some, it is." He nods. Robert glares at him as Jason kicks the dirt path once again. "Well, I will keep an eye out for you. We will see you later tonight then, Captain."

"Good," Robert says with finality.

Jason wanders off of the path and disappears.

"You didn't have to be so harsh with him," I complain. I watch him disappear from view as the trees swallow him. I trail behind Natasha and Robert.

"He is young. The harshness is good for him," he says.

"You seemed lighter and not as harsh as Zeek would be," I say, barely a whisper.

Robert pulls up on the reins and stops Lucky, waiting for me to catch up. "I am in charge of these people's lives. If I make a wrong call or let the younger ones ease off duty, they or their friends and family could die because of it. I would not wish that on my worst enemies, that guilt can bring a person down."

"You speak as if you have lived that path." I continue on by not wanting to stop and have this conversation.

"It is a path that is too well-traveled in some instances." He pushes Lucky forward, trailing behind us and looking where Jason disappeared.

We continue for many hours until we come across a large hill, which I remember quite clearly. "We are here, aren't we!" Gem trots happily forwards. I kick my feet lightly so she moves into a jog, pushing past Natasha.

"You remember?"

"Yea, you said this is a big hill, but the other side is an enormous cliff."

"Right, right." He rubs the back of his neck as the sun peeks through the harsh greenery and the heat is sweltering.

I fan in front of me, trying to keep bugs and other critters at bay. The heat is not helping anyone around here. Though the trees provide shade, the warmth is not letting up.

Natasha moves past, not stopping at all. "I bet you guys wish you had my power now." She sits up tall. Sweat does not roll down her face like it does us.

"Why aren't you miserable like the rest of us?" I ask.

"My powers help me stay at a comfortable temperature. In cold and heat. Hotter temperatures can keep me cooler as long as I stay hydrated." She grabs from a pack that is on the back of her saddle and pulls out a large water bottle. Guzzling the water down.

Robert rushes ahead to the top of the hill, and we are still halfway up the large hill. I nudge Gem into a faster run, passing by Natasha while she is still drinking. I knock a hand on her back as I pass her. "Race you to the top!"

Natasha coughs a bunch. "You cheat," she says as she fiddles with putting it away. She trails behind, unable to catch up before I reach the top.

"I win."

"Of course, you win. You cheated." She glares. "I could have slowed you down with my powers to beat you."

"Shoulda, coulda, woulda."

"Though there have been no sightings of anyone around here, do you two want to keep it down just in case?" Robert says in a low voice.

"Always ruining the fun," Natasha calls out.

I move past, making my way over to a house that sits close to the woods. Trees surround the few houses that were out this far. All words and fun leave me as I take my first proper look at what this place is. Nothing was left untouched. It all has fallen and been left to rubble. The only house that has parts of it still standing was the main one on the cliff. "Our destination."

The other houses are bare, and you can only see an outline of what used to be. The vegetation has taken over and started growing around the structures. I lean over Gem and call her to a stop as I swing over my leg and slide down her side to the ground. My legs feel weak as I crouch low on the ground. I slowly stretch my legs out and stand fully, patting Gem's neck; my feet move towards the towering house at the back. My eyes taking in the view along with darting from side to side. Wondering which part of the house I would go through first.

Robert and Natasha exchange pleasantries, but their words drop off as I continue down the way. Their words lose form and are just noises I can't make out. After fixing my trajectory, I feel a pull to the left. I hop over the rock fencing that surrounds this place. My hands run through the tall prickly grass as it is up to my knees. The minor wind made it rustle against my legs. The sun beats down on my head as I make it to the side I need. There is a large hole in the side. I step inside. The sun fades away and I am greeted with dust and shadows.

"Do we have a flashlight or something?" I yell out.

A match is struck, and flames burst to life, framing Zeek's stern face.

"Zeek," I squeak.

He holds an old fashion lamp up and lights it with a ball of fire. He scoops out of one of his many hidden pockets. The light pools and lightens up the darkest corner that he hides in. "What took you guys so long?" His rough tone is low.

"I didn't know we were meeting you here. Why do you use that? Why not something that creates more light, like a flashlight?" I say as I pick my way closer to the light and search the debris.

"Flashlights are harsh on the eyes, especially when pointed directly at someone. They are also harder to adjust your eyesight back to normal night vision after the area is lit. We use torches and these lanterns, which is a lot easier on the eyes and those that need to keep hidden and careful."

Robert and Natasha come rushing through the hole in the wall. "What? What is it?"

"Nothing Zeek scared me. I didn't know we were meeting him here."

Natasha stops dead in her tracks, then glares at Robert before picking her way back out of the hole. "I will keep an eye out here."

Zeek watches her leave, his eyes worried. "You guys should have been here sooner. Did something stop you?" He places the lantern in front of him and pulls back into the shadows.

"No." Robert comes over to our dark corner. His eyes flit around the ceiling and doorways. "This area looks strong and stable enough. Jason stopped us about halfway to give a check-in. I told him we would stop by the camp on the way back."

Zeek nods, satisfied with the diversion.

"Also, these two like to bicker and argue back and forth. You keep a watch on both of them. I am going to go keep a true eye out." The last part, Robert calls out loudly so Natasha could hear him.

"Perhaps I should let Margaret know your opinion of our chat."

"You leave her out of this!" Robert growls as he makes his way back outside. "Do you need every woman to hate us men? I can make your life a lot worse. Just test me," he bites out as he continues to pass her. She is leaning against the side of the house. "Get off of that. You could cause the house to shift and be unstable." He stomps away.

She slides to the side and comes into the room again since two people do not need to keep watch. She moseys around the outside of the room, keeping as far as she can from Zeek.

"Why has the light or dark side not come back here to finish this place off? Or why don't they know of the village just down the way?"

"We have strong magic covering the village, along with people hunting and tracking, to ensure we are not found," Zeek answers. "We are also careful of this place, and so are others. Most think of this as a graveyard of sorts since so many perished here that night. They respect the place and want to let the ghosts have their peace or as much of it as they can."

"The place is said to be a very important dwelling for your parents. That is why they chose this area to build their kingdom," Natasha says in awe. "Most rogues try to honor your parents by protecting what was there's."

"Can I take that?" I point to the light. "It's the only way I will be able to see well. To find what is pulling me to this place."

Zeek nods. "That is why I brought it with me since I knew you could not still use your animal eyes on command." He nudges the lamp with the toe of his boot.

I grab it by the handle, pushing the light out in front of me. Trudging through the doorway into the next room, my eyes rove over the empty chamber. Rubble is the only thing that litters the floor.

I keep close to the wall to hear what Natasha and Zeek will talk about, making sure they don't kill each other or Natasha won't run away. This is also to understand why she detests him so much.

"Did she have any other messages or tricks for me?" Natasha's voice carries well to the other room since she was close.

"No," Zeek's voice is low, and further away, I struggle to hear him.

The silence between them stretches and becomes uncomfortable. I almost rush in there to break it myself but hold myself still. I keep searching through piles of rocks, making noise, so they think I'm not listening.

Natasha mutters something, but the rocks clatter and cover up her words. She has moves away from this wall, closer to Zeek.

"Why are you so horrible?" Zeek says.

"Have to be. You know more than anyone what this life can do to someone."

"Only if you let it."

"You don't get to call me horrible; you have been a part of the dark side. You have done things that are horrendous compared to me." Peeking around the wall, I see her pointing furiously into his chest. "You have done things on behalf of others so they could sleep better at night."

"I know who and what I am." Rocks shuffle as he moves. "Do you?"

"No," Natasha breathes out a sigh. "I know what I am," she says with more force.

"But do you know who you are, what you want from this world? What do you demand of it?" His voice is so very low.

I shuffle around, searching for a way to hear them better, wanting to keep with them. Soon, I would look through the house, and what I actually came here for. I needed to make sure Natasha would be all right. She was the only friend I had around here. I wasn't letting her go willingly just because Zeek wanted something more. Crouching behind a half wall crumbling across from them, I peek and see them facing one another; close together, I can see the sides of them easily, the sunlight still casting brightly, lighting them up.

"Stop," she whispers. He inches closer. "Please." Tears fall from her eyes.

He stops moving forward and really looks at her. "I will stop." He thumbs away the tears streaming down her cheeks. "I would not force you to do something you truly do not want."

"I can't play into their game." Her face is full of pain. "I can't play into any of their games."

"This is not a game." His hand darts out and grips her waist, pulling her into his cloak, and hiding them from view.

Her hands come up; she places them on his chest. I can only guess from the position they were in. Stopping her from coming any closer. "Why then?"

He takes a step back, taken aback by the statement. "Why what?"

"Why me? Why do you care? You don't even know me."

He looks above Natasha's head outside. "Those are not the answers you are searching for. How about a deal?"

She looks up at him with distrustful eyes. "What sort of deal? I don't much care for bargains."

"Even one that could get rid of me for good?"

"I could only be so lucky." She steps back out of his cloak and crosses her arms in front of her chest.

He smirks. "We will see. For this deal you give me... let's see." He leans back against some fallen rubble and thinks for a moment. "What is it Fae like to keep to? A year and a day, right?"

"Go on," she says.

"For a year and a day, you only call on me if you need companionship and we get to know one another during that time. If you still dislike how things are after that, I will leave you alone forever, and you won't hear from me. You can also ask me to go away if you need the space. You are in the driver's seat during this time."

"Sounds good on my side. What are the cons?"

"If the bond is at risk of failing." His dark eyes bore into her, forcing her to know what he is talking about without saying.

"If I go to someone else, yeah, yeah."

"Then the bond will force me not to stay away. But we have to converse with each other since you think we do not know one another enough."

"Converse how? If I want you to stay away." An eyebrow arches.

"Phone, in person, your choice." His lips turn up in a grin. "If you need me in person, all you need to say is Zeek, I need you." He flourishes his hand at his side. "And I will be there."

"You would like that, wouldn't you?" She glowers. "If I do this, you keep me out of all your past, present, and future deals. Other than this one and the one that just happened that I know of."

He hisses a bit as if he got hit with something. "Fine," he wheezes.

"No tricks or traps. You have to follow things to the letter, as I specify."

"Why do I feel you are going to make me pay?" He grounds out.

"You forgot who you are playing with. I know the specifications of a deal." She raises her head up, and even though he is taller than her, she can still look down her nose at him.

"I know who the players are. Do we have a deal?" He invades her space.

She thinks for a moment before her eyes fall on mine. She holds them there for a moment before looking away. Does she want me to continue to stay here and eavesdrop to have a witness to things?

"Yes, those terms are agreeable. One stipulation, though, you also can't stray through this endeavor."

"That is not a worry."

"You also will not lie to me throughout this entire time and cannot avoid a direct question. Otherwise, the bond will be null in void."

"I can agree to that as long as you don't ask questions about my job."

"Uh uh uh. No changing the agreement. Take it or leave it." He stares at her with intensity. "I promise not to ask questions with your work if it doesn't tie back to me. How about that?"

He clenches his teeth, thinking things over. "One other stipulation the conversation each day has to last an hour, and there has to be an active conversation."

"Ugh..." She breathes out a sigh. "Fine."

"We agree, then." Natasha nods. "Then we just need something to seal the deal." He gives a sly smile once again.

"No." Her eyes narrow in response.

"Yes. A kiss is required."

"No, it's not. You do not seal all your deals that way."

"That is true, but this is the way I want to seal this deal. Your other option is that you could hope I lose interest and leave on my own, or deal with me being around whenever." He shrugs, keeping back a bit, letting her come to her own decision.

"Why are you doing this? Why even want it this way?"

"Would you trust or do it otherwise?" He waits for her to shake her head. "Then this is the way it must be," he says.

She moves forward, his cloak encompassing her once again. Her hands snake around his neck and pull him down to her lips, smashing hers into his. He freezes for a moment, but it does not take long before his arms wrap around her, pulling her closer to him. He deepens the kiss, and she allows it to keep going.

Looking down at the floor, I ease back around the corner. "Well, there has to be something else I must do now," I whisper. There are rocks and wood that have fallen overtime. Not hearing much noise coming from the other room, I hope it will stay like that. I bring the light back up, trying to see if there is a way around this crumbling building. The primary way is open, but there is only a small opening to a room that the debris sits in front of. As I try to wiggle my way through, my foot gets caught between the rock and wood as which causes me to slip. I lower the lamp in the next room, which sits in darkness. The pool of light not reaching anything remarkable. I slide back out, freeing my foot, and maneuver carefully through the rubble.

I test the durability on the other side, ensuring the floor will hold since it doesn't look like anyone has been in this room since before the house crumbled. It holds. I bring the rest of my body and foot through the small hole. My foot catches and pitches me forward.

"Crap!" I puff out as my hands catch me, holding me in place. The house creaks and moans in complaint. I freeze, not wanting to disturb anything further.

I push up away from the ground and dust off my hands that were now covered.

"Lexi," a whisper pulls me to a stop.

"Hello?" I call out just as softly. I wait, expecting to hear Natasha or Zeek. "I am alright, guys, no need to worry, just searching in this room. It doesn't look like anyone has been in here."

I wait for a response. I look back out the hole. No one is standing there. "Natasha? Zeek? Did you guys call for me?"

"Lexi," another whisper comes from right behind me as something stirs the hairs at the back of my neck.

I freeze in place, not wanting to turn around and see something that will horrify me. "Where are you guys?" I call out a little louder, hoping to get someone's attention. Looking through the hole, I see only darkness.

Nothing, no noises or sounds answer me. Dark shadows creep in, attacking and dulling the light. Is the sun going down already? Did the sun disappear behind some cloud covering?

I take a few breaths and slowly turn my head, fully expecting something to be towering over me. I pull the light off the floor, extending my arm fully after noticing nothing was directly behind me. There were stacks and stacks of books with cushioned benches built into the walls to sit and read. There are papers strewn about, and an inch of dust covers everything. The room was large and went far back. There were rows and rows of books.

Making my way around the large room, the light only illuminates a small portion of it. My hand shakes as I step into the room, moving past the rows of books.

"Lexi," a voice calls from in front of me just beyond the light. I hear steps race away and something slamming to the ground. I jump and hide behind one bookshelf that was still upright. My breath puffs in and out. Looking down at the lamp, I crave to extinguish the light but am afraid I would not get it to turn back on, plus I didn't have a fireball handy. My legs knock together. I close my eyes, not wanting to hear or see any creepy creatures. The darkness was becoming a cruel mistress. My heart ached with the amount of loneliness I felt at this very moment.

"Stop," I whisper back, my voice and breath shaking. I hear no more noises or my name being called. I wait there for several minutes, not able to move.

"Come on, come on. I can do this." My teeth chatter.

I scoot the light out and look around the edge of the bookshelf. Glancing down the corridor, I don't see anything standing there. There is a board on the floor. The side panel must have fallen down from the bench. The light flashes and catches on something shiny. Something is sticking out as I look down. I walk a few steps further, making sure I can't see footsteps in the dust or see anyone hiding the next shelf down. I walk back, curious about what had caught my eye earlier.

Before kneeling, I set the light to the side closer to the entrance, but still gives me plenty of light to see.

"What do we have here?" I question as I bend down to sift through the cobwebs and pat at the large object. Bringing it out, I remove years of grime and dust just from disturbing it. The box is tarnished and silver. It would have been very shiny if not for all the grime and dust. "How could the light catch any of the shine on this thing?" I pry at the seam and pop open the lid to the box. It opens up easily, and a large book is inside the metal box. Crawling closer to the center of the light, I sit down with the book across my legs, the box I set beside me.

The book is thick and sturdy. I flip open to the first page and see feminine handwriting staring back at me. It scrawls across the page written at the top is dear diary. I quickly scan the page and see Sera's name signed at the bottom. I flip a few pages through and turn the book over, and scramble to see the last pages are empty. This book was filled with my mother's writing. I look back at the bench I had found this under and make sure there is nothing else hidden there.

I turn back to one page in the middle, needing to see what this is all about.

Dear Diary,

They signed the treaty papers today. My life is officially over and is no longer my own. The marriage will be soon. How can they expect him to marry someone he doesn't even know? My half-sister doesn't even like me, and only because I am half human and half witch am I unable to be a contender. Father says I will grow to understand one day and that it is best for both groups. The Shadow and Light groups have been at each other's throats since before I was born. We are no longer in ancient times. A prophecy was foretold that if the strongest from each side combined, a Savior would emerge. There is another foretelling, though, that explains a world destroyer. Who is to be believed? No one truly knows?

I didn't mean to fall in love with him. It just happened. He feels the same... or says he does. We should be free enough to be with who we want. We both should have a say in our own futures. People are hard to change after so many eons of war. My older half-sister seems fine with it all. Even though she despises him, she understands her place in things. That is what father is always saying to me, to corral me in place. She says it is our duty and must be done to better the world's future. We must be the beholders of change. She thinks I am just young and dumb for wanting to follow my heart.

That's fine with me!!! It's okay if she is fine with not marrying for love, but she is not me, and I need that in my life. I refuse to bow down for this. I will speak to Ivan and possibly Flit; his father must know something we can do. He is the true ruler of the dark side. No one would deny him. I just have to find a way to talk him into this. They will be here soon to make plans and pick a date. Part of me is sick to my stomach with worry. Another part of me wants to just run and never stop, only if Ivan would come with, though.

Great, now I have depressed myself and don't want to continue writing. Hopefully, I can find a way out of this chaos.

Life sucks, and then we must continue on,

Sera

I reread the entry, ingraining each sentence into my mind. My eyes fill with tears as I caress the thin pages. I shut the dusty diary, looking at the box and finding a note at the bottom that says, "You will know when you need this. Love Mom."

I crumple the small note in my fist and let fresh tears run down my face. There has to be more hidden around here. This couldn't be the only thing pulling me here the whole time. I hold the book to my chest and squeeze it tightly, not wanting to get up or ever leave until I have finished it all. It was a very large book and covered in writing. This would take me a while to get through.

CHAPTER 3

Something brushes against my shoulder. My face is down and hidden in my arms as I sob. Startling from my position, I bring my head up quickly.

"Whoa, what are you doing? What did you find?" Natasha steps back quickly.

"Where did you come from?" I ask, looking around the quiet room.

"We heard you sobbing and came to check on you. Zeek couldn't fit into this room through the small opening, so I came to see what was happening." She looks back towards the scar in the wall. She steps closer, so she is in full view of the hole, and waves a hand. "We are fine to go ahead and look around out there. I will call out if we need you."

"You guys didn't hear me yell out earlier?"

Her cheeks burn red. "No, we were preoccupied. Though I don't doubt you did that with all the ghosts that tread through these dusty rooms."

"Like actual ghosts." I keep my arms around my knees, unsure of what a ghost could do.

"There could be," she shrugs. "What did you find there?" She stares at the box next to me.

"That piece of wood fell, and I found this hidden inside." I point to the hidden nook under the bench where the wooden board was still in front of me. "The metal box contained this journal, or diary, from my mother." Unwrapping my arms from around my legs, I show her the large book I still have huddled in my center.

Her hands reach for it, but I pull it back, covering it.

"Can I see it?" She cocks her head.

"Umm." I look between the book and her.

She gives me a questioning look.

I sigh. "Here, let me show you. I have only scanned some of the pages and this note." I shove the crumpled letter that I still have grasped in my hand. "That was under the journal."

She smooths it and reads the same note I did as I open the journal slowly and carefully. "This was meant for you. Or seems like it."

"It has to be! Right?"

"I think so." She hands me back the flattened note. Sitting beside me to look at the pages. "These are so frail."

"That is why I don't want anyone else reading these until I have time to go through and devour the knowledge. This is my only connection to her." My fingers grip the book. It digs into my skin, and my fingers turn white with the pressure.

Once we flip through a few pages, I raise the box up so that I can put it away. "Let's keep looking around. Make sure there isn't anything else we should bring back with us. Might be a little while until we can come back here. If Jazmin gets her way, we will leave sooner rather than later."

I place the note and the journal back in the box and cover it up, tucking it in my arms, keeping it safe. Natasha grabs the lamp and looks around the row of books.

"There has to be a reason I was pulled here and found this? Did my mother have foresight? Or any powers other than vine magic?" I ask quickly, my mouth hardly able to keep shut.

"I don't have those answers. I know she is a strong magic user with the earth element. Other than that, Quintan or the council would be better to ask. They were the elite members and started this whole movement with your parents, to begin with. They had to be close to them."

I comb the halls of books and shelves, searching for anything of use. I find a satchel and test its sturdiness of it. Placing the dusty box inside, I sling it across my body. Natasha pulls some books and papers free, taking them with her. I look at the titles. Some are in an unfamiliar language, and others talk about things I don't yet understand.

We make our way back through the hole a couple of moments later. Zeek is on the other side, still rummaging through things. He has moved deeper into the house. We follow him down the hallway. I want to see more.

"Where is the dungeon they kept me in?" I ask.

"Those are heavily damaged and on the other side of this place. There is nothing much there other than the cells that have been long forgotten," Zeek answers.

It's not like I really wanted to go there, anyway. I wasn't ready to relive that part, and I didn't want to stir up those memories and feel that anger and pain yet. "What about a great hall or a room where thrones would be?" I ask, unsure of what to call it. My memories had only shown me two rooms. The need to see these rooms in person was boiling up inside me. I needed to see if they stirred something up in my memories.

"Yes, that is close by. This way." He leads.

We follow behind. Zeek went first, followed by Natasha and me. The beams and ceiling had crashed down in places. Chunks were missing from the walls and floors. The second floor was caving in at spots as we made our way through the debris. Most of the hallway was intact and held steady. We come to a main room, and to the right is a staircase leading to the upper floors. The stairs were in disarray and didn't look stable.

"Please tell me we don't have to go up there." I stop at the bottom of the steps.

"Only if you have wings or climbing gear," Natasha says as she brings her wings out. She flutters and stretches them as if they have been resting for a while. She flies up over the crater that is in the middle. There is a sizeable gap between the top of the stairs and the bottom.

"The room you are looking for is this way." Zeek calls our attention in the opposite way, away from the broken stairs.

Natasha flies past me, zooming down the hallway where Zeek is heading. She stalks down the hallway, darting into the rooms to check them out, and then moves on to the next one. I watch her for a moment, then follow behind.

"What are you searching for?" Zeek asks.

My eyes slide to him as he waits on my fumbling. "I could ask you the same thing."

"I already explained what I am searching for. I don't enjoy repeating myself." He eases back, letting me go forward.

"I'm sorry. You are just trying to be helpful. I just don't know how to process all these emotions at once. Something is pulling me here, but I only have one memory of my past from this place. I wanted to see it in person, feel it maybe shake something loose." My teeth worry at my lip, biting the skin there. "I was hoping for more answers than questions this time."

Wind curls around me and pushes me toward a room that Natasha disappeared into. I look at him, making sure it was safe to follow. His hands come out, feeling the wind in front of him. He looks around the hallway and checks the shadows. "Go on. I will check this out." He walks into the shadows, and they cover him completely. He is there one moment and gone the next.

I jog my way into the room, seeing Natasha sitting perched on one throne. "Imagine me ruling. Lick my boot, you sniveling weasel!" She calls out.

Leaves and rocks roll as I slow to a walk, seeing the thrones up close and real. They are toppled over and banged up, but both are in one piece as if they were made of something unbreakable.

"We would all be in danger if you were in charge." I chuckle.

She rolls her eyes. "Not too much danger, only if everyone pissed me off."

"And how does one not go about pissing you off?"

"Showering me with attention, but not too much. Not in like a creepy way. Wait on me hand and foot and do my bidding as I ask."

"And you don't see a problem with that?"

"Nope." She stomps one of her boots on the ground as she stands. She places her hands on her hips. "Don't I deserve good things to happen in my life? I should have people fawn over me; I should get what I want."

"You deserve good things, same as I do. But do you really want someone that dedicated to you? Don't act like you wouldn't run away the first chance you got."

"Only if it got too serious."

"What are you going to do with that one?" I point behind me with my chin and motion with my eyes.

"Beat him at his own game. Or try to."

"Careful with that."

"I have an entire year to figure things out. I'm not in a hurry. Maybe it's time to stop running." She shows a part of herself that not all get to see. Her eyes become weary, and her shoulders slump. "I am so tired. So tired of the games and having to watch out for all the knives coming at my back."

"You have me. You're not running away from me yet. So, there is that."

"Only because you're so innocent and new to this world that I don't even think you would know how to play the types of games going on here. When you first came here, you were naïve and knew almost nothing. I knew it was either the biggest ploy I have come across or you were that blind to this world."

I walk up to her and, careful of her wings, wrap my arms around her, hugging her close. "I am only letting you get away with calling me naïve because I feel your pain."

"Stop, you will give me hives." She rolls her neck and backs away. "Keep that up, and you will see me running away. I don't do hugs."

"Keep it fun and lewd, and you won't run. Show some actual emotion or care, and she runs the other way. Got my Natasha directions now," I say it louder than I was speaking previously, hoping

Zeek was around and hidden in shadows, where he could still hear what we were talking about.

I run my hand across the chairs, feeling them and making them more solid in my mind.

"Is this their throne room? Wasn't there a room behind somewhere that you told me about? I can't recall it too well. You were talking pretty fast and with your hands a lot," Natasha asks.

"Yea." My mouth is parched. Behind the thrones, there is a bit of space and then dirty, ripped curtains in disarray. The room beyond is caved in, and rubble has blocked the way forward. "No," I cry out in anguish. Racing to the busted doors. Rocks and broken wood lay packed tightly, with no small place to fit through. I bang my hands against the rocks. "Why?" There had to be something there.

It's where they had kept me protected. I scrabble at the rocks to move one to see if there was any wiggle room through. The house groans in answer and the clutter rumbles, causing other stuff to move over our heads.

"Alexia don't! You need to stop. This place is not stable and if you move too many, it will cause things to shift and could cover more area up." Natasha flits around, dodging small rocks that shake loose from the ceiling.

"What if something is back there?" I cry out. The skin on my palm scrapes when I rub my hand against the sharp rocks. I kneel and hold my hand to me, moving back and forth, feeling anguish run through me. "It could have been another piece to the puzzle."

"Come over here, Alexia. Come away from there." Natasha dashes forward, grabbing at my good hand.

I follow her. She raises the thorny chair up since it is the least banged up. She urges me to sit. The rumbling and dust settle.

I sit down slowly, not wanting to sit on thorns. The cushions have long since been eaten by vermin and bugs. Though there was a bit of stuffing, not enough to keep the thorns from poking. My roughened hand catches on the thorns, slicing through the first couple of layers of skin.

I stare at the blood that wells up out of my hand. I dab my palms against at my pant leg, holding it there to staunch the flow. The wind kicks up once more. Causing the house to groan in answer all by itself. The shadows elongate, and the light diminishes. Natasha has gone over to the rocks I had messed with earlier to ensure nothing else stirs.

The walls move in and out as if they were breathing. My breath comes out slowly. "What is this?" I ask, but my tongue barely feels as if it can move.

"What did you say?" Natasha asks, but it sounds warbled and far away.

My tongue and mouth are still dry, no matter how often I try to wet my lips. My eyes droop down. I try to shake my head to clear it, but the room begins to spin.

Water surrounds me. My hands scrabble for purchase, but there is none. The water crushes me. My body fights to get free and breathe in the cold, fresh air. I had to let the air go and breath in. Cool water pours in as I open my mouth to breathe. The coolness dashes the fire in my lungs. I try to swallow the water instead of breathing it in but end up choking. My limbs become heavy; my movements slow. Someone grabs at me harshly whisks up out of the water. The water is in my throat and lungs, which makes me cough. In between the coughing, I gasp, heaving breaths of sweet oxygen.

"Worm, you work for me!" A voice says beyond. I can't see who it is, but their voice is mesmerizing, her voice feminine and sweet. Sickly sweet.

"I know," a gruff voice answers.

The voice comes from behind or below me. I try to look around, but my eyes stare forward and on the floor. What is going on? I try to ask, but no words come from me.

"Your job there was finished. Now you have another job and are what? Saying no? Did you not want to pay off your debt to me?" Her voice is almost musical, calling her prey to her.

"I do. Just not this way." His voice still comes out rough.

Is this Blaise? I look down at myself and see powerful arms covered in scales. Did he know I could see or hear this? Did he know I was here?

"You have before."

"That was before. It's different now." His voice sounds dejected, almost lost.

"What power does she have on you? If she affects you this much, then she affects my business. I kill what hurts my business," she sings.

"She has no power. She is nothing."

Would he say things like that if he knew I was here and could hear him? I push with all my might, wanting to move and attack him for what he said.

He hisses out in pain and grabs at his arm. His eyes flicker to the sides of the room. They slide over where the voice was coming from. Black high heeled-boots that are kicked out is all that can be seen.

"Prove it," she purrs. "If she has no power over you, then you will not have a problem doing a job you have done many times before."

"Find someone else."

Fingers snap, and he is raised up and lowered back into the cool water. He takes a deep breath before he goes back under the water. He thrashes and struggles against what is holding him under.

I didn't like what he said, but I didn't want him to feel this pain either. I brush up against him, wrapping my mind around his, pulling him in close. "Come away from this. Hear me," I whisper. Closing my eyes and concentrating, trying not to feel what he is going through and instead have him feel what I am.

"What are you doing here?" Blaise snaps at me.

I open my eyes and see him standing next to me. They soaked him from head to toe, but we are not in the water suffering.

"Where are we?" I ask.

"You brought me out of my mind into yours. Why are you here? You can't be here." He looks around, searching for a way back to his body, his own mind.

"Why am I here? You brought me here. I didn't do this." Something was different. This did not seem like the Blaise I had known.

His body shook, most likely due to losing air again and on the precipice of death. He pushes me back gently, making the distance larger. "I need to be present when she brings me back around."

I fold my arms in front of my chest and take a few more steps back, the hold weakening the farther I get. "I'm staying as long as I can." I eye him, making my point.

"You can't stay if she senses you if any of them do. Your life is null in void. If you ever see me, act as if you don't know me." He rushes up to me and grabs my chin with the force of his fingers. They do not bite into my skin. "Promise me, please." His eyes soften. "You will not like who you meet."

"Why wouldn't I?" My hand reaches for his, but he quickly steps out of my reach.

"I am not who you knew." He throws a worried look behind him and at the ground.

"Then be someone I want to meet in the future and make sure you live to get there," I growl out. His voice fading and his form wavering. "You can explain later."

"No, I will not do this." He thinks for a moment. "I can't do this."

"You can. To get where you need to be." I am stern and hard with him since he could not be.

He disappears altogether before he can respond. I appear next to him instead of inside his body. I look down at myself, a transparent sheen. "Is this magic? I thought I had lost all ability from it." Shaking my head back and forth, I look around, trying to see all that is possible. We are in a large, dark room. The floors are all cement and are slightly slanted into a square pool of water. The square is large enough for a couple of people. There is a grate that hangs on hooks hanging above.

"Worm? Have you changed your mind yet?" Blaise coughs and sputters back to life. Her voice coos to him, murmuring. Blaise looks around the room, but his eyes do not land on me. I touch his shoulder to let him know I am here.

My eyes land on the woman with boots. Her face is still in shadow even as I try to move closer. Something was blocking me from her. Kneeling beside Blaise. "Are you keeping me from her? Are you keeping me from knowing who is doing this to you?"

His eyes still do not land on me; he doesn't even acknowledge my presence. I try to sink back into him so we can still be connected, but nothing happens. He has blocked me out. I wasn't sure how to get back to my own body from where I am now.

"I will do this on one condition," he sputters finally.

I look over my shoulder, expecting to see a tether of some sort, but do not. The boot I see swaying in the air stops. She uncrosses her legs and sets her foot down. Only her toes and knees are in the light.

"You think you have power here, worm?" I don't see her move closer, but her voice comes closer. "You do as I say until your untimely death, or you have repaid what is needed."

He coughs again and looks down at the concrete beneath his hands and knees. He sits back on his legs, just breathing raggedly. "I will do this job for you. But I will not do others like this again," his roughened voice breaks.

Cloth rubs against something as she settles back and crosses her legs again, the boot swaying. "We will see." She snaps her fingers once again.

He is picked up and thrown into the water once more.

I stand there stunned a moment; she laughs it is almost lyrical. I jump in after him and feel the cold water caress me. He was my only way home that I knew of. I swim down, trying to grasp him, a cage coming down in the water trapping him below.

I curl around him, not knowing what else to do. He thrashes, but they don't connect. I keep close to him, holding him tight. Eventually, the fight dies out, and he can no longer keep the wall up that blocks us. I am falling into him, but quickly pull him into my mind, not wanting to feel the pain and loss of air that he is going through. I bring him away from the pain and abuse that his body is experiencing.

"Why?" He croaks.

I grab his chin and force him to look into my eyes. "Why not?" I ask.

His hand comes up, and cups my cheek, his thumb caresses my lip, and he licks his lips, staring at me, staring into me. I can feel the pain, but I can also feel something else that he craves.

"Fight for what you want," I whisper as my tongue darts out to swipe at the pad of his thumb.

He lowers his head and brushes his lips against mine.

I deepen the kiss, raising up on my toes and clutching his shirt to me. He wraps his hands around mine and presses them away, making me let go of the shirt and look down at our hands, breaking the kiss. "Know I block you for a reason."

Darkness pulls me in, and I am flung backward. "Don't." My voice breaks.

"I need you to stop looking for me. I need you to stop talking about me." His words waver as the darkness envelops him, fully striking him from view. "Stop talking to me in these dreams." A whisper echoes after him.

I am thrust back into my body, coming back. My eyes blink rapidly, and I spring up, swinging my fist. Standing up from the chair I had been sitting in. Natasha is still behind me.

"What gives?" She gives me a curious look and is on her way back. "Who are you punching?"

"How long was I gone?" I shake my hand out of its fist.

"Gone?" She looks back at the rocks piled in the broken doorway. "You didn't go anywhere. I was just checking out the rocks you had pushed at me and coming back to check on you since you were so silent."

"No, that's not right." I shake my head; my fingers massage my temples. "Blaise. I think he is in trouble. Was in trouble?"

"Blaise, who you haven't heard from in what a couple of weeks?" She asks.

"Yea, I was pulled to him. He was drowning at first; they were torturing him."

"Are you sure it wasn't another trick from Tom? You know, last time he tricked you. Where he looked like Blaise but was not."

"Why would he do that? This didn't feel like that. He gained nothing from this meeting. He asked me to actually stay away. And if we meet in the future, don't act like I knew him." I caress the shoulder bag still across my body, craving to open it and read. I needed comfort, and I felt like my mom's words would help, help her be here when I needed her the most.

"Him telling you not to come may be his way to get you to come. Well, we are going over there. All we know is he is somewhere on the dark side. Maybe we will see him along the way."

"It didn't seem like that," I pout. Second guessing myself and what I saw.

"Tom is a master illusionist and has tricked you before. What makes you so sure it wasn't him? He would try to trick you. If he knew you saw through his illusion, then telling you not to come, you would do the opposite," Natasha chimes in.

"Why are you so against him, so against this, and what is between us? I am being careful. I am listening to your and Quintan's wisdom of not jumping into something before having myself and others covered and going in with a plan."

"If you don't want my opinion on things, then I won't give it." She backs away as if I slapped her. "Did you want to look around anywhere else?"

"No, let's just get going." I kick at the pebbles littering the ground.

CHAPTER 4

WE POKE AROUND THE house and town a bit more than make our way back. The sun is going down and is almost set by the time we were to get going. The sun disappears from view, and it is dark as we return to the tree line. I trail behind both Robert and Natasha. Zeek decided to travel by other means, and he would see us later. He had a job to do or something more important. I fiddle with the bag I still hold and caress the metal box inside. I found some other interesting trinkets just to bring back with me but wasn't sure what they were, just stuck them in the bag and would look at them later.

The path looks different. "Did we go a different way than when we started out?" I ask Robert, who is ahead of me. Natasha is out further, not wanting to speak to me after what I said.

"We like to keep our enemies on their toes and never be sure which way we are coming or going. We don't want to make things easy for them, so we try to keep things chaotic so they can't guess our moves."

"Other than what happened with Tom, it doesn't seem like you have too much to worry about here. Have you ever been under attack in this place since that night?" I notice a dim light up ahead and a chattering noise that accompanies the unfamiliar sight.

"No, we have not been under attack since that night with your parents. We had before then, for this is not a new town. But just because we have not before this, doesn't mean it can't happen and I will not be the one in charge and not be prepared. Better to be prepared than slaughtered."

Robert makes the same chittering noise back. I squint up ahead and notice it is Jason waiting along the path. I look at Robert then. "What kind of noise are you doing, and why are you doing them?"

Robert looks at me and eyes me carefully. "They are warning calls. If the person answers back correctly, then we know it is one of our own. It is a certain bug that travels at all times of the day and night but is rare. Most people don't pay attention that much and only think it is a normal woods sound."

I stop Gem a moment later, thinking back to what we were talking about before. "Were you there? That night? When my parents died? Do you know if they are dead for sure?"

He stops and turns his horse back to me. Natasha rushes up ahead and is already with Jason. "Yes." His voice is deep and sincere. He sees my look of confusion. "Yes, I was there that night, no, I did not see your parents perish, but I have not heard news or heard from them. We assume them to be dead. Both sides think the same. Spells were done, and they could not be tracked. You saw the house and village the bodies could be crushed anywhere in there. It is not stable enough to search thoroughly. You know you've seen it."

"Did you know them well? My mother or father?"

"Yes," he says simply. Turning his horse away from me.

"I'm sorry."

His face contorts into rage. "Why are you sorry?" He turns fully in his saddle to better see my face; Lucky tries to pull forward, wanting dinner.

I move Gem up alongside him and gently place my hand on his raised arms on the reins. "We all blame ourselves in tragedy, but the short answer is even if we did something else to try to sway fate, it most likely wouldn't have made a difference."

"Fate is a wicked thing and won't be denied easily. I know that more than most."

I ride ahead as he lets his reins fall limp. "Don't I know it." I call back as Gem slows to a walk, not wanting to leave Robert too far back.

His words barely reach me, but I hear them. "But we can deny it. Just ensure you are ready for the scars that will come with the repercussions."

Jason waves as I come closer and walks us into the trees, away from the path. He leaves Robert back there. "He probably wants to be left alone and scout the area to keep everyone safe."

Jason might answer my questions since he was so interested in me earlier. We leave the horses and walk slowly over to a small clearing and camp. The fire is nice and warm as we grow closer to the center. A lone figure is huddled there with a pot over the fire.

"Why hello there again." Charles looks up from stirring something that smells delectable.

I breathe in the aroma and sit on one of the many chairs they have surrounding the fire. "Smells good. What are you cooking?" I ask.

"Stew." He smiles. He is still wearing his cowboy hat and tips it down in greeting.

"Do you help with guarding and protecting as well?" I lick my lips, staring at the food in front of us. I watch as Natasha and Jason also sit down around the fire.

"Where're the dishes? Is it done?" Natasha asks. "I didn't get to eat this morning." She glares at me. "Because someone didn't want to get up, so I had to assist."

"Ariella is coming with the dishes. Jason warned us you would come by soon." He looks around the treetops above us and the clearing, looking for someone.

I stretch out my legs, rubbing at them. They are sore from all the walking and horseback riding I have done today. A tall redheaded woman comes out of a large tent with many bowls and though her hair is very curly, she has it in a tight bun. Her hawk-like eyes peer at the group before her, not missing a thing. "Robert is scouting?" She looks at the trees around us as if she can see which direction he went.

Charles sips the soup from a large spoon that he is stirring with. "It's ready, boys and girls," he calls. She steps closer, bringing the bowls to each of us. We give him our bowl to spoon some into so we can all get some. "This here is Ariella. Ariella, that is Alexia, and Natasha is the other one."

I wave as she nods to us but does not say a word more. I reach out my hand to shake her hand as I wait for him to fill my bowl of stew.

She looks at my outstretched hand and backs up, shying away from my touch. She backs away into the burning fire, being consumed entirely by the licks of fire. The flames scorch her form, and still, she does not scream. Her form flickers but stands there unaware of the fire, unaware that the flames are even touching her.

I gasp in shock and look back at the two men and even Natasha. She gives a curious look, but since no one else is doing anything, she stays sitting and remains calm. I scramble closer to the fire to yank her out. She backs up deeper into the flames, not wanting me to touch her. "Wait!" I move forward. "Sisters." I call out, calling them forth. We had to work on a better technique if I ever needed their help without verbal cues. They should be able to help me with the flames and withstand the heat of the fire to rescue Ariella. What the hell was wrong with everyone?

Laughter erupts from the trees above our heads, echoing and bouncing off of the timbers. I retract my arm and hand from the flames, the form in the fire no longer there. I look around, searching.

"Damn, Charles, you were right about this one. She knows nothing of this kind of life or us," a female voice calls out.

I move away from the flames and rub my arms, letting the sisters know they do not need to come out. Though Trill disappears back down to wherever they go while residing in me, Tina leaps from my arm into the large flames of the fire. She dances around and plays in the fire, becoming larger herself. She stretches and seems happy and content to dance within the flames.

I look at Charles. His eyes flick to a branch above us, and to the right, Foliage is tight and covers around it, making it hard to see past. He gives a hoot of laughter.

"What is going on? Where did she go?" I look at Jason. "Why are we not helping her? She might be hurt. Did you not see her in the fire?"

Natasha glares at both Jason and Charles. "Sure, pick on the new people," she grumbles as she sips her stew. She licks her lips and quickly goes for another spoonful.

"Just wait." Jason lights up with laughter. He comes forward and turns me toward the tree that Charles is watching.

Four Ariella's appear around the tree, two coming from the top and two from around the base of the large tree. The two from the top land on the floor, barely disturbing anything on the forest floor as she moves with no noise. A fifth one appears from the tent that the original one came from with more dishes. They all move closer once they come so close they combine into one form. The other copies disappear into one. The last one that drops from the tree comes forward and disappears through the one with the bowls, making her flicker and disappear. "Seriously, chill! They are not real, just projections. That is why we stay away from touch. It interrupts the form and doesn't make it real anymore."

A brush of Jason's hand touches my shoulder as I step away, not liking how close he is crowding me. I glance at him, but he chuckles at Ariella.

"What is wrong with you people? Do you get off on scaring me half to death?" I ask.

"Do you get off on other people's pain and fear?" Natasha also asks.

"Oh, come on. I had to. It was too easy. If I didn't, I would have felt incomplete." Ariella comes around by Charles, kisses his cheek and sets the other bowls down before taking her own and digging in to get some grub for herself. "Think of it as an initiation of sorts if you must." She shrugs and pours multiple helpings into her bowl, topping it off.

"This isn't college," I mutter.

"Leave her alone, love," Charles says smoothly as he stirs the pot of left overs, keeping it moving. He grabs a cloth and takes the entire pot out of the flames, letting it cool and placing a lid over the rest. He brings the bowl he was holding and holds it out to me, waiting for me to grab it.

"Love?" I look between Ariella and Charles, lost in confusion once more.

"Yea, that old coot is my sort of stepfather." She shrugs. "Helped me find my place here. What is college?"

"It is a school system in the human world where young adults like yourself go to learn and have fun," Charles answers. "She has never been to the human world, and we do not have colleges here in this one. All she has known is this town. She is around the same age as you, Alexia," he answers my silent question.

She sits beside Jason but far enough away that he would not accidentally touch her. She digs into her meal and does not stop, done with talking for now.

I take the bowl that is still extended to me, sitting next to Natasha. I want her close in case we have to get out of here at a moment's notice. She was the only one I truly trust.

"Do you know anything about her?" I whisper to Natasha.

She shakes her head and makes noisy slurping noises, covering the sound of my voice.

"You probably want to know the reason I am here. Yes, I also help guard the town and am the only decent cook for these young ones. But I also wanted to know more about you. I take it you would also like to know more about us, the council members."

I nod slowly. Not sure how to take him.

"Ariella, there is sort of a mimic. She can make multiple copies of herself. They can touch and hold nonlivable items but cannot hold the illusion when touched."

"But why?"

"Something about the electromagnetic fields around a person is our best guess. She can also speak through the clones, though only one at a time. Her mother is a skinwalker, so she got a bit of that power mixed with her father's power, which is an illusionist." He frowns.

"You know you are my true father," Ariella pouts. Holding off on the next bite.

"Yes, I know," he waves her off and continues to get his own bowl and take a seat. "Though most people on the guard team have an animal to call, not all do. She is an exception for the team, and they are better for it. You don't need to have eyes or strength when you can create copies of yourself from long distances away."

"You just need to be more cunning than your opponent," Ariella chimes in. "Dad, stop giving away my secrets, give some of your own away," she complains.

"Fair enough pet," he harrumphs. "I am great at training animals, both shifters and actual animals. My skin is impenetrable when I am concentrating. So even though I may look frail and older, I am not." He gives a wicked wink.

"I figured something was going on. Everyone in that room earlier seemed dangerous, maybe not in looks, but underneath. Even the older woman with healing properties looked strong, very cunning, and willing to fight for what she believes in."

"Yea, Greta has some bite, always has." He chuckles. "In this life, you have to fight for what you really want."

I give a sad smile. "Sounds familiar," I say.

"How so?" Ariella asks.

My eyes fill with water. I concentrate on fighting them back. I look at Natasha. She just pinches her lips with worry.

"I said that to Blaise once."

"Blaise, who is that?" Ariella asks.

"Just someone that I don't really know. I said something very similar to him." A lone tear trickles down my cheek, but I quickly brush it away. No one says anything or comments, so I continue to eat.

"Did someone die?" Robert walks out from the darkness and leans against a tree as he throws an apple up into the air before catching it.

Natasha jumps into action to get the spotlight off me. "Just being my obnoxious self." She gets up and grabs some more stew, helping herself to seconds. "Ariella likes to watch how people react to her in dangerous situations. She was showing off if you ask me," she says snidely.

"Sounds like something you know about," Robert comments.

She stops and thinks for a moment. "It does, doesn't it?" She gives a tinkling laugh.

"Oh, another troublemaker for our town, eh?" Charles replies.

Ariella glares at her father.

"The younger pups are overrunning us older generation," Robert states.

"Hey, I'm a part of that generation, and I listen and am not a troublemaker," Jason chimes in.

"That's because you're a goodie-two-shoes. And never get in trouble," Ariella scoffs.

"Do not."

"Do to," she says back as she wiggles her delicate nose. "But that's okay. I like you a lot more than anyone else of our generation."

"Thanks a lot. There aren't that many in this town that are our age. Just adding salt to the wound."

Ariella brushes her fingers against his hand even as she cringes away slightly. She lays her hand on his, keeping it there until she can control her facial features, and ends up curling her fingers around his.

He freezes on the spot and looks down at her hand on his. "Ariella?" He asks in amazement.

"Just shut up," she states in a hushed tone. She takes her hand from his and returns to eating without looking at anyone in the circle.

He coughs into his other hand, the one not still sitting on the bench between them. "How is the perimeter, Robert?" He asks, trying to lighten the mood along with changing the subject.

"All clear." He nods.

I stand up after finishing my bowl and place it near the pot still holding some leftovers. I leave the group and walk over to Robert. Understanding that Ariella and Jason may want some time alone specifically. I lean against the tree that he is also leaning his shoulder against. He takes a bite from the apple he has thrown in the air.

"What do I need to learn about the perimeter and this town?" My gaze lands on each person in the group. Natasha, of course, has to break the tension. They are all once again chatting around the fire. Charles gets up and disappears into the woods, grabbing a bag that has been lying beside him.

"I am going to go feed the horses some apples. Are you wondering, because it is a leader's responsibility to know how their kingdom works?" He looks away a moment. "Or do you truly want to know?"

I blink a few times in shock. "Um, what? Why would I ask if I didn't want to actually know?" I question.

"Sorry, I am used to the younger generation wanting big jobs but not ready for them and them taking on too much too soon. You're a lot different from what I was prepared for."

"Someone like Natasha?"

The right side of his lips pick up in a half smile. "Yea, kind of."

"Sorry to disappoint."

"Don't be sorry. Just keep your eyes, ears, and mind open. Learn all you can and use it to the best of your ability because only you can protect yourself when it matters. If you hold on to that, maybe you will have a shot at this whole thing."

"Why do you say that?" I look up at him hovering beside me.

"This whole world needs change, and I think you have the makings for that change that the people need." He takes another couple of bites, almost halfway through the apple.

"Tell me how you and Zeek are brothers without actually being brothers, then?" I try to ask a question that has circled my mind since we got here and first met Robert.

He finishes the rest of the apple before he walks close to where the horses are tied up. He looks over his shoulder. "Perhaps one day, but that day is not today."

"Normal of nine tails to not give any useful information. What do you expect from a trickster like a fox?" Natasha comments, keeping her eye on us but still closer to the group and the warmth of the fire.

"You're horrible, Natasha!" I say.

"Who?" Ariella peeps up, peaking at us. She had been having a very in-depth conversation with Jason next to her.

"Your boss man, there," I say irritably. Pushing off the tree, I walk back over to the group. Leaving Robert to feed the horses their treats.

"He is pretty horrible, isn't he?" She gives an evil smile and quirks her head to the side.

"You will be glad I was tough if you are ever in a fight for your life," he states. He gives a serious look.

"It was just a joke. Forget it." I wave my hand absently at the side of my head near my ear. "So, are we camping or heading back to the house tonight?"

"No, I should make you all sleep out here under the stars," he grumbles. "But this is just a stop on our way back to the town. Tomorrow we will meet some other council members tomorrow. Along with someone that you may remember."

"Remember how? Who would I know here? Or do you mean someone from Morning Star?" I ask.

He moves toward the fire and reaches out his hands toward the flame. He eases into one of the chairs. Tina twirls about and dances up his jean leg. "You will see tomorrow," he says cryptically. "Hey Tina, is Alexia taking care of you guys?" He peers at her closely.

Tina nods. "We are doing fine, though we have never been this far from Taz. Trill is anxious about her and what kind of trouble Shade is getting her into."

"I bet Margaret would like to talk to you girls before Alexia heads out, if you have time to go see her. I have another working on their location to locate Taz. Don't worry." He reaches out a finger for her. Her flame hands reach for it as he twirls her around.

"I won't and I will go see her," she says.

Since Tina and Robert are catching up, I let our conversation die down and let go of whoever I would be reuniting with tomorrow.

"Jason and I will take you guys back; Robert and Charles will run the perimeter until the next team changes out later," Ariella says.

"When will we be leaving, then?" I pick up a stick near the campfire. A medium-sized stack was sitting close by to throw into the fire whenever it got low. I peel off the bark and throw it in the flames, eating the crumbs that come off in my hands.

"Ready to get rid of me already?" Robert asks.

Jason's eyes light up as he looks at Ariella. "We can head back a bit early."

Ariella gives a shy smile.

Charles focuses on Jason. He growls low in his throat as a warning. "That better be all you are enjoying, hatchling!"

"Dad! Stop!" She kicks the sticks into the fire, diminishing the pile quickly. She stomps off. "I am going to scout ahead through the trees," she grumbles. "So embarrassing."

"How will she keep up?" I ask.

"Don't worry about that. I can skip through the clones I send out, deciding which one I want to be a part of and be real."

I nod and see Jason has followed close behind Ariella, trying to talk to her.

"How old did you say those two were?"

"Yea, they seem pretty childish for soldiers." Natasha looks at the tree line.

"Ariella just turned nineteen, and dragons age at a very slow rate compared to others, so you can say he is about that age."

"So not quite my age then," I let him know.

"What young twenties?" He asks.

I nod.

"Still the same, then. You guys don't even know yourselves, let alone others at that age," he chuckles.

"Old coot stuck in your ways, are you?" Robert mutters to Charles.

"You're one to talk," Charles chuckles back.

"Now go on, get out of here. Go catch up with them and make sure they aren't making out or something like love birds. If Charles catches them, there really will be a fight. That will not go well," Robert says.

"I've taken on a dragon or two in my time, so don't count me out," Charles grounds out.

"No, my friend, I am worried about the dragon and his family who entrusted us with their son," Robert barks out.

"Don't worry, we won't be out here very long and you will be back to warming your wife's bed in no time."

With that, I shake my head and grab Natasha, staying out of their banter. I throw the rest of the stick behind me and whisper. "Let's get out of here before they pull us into their craziness."

"I agree."

Robert raises his voice, catching me before I leave. "Aren't you forgetting something?" He glares at me.

I look around; I tap the bag I am still wearing around my side and look at Natasha. She shrugs her shoulders, not knowing what he is talking about. Robert holds out a finger, and the flame jumps up and twirls around again. Tina is still dancing around near Robert.

"Come on, Tina. We are heading back to the house. You want to go visit Margaret with your sister tomorrow?"

Tina looks back at Robert. She snuggles his finger in a hug and then skips off from him, hopping back to me in little hops. I wait for her to catch up. Kneeling, I let her hop into my hand as she melts back into my body.

I head back to Gem and see her shaking her head and pawing at the dirt. I grab the reins and pull myself into the saddle, not having any trouble this time. "Yes," I cheer to myself. My legs already bark in pain, and my back needs a good stretch after all this riding. Gem seems like she is more energized just after that small reprieve.

I wait for Natasha and Jason is already waiting for us both. He keeps a lookout in the trees. "Can you sense where she is?" I ask.

He nods. "We have always had a bond since we met. We just get each other and can sense one another."

"That's kind of weird, isn't it?"

"Guess we never really thought of it."

"Are you going to turn into a dragon or just your misty form?" I ask, eager to see his full form. I had never seen a dragon before.

"I will walk you back to the path and then go into my misty form. I will change back if I encounter any trouble or need you. You can just call out quietly. Either Ariella or I will be close by and can come to check on you, but mostly, it will just be you two."

"Which way?" I bellow out and look around, unsure where the path was from here. I have already gotten turned around. My muscles are tired, and I want to call it quits for today.

Jason looks at me with wide eyes and points to a break in the trees he had gotten closer to, Natasha coming up behind me. I trot past him as he is still double-checking things, moving on ahead. "Don't stray from the path. This will lead you directly into the town. Then we won't have to come to find you since you will get lost in these woods, obviously." He gives me a pointed look, having already gotten turned around.

I nod and re-enter the maze-like woods. The fire is not visible when I look back. I try to peer behind the leaves and can't tell where the camp was or where we have even come from.

Natasha and I continue forward in silence, and Jason mists away, leaving us to converse on our own.

"Are we okay?" I ask, knowing things were rocky today, but I still needed her.

"Yea." She deflates against Powder, just relaxing against and holding around her neck. "Today was just a lot, you know. For both of us."

CHAPTER 5

T HE NIGHT PASSES BY quickly, and once we get back; we are so dead tired we fall into a heap. My clothing forgotten. I just drop into my bed and pass out.

I wake up late since I want to relax and just read. The spell books call to me, begging me to find a way out of this mess. "I don't know why I even try with these since my magic was taken from me. I should have talked to Charles about controlling my animal when I had the chance." The next time I see him, I will have to remember.

"Trill, Tina. Did you want to go see Margaret today?" Tina pulls up immediately and hops around, keeping her heat to herself and not scorching my clothes. Trill pulls up slower and sits on my leg, staying there.

"Come on Trill," Tina says energetically. She skips out of the room, not waiting for her sister.

"You going to follow Tina and go see Margaret?" I ask. "Make sure you guys get plenty of time with her before we leave. I am not sure who will come with us yet."

"Yea, I am just worried about Taz. I have never been this far from either of them." Her light is low, and barely any heat comes from her.

"Are you okay?" I rub a finger down her small back.

She sighs, and her light brightens. "Yes, I am physically okay, but in here." She points to her chest. "Something is not right."

"You are not alone there. We have this in common."

"I am the oldest Mama made me promise to take care of them. I don't think I am doing an outstanding job."

"Why do you think that? Why is your mother not here with you?"

"We are not altogether, are we?" She gives me a look as if I am crazy. "Mother had to stay in her world. She made a bargain with someone for us to be created. She always wanted and loved us. Would do anything to make us a reality." Her glow diminishes with her mood. "She has to live out her bargain. Something took us away from her world. We are too young and not strong enough to find our way back. We almost perished. Margaret and Robert, they both saved us."

"I am glad Margaret and Robert are here for you girls. Maybe your mother will come for you one day. Perhaps like you can sense your sister; she can sense you three."

"That won't be for a long while, then." Her face falls. "Margaret has done her best with all three of us. I am sad we can't stay with her since she can't have her own kids."

"What? She can't."

Trill shakes her head. "I don't want to see her and make her sad."

"You will miss her and regret it if you don't, though. What if something happened while we were out, and you never get to speak with her again?" I pick her tiny form up and place her on the bed next to me. "Wouldn't that make you more upset with yourself?"

"Can you come with me?" She scoots back close to me.

"Sure, I can help you find her and then leave. I will have to meet Quintan and Jazmin later on today, but other than that, I got nothing."

"Yes, please." She waits for me to put my hand back down and climbs into the middle of my palm.

I cup my hand around her and raise up as she sits down in my palm, keeping my hand up so a gust of wind doesn't blow her out. Going through the hallway and downstairs, I check a couple of places she could be.

"Do you want to help tell me where Tina is? She might be with Margaret already?" I suggest after the second room is empty, with no one to help point me in the correct direction.

"She is down on this floor, down that hallway." She throws her arm straight ahead. The library was down this way, along with the training rooms and kitchen.

I stick my head in the library first. "Margaret!" I call out.

"Alexia, is that you, dearie?" A loud voice yells from deep within the library.

Who is that? That voice seems familiar, but where did I hear that voice before? "Who's there?" I call back.

"It's Greta from the council meeting."

"Greta?" My voice echoes back to me.

"Come back here, dear, I don't bite."

I look down at my palm. Trill gets up and holds on to my thumb, looking down the hallway. "Go on. They are close by. I can do this on my own." She squares her little shoulders and jumps down from my palm. Her flame flares up so the draft would not blow her out. She lands, and the wood scorches beneath her. She dulls her flame and hops forward quickly, making her way down the hall, out of sight.

I slip into the library and look around, trying to find where she is hiding. It isn't such a big place, but the rows of books and high desks with individual stalls make it hard to find where she is right away.

"Where are you?"

"Back here at one cubicle in the stacks."

I round the corner and amble back towards the desk. I see her white hair braided down her back. She pushes her glasses back up her delicate nose. Looking me over with cold, calculating eyes. Many books are strewn about. She picks one up and tidies up as she flips open to another. Her eyes never waver from me as she arranges the books in a better stack, keeping it clean.

"What are you doing back here? Someone could get lost in this place," I say, picking up one book and reading the title. A long word is scrawled across the book, one I did not know the definition of.

"Wouldn't that be grand to get lost in a place with all these stories? All this knowledge!" She says with a smile.

I put down the book and rub my hands and arms. "Guess this place kind of gives me the creeps."

"To me, this is a calming place where I come to think and get answers. Sometimes it even helps me be a better healer." Her smile falls, and her face is back to business.

"Well, I was just helping the fire sisters meet with Margaret before we set out to go to the dark side."

"Oh, that's nice, dearie. How are you feeling? I know you were out of it for a few days when you were brought back?" She gives a hard stare as if she could see more.

I pull my ponytail forward and split it down the middle, pulling some darker hairs forward. "The only thing that seems to be left over from that time is this." Black highlights streak my brown hair, only a small piece, so it is easily hidden from sight. "Black highlights showed up in my hair. I didn't get to ask if that was from my transformation. Will that happen more and more once I go full animal?" I ask flipping the hair back and tightening the ponytail.

"It's been a few weeks. It may eventually fade. I am glad you are doing well, though. Charles would be better to ask about the animal part of things, but I can say it has to deal with control of how much changes or doesn't." She picks up another large tomb that is towards the back of the desk, pulling it forward. "If you would continue to rest, it should all go back to normal."

"Do you think people would wait that long? During the council meeting you were all in, the entire group wanted answers."

"Yes, Quintan brought us to discuss the situation with you and your wants and needs." She closes the book she has been reading. She swivels from her seat to face me.

"I am trying to get to know the people and what must be done. Losing myself is not an option, especially since I don't even know myself." My hands fiddle with the books on the desk. "I knew this would happen; I don't even know if I can be what you all need me to be."

"I agree with that. I think you must know yourself first." Her cold, calculating eyes never waver from me. "That is why I told him you should go on this trip."

"What? You have been against me running this group since the beginning. Why are you helping me?" I back away from her, making sure there isn't a trap being set.

"Dearie, I may be old, but I am not senile and have only gotten to this place by being knowledgeable. I can see that you are anything but."

"That doesn't mean I can't learn or be guided," I argue.

She cocks her head to the side. "Could you? Could you forget Shade, not go looking for your lover and be who the people need? Could you turn your back on yourself? Quintan thinks it's a possibility he is talking to the masses right now."

"To everyone in town? Right now?" I gulp. Paling at the thought.

"Yes. I think you should go on this quest to find out what you really want, find out who you are working with, and see if we align with what you want. I don't want to be your enemy, but I am not your friend either, and you will have to learn that being in politics and war."

"Let's go, then." I pick at the skin near my nails, unsure of my next move but willing to try.

"Really." She raises a surprised brow. "To the town hall Quintan is holding?"

"Yes. What are we waiting for?" I huff as I straighten my shoulders and let my hands dangle beside me, looking more sure.

She gives a smile. "I am waiting for you to think better of this idea and tell me you are still unwell or that you will go on this journey and learn yourself before you decide on what you want to become."

"What good will that do? Other than giving everyone else time to solidify their place or work on the way to make sure I can't take back my family's legacy," I say in aggravation.

"Your mother and father set you up. Well, that is true. With a reliable council, we could handle it while you are away. These people believe in this cause. Do you want them to question you as we did in that previous meeting? Are you ready to stand before them with those kinds of questions?" She pauses. "Go on your journey and live a little. Learn this world, and know you will gain the knowledge you seek. Quintan will stay here and make sure we all stay in line."

"But you have all been waiting so long."

"We did not wait for you all this time. We survived and persevered, child. Yes, they want to know if you are the savior or destroyer at the end of it all. But they can wait a bit more. I don't think it will kill them."

"Lead the way." I motion for her to go first.

Her mouth forms a thin line as she looks at me and nods. "Remember, I gave you your out." She moves gracefully through the stacks; her plain clothes pants and a shirt hang off her tiny frame. They move in time with her slow steps.

I glance back at her books and bite my lip as my fingers itch to check what other books she is reading. Wanting to know her true intentions. Everyone else was out for themselves. I was starting to see that. My curiosity pulls me to the books. Something in me needing to know for sure. I glance at one on the desk she had opened but do not see a title on the front. This place has some weird books.

"Are you coming?" Greta calls back.

I stride down the rows of books, quickly catching up. "Right behind you," I comment.

Silence surrounds us as we turn the corners. Our talk still bouncing around in my head. We twist this way and that before getting to the front of the house. I trail my fingers along the walls, the wood smooth to the touch.

"This meeting place you said is in town?" I ask, unsure of where we are headed exactly.

"Since we are on the outskirts of the town, we have a bit of a walk but we will be there in a few minutes." She holds open the door for me to walk through.

We walk for a bit, not saying anything more. I concentrate on my footing and keep my eyes glued forward. My mouth is dry, and I can't stop my right arm from shaking.

"You're awfully quiet back there," Greta remarks as we spill into the main square of the town. A large building sits off to the right, with a bell at the top.

"I stand back in awe. That is beautiful."

Greta stops to look at where I am and nods. "That is where we are headed. That bell is used to warn our town if the perimeter is lit up. It warns of an attack or danger that is nearby."

The building was bigger than any of the others. It is meant to hold many people and large meetings.

"How many am I meeting with today?" I lick my lips, trying to get some moisture into my mouth.

"All and any who could make it, some might have spelled their way in that have a device to do so. Quintan opened this up to anyone who had questions or wanted to know the plan."

I come to a standstill right outside of the tall and heavy oak doors, or at least they looked very heavy. I gulp down the saliva that is now running down my throat. My stomach is in knots. "Tell me that will not be a lot of people."

"I saw quite a sizeable crowd here earlier, and Quintan said a few would be spilling in. That was before I came to Margaret's for her library. So, who knows?" She gives a wide smile.

"You could be nicer and not as devious. Can I change my answer to how I am feeling right now?" I bite out. "I think I'm going to be sick."

She laughs at me outright. "I tried to warn you. Quintan thought it best to get this over and done with all at once, so it wouldn't be as draining. People were getting rough around the edges. He wanted to set them at peace before you left the community in case you needed to make an appearance. He would understand if you did or did not show up."

"But I found you. You did not seek me out."

A cruel smile forms upon her lips. "That is correct, child. You caught me. I was going to explain to him I could not find you or tell him outright you were not feeling up to it and not bring it up to you. You did not need to be bothered with such things when he can handle it.”

I glare at her. “Do you always line things up, so you get your way? This does not help me trust you.”

“Yes, I usually maneuver things my way. Good thing you don’t have to trust me, per se. You just have to trust the knowledge I have. I want our group to succeed. I think our thoughts and ideas will align not at the moment but eventually. Hence why I am pushing you towards this trip.”

“Are you all like this?”

“No, I am a breed all my own,” She cackles. “Power always corrupts.”

“I am beginning to see that,” I nod. Stepping slowly away from the door, not sure if I want to go in anymore.

“Alexia!” Natasha yells out.

I back up and give a startled look. “Hey Natasha.” I wave, seeing her rush between two buildings. “How are you? Are you sore from the horse ride still?”

“A bit. Margaret saw you guys leaving the inn. She thought it would be good for me to come check on you.” She gives a side glare to Greta before walking over to my side. “Margaret and I talked a bit. The fire sisters have let us know how you intend to track Shade. Smart.”

I wonder how much confusion he is feeling or the pain he is in. He was just a shadow, and now he is an actual person. Even I did not have control over my powers. Does he? Could he possibly be doing better without me? These were all questions that were going around in my head, and the ones with Blaise never stopped, either.

“I have been searching for answers that can help us or help me connect to him when we find him.”

“Then you definitely don’t need to be here for this. I wouldn’t worry about these people quite yet.” Natasha urges me to follow her back to the house.

"If there is no way to fix Shade, then what? If there is no way to contain what Tom has started? He must be dealt with." Greta frowns. Shaking her head.

"He will be dealt with," Natasha states calmly.

I move toward Greta, hearing the threat in her voice. My fists curl into themselves. "What if there is a way to keep Shade human? He was a part of me and helped save me multiple times. You don't think that is worth saving? Just because he is a variable that you can't control." My anger rising to the surface. She has tested me throughout this ordeal, and I am getting a little tired of her games.

Greta's hand stops me in my tracks, her hand firm on my shoulder, freezing me in place. "He is human now. With your powers."

"What did Quintan not tell you?" I gasp. "What if he is human and has my magic? It's not like I could access it or do anything with it. Maybe he will be better equipped to handle it. What's the big deal?"

"He is other, and many of the people remember what happened the last time we allowed other to taint this land." She looks off into the distance, trying to see something that is not there. "It's best if we turn him back into what he was. He is not safe otherwise."

"Why not?" I huff.

"Both of you will not be safe if this is not the case." She looks at me, forcing me to stare at her. "You have to know that."

Natasha lays her hand on my other shoulder, edging me away from Greta. "You don't have to do this right now. This is a problem for another day."

"Wrong you are little fairy. It's a problem for now if she doesn't figure things out quickly. She has two men that could be her downfall. Quintan and the council know they are her weakness. We know the light side knows of Blaise and his weakness to her, but what will happen when the dark side learns of this weakness? What will they do to her other than shred her to bits?" She bites out.

I turn away from her. "First, she wanted me to go on the adventure, and now she wants me to give it all up." I turn back to face her. "What do you want from me? Give me a straight answer this time.

No walking around the truth!" I scream in her face. My voice echoes around the empty square.

Murmurs can be heard behind the large oak doors. I glance at them and then back at Greta, then at Natasha. I place my hand over my mouth, afraid of letting out my frustration and being loud once again.

She raises her head and gives me a level stare. "For you to understand, you are still new at this all. You have many weaknesses. You need to know what they are and how others may exploit that. Now you must be the protector instead of being the one being protected." She eyes the door and hears a louder commotion coming towards the door.

I turn on my heel, away from her, walking back to where Natasha stands. "I am doing what I can." As I walk away, I whisper in a quiet voice.

She looks nervously at the doors, hoping they will stay closed for a little longer. "I know."

"Let's go," Natasha says.

CHAPTER 6

"AHH, YOU FOUND HER," Jazmin calls out.

She comes up behind Natasha and me, crowding us forward toward the extensive building instead of away from it as we wanted. Greta's lips thin out in contempt.

The big wooden doors open slowly, and Quintan is there at the front of the room. His bulbous body totters back and forth, sweat pouring down his face as he exerts himself.

The others behind him wait patiently to see what is going on, only some throwing questions back at him.

Jazmin grabs my arm into hers and walks me forward. Natasha is on my other arm, but let's go, standing still, not wanting to go towards the crowd. Greta moves out of the way before others walk over to her.

The group whispers loudly. I can hear many questions being asked at once. "Is that her? Was she going to come to talk to us? What is she doing? Why does she look so confused? She is so small? How is she going to help us?"

Jazmin pulls me forward by the arm, squeezing me through the people. We make our way back into the building up to Quintan. "Greta wasn't able to follow through. I made sure that she did." Jazmin bats her eyelashes. Her dress swaying in tune with her motions. Her nails cut into me as she holds me close to her.

"Jazmin," Greta grumbles as we pass by.

I stumble between the people trying to keep up with Jazmin as she picks up her pace. She shoves me forward, closer to the front of the room, where a small stage sits. I grab onto the corner of the stage and catch myself before I can fall face-first and embarrass myself in front of everyone.

Quintan catches my movement. His eyes light up as he addresses the crowd. "Alexia is here and in full health today. She is now ready to hear what everyone has to say and all the questions you want to have answered. But let's keep them to a minimum and not scare her away immediately. I wanted you all to meet her and see how she will help." He motions me forward to climb the stairs on the stage side and come up.

I climb the stairs. Whispering to him as the people clap. "This is payback, isn't it?"

"Of course not," he smiles, whispering back. "The people wanted to see you and know your face. Though I thought Greta would have made sure you did not come by." He looks between Greta and Jazmin. "Seems like someone else is playing a different game."

I roll my eyes. "And I am stuck in the middle of it." He takes something from his suit and clips it on my shirt. "When you talk, this will make your voice louder for everyone to hear you."

I nod but tug the neck of the shirt away from me, covering the item. "You better stay close by," I hiss out.

"I will be right at the edge of the stage near Jazmin and Greta." He points to the side.

Giving him an evil look, I dare him to disobey my orders. I face the crowd and let go of the neck of my shirt, pulling it down, hoping it fixed the wrinkles my hand had left.

"Hello?" I test. My voice echoes through the full room. Cringing, I hear my voice echo back to me. I cough. "Ahem, that better?" I see some nods in the crowd but no one answers all stare up at me as if waiting for directions.

My hands shake as I take a step back, unsure if can do this. Natasha would have a better time with this. She always knows what to say. I look for her.

"My name is Alexia," I stumble over my words.

"We know who you are," someone calls out in the crowd.

I lick my lips and take another step back as I look to Quintan, who urges me forward. I search the crowd trying to find one friendly face.

"I will try to answer any questions you may have. Please speak one at a time. I will try to get to as many as I can." The ball is in their court. I have no words for them, nothing that can help them. Greta's words hang heavy in my head. I don't know what they need, let alone what they need to hear.

I look over the tightly packed room. It falls quiet. Sniffling and coughing are the only noises I hear. I scan the room once again since I don't see anyone offering questions.

I try to keep my hands at my sides, but I fight back, wanting to fidget with the sides of my shirt or a loose string on the side of my pant leg.

This is worse than them throwing unending questions at me. Even ones I can't possibly answer would be better than nothing at all. My palms moisten, and I rub one on my side. I stop, not wanting them to physically see that they are causing me anxiety. I look once again at Greta and Quintan. They are just staring at me like everyone else, no help whatsoever.

Natasha flies up from the back in her ice form, not caring who sees what she is. She hovers over me, causing ice to rain down on the stage. Lowering beside me, she smiles. "Looks like you needed some help," she whispers.

Giving a smile back, I nod. Holding my hand out, waiting for her to take it.

She gives her support with that minor act; she didn't even want to come in here before this. Natasha clears her throat and projects to the crowd. "Hello, how is everyone today?" She gives them a winning smile with sharp teeth.

Quintan's brow furrows, and has worry lines all over him. He shuffles forward but steps back as Jazmin places a hand on his elbow, asking him to wait.

Turning to the crowd, some are smiling, others are nodding. Some belt out how they were doing today in answer to her question. Others leave out the back. I hear some displeasure and some murmurs of surprise.

She is a natural.

"I know what all of you are thinking here," Natasha scoffs, and laughter bubbles to the surface. Some that were at the door turn back to see what she will say.

"I'm an outsider," I say.

"We don't belong here," Natasha states right after me. She looks at me, giving me eyebrows but moves forward with me in tow, our hands our link and the audio covering both of us.

"Got that right," a few people call out. Others murmur approval, and some grumble in anger.

I call out before Natasha can continue, wanting them to know I have things to say as well. "And you are right to think that way and trust how you feel." Some have stepped away from the door and begun to actually listen. "But weren't you all outsiders? Is this how you would want to be treated when you first came here? This group was made because we were not wanted where we were placed. We didn't feel like we belonged, but found others that agreed in needing a change."

Natasha squeezes my hand, liking how I went with the thing, and she adds on. "I, like many of you, come from a broken home because of everything. Worlds and families are divided. We shouldn't have to be anymore!"

I feel like with Natasha by my side, we can conquer anything.

No one spoke up. Most people have their eyes downcast, knowing what they are doing is wrong. But prejudices don't just disappear over a few words that were being said.

Someone raises their hand in the crowd and tries to move forward to speak. The crowd parts around him. I wait for him to come toward the front to hear him better.

"You have your own problems that you haven't even solved yet. You are new to this world. How do you think you will take care of our problems when you barely even know how to handle your own? You don't even know everything about yourself, let alone this new world you got yourself into."

His words sting, but Greta had warned me they had these types of questions. But he made it sound like I asked for these problems to happen and that I asked and deserve the consequences that come with them.

Natasha moves forward, but I hold her back. I laugh, covering up for her anger. "You are right. I have a lot to learn in a small amount of time. But I think I am up to the challenge. I have a good council and Natasha by my side." I hold up Natasha's hand. She smiles, but her eyes are slightly surprised as they glance at me.

"I come from another world that is also divided. This does not work well, and they are always fighting for ground," Natasha comments. This is her way of fighting for them to let them know she belongs here and has knowledge they need.

"I am working with everyone here to learn the individuals on the council and others on both sides. It will take some time, but know I am working on this always." I watch as some walk out and the crowd thins.

The room seems really large with all the people that empty out of it.

Another calls out from the back before heading out the door. "We don't have time to educate a child and hope she ends up helping us," her crabby face exclaims. She looks familiar but falls into the crowd and is gone.

"I am young, but I am not a child," I seethe. "If you do not wish to teach me, I can shadow people and learn from them, regardless. I am a byproduct of this war and know I can show you what I have, even if you think I do not have any gumption." I try to reign in my anger.

"Would you say the same to me?" Natasha calls out. "I am more than adult enough. I have seen much of this world and too much of my old one. Trust the council and I that we will guide her and ensure her training is complete." She glares at Quintan. Obviously, she was kept unaware that he wanted to hold this kind of ceremony.

Quintan speaks up before the older woman can get away. "Mrs. Moshner!" He waves.

She stops moving towards the door, the others around her make room and bow around her, making sure we can see her.

"It's Ms." She speaks up, her body is hunched over a cane.

He speaks loudly so she can hear him. "Then it is settled. Alexia will meet with you, Ms. Moshner, tomorrow and will shadow you while you go about your day." He looks at Natasha and me. "Ms. Moshner is a jewel crafter. Learn what you will from that." He nods and continues. "Would others like to have Alexia around to help and learn from her?"

None speak up, but no other questions are thrown at her or grumbles of disapproval. Ms. Moshner taps her cane on the hard ground. "This is preposterous. I have a busy day ahead of me. I barely could take time out of my day for this silly outing," She complains.

"Then I would think you should welcome the help. For I will come along. Two pairs of hands are better than one." Natasha smiles coldly. "If you have any problems, we can take care of those for you." She winks.

Ms. Moshner grumbles as she leaves. "Never get my way... Always... babysitting someone. One Child per day is my limit ye hear?" I can hear some snickering from outside as the crowd moves. Another person yelps as she hits someone with her cane in punishment.

I glare at Greta, Quintan, and Jazmin. I drop Natasha's hand and take the little device off my shirt, throwing it at Jazmin. "Thanks for nothing."

"I warned you." Greta eyes me with a serious face. "It wasn't as bad as I thought it would be, though." She smiles, a part of her surprised by my speech.

"They will come around," Jazmin pipes in. "It was better for them to see you as you are, so they know how to react when you are much more than you are now."

"That is a very intriguing way to think of things," Natasha states.

"Though most of everyone in town came, the people that were meant to spill in did not end up coming. Other rogue outposts will meet you along your travels. It was good practice for you. You will have many more to come."

I shake my head quickly. "Nope, not going to happen. Greta was right. Before I go back out there and do that, I need to learn a lot. I am not ready. I need to experience first, and then perhaps we can discuss this."

Greta's eyes light up, and she gives an actual smile that reaches up to her eyes. "Finally, seeing it my way?"

I ignore that and continue with Quintan. "What is it that Ms. Moshner does exactly? I know you said she crafts jewels. Is it just jewelry or something else?"

"Or something." Jazmin gives a wicked smile and winks. "I will meet you there later so we can have a proper talk."

"Cryptic much?"

"Yes, she makes jewels, and sometimes she sets them into jewelry or trinkets. Sometimes they are also embedded with power and spells. She helps a lot of witches and other magical creatures that store power and spells into things." Quintan steps in.

"Many go to her if they want a glamor or even something more mundane done if they can't perform it themselves." Greta adds on, giving an angry look to Jazmin, watching her walk away.

I look at the windows and notice the sun is high in the sky. It feels like the day just got started. Well, that is what I get for not getting up earlier. I shrug to myself, thinking it will be okay. The later hours will be best to start in on the book. I have put it off long enough. I crave to hear from my mother and more about her life here.

"Am I free of my duties here, then?" I ask Quintan, unsure what else they all have planned for me.

"Yes, but make sure you meet up with Ms. Moshner soon." Greta asks Quintan a question. He turns to her but thinks better and turns back to Natasha and me. "Today, that is sometime today. You have plenty of time. We are still getting the final plans together to make the trek into the dark territory, so be patient," he says.

"Sure," I throw over my shoulder as I push the door aside, exiting with Natasha.

"We are not going right away, are we? Do I even have to go?"

"No," I snicker. "First, I don't even know where Ms. Moshner lives or works. Second, I don't want to. Third, let's head back to the house. I wanted to read a bit of what I had found the other day. We can also grab a bite to eat."

Natasha nods. She shakes her blue hair, and her wings disappear into the glamor she wore. "Much better." She stretches.

"That is better? Why did you let your wings be visible back there?" I ask as we walk back to the house.

"I needed to make my way to you quickly since you were bombing things. I also wanted them to know I had my own powers. They may not know who my father is, but they should respect the power I hold. Yes, it feels better to have them hidden away from anyone that could harm them." She massages her shoulder in worry.

We make it back with no one stopping us, and the walk is very nice; the sun is shining brightly, and seems like it will continue to do so for the rest of the day. We go in. Natasha breaks away from me, and I am soon twisting through the hallways, trying to make it to my room before anyone can stop me.

I twist down hallways and hear a tiny voice light up behind. "Play?" Tina skips down the hallway bobbing in time with my steps next to me.

Her tiny body of fire hops and skips, jumping long jumps to keep up with me.

I tilt my head slightly down, and to the side so I can monitor her and not accidentally step on her. I could easily tell between the fire sisters not only by height but by hairstyle as well. Taz had the longest hair and the craziest. It erupts from her body like a cloak. The middle sister Tina has hers on her shoulders. It made her seem like she wore a hood instead of hair. The oldest Trill had the shortest hair. It was short and spiky, cut in a pixie cut style.

"Kind of busy."

"I won't take no for an answer." As she lands, little flames dance around. I have to stomp on the embers once she moves away.

"You won't always get your way this way. But I guess I can play for a bit. Did you have a wonderful talk with Margaret?"

"Yea, but she was too sad. Trill is staying with her right now. I had to get away." She looks back down the hallway but turns back to me. "Play?" She reminds me.

She could be a problem as she grew up. I would have to be careful with how much I said yes and how much she coerced me into doing things. They are just children, though, and they deserve to have some fun.

A light giggle flows over me as she shakes her head.

We both are at a standstill staring at one another. "No one else can play with you at the moment?"

"Nope." She swivels and kicks her flame foot out in a wide step. "Trill is no fun. When are we leaving?"

I move forward, walking to my room. We could play there. "Soon, I am getting antsy as well," I say.

I enter the room and close the door so no one will interrupt us. The books litter the table top as I sit at it. I push them to the side and make room. I tap the top of the table, hoping she can jump up there.

I watch as she jumps up and comes closer to my chilly hands. I wriggle my fingers near her. She dances in and around my fingertips, grabbing onto them. My icy fingers warm against her dancing touch.

"What would you like to play, then?"

"Hopscotch, hopscotch!" She squeals. She pulls herself up on my fingers, jumps from finger to finger, and falls back to the table at the last one. She crouches low as she takes the impact of the fall. She rises to her tiptoes and dances once again in little hops, grabbing onto my dangling fingers once I lower them back down to her.

"Though you have good control of your flame, you do still leave marks when you aren't careful." I look at the one mark she left when falling to the table.

"Oopsie," She giggles.

"We will have to start training soon to figure out what we can do. Can I call you guys without words, or can I just think it, and you come?"

She stomps a foot, and another streak of smoke steams from the wood.

"But we will play first, I promise. How about hopscotch on candles instead?" I ask.

She tilts her head, peering up at me. "How would that work? And yes, you can just call to us in your mind, and we will be there for you."

"Really?"

She nods.

I take out some candles I have around the room.

"So, remember the course Margaret and Robert had set up for you? We could do something like that."

"How would you play?"

"I am too big for candles, so I can." All the pillows are on the seats and bed. "I can take these." I pull them and throw them to the floor in a pattern. "After you go, I can follow with the pillows. We can play that way."

"Poo, I wanna play on the pillows."

"Remember what happened last time when you got too excited and almost started a fire in here?"

"Yes," she whispers back in a very tiny voice. "Margaret screeched really loud, and Robert hollered."

"Only because they were worried. We must be careful, but we can still have fun."

"I know. At least I am not like Taz. She ruins all the fun. She is not careful." Tina sticks out her tongue.

I bend down and whisper as we conspire together. "Let's not do that again, or else Robert might kick us out." I give her wide eyes.

"No, he wouldn't! Couldn't!" She gives a high pitch screech.

"You're right, he wouldn't, but do we want to test what he will send instead?"

"Where you go, I go. They will be sorry for not having us in their group. They need us!" She hops from candle to candle. "Think of the adventures we will come across."

"I hope you are right. Until then, we will have to be on our best behavior and try not to get into too much trouble. You and I can work on a miracle for these people later on."

"We will rock this!" She pumps her small fist into the air, the flames on her body grow and jump with vigor.

I give her a half smile. I walk back over to the pillows and go to the start. She does the same to the candles that are set up. She catches on the wick and twirls around it.

We play for a few moments before she wants to talk to Margaret and Trill again. I pick up the discarded pillows and place the candles back off the table around the room. I want the table clear so I can go through more of my mother's journal.

I pull out the pack I got from my parent's home from under the bed. I hold it carefully against my chest, gripping it. The metal case contains what I really want. I have wiped the metal clear of dust and grime, though it is still dull and not shiny like new. I pull the lid open with my fingers. The journal lies in there. Nothing is disturbed.

I turn open to the first page, this time since I had started from the middle last time. I look at the closed door, making sure I will not be disturbed.

Dear Diary,

Soon my sister's future husband will be here. Papa says they should be here tomorrow night and we should all be on our best behavior. Flit is supposed to be the most terrifying of creatures from the dark side. It is why he is in charge of things over there. Once she weds him, I can follow my dreams, do what I wish, and be with who I want. He has a brother, though, and I fear father will make another deal for me. He has a problem being indebted to others; it is like a drug to him. A rush, he says, makes him feel alive. The son's names are Ivan and Ian. That is all I know about them other than they are from the dark side, badger shifters and might have some dark magics. Their mother was not a full badger, but that is not really known or a fact. Just speculation.

I am trying to be like my sister and give them all a shot to stop all this warring. I am only eighteen. This is too much for one girl at this age. Perhaps they will be nice. Perhaps I am freaking out for nothing. I spoke to Jade. She is very intrigued by how things will go. She has always wanted to marry a prince. She sees a picture of Ian and Ivan from some magical report and thinks they are pretty cute. I think he has cruel eyes. If she is so inclined after all this, she can have him. As long as father does not break his promise to me and makes me marry him, that is.

Jade is better than me. That is why she is doing all this. She is a full witch and knows her duty is important to her and her people. It is why father cares about where her future is headed. I am just the lone wolf, the mistake that is kept around in tolerance. I will never be enough for any of them.

I want to run away from it all. Did, in fact, the other day since I'm not really needed. They sent Robert to fetch me. Even though he is a newer guard here, he does his best to prove his worth. I ended up spilling everything to him to fight coming back here. He understood but wouldn't have any of it. He kept his word and hasn't told anyone about what I told him. I told him I would remember that. But what does my word mean?

I only got away for a couple of days, not enough to miss our royal meeting! Earth is my element to call. It should have been enough to hide from almost any creature. Robert is special. He is a spirit creature and can find people regardless, as long as they have a soul.

It's too bad he works for my father; I could almost like him.

Life sucks. Where is my helmet?

Sera

Robert! He had said he knew my mother, but even before that before she became what she was. It had to be the same person. Right? Could he sense others? I reread the passage in front of me. No, she states that he can track them as long as they have a soul. Shade is a soulless being, but could he find the flame spirit, Taz? What about Blaise? Why were we not asking for his help in all of this? He could find them right away? Others had to have thought of this before, now I would think.

I scrabble to shut the journal and get it back in the metal box. Taking care to make sure it is fully in the satchel before wrapping it up and putting it back under the bed where I hid it. I could wait and read some more, but this was too good to pass up. I had to find Robert and ask some questions.

The last time I remember seeing him was the other night when he took Natasha and me to the ruins of my parent's place. I wonder if he is around. I pace in my room, growing closer to the door and back toward the bed. Margaret! She will know where I can find him or when I can talk to him. She has to. I race to the door and fling it open wide. I catch it before it bangs on the wall and hurry down the hallway. I skid down the stairs, almost jumping past all the steps.

"Margaret!" I call out.

"Alexia?" She calls out, her voice laced with worry.

I run to the kitchen, where I heard her voice coming from. I race past the training room Natasha and Zeek are sparring in. I don't slow down. Not wanting to interrupt them or my quest as I race past the room.

Margaret chuckles at something one of the fire sisters says. They are all giggling once I slide into the room. Both are skipping around and balancing on twigs and strings that are strung across cups and other objects.

"What's going on, Alexia? There is no fire, as you can see." She splays her hands out in front of the sisters.

I gasp out my breath, wheezing in and out. "Man, I need more cardio in my life," I huff as I bend over and place my hands on my knees.

"Many of the people that keep guard do a run every morning you could join them."

I shake my head politely. "To have them laugh or have to slow down for me? No thanks. Do you know where Robert is?"

She looks up in thought and concentrates really hard as if she is trying to reach him.

I give her a worried look, but she continues staring at the ceiling. I wave my hand in front of her face. "Margaret? Are you okay?"

"Oh. Yes, sweetie. I was tugging on our spirit chord to see if he is around. He is close by, but I think he is in his other form. You can wait for him here; he will come when he can." She pats the table next to her, wanting me to sit and wait.

"Why can't we go wait for him where he is?"

"No, that is rude. We will wait till he is less vulnerable and safe." She nods, winking at Tina.

"Is he doing something dangerous?" I tap on the top of the chair, not wanting to fully commit to sitting down. I stand behind the chair, leaning into it.

"He could be, yes. That is why we should wait here. Make sure nothing follows while he is spirit walking."

"You said spirit chord." I watch her nod to me. "What is that? He said you are not mates. How can you be bound, then?" I ask, really confused. Was this bond kind of like how Zeek does some bonds when doing deals?

Something shifts behind her eyes, and she stares at me. Her eyes grow darker and wider the longer she stares. I blink and look down, unsure of myself or what is happening.

She shakes her head and smiles at the flame sisters. "Let's get some tea. You girls want to help?"

Squeals of laughter come from Tina and Trill as they make their way to the stove. They already have things lit. Margaret goes to get the water in the teapot. Their flame bodies bend and sway as they play in the flames, dancing in and out. She tsks at them and tries to calm their voices. Margaret places the teapot on the stove and waits for it to heat up. The girls make themselves even smaller and dive in and out of the rushing flames. Daring the flames to grow higher and hotter.

"I apologize for my rudeness. I didn't have the best time before Robert came into the picture. That part gets to me sometimes." She pulls at her blond hair and tucks her long bangs back behind her ear.

"What do you mean?" This time I pull out the chair, taking a seat. "Robert didn't really explain anything, so I am unsure what you are talking about."

She let loose a loud sigh. "It is a very long story and not a very nice one at that." She looks up at the ceiling once more. "But I think we have time for some of the story, at least." She gives a wry smile.

"When Robert and I met, he was with your mother and her family, guarding for them. We were so young then."

"I read about that in my mother's journal," I blurt out.

"You found one of them?"

"One? There are more?"

"Oh yes, that one was always writing any chance she could! It surprised me she never wanted to write stories or books," she chuckles.

"Yea, just one so far. It said Robert was a newer guard, and he brought her back to her family after she tried to run away once. I haven't really read much more than that yet."

"Keep reading. You will find a lot of information you may need throughout your journey. Yes, he was a very new guard for your family when we met and was inexperienced with more wild women, too." She shuffles her hands and sits back down in her chair, waiting for the whistle to blow.

I lean forward, intrigued by what more she has to tell.

"I was mated at the time. So, as good as married. We traveled with Ivan and his father when your parents met for the first time. I was there to help with the boys and keep them in line while their father worked his magic, so to speak. Jeffrey, my mate, was the dark sides right-hand man. He was as sly as a fox, you could say." She winked once more.

She said things as if they were jokes, but I was out of the loop on the punch line. I smile and nodded, unsure what more she wanted from me.

"He was not a suitable mate; we were not a good fit for one another. Once mated, breaking that bond and remaining whole is almost impossible. He was a terrible man. We were both fox shifters. Our animals fell for one another before our human selves did. Those rarely turn out right." A tear falls down her cheek. She swipes it away quickly, gets up to walk a few steps, and then turns back again. "I was young and naïve back then. I thought it was love. I thought it was right. I thought that was what life was supposed to be like."

"I.. I.." I stutter to come up with something decent to say. "I get how that can be. Not all people are good, and they all don't stay that way either."

She nods, wringing her hands in front of her. She picks up a dish towel, wrapping it around her hands and then folding it and un-folding it, keeping her hands busy. "Robert found me at my worst, at Jeffrey's worst. I mentioned he was a spirit walker, correct?" I could tell she still had a hard time speaking about this trauma that happened to her.

I nod eagerly. "Though I am not sure what a spirit walker is or does. Though I have seen him in a fox shape with many tails, he looks like a ghost," I point out.

"Yes!" She exclaims in a loud, boisterous voice. She rushes back to the table and sits down with the towel so that her hands have some-thing to do. "He has a fox shape but is a kitsune, a little bit different from a fox shifter, which Jeffrey and I were. Kitsune are spirit walkers and can manipulate and do things with spirit that aren't always an option for others. Again, I state this is a very complex and lengthy story, but the gist of it is he saved me. Usually, when one of a fully mated pair dies, the other soon follows. Robert cast me in his own spirit net and used it to create a link when there were none. That helped anchor me to the living, to him."

"So, you are kind of mated, right?" I ask, highly confused.

"I would not use those words around him. It is more freeing than formal mating. Shifters, many of the animals, have evolved and become laxer than they used to be. Though there are still expectations that are still held. Like in my case, even though you find your other half or soul, it doesn't necessarily make them nice or treat you how you deserve to be treated. But you have a tie that normal means can't destroy. Though there are some darker magics that you can try, they are not promised. Death is one surefire way to break the connection, but it results in the death of both parties. Robert refused to accept this and made his own way."

"But you are tethered to him," I state.

"Yes, but he has ensured I know I have all the slack I could want. I can leave if I wish and do what I want, when I want. He has pushed all the slack to me, and I can go or not go. He expected nothing to come of this. He is a very kind and gentle man. Probably one of the few reasons I have stayed with him all these years." Her lips quirk up on the side. A high-pitched whistle sound emits around us.

She jumps at the sudden noise and goes to get the kettle. The girls continue to play in the fire. She leaves it for them to turn off when they are done. She pours the hot water into some cups, sets some tea bags in them, and brings them over to sit in front of us.

I also take mine and dip the tea bag in and out of the water, letting the water grab and pull the contents to the bottom. "He didn't do it to have you be with him instead?" My hands wrap around the warm mug.

"No. Not really. Oh, he probably hoped all the while but did not want his thoughts or dreams to manipulate mine. He didn't want me to be forced to live another life that I would not be happy with. Not when he saw me try so hard to escape my current predicament and fail."

"What made you want this life? What made you decide to choose him in the end? What made you decide to go rogue?" I ask, wanting to know more about what made up her decision and pushed her to this place. I wanted to hear and understand more of her story.

"The dark side is a harsh place, and many go back to age-old practices. It is truly the dark side of things. We were ridiculed and thought to be horrible. Why not go along when you will be blamed for such things, anyway?" She raises an eyebrow as she takes a sip of the still-steaming tea.

I continue to swirl the bag at the bottom, not wanting to take a sip until it cooled down further. "So why not try a different world? Natasha explained she came from a different world to here. Could you not do the same?"

"I could have. It would have been tough; you see, only the higher-ups or certain places have portals to other worlds, and you have to know how they work to get to where you are going. Mostly, you stick to the safe ones, and those are governed by each side and those who are in power. I didn't want to move away from all that I know. I like this world even with all the flaws it has. No, my place needed to be here. Just the dark side was not somewhere I wanted to be. They would never accept me as part of the light side. Robert, Ivan, and Sera explained what they were trying to do, and it sounded like something I wanted to be a part of. After that, Robert and I spent more and more time together and grew closer than we had ever been before, and the rest is history, as they say."

"Wow, so you and Robert were just friends when it all went down, and he still did all that with nothing more promised."

"He is a guard, true and true. He is noble and prideful in what he does. Who he decides to protect, he protects with everything in him. His devotion, dedication, and determination are unbound like no other. Once he puts his trust in you, there is no going back, and he does not turn on his friends or those he calls his. Don't get me wrong, it took me a lot of time to figure out my own mess and not feel as if others were trying to force me into something I did not want. I questioned a lot in those first years. He was patient and understanding."

"Don't be lying to the girl." Robert walks in his boots, hitting the floor with a heavy thud.

I finally pull the mug closer to me and inhale the aroma of the tea. It is a lemony scent. I blow across the steam still pouring off of it. I sip on it gently.

He comes across the kitchen, kisses the top of Margaret's head, and then kisses her on the lips in greeting. He walks across the way, picks out a cup of his own, and makes his own tea. She pinches his butt before he gets too far away.

"I am telling her the truth," she says. "You were very kind and patient."

"I was ruthless in my own right. She made me out to be some hero, didn't she? She made me the white knight."

"Because you were!" She pushes.

He walks over and holds the cup in one hand as he places an arm around her, comforting her with the other. "Hun, anyone could have been in that situation. We are past that now. There is no way that will ever be your reality again." He rubs her arm in comfort.

"I know." Her eyes go distant for a moment but pull back to him. "If I get to talk about you being my hero and how amazing you are at it, I damn well will!" She puts force behind it. "And you will like it."

"Of course, I will." He nibbles the tip of her nose and snuggles with her. "But a white knight wouldn't burn the world down for you like I would. Just saying." The heat coming off of him intensifies.

I keep my eyes focus forward and sip on the tea, hoping not to breathe too deeply or loudly so they can have their moment alone. I almost think of leaving but know if I move, the screeching of the chair on the floor will ruin the moment, so here I sit, feeling a bit awkward.

Soon there is a whisper and something I try hard not to pay attention to. "Robert!" Margaret says sternly. "Alexia needed to talk to you, and I was keeping her entertained while you were busy. I will remember next time that you would rather be disturbed."

"You still here girly?" Robert's voice is low and rumbling. "What was it you needed?" He eases back and sits on the tabletop in front of Margaret, who glares at him.

I gulp. "I read in my mother's journal that you could locate souls that no one could hide from you."

His eyes slide to me a bit and just take me in before continuing. "That's right." The heat no longer there.

"Are you able to track Shade?" I ask, my voice barely above a whisper.

"I have tried. The answer is no. Whatever he is, yes, he is human, but he is still without a soul." He frowns. "And before you ask, I have tried locating Taz, who he carries with him. She is not registering with me either. He may be keeping her hidden or off the charts somehow. So, I cannot locate either of them."

"I had thought you guys hadn't thought of it since no one really was bringing up finding them other than me."

"It is not that we haven't been working on this. We just do it in private. We don't want you to be disappointed if it doesn't work out," he says.

I nod a little. Sadness shines through. "Have you then tried locating Blaise?" I ask hesitantly.

"Blaise, are you sure you still want to find him?"

"Wouldn't you... Maybe you are not the best person to ask that question, but wouldn't you for Margaret?"

"That is different." His voice goes low, and anger radiates through him.

Margaret places a hand on his knee, calming him instantly. His body curves over hers, and his body settles down. "She did not mean it that way. Alexia, if you have that urge or something that tells you this is the right path to follow, then you need to follow it. I almost didn't listen to mine and almost lost out on this amazing ride."

Robert whisks away a few strands of hair that have come loose from behind her ear. "You never said that before."

"I did, but not in so many words." She gives a hint of a smile.

"In short, I can find Blaise, yes. But the question is, do we want to, and when? When we get over to the dark side, we will look for him, but know that we also need to find out the truth of the matter and how he fits into all of this."

"I think he is just a pawn in all of this." He is frowning. "I will play this smart and learn the truth before giving my heart."

"Have you been over to the Jewelers yet? It's getting pretty late."

"No." I put down the rest of my tea and place it on the table. "I am not sure where it is, and Natasha looked like she was in a pretty intense battle with Zeek." I look over my shoulder down the hall.

"I can take you over there. It's not too far. Margaret, you want anything, or do you want to come?" He asks, keeping things open for her to make her own decisions.

"No, I want to spend time with the girls while they are here." She shoos us away. "You can stop by the bakery and grab some cookies. I would like that very much."

"Will do." He nods and stands up, giving her a peck on the lips before he walks down the hallway. "Let's get going. No time like the present."

I scramble up out of the seat and push it in. I walk a few steps toward the hallway and then stop and step back to the table.

"Don't worry about the dish. I got it," she says calmly.

"Thank you for the story. I would like to hear the full one sometime."

"Anytime. Perhaps in time, you will come to know the story."

CHAPTER 7

I WALK WITH QUICK feet down the grass-covered hill with Robert in tow. Instead of going straight like I did last time further into town, we headed right down the hill that led to a few shops. Jason stays silent mostly. It unnerved me how quiet he could be.

"You can get anywhere in this small town with just a short walk," I state.

"Yea, we like it quaint and small. Fewer problems that way. There are larger rogue towns to the south, near the mountain range. They are so large because no others want to live down that way, so they pull together instead of spreading out. The land is treacherous and dangerous, and hardly anything lives there."

"Good to know. Great place to hide a town is somewhere no one wants to go," I say. The tea calms my stomach, but it works itself back into knots on what I am supposed to do with Ms. Moshner. Meeting new people would be the bane of my existence and my stomach. I am curious about where Robert has been spirit walking, but I don't want to bother him with things he doesn't want to talk about. He seems sad. "What's wrong?"

He smiles sadly and shakes his head, continuing on our way. After many minutes of silence, he throws out what is on his mind. "Some people are dealt a bad hand and don't deserve the things that happen to them." He breathes out heavily.

"Yes, but it is better now for her and you." I give him a curious look, then look away quickly, not wanting to see the pure anguish on his face.

"Not all get that, though. She almost didn't make it, as she stated. To think what could have been."

I place my hand on his lower arm and stop him from walking. He stops and turns to me, keeping his eyes down. "What could have been is the worst to think about. There are so many paths to pick, a different way may have led to worse consequences you didn't think of. You can't think about it like that, be glad about how it turned out. Enjoy the happiness you have. If you do not, then even that you could lose, eventually." I let my hand drop away from his arm.

His eyes raise to mine in surprise. "I forget sometimes you are not just a child and do have wisdom hidden within. It just needs to be nurtured to grow. We will help you with that. Thank you." His giant hand claps me on the shoulder as he pushes off. We continue walking, and soon there were four buildings up ahead. Signs were in the windows or off to the side to explain what each of them was for.

I did not see a sign for a jeweler or anything like that. "Which one are we headed to, my fearless knight?" I call out, trying to lighten the mood.

He chuckles and shakes his head. "None of these. Ms. Moshner's place is around the corner."

We progress down the well walked road. I jog ahead to the corner to see what is down that way. The inn and the main building I was in before were huge, the biggest in this small town, but this one is very peculiar. It wasn't huge by any standard, but it is shaped weirdly.

I knew which shop only because it is the only one around the corner. The rest of the street disappears into the woods. She lives on the far edge.

"This is it?" I ask, unsure how to categorize this place.

"Yep." He stands back behind me, wanting me to go in first.

I stare at the building before me. There is a mix of steel and wood. It looked like it was being eaten by the woods and the hill we have just traveled down. The lines and front look clean, though some parts of it are sticking out where others are further in some places are rounder, and others are boxier looking like a building usually is.

"This building makes no sense."

"That is the way she likes it. Keeps people on their toes, and no one knows what they will get when they enter." He bends down and whispers. "Keeps thieves at bay, too." He raises his eyebrows.

I advance towards the window, trying to peer in through the colored glass to see what the room will be like. They are tall and skinny; I squint, trying to see past the glass. Only wisps of shadows move behind the panels.

A bell tinkles as Robert opens the door wide open, wanting me to go through first. The door is the only thing that has clear, see-through glass. I shake my head at Robert, unsure of wanting to go into the store yet. I peek my head in and soon follow through the door.

The store is immaculate and pristine. I have pictured something stuffier and more cramped, or something very dusty and dirty. Some parts of this town seemed like a small village; others were more sophisticated. I wondered what an actual town looked like on either side.

There are numerous tables covered in thick cloth, and tons of jewels are scattered across each table. All kinds of colors from each side of the spectrum glitter and sparkle before me. Some jewels are huge, and others are very tiny. I walk over and pick up one until I feel the thrum of something zap at my fingers.

I drop it quickly. "Ow." I rub my fingertips against my leg, trying to release the sting of it.

"That will teach you," Robert murmurs.

"Is that girl already causing problems in my store!?" A loud voice rings out from the back.

"We are out here, Ms. Moshner!" Robert calls out.

"What did she touch?" She hacks as she walks forward. A loud bang comes from behind the counter in the back of the room. She grumbles loudly and curses under her breath. "What if I say we aren't open? Will you take her back with you?"

"She didn't touch anything dangerous, just knick-knacks you keep at the front here. She is here to shadow you in your day, so you can't say you are closed when you are clearly open." Robert stares at her before she accepts, I am not going anywhere.

Ms. Moshner doesn't back down and throws out her hand in my direction. "What am I supposed to do with this? She has no magic from Quintan's little speech, and she can't even call on her other form from her father's side."

What was Quintan doing, airing out all my dirty laundry? Did everyone know what my faults were? Was anyone going to give me a chance or accept me? My eyes narrow at them both. They both move past me to yell about the situation. I ignore both of them and walk around the store instead to check out more dangerous gems. Oh, no, what if I touched one of those? I skim my fingers barely above, touching the jewels around the store. They didn't pay me any attention. My lips quirk up into a smile.

My eyes rest on a couple of beautiful rubies that sit in a pile to the right of some other jewels of all sizes and colors.

"I suggest you give her something easy for the day. Teach her something about your trade or use her to move around stuff that you want to get to but haven't. There has to be something," Robert pushes.

I ignore their squabble as I move closer to the deep red rubies. They glisten and sparkle like stars or little fireballs as the lights in the room reflect the rich color. I reach out a finger and barely touch the large stone that is propped up in the middle of all the other jewels, wondering what this one would go to. I lightly caress the stone and hear a voice sing, a wondrous melody that enchants me. I shake my head, take my hand off the stone, and look around the shop, checking to see if anyone is paying attention. The singing stops once I stop touching it.

Robert and Ms. Moshner step further away from me, their backs toward me. I look down and feel the urge to pick up the stone. I press my cold fingers to the smooth stone and pick it up from the cloth. I hold it and bring my other hand up to caress the jewel. The singing starts back up again, bringing me closer. I close my eyes and sway to the tune. My breath catches.

The lure calls me deeper, and the song catches me and pulls me further into the depths.

"What a pretty thing to have, my jewel." His voice is cool and in tune with the melody that still hums in my head. Though his voice is cool and calm, it stokes the fire further down inside me.

I gasp in answer, but my hands cling harder to the jewel. "Who are you?"

His rich laughter pours over my ears. "Wouldn't you like to know?" On the nap of my neck, I feel a warm breath.

"I would," I say almost automatically.

"Such a pretty thing should be rewarded for finding what is mine." Something huge and firm brushes against my back. "How would you like to be rewarded?" Something further down and large brushes against my pant leg. This felt like a dream, and nothing felt real or substantial.

"I... You..." I pant.

"Minx," A soft voice calls.

I look down and see a tether of some sort. I grab it with my hand that is free and pull it up closer to inspect it. It becomes more solid as I touch it.

"What are you doing, Minx?"

"This voice is entrancing," I answer. The darkness is too thick to see Blaise, but I know his voice.

Laughter rumbles from the man behind me, and his hard chest pushes into my back. Low humming whispers past my ear closer, lulling me. I lean back into his embrace. "Let go of that string, my sweet. He won't bother us here if you don't let him."

I almost let the chord slip from my fingers. "He did say he didn't want me around; he didn't want me to find or know him," I whisper as I let the string swirl through my fingers. "The string is barely even there as it is. The rope is rough and fraying at the edges. It is so frail."

Rough fingers scrape against my jaw and pull my face and eyes away from the chord. "You, my treasure, deserve untold riches and someone to want you with them, whatever the cost."

The chord slips from my fingers as he turns me away from the chord. He turns me fully into his arms. It is the first proper look I get of this man. He is tall and has wide shoulders. His blond hair is cut short and styled. His eyes are gray and haunting.

"I could give you so much more than he ever could. If only." His fingers rub over my jaw and down my arm to where the jewel lies in my hand.

As his fingers come closer to the jewel, the fire intensifies within me. "If only what?"

"You are so far away, beautiful one," he calls. His other hand caresses strands of my hair.

"Where are you?" I reach out to place my hand on his arm, but it passes right through. "Wait, what is this?" The mist envelops him, and now only I can see his face which is close to mine.

"None of this is real," he answers serenely. His eyes turn sad as warmth envelopes me. "The jewel holds my heat. I can manipulate it for small things and converse like this with whoever is holding it if I wish." His hand travels back up my arm and passes his warm hands over my sensitive nipples. "The heat can do some more delicious things," He answers wickedly.

"Yes," I pant. "More." The fog wavers and pulls back a bit but covers everywhere. Everything is becoming hazy and hard to make out.

A melody belts out of him once again as the heat skims over my stomach and wraps back around my back. He turns me in place and melds all of him and his heat to my back. His hand roves to the gem. "Grip the stone tightly, my sweet," He continues to hum into my ear. The music making me drift further off.

The edges of the stone press into my palm. I feel the heat get hotter, and his touch becomes more solid. "Where are you?"

He turns me back around and wraps his arms around my stomach. Relaxing back into him, I feel him solidify there with me. The fog and darkness begin to drift away. There is no longer any rope around me, and his hands slide to my breasts as he feels me sink into him. He massages them, and his warm breath whispers to me. "Some woman has me trapped. She sold my warmth so I could not get away. But you found it. Oh, how you will be rewarded." He tweaks my nipples in response.

I cry out in response. Bucking my hips and push back against him. His song stops for a moment before it resumes.

"You are a strong one. You must bring this back to me so I can escape this wretched place." One of his hands travels down mine, the one cupping the jewel. He pushes my hand down further, tucking it into my pant pocket, but he makes sure to hold my hand there, so it doesn't let go. "Can you do that for me? Bring this to me?"

I nod.

"Do not tell anyone about our little deal, my pet. If you don't, I will make it so much more worth it." He caresses my arm as he takes his away and places it on my throat, tipping my head back, making me look into his cool gray gaze. He hums a little in response. "Tell me you understand." Light pressure presses on my neck in answer.

I swirl my tongue around my dry mouth, trying to form the words needed. "I understand." I say in a faded whisper.

"Good, my pet. I will visit you again, my sweet. I have not had quite enough time with you yet." His hand again loosens, and he pulls my hand away from the stone, making this reality disappear from view and the humming and singing stop.

As I open my eyes once again, the store and jewels answer me. My one hand is flat on the table right next to the other jewels. I quickly fling my hand away from the other ones, and my body quakes. What the hell was that?

"Don't you dare, girlie," Ms. Moshner wails. She hobbles over to me and slaps at my hands, which are shaking.

"What?" I shake in a daze.

"Which one did you touch?" She turns back to Robert. "How can I work like this if she touches everything?" She hollers.

Robert is not where he was previously. The door swings open, and the bell above the door gives a loud ring with another bang as the door slams shut in answer. I watch Robert's form turn down the corner and vanish from view.

Ms. Moshner screeches in anger. "Oh, he's gonna be getting what is comin to him. Fer runnin away from me. He is a big chicken, that one." As the anger rises, a thick accent kicks out.

I clear my throat as she shambles away, picking up this and that as she heads back to the back of the store.

"Don't ye be touchen anything else in here, girlie. Unless I tell ye to."

"Yes, Ms. Moshner." I cast my eyes to the floor, away from the sparkling jewels. Done with touching the gems, I pull my hair tie out and fix it to where my hair is up in a bun off of my neck. Hoping to cool the heat that has been stoked inside me.

She grunts and wobbles her way around the corner. I follow close behind, her pace a little faster than that of a turtle.

She ducks behind a curtain. It leads to a large back room. Machines that are far in advance litter the space, making it seem smaller than it is. It clutters the workspace, and shavings and sparkling dust litter the floor. Another door is set into the back of this room. The door is heavy and solid, unlike the front door and cloth separating the store from the back room. The door shines. It is thick and fully metal. The silver makes it look impenetrable.

"Ms. Moshner?" I ask tentatively. I am unsure if she realizes I am still here. She hasn't said anything for several minutes, and I am unsure if she meant for me to see all of this.

"Speak up girlie," She hollers back as some machines make noise and start-up. Gears grind together and make a screeching sound. The tone resonates through my sensitive eardrums, causing me to shudder in pain. I fan the back of my neck, trying to cool the inner heat that still thrums through me. My fingers itch to delve into my right pocket where the jewel is hidden to play with the person inside.

"I was wondering what your name is?" I speak a little louder this time so she can hear me properly.

"Are ye daft woman? It's Ms. Moshner." She gives me a cruel look.

"No, I get that... I mean your first name. What is it?" I ask, trying to explain differently.

"I know what you meant, girlie. I am not the daft one here now, am I? Everyone has a first name, but not everyone deserves to know it. Ye have not earned that right as of yet. So, first name Ms. Last name Moshner to you," she scoffs.

I rub my fingertips in slow circles across my forehead. The rest of the day is going to be very long. I follow behind her as she pokes and prods her way through the machines.

The bell chimes once again. I look at Ms. Moshner and watch her fiddle with a machine. I shuffle back to the hanging cloth and peek through the curtain.

"Hello!" A lady wails out.

I look back at the owner of this store to see if she heard the new person out there. She instead pulls up a chair next to some jewels in a machine and sets her sights on them, pulling them closer without touching them.

"Hello?" The voice howls out the question, a little less sure that someone is around. The purple dress is a dead giveaway to who stands inside the shop.

"Well? Go see who it is, girlie. Yer here fer some learning, aren't ye go check out what they want?"

I let out a pent-up sigh and turn to head back to the front of the store. I bat at the cloth as I walk out. No wonder she had a problem with thieves if she treated everyone this way. I can see why she did.

"Yes, can I help you?" I inquire, pasting on a fake smile.

"You are not Ms. Moshner." Jazmin chuckles. "But I told you we would see each other here, so there you are."

"Hi Jazmin. Yea, she is in the back. I can get her if you need." I wave my hand behind my back at the cloth.

Things start to hum, and it feels like a charge in the air. One that I have not felt before now. She is wearing a strange metal covering that is over her right eye. It looks like an eye patch.

"What is that? You didn't have it on earlier today?" I ask.

She tilts her head to the side as if she is listening to something in the distance. Her long purple hair swishes forward, covering that part of her face.

"Actually, they are telling me she is needed. We can chat later. Can you go get her for me...? Please?" She adds for emphasis when I do not move.

"Come again?" I ask, unsure of what is happening. It is as if a switch flipped in Jazmin.

Her fingers twitch. "The dead."

I back up a step; the cloth tangling up on my back as I move.

"The dead talk to you?" I ask.

"What else do you think a necromancer does? She is new here." The last part, she looked to the left of me.

I look to my side and see empty air; I scoot away, smashing myself up against the frame on the right. The cloth catches against me. I have it twisted, and it causes me to trip up. My arms pinwheel, and I lean way back.

Jazmin catches my arm before I fall. "They say you have many paths before you. Some are not what they seem." Her head tilts to the side, not looking at me anymore. "They also know your story; the dead are very eager to see the outcome and if some will be avenged. Spirits are heavy around you."

I cringe at the added pressure continuing on my bicep that she still has a hold on, even after righting myself. "Do you not just conjure the dead?" I ask, a bit horrified at what is happening.

"Why do the dead follow you so?" She questions and smiles right back.

"I don't know. Why not ask them? Apparently, you talk to them." I yank my arm free from her vice-like hold.

Her arm comes free and out from the billowy sleeves of the dress. A red tattoo is scrawled up and down her right and left arm. Last couple of times, I had just seen her briefly, and she was fully covered and didn't have the eye patch. This was a bit too weird.

"They like to keep their secrets. The living is much easier and better to play with." She gives a cruel smile. "But they are interested in you. Isn't that fascinating?"

"I don't know why they would be."

"You can ask them for yourself if you would like." She fingers something in the folds of her dress.

I back up, clearing the cloth before going through the doorway this time.

"Leave the poor girlie alone, Jazmin," Ms. Moshner barks out.

"There you are. We must talk to you right away," she pouts. "But they wanted to be distracted by Alexia instead. They whisper about her."

"Well, let's talk out here. Girlie, you saw how dusty it was back there. Get to cleaning up might as well be useful." Ms. Moshner walks up to Jazmin, wraps her arm around hers, and guides her across the room further down the counter so they can talk in private. "You know you should stop ye talking with the dead and try living amongst the real people." I hear before crossing into the back room.

I hover by the doorway, hoping to get more. "They are real enough." She bites back, but her voice keeps moving further away.

"Come this way. Your order is ove' here." I peek my head out of the curtain to see what she has ordered.

Jazmin catches me looking at her and at what they are doing. "So many paths for someone so young Alexia... no, Lexi.... No, Lex" She shakes her head, causing her purple hair to pull in front of her face. "Why do they have different names for you?" Her brow furrows in concentration. "I need you to stop!" She yells out. "One at a time."

She quirks her head as if listening intently. Ms. Moshner shoos me back, wanting me to leave them in peace. I ease back, but the cloth has gotten caught on something. I reach up to tug at it and bring it back down in place.

Something black and purple wraps around my wrist, pulling me and yanking me out of the doorway. "Ah. Ah. Ah. No, you don't." She whips out the thing that Ms. Moshner had completed for her. It has a black handle at the end. The rest of it is a black chain that is littered with jewels and spikes spinning down the whole chain. She flicks the chain, loosening it around my wrist. The chain comes free from me when she flicks it once more. She pulls her arm back and lashes out once more.

I squint my eyes shut and lift my arm to block the hit. I don't feel anything come down on me, so I lower my arm and open my eyes with the barest of slits. I see the chain hanging to the side of me near the doorway it was wrapped around a ghostly figure, one who also held a part of the curtain, keeping it from falling close. "What is that weapon?" I ask in wonder.

I shuffle back away from the form as my eyes dodge to Jazmin, who still has a hold of this ghost. She pulls it closer to her, muttering something under her breath. The spikes impale the ghostly form when she twists and tightens the chain. She wraps the chain around her own arms, gaining traction on them. The form, as Jazmin speaks and brings it closer, starts to fade and dissipate into nothingness.

"What was that?" I ask.

"Don't you know Jazmin is a necromancer?" Ms. Moshner tsks. "That weapon is her whip with the added improvements that help her attack the spiritual plane." Ms. Moshner puffs out in pride.

"Yes," I say, stunned.

Jazmin butts in. "Along with raising the dead, I can also commute with them and see them. I can also interact with them." She rolls her whip up and collects the chain. "I imbued certain objects and jewels with my power to have weapons that affect the spirit realm. That is why I come here for the jewel makers' help."

"And what did you just do?" I point a wavering hand in the direction of where the ghost was last seen.

"Saved your ass." She giggles. Her fingers caress the chain and whip all in one, looking at it with love and affection.

"Could the dead harm me?"

"Of course, they can in lots of ways." She waves her hand away. "None of that now. I promise, Ms. Moshner, they will behave now. Let us continue with our conversation. This whip will do what I need it to."

"Yes, right this way." She shambles further away from me and glares daggers my way. I dip back into the back room, wanting to get away from the dead and Jazmin as fast as possible for right now.

A shiver runs down my back from all that has happened.

"How am I supposed to learn from these people if they won't even give me a chance?" I grumble to myself. Looking for a broom and dustpan to clean up this mess. The shininess from the metal machines distracts my eye. I keep them to just the machine, not the jewels on the tables or machines. I look back at the cloth covering the door, ensuring I am still alone. A computer is on the other side of the room, near the big metal door. I make my way to the computer, also keeping an eye out for a broom.

"I have not seen a computer. Since back at the fancy library. It feels like it has been so long since I was at Morningstar." I move the mouse, and the screen lights up. An order receipt is being displayed plainly on the screen. I scroll through the jargon, scanning my eyes over the words, hoping they catch on something of interest. The name on the top is Jazmin.

"This is her order. It must be," I whisper. "This must be what she is going over with her right now, along with the whip." Glancing down at the receipt, it is just a bunch of words that don't really mean much to me or are words I have never heard before. Didn't Quintan say she could also work magic into the stones? "So she doesn't just manipulate her own power or spells into an item, but others as well."

"Well, this is useless." I complain. Spinning around in the chair, I look yet again for a broom but can't find or see one. Perhaps it was behind this door. I look at the door a few feet from me. I march over to it and test the handle to see if it would open. It turns with ease. I open it to pitch blackness. A clatter and bang pierce the darkness and echoes into the room. My head jerks up, and my breath puffs out in terror. I drop behind the door, keeping most of my body covered by the metal door. I glare into the darkness, but nothing moves or is seen. My body shakes, not wanting to go into the room even a little bit to find a light switch to see what they kept in there.

"Nope, nope, and a big hell nope." I recite to myself, shoving the door shut. I walk back over to the computer, shaking my head. "I am not going in there, no way, no how." I settle my sights on the computer once again. Trying to ignore the creepiness from the room. I didn't feel like I was alone. I could feel something peering at me from the darkness. A crack of the door stands open. The door did not snick shut when I closed it.

Another clang resonates through the room, followed by a screech. I stare at the door, watching it intently. I continue to back away; my hands skim over things as I go back to watching the door. My fingers land on something hard and wooden. My eyes glance down and then back up. Did the door move open a little more? I grip the wooden broom I have found and turn it with the bristles in the air, holding it like a bat.

The door moves open another inch, but I don't see anything come out. The machine and table cover the bottom part of the door, but I don't see anything come through the top part of it. My arms shake, but I stand steady and firm, unable to back up any further. Something hard and cold keeps me in place.

Nothing happens for several moments. I look around the counters where I am, seeing if there is anything else I could use. There is a flashlight. "Great." I grab it and yank it from the counter. I flick on the switch and angle the beam at the door. This far away, it does not illuminate much. "Come on; I can do this." I try to psych myself up. My legs feel like Jell-O as I slowly reach the door, inching my feet closer to the room. I swing the beam into the darkness, pulling open the door. The beam penetrates the darkness like a knife cutting through butter. Walls of rocks illuminate. The light flickers over dull shiny jewels still set in the rock. "Is this the hill that this building is built into?" I whisper to myself.

I stick my head in further, hoping to see more. The light shines on tools and other things needed to get the jewels out of the rock. A black skull sits on the floor right in the middle. Giant red rubies fill the eye sockets. The light from the flashlight makes them seem as if they are glowing red.

"Lady master!" The skull's teeth click together as the words flow from its mouth; it raises and hovers up in the air, bouncing closer.

My mouth hangs open, and a whisper of a scream wisps out of my open mouth.

"Don't you remember me, lady master?" It twirls in the air but doesn't come closer this time.

I didn't want to scream and make Jazmin and Ms. Moshner come back here and berate me. I do a low screech out of my closed mouth instead of not being able to hold it in.

"I know you are probably angry with me. The last time I saw you, I helped destroy the people holding you. But to be fair, I just gave you the key. You took it the rest of the way," the skull chatters.

"You helped me kill people?" I say again, trying to wrap my head around why this skull is talking.

"Survive those people is what I think you mean. Yes, that was me, my lady," he charms.

I walk around, giving a wide berth. The skull is still floating at the edge of the dark room. I keep the light trained on it but come closer. I shove my shoulder against the giant door, begging it to close before the maniac of a skull floats free. The door hardly budges as the skull passes right through the open crack.

"Thank you for letting me out of that horrible dark room. I thought she would keep me in there forever!"

"Let you out. I was trying to keep you in." I say through my teeth.

"You wound me, my lady." He floats low to the floor, crying, though no tears flow down his ruby-crusted eye sockets. "I only wish to help," he wails.

"Help?" I lean fully against the door, and it shuts. No problem. "Help how? Who are you? What is your name?"

"You truly don't remember me?" He stops mid-cry. "Well, you had some nasty spells placed on you. I guess I can understand that, well, then you are in luck, my lady!" He floats higher into the air, dancing around. "It will help you understand what is happening and who I am. Trix, at your service." He does a little head bow.

"Trix, that is your name? How is any of this lucky?" I ask, flabber-gasted.

His head perks up from the bow. "I have a gift for you," he crows. "Well, two now."

"What sort of gift?" I ask, my voice going high in doubt.

"One that will help, silly." He grins. "Look into my eyes, please, my lady. It will show you what you want to know."

I give a hesitant look, glance back at the cloth-covered door, and then look deeper within the rubies.

The scene changes, and I see things happen in reverse. I am at the top of the stairs and then at the bottom. Something is different about my form, more so than the claws and teeth. Things reverse faster, the shadows passing over everything.

"Follow me, my lady." The skull bobs into the wall, going through it.

I look around the empty basement. The door is now closed. My past self has already gone back to the tiny room. "What is going on?"

The skull comes back through the wall and spins around me, pushing me towards the wall myself. My feet move forward, and I bring my arms up to block the wall coming at me. I don't feel any force or stopping from the wall. I squint through my eyelids, checking on what is happening. I am in the small room that they kept me in.

"We went through the wall?" I screech.

"Of course, you are seeing the memory of when we first met. Well Shade, you, and I," the skull reiterates.

I see my younger form laying there. No chain is around my leg this time. The chain has been fully removed, but the ring sits there in the center.

"Why am I just sleeping there?" I ask.

"Zeek put you in a coma-like state until such a time when your powers could be unlocked. He spoke with Jazmin to send me to unlock them. He did not know that the people upstairs are also trying to break the curse to end your life."

I look up at the ceiling as if it could tell me what is going on up there. "What?" I ask, still confused.

"Shhh. The good part is about to happen." He floats to the top of the ceiling and looks down as if he is getting the angle right for shooting a movie.

"Oh, boy, oh boy. What do we have here?" A skull comes through the outer wall on the other side of us. This skull is still black but has no rubies in the eye sockets.

The skull looks around the room. "My lady, how have they treated you?" The skull floats up to the ceiling and goes through to the next floor. He comes back just as quickly. "They look like they are having fun upstairs and leaving you all alone and behind. We must change that, shouldn't we?"

He flies down and comes closer to the girl sleeping on the pallet. He scoots, barely hovering over the floor, just scrapping by a bit. "Now, I do apologize in advance, my lady. I wouldn't cause pain if I could avoid it. But Zeek explained along with the spell that there might be toxins in your bloodstream, and I have to bite directly into your skin to make sure you can wake up and get out of here on your own. That is all the help I can give with this," he wines.

"See, I feel terrible about it!" The skull from my time persists. I glance up at his form there, still in the ceiling's corner, and then flick back to what is happening.

A red aura appears around his dark form, shimmering around us. His teeth elongate and drip with some sort of black liquid sludge. He gently places his mouth around my arm and presses down as gently as possible. The black sludge pours into the puncture wounds and over my arm. Black shadows pour over my form, covering me from head to toe.

Once the black liquid, the skull has stopped unlatches from the arm and lets go completely. "Zeek warned me of your shadow, my lady. Shadow creature, do not worry. I do not want your lady to be in pain. I am helping."

"Helping?" A garbled voice emits from the shadow. It did not sound like mine.

"Yes. To get free."

"Who are you, worm?" My garbled voice belts out.

"I am Trix. I was sent to help wake you up and give you enough power to free yourself. These people are holding you against your will, and they look to be in good spirits about wanting to end your life tonight."

"My life?" My past self-roars. Shadows flow and become bigger on my slight frame. Claws become longer deadlier; the shadow even covers over my head. "Shade and I, Alexia, will not stand for this." A mix of our voices combines to make one loud, angry voice.

Darkness covers me completely as I move forward. My past self places her palms on the metal door and presses. It dents as the darkness pours over it. The door flings from its hinges and crashes into the basement. The shadow of myself walks slowly making her way toward the stairs. There is singing and chanting up above that can be heard now. Just like last time, I hear it swaying and calling to me. I growl out and mumble to myself. I can't even fathom what I am thinking. I do not remember this. The only thing I remember is when I saw Blaise's knife on his wall that called to me. I remember the singing and chanting. What came next would be a bloodbath! I didn't need to see that take place. I already knew what the after would look like.

I look up to Trix from my time. "I've seen enough. Take us back." I stand at the bottom of the steps watching my shadow form disappear around the doorway, making her way toward the festivities. Screaming would soon begin.

Though Trix looked different, his manners and voice were still the same. I would believe what he showed me for now.

"Zeek kept his word then and helped me get free of those people," I ask in shock. I cast my eyes away from the skull, not wanting to meet its ruby eyes again. "I mean, I know he did just not the how of it." Both the flashlight and broom clang to the floor.

"That he did, my lady!" The skull does a flip in the air. "He is most honorable and lives by a code all of his own."

My dull eyes raise up, my body empty of emotion. I felt so tired. "You said you had another gift."

"Cheer up, my lady. This gift you will like, I promise, it is not as dark and gruesome as that one. To be fair, I didn't mean for that other gift. I only did that so you would know where we met before," he whines.

"Is this gift going to hurt or cause anyone harm?" I ask, unsure if I could handle any more gore. A part of me craved it, but another part didn't want anything to do with it.

He hops over and twirls around my legs. He rubs against my legs as a cat would. "Of course not," he gasps. "How could you think I could do something like that?" He looks up with saddened ruby eyes.

"Well, after that last memory, I don't think you have the best track record. But hit me with this gift." I glance away, not wanting to meet his gaze. I didn't want to be trapped like I was before.

He gives a coy smile that I see out of my peripheral. Then swooshes up underneath the billowy shirt that I wear.

"Hey! Cut that out! Get out of there!" I swat at his skull under my shirt. He shrinks in size and dodges my hands easily. "What the hell are you? The skull of a dead pervert?" I yell out, no longer worried if my voice brings Jazmin and Ms. Moshner. I would rather hear her wrath rather than deal with a dead pervert.

His head rises out of my shirt with the necklace I keep hidden underneath. A simple metal flower sits at the end of the chain. He has a flower between his teeth. His red aura becomes darker and more sinister. His teeth elongate again and drip with the same shiny black liquid from memory. It pours over the pendant.

I grab at the chain on the back that secures it, holding it there. I try to yank the pendant back from his mouth. His teeth stay fastened around it. I didn't dare pull harder for fear of ruining the pendant or destroying the chain. I didn't want to ruin the necklace I received from the Teager as a gift. Also, if Shade ever did return to his natural state, this would be the only way to communicate with him.

"Let go! Now!" I thwack him on the forehead of the skull.

His teeth click together. "Owww. My lady, I was only helping," he howls and lets the medallion fall free. The pendant smacks against my shirt with a wet plopping sound.

"This stuff is disgusting," I complain as I brush the black sludge away from the pendant. The metal of the flower is dull. I pull the necklace up and away from my neck, pulling it over my head. I take a corner of my shirt that does not have the black muck on it and clean what is on the petals and the center of the flower. This shirt would never be the same, anyway.

"But that is what breaks down other spells and makes it useful, or gives strength when needed." He bounces there in the air, unsure if I would allow him closer. "The grime is good."

The black goo wipes away easily enough, clinging to the shirt instead. There is still some black sludge in the crevices, but I will have to clean it more deeply later. Maybe borrow something in here to help with that.

Once I clean all the black stuff from the main pendant, it hardens on the shirt. "What is it doing now?" The stuff hardens on the necklace as well. There isn't too much left, so the crevices are the only part that has the black liquid. Peering at the flower, the black liquid hardens and sparkles, making a dark outline on the silver metal flower. "It's gorgeous." My shirt is laden with the weight of the hard substance. I pick at it carefully. It reminded me of obsidian stone. Where had I seen something like this? I peer through squinted eyes, trying to think.

I had had something dark like this that I had gotten from my first session with Quintan. I have hidden the stone in my pant pocket. When getting here, I hid it, unsure what it was or what it did, but I kept it with me during my waking moments to keep it safe in case someone came sniffing around for it.

I reach for my pockets. In my right pocket sits the new red ruby, and in the left, I grab the black shard and pull it out. How can I attach this to the chain? I glance around, seeing crumbs of things, nothing that could be used.

"The necklace is okay, correct?" I ask.

The skull bobs in assurance. "Of course, my lady. I only help."

"And help you shall. Please come closer." He comes closer, dancing a bit in the air, getting excited. "Get me something that I can tie around this or hook this too, so I can attach it to this chain and keep them together."

"Yes, my lady. Right away." He zooms around and accidentally crashes into something.

I look up, ensuring no one comes through the cloth doorway and then back to where he had zoomed off. "I guess they did not hear me from earlier." My curiosity begs me to check on them.

The skull rolls around on the floor in the background, howling and wailing to himself.

"So dramatic," I hiss. "Be quiet while looking, or else I will step on you." I call out. I grind my shoe against the grit on the floor for emphasis.

"Here, I only help." He brings a tough cloth chord and throws it into my empty hand.

"Thanks." I grab it and wrap it around the black shard, securing it in place.

"Lady master is much meaner than other masters. Mayhap I leave lady master defenseless." He mumbles to himself. "No, then main master will be even angrier."

My eyes zero in on him, and my hands slow with what I am doing. "What did you say?" I use some tools I find nearby and keep working on binding this stone into something to connect it to the chain.

"No, no, no. Main master will destroy me if I don't help the lady master. Tall master doesn't know they are all angry sometimes!" He crows out in pain as if we were all hitting him at once.

"What are you babbling about?" I ask, pulling the thick chord tight and then grabbing a metal loop to loop under the string and connecting it to the chain.

"I am helping. I swear, my lady." He floats back up to eye level, watching what I am doing. "You must know about master you wear what is his."

I cock my head to the side in question. As I finish connecting the shard to the flower necklace, they are on the same chain. I pull it back over my head and let both baubles land between my breasts on the top of the ruined shirt. "I wear something from your master?"

I grip the chain and push it under the ruined shirt.

"Well, yeah, it is right..."

"Trix! How did you get out? Why are you always such a drama queen?" Jazmin yells out. "You know Ms. Moshner can't stand your constant chatter."

"Lady master got me out. She is sweet, but also brutal." He swirls around Jazmin's fingers when she sticks them into the air, calling for him.

I turn around slowly, ensuring the necklace is hidden before I show my appearance.

"No!" Jazmin scoffs in horror. "Trix, did you do that? Why, you beast? This is why people lock you up and do not welcome you in certain places." She places her fists on her hips, but in one fist, the end of the whip is still in her hand.

"He belongs to you? Are you the main master or the tall master?" I ask right off the bat.

Jazmin unfurls the new whip and glares at Trix. "Multiple masters? Are you two-timing me?" Jazmin growls out. The one eye looks at me in surprise. "Fiend! Though I do like the new ruby eyes, anon, I mustn't break. You must grovel at my feet, fiend!" She flicks her wrist loose, and the rest of the chain comes undone.

"You might want to leave," I whisper to the skull, which hovers in between both of us. I step away so as not to get hit by the spiked chain.

"You can't leave. The queen of the dead wants to play!" Jazmin calls out.

"Queen dead wants to play!" Trix screeches as he loops under and over the machines, making loops in the air.

"Be gone from my sight, infidel. Your kind is not welcome until I see some groveling!" She says.

"His kind?" My brows lift in question.

The skull laughs as his red haze fades behind his flying head. He rushes out into the store, and a tinkling of the bell above the door goes off, proving that he has left the shop.

"Yea, the dead." She shrugs as she rolls up the coil of the whip once more. "Ms. Moshner, you left him in storage too long, and now he is bored and causing havoc once again."

She shakes her head. "What he does once you have him back is your own problem." She waves. "What else did the girl get into back there while discussing your next shipment?"

Jazmin turns her head and looks at me with the one good eye. "Nothing. It still looks much the same as you usually have it."

"She didn't even clean! Ugh. This will not work, not going to work at all." She mutters.

I grimace and look around at the floor. I was supposed to have been cleaning up. "Well, it took me a while to find the broom, but I found it." I motion to the broom lying on the floor, all but forgotten.

Ms. Moshner finally makes her way to the doorway. "And ye are filthy as well for doing nothing!"

"It is just some sludge from her skull." I point to Jazmin. "I will go clean up and come back to help."

"Don' be botherin, girlie." She looks at Jazmin. "Take her with ye."

"But Quintan wanted me to help you today. Learn and get to know others and why they have joined this rogue group."

"I have always been here; I will always be here. Ye brought this on. I will be closing for the day. No need to come back. Yer work is done here." She says with finality.

"I thought it would be busy since you took most of your morning off." I say softly, not wanting her more riled up than she already is.

"Things change, girlie. Roll with the punches." She shambles over to me and pushes me closer to the door and the front of the store, showing me my way out.

"Fine," I admit. I could always get back to my mother's journal and learn more that way. I wave to Jazmin as she stays there to pay or talk more with Ms. Moshner. I exit the building and notice the sun is close to setting. Night is about to descend once again. I fear my animal side will get the better of me if I don't find a way to cool down.

CHAPTER 8

THE FIRST THING I do when I get back to my room is change out of the clothes I am currently in. My pants thud on the floor. I bend down and find the red ruby in my pocket. I think back over my time at the jewelers. "How is this real?" I question myself. I carefully pick up the ruby, keeping cloth between the jewel and my fingers so he wouldn't pull me into whatever dream or reality that he had before. "Did Blaise try to stop him?" I place a hand over my forehead, feeling the heat.

As I kneel on the bed, I pulled out the metal tin that holds my mother's journal. I place the ruby inside with the journal to keep it safe. I didn't want the ruby on the necklace with the flower and the black shard. It didn't feel right. He also said to keep it hidden.

This would be as hidden as it got. I skim through a few more entries. Most of them were about how my mother's life was unfair. Or about Robert not letting her do this or that. It spoke some about Jade, but nothing personally other than that they were sisters.

My eyes droop forward, slumping lower into the soft bed. I breathe deeply and try to pry my eyes back open. Blinking them wide. Must stay awake. I wanted to know more and get through a substantial amount of the journal rather than one or two daily entries.

I scan the page before me and watch as the letters blur out of focus. My chin slumps forward, resting my head against my arm as I lay on my stomach. Maybe I just needed fifteen minutes to rest my eyes at least, and then I would be refreshed enough to finish reading a good chunk of the journal. I set the book aside and rest my head, pulling one pillow under me. I doze off.

The last thing I think about before sleep takes me is the overwhelming desire to run away from this place and all it holds. To be as free as Natasha likes to be and the ever-present heat that refuses to let up.

I snarl at the dim lights that surround me. The smells were off in this place. A chemical smell. I wanted to smell fresh smells, more nature than what was surrounding me. There was no hard ground beneath my claws, only fluffy softness. Where was I? What am I? Scenting the air, my nose reaches up to catch the fresh wind-blown smells. Fresh air! I shuffle forward, my arms and legs getting caught in the softness. I scramble, wanting to be free.

Trap!

Fear zings through me. I growl, scurry against the cloth, and slash out at what holds me.

Let go! Now! I snarl once again and bite at the blankets cocooning around me.

I bite into the rough fabric, yanking it from my short legs, and shake my head back and forth as it curls around me and pulls me down over the edge of the bed and onto the ground. I spill out and shake my head once more, slapping it against the floor. Rendering it, limp and lifeless. I raise a claw and shred the rest to pieces. Blue bits fly from the covering. I scrape my claws, shoving it under the bed.

I lick my front paw, smoothing out the fur there. A whiff of something delicious crosses my nose. My ears perk up as I twist my nose, searching for the smell. Saliva fills my mouth as I intake the husky and coppery smell. I tongue my sharp canines and lick my chops in anticipation.

Skittering across the ground in a rush. My claws clatter against the hard wooden floors. I sniff the air again when I swipe at the door to the outside. They push open easily enough. The warm smell fills my nose and increases my need.

Food! I howl.

The sweet smell is more pungent in the wind than in that death box. The wind rustles my fur as I raise my face, enjoying the feel of my fur. I look up to survey the surrounding scene. Going out of the room and the hardwood floors follow me onto a small ledge. I look lower and see the ground further below. I wait and watch, watching for a predator to show itself. My claws grasp at the soft wood. Trying to judge how long of a fall it would be. Dark greenery of a bush is off to the side. I push my hide against the slats that box this wood in. They were thin railings and easy to climb through. I push all my paws to the forefront, making a jump for it to the ground. A high-pitched whine emits from my mouth, but I bounce onto soft green and flower bushes. Sticks poke at me, but I brush them off as I move away from where I land in case something follows the noise I make. My eyes squint close, causing them to blur. I shake my head; flower petals dance around me as I move.

I pick myself up, assessing each of my bones. Slapping a claw against the hard packed dirt ground. Dust rises from my paw. I sneeze and back away from the dirt that has risen. I walk away from where I have stirred things up, clearing my nose and trying to find the scent I had smelled earlier. My claws dig into the ground to grip it, pushing me forward faster. I lick the nail and taste salt and a tang of metal and dirt.

Not food. I place my paw back down.

The air felt better on my fur and my mind didn't feel caged as it once had. Needed out of that place. I glare at the box over my shoulder. I chatter at the door noisily but soon scoot away when I hear noises pick up nearby. A loud bang erupts as I scoot by another building on my way to the woods. My heart thuds in my chest, and I take off, my paws scrabbling over the ground gripping easily, pushing me forward quickly.

Once in the woods, there are many open paths going in all directions. The openness of it all worries me. I hide under dark leafy greens, puffing out quick small breaths, trying to keep my pants shallow and quiet. I gasp and slow my breathing as I return to myself and calm down. My heart thuds against my small, furry body.

Inhaling deeply, I try to fill my lungs as much as possible. Trying to smell that sweet smell I had in my nose earlier. A sweet, cloying scent is all around me, very different from the meaty tang I had smelled earlier. This seemed fresher and almost floral.

Different food?

I burrow into the leaves and exit out the back to find more bushes I can dodge and weave under. I hunker down after each one and rush from bush to bush, searching for the sweet smell. All the while trying to find the original smell to see the difference.

A hoot of an owl stops me in my tracks, between my travel between two bushes. There are black orbs next to the leaves. A sweet scent fills my nose as I sniff the item. I lick the thing and taste sweet juice running down my throat. I gobble up the berries that were there. I push myself further into the bush, hiding and getting more of the berries. Two birds, one stone. The sweetness from the berries makes my mouth water as I gobble more and the rumbling from my stomach quiets down. The wind shifts and my nose twitches as I smell the tang of the heavenly scent from before.

A high-pitched squeak makes my ears twitch, and my body freezes in fear and in excitement. I fall gently on my front paws. And dig my claws into the cool dirt beneath them. My ears twitch back as they lock onto the small sound of the vermin close by.

I squat down on my four short legs and try to blend into the darkness and the bushes. I lie in wait for my prey.

A small mouse scurries into sight. The moonlight shines brightly over his little body; illuminating its smooth fur, and acting like a beacon. The copper smell fills my nose, enticing me forward. My paws move in quick silent motion under my body, getting my body ready to launch.

Why did this mouse smell so good? Did it hurt itself, and I was smelling its blood? Is this what animals smell like? These are all questions running through my mind, but the animal in me soon take over and my mind thinks of only prey.

A mouse stops to sniff the air for enemies. I stay downwind. It cleans its face with its front paws and sits back on its hindquarters, content and thinking it is safe.

I inch forward, careful of where my paws land. My whole intent is coursing through my veins, and my single thought is of this mouse and how I would make him mine. The fur on my back roughens as it stands up in anticipation of the hunt for the kill. My legs move quickly through the shrubbery, the dirt flinging up from my claws as I tear at the ground and fly at my prey. My mouth and teeth open wide to bite down.

The mouse sprints away as it feels my thunderous vibrations through the ground. It's exciting to chase the small body. The mouse tries to lose me as I close in. I burst forward, forcing myself to run faster.

I give one final push and pounce on my target, easily catching it. My nails puncture the furry body, bringing the coppery smell straight to my senses. The smell deepens there as the eminence of death takes hold of the small creature. I nudge the struggling mouse, going in for the final blow, the bite that will mean certain death. My jaw clamps down on the frail bones, and I hear the crunch and snap of the bones through my teeth and skull. The blood bursts onto my tongue, and my eyes narrow in bliss. I continue to chew, and pull at the body, getting at the deliciousness further.

The liquid fills my gullet more so than the berries did previously. I pull the body under one bush and enjoy the rest of it throughout the night. The small meal of this and the berries fill me up, and I am content. Though I don't leave this spot for many hours, I continue once thirst becomes a need, along with having to relieve myself. The night passes with many more things for me to see and hear. I stick to the woods, not wanting to be near people. My eyes feel heavy.

My body gets too tired, and my movements are lethargic. I burrow under some leaves and brush deep in the woods to avoid being seen. The sky was becoming lighter now that the night would be over soon. I yawn and am soon asleep.

I hear murmurs and low voices nearby, and a bird's screech flies overhead. I open my eyes and squint against the harsh, unforgiving sun. The light that slips in between my lids makes me cringe away. Something rustles near my head as I move to block the light with my arm. "What the hell is going on?" I ask. Pain radiates through my arms and skull; I lick my chapped lips. "What is that horrible taste?" I bellow. I wipe my mouth on my arm to make the taste disappear.

I moan and grunt as I bring my hand up to shade my eyes and roll over onto my side. "What happened? Where am I? Why do I feel like crap?" I question, unsure of where to start.

"How do you think you should feel after the night you had last night?" A gruff voice answers in return.

I screech out in horror, my hands searching for the blankets. "What the hell, Charles!" I shift onto my other side to better see him and why he was in my room.

"Indeed." Charles tosses a blanket down on my naked form.

I shriek for an entirely different reason now. "Why am I naked?" I look around at my surroundings and where I lie now. "Why are we outside? What the hell happened last night, and why am I not where I fell asleep?" My hands shake, and I get up from the hard ground, my legs almost buckling out from underneath me. The blanket slides to the ground off of me.

I hold on to the trunk of a tree to keep myself standing up. He raises an eyebrow as I have not reached for the blanket. He gazes at my form, getting an eyeful.

"Ass!" I yank the blanket from the ground twigs and dirt clings to it. I snap it open, clearing it of the small debris. I wrap it around my body and tuck it under to secure it around me. "Shouldn't you be leering at someone else? It's not polite to stare."

He bursts out laughing as he continues to stare. "If I didn't get my looks in, they would take away my man card. Plus, I am old and married. Let me get my fun in any way I can."

"At my expense, of course," I growl. The horse blanket scratches against my skin. It reddens with irritation, but it is better than being nude. It also covered me pretty well, and hung down to my knees. "How far away is the house?" I ask, hoping I wouldn't have to walk much to get back. I didn't see any horses around that Charles had brought.

"It's not too far away," he comments, still smiling.

"What happened last night, and how did I end up here?" My body is sore, and I hurt with every move.

"You don't recall?"

"If I remembered, do you think I would ask?" I lean back, trying to get used to the bright sun. My eyes water right away.

"You are your mother's daughter," he laughs.

"Am I, so you knew her as well?" I ask.

"As much as any of us could, I suppose." He looks up and around, a dark shadow cast over us.

I look up and see a giant dragon flying by. "Is that Jason? Did he see me also?"

"Nothing major. He saw you, yes, but came to get me to make sure you shifted completely and you were okay. New shifters have difficulty staying in one form and sometimes get stuck in half forms. Touch can be really painful and, not to mention, moving someone during that time can cause them to have a severe problem."

"I don't think your daughter would like that he saw another woman naked." I bite at my lip as my stomach does a flip.

"Shifters are comfortable with their own body, let alone others. He is a dragon, yes, but he shifts just like you do, so it doesn't really bother him as it would a normal person not used to it."

A great roar call comes from nearby. I look over but do not see the dragon anymore. But I am curious why he is roaring and giving away the location.

I can hear crashes in the woods. Ariella appears in between both Charles and me. I jump back, hugging the blanket closer to me.

"Dad." She gets his attention.

His firm eyes go straight to her. "Why is he making all that noise? He isn't new. Are you okay?" His eyes zero in on her.

"Yes, I'm fine." Ariella rolls her eyes; they land on me. "She, though, is in heat." She glares at me.

As if her words unlock something in me, a heat blooms lower in my belly. My stomach flips once again. I place a cool hand against my forehead. Feeling the heat that had been building yesterday, it continues today.

Charles' eyes zero in on me. He moves to feel my forehead as well. I lean into the touch but then shake myself away after I realize what I have done. "What does that mean?"

Charles looks into the woods. "Go, keep Jason downwind and away from here."

She nods. "He already is. His roar was a warning to every shifter that might be susceptible."

"Great, go get Robert and let him know what is going on so we can prepare." She blinks out of existence a moment later.

I pull the blanket around me and stand tall and proud. "What did she mean?"

"Let's go." He grips my upper arm.

I snarl and slip from his grasp. "No, you are supposed to be the animal helper here. You help all the other shifters. Help me, help me now!"

"I can't not with this."

"What are you not telling me?" A wave of heat washes through me, making everything harsher and hotter. The blanket is becoming too much. The blanket is not soft enough to be kept against me. My fingers fumble at the edge of the blanket, it being too much and not enough all at the same time.

"I don't know what state you are in or the cycle of your animal since you are the only badger shifter in our area. But all shifters go through a time when the heat cycle in their respectable animal is high and more prominent. Your animal tries to take over and take care of things, especially if you ignore them in your personal life."

"I was in animal form?" My fingers freeze at what they are doing.

"Yes, you transformed last night into a full badger."

"I have only changed my hands, teeth, or eyes." I look down at my feet and legs. "I didn't know I could do that."

"It looks like Quintan was wrong about you not needing shifter training. He wanted to hold off since you had lost a lot of your magic. He thought that would affect you and diminish your power."

"Obviously, he was wrong in that thought." I stomp.

"He also doesn't know that when a female shifter is in heat, she sends out pheromones for potential mates. The strongest will be to their own kind, but as our races have mixed, the power pull does not restrict to just your own kind. Some are more resilient than others, and some stay away as much as possible." He glances off into the woods where we had heard the deep roar earlier.

"How come I am just feeling this now? Shouldn't there have been a warning or instructions that come with these powers?" I gesture furiously under the blanket, trying to keep things covered as I do, my agitation rocketing.

He sputters, not sure what to say. "There are too many variables that could have thrown things off. It could be because they imprisoned you for so long, it could be because you did not develop as normal shifters and magic users have. It could be a multitude of reasons."

"Alexia!" Natasha calls out.

"Natasha, what are you doing out here?" She distracts me from the anger that is building inside me.

"Margaret and I have come to help!" She calls out closer.

"I thought Robert was supposed to come?"

"He is not a true shifter. He is not the best person for this problem," Margaret's small voice calls out.

Charles walks over in the deep brush. He bends and breaks back foliage so they can get to where we are hidden easier.

Natasha rushes over to me. Her cool skin calms the fire that is raging inside. She hugs me close; I rest my head on her shoulder as she brings her temperature down to combat my fever.

Margaret waves to Charles and rushes over to me, only a few seconds behind Natasha. She checks my pulse and my temperature. She gives me a once-over. "Charles, will you give us a moment? You can wait for us on the path."

"Are you sure?"

"Yes, please go." She waits until he is away and out of hearing range. "Natasha explained you were with a snake shifter before you came here."

I nod, not sure I can trust my voice. I lift my head up and step out of Natasha's embrace to face Margaret.

"I have known a few badgers in my day, so I am aware where some men are not. Also, the thought of a woman that is not their own sometimes makes men a little wheezy." She smiles and chuckles to herself.

I chuckle along with her, not sure what else to do.

"Since we are in the late spring season, that is the time for badgers to go into heat usually. When you have a willing partner, there is no issue other than you may be more easily angry or sexually charged."

"When I met Blaise, I felt like I had the choice to either put him in the category of prey or mate. I didn't want to hurt people anymore," I say sadly.

She nods. "Since Blaise is not around and you are not fully mated, your pheromones will start calling to other potentials, usually only shifters, though your normal sexual prowess can call to others alike and be satisfied." She gives a hint of a smile. "Some choose to sleep this time away, but it can be dangerous and time-consuming."

"Has anyone ever just suffered through it?"

She gives an unpleasant face. "None that would talk about it."

"I can keep her cool if that helps." Natasha pulls me back closer to her frozen skin. It is not as cool to the touch, but it is still a pleasant feeling against my hot skin.

"Even that will not help, eventually."

"How long do I have?"

She shrugs. "It depends. Badgers can sometimes be in heat through the entire spring season. It depends, and I worry that you being caged as long as you were, it has boiled up to this point. Are you normally attracted to women?" She asks.

I look at her and then look at Natasha. "What does that have to do with anything?"

"Just answer the question."

"No," I answer, simply not sure where this question is going. I eye her suspiciously.

"I would suggest surrounding yourself with women then until something else can be figured out. Any male that is not taken will be up for grabs, and your body might push you into situations you wouldn't usually find yourself." She puts emphasis on taken.

"So, keep her distracted?" Natasha reiterates.

I yawn, still tired since I didn't get much rest the night before. "I am so tired."

"Yes, that will also happen, especially right after a shift. We should get you back to bed and some food and water in you."

"Food?" I burp, and my stomach turns nauseous. "I think... I think that already happened." I turn from Natasha and bend over, unsure if I am going to empty what was in my stomach.

"Okay, no food. I guess your animal took care of that need last night. Be really careful if your beast does not think you are handling things well. It will take over and make sure you get everything you require." She grips my upper arms roughly and pulls me up to meet her eyes. "And I am serious. I mean, everything your body requires!" She gazes intently into my eyes.

My eyes and mouth go wide with horror. "So, you mean. I could do that, but in animal form and not even know it?"

"Oh, you would know, but you wouldn't want to. It is why shifters are taught to be free and live their best life. If we are not careful and do not learn to control ourselves and our urges, the animal within will take care of it."

I lean to the side, and only Margaret's firm hands on my arms keep me from falling over. "I'm not feeling too well," I say.

"Quintan should have known better, but men, especially non-male shifters, do not want to believe the things us women go through." She shakes her head.

"How's the journal that you found?" Natasha changes the subject, seeing I have had enough.

My head swivels to Natasha, and I stare at her with listless eyes. "Fine, I haven't gotten very far into it."

Natasha pulls my arm over her shoulders and hugs me close to her cool body. Margaret comes up on my other side but does not crowd me.

"Was Robert really my mother's guard? You said something about that yesterday, right?"

"Yes, he was and ended up being a great guard to both your parents and this town." Margaret beams.

"Did Charles also work for my mother?" I ask, seeing as he knew her before I was even in the picture.

"He actually didn't come in till much later. When your parents were young, he didn't know either of them. He came around because of a certain woman that had a feisty daughter. He promised a friend to be better for them than his friend could provide."

"Charles married his friend's wife?" I stick out my tongue and shudder.

Margaret laughs once again. "Oh, to be young again. Love is a fickle thing and will happen regardless of whether you run away from it." She looks at Natasha before shaking her head.

"Distractions!" Natasha hisses through her teeth.

We continue forward, making our way back to the dirt path. Soon Charles' head comes into view. He is bending over to dust the dirt from his boots. "Don't hurry on my account. The sun is just getting higher in the sky, getting steamier out here by the minute."

"I demand all the answers to my questions." I keep one hand on the blanket that is around me. The other one I keep light and around Natasha, her coldness keeping the heat at bay and doing the trick. I didn't care that it wouldn't keep working, it did for now, and that is all I needed.

"Who are you to demand answers from us!" Natasha says in a burst of laughter, her shoulders shaking my arm.

"You claim I am the heir to this whole place, which makes me queen of these rogue encampments. So, you guys have said that I am the one who can demand these things. That's who."

Charles chuckles. "You are no queen yet, my dear."

"Close enough." I look at the path where twigs and rocks litter the area.

"Queen of no one then," Natasha comments.

"Why? Because no one will follow what I say, yet they want someone to go to for help when things go south. Sounds like a queen to me."

"Welcome to the real world, where people will always seek someone else out for the answers and who to blame their problems on."

I scrunch up my face in distaste. "Then, to paraphrase my mother's writing, 'this sucks'."

"Yes, yes, it does." All three of them agree.

"Well, I am glad I have some around who care about me and what happens." I look at the ground, not wanting them to see how much they affect me. "Some people around here don't seem to like me very much."

"They don't know or understand you. They know you don't know or understand them either. As you grow and learn, they will see what kind of leader you will be. What kind of person do you choose to be?" Margaret says.

"I can tell when someone is just following orders or doing their job, Charles." I lick my dry lips, waiting for him to turn back to me from up ahead. "Why do you not like me? Perhaps if you tell me, I can stop doing whatever it is I am doing that seems to annoy or piss people off."

Charles' eyes widen in surprise, and the three of us women stop before him. "I don't hate you." He raises his hand to shade his brow in the direct sunlight.

"Then why have you not pushed to train me and tell me about my shifter side? You are supposed to be the go-to person for this sort of thing, right?"

"It's complicated." He looks off into the distance.

"Try me. It can't be that bad."

"It can," he says simply, with a small smile peeking out of the corner of his mouth.

"Fine, have it your way. How far are we from the house? Can we talk about last night and how I got out here?"

"We're not far," Charles calls back.

"When you changed into a badger?" Margaret asks.

I rub my upper arm over the blanket in an absent-minded manner. My feet and legs were scratched up and not doing much better going through brush and trees in the woods.

"Did anyone see me in my badger form?"

Margaret shakes her head.

Charles picks up when he hears nothing coming from us behind him. "Jason did that is when he came and got me, he saw you changing back into your human form. He did not get close enough to see it was you, though. He found that out from me once I got closer."

"Like a badger, badger!" I ask in exasperation.

"Yep. If you think of it, it's like a little bear with claws. It's kind of cute." Natasha hugs me close.

I push away from her and roll my eyes. "I have never shifted all at once like that before. Just a half form." I run my fingers through my snarled hair. My fingers get caught halfway through. I pull the strands forward, checking to see if I can force them through. My hair did not change color from its normal reddish-brown color. "Will my hair color change?" I comb more strands forward, making sure the black patch of hair has not grown in size.

"Not unless you stay in your form for a much longer time," Margaret assures.

"There is always the first time. You will do it more often as you learn control. The memories will come back to you throughout the day, and as you learn control, you will be able to control your animal or have a say about things." He comes to a fork in the road before choosing the left path. He holds up a hand for us to wait and checks the right path first.

"I just started to accept life here and magic. Why do I have to do this now?" I whine. "I just got my magic, or most of my magic, drained from me, so I am useless there. I have no idea how to fight or really use the fire sisters, and this side of me only comes out when angered or afraid, which is not a good start. Now add on to it, apparently, when I am horny."

Charles moves on the left path and motions for us to follow him. Margaret shrugs and continues forward. We all three walk near each other. I no longer hang on to Natasha and just make my way.

"You must have been comfortable enough to deal with it, or your animal thought you needed to listen more. She could have thought you were ready for this or you weren't doing a good enough job, so she took over," Margaret states.

"I want to talk to whoever deals out this punishment and give them a piece of their own medicine." I shuffle my feet under the blanket, shambling forward slowly.

"Poor little princess having a rough day?" Charles shoots back.

"You know what, on second thought, I think I will walk back to the house by myself instead." I turn around on the path away from them, hoping to just get away from them for now.

"If you wish." Charles motions ahead of him. "But you might want to try going this way instead," he states.

"Can you just stop!" I exclaim.

"It's good for you. Now come on." His face sets into a frown. "I am done playing nice. Let's get back to the house."

"Thanks for nothing," I grumble as we all follow behind him.

The birds chirp loudly, and the morning light pierces between the greenery. The sound of the birds seems to echo back and forth as if in calling. I groan and shuffle the blanket up higher, hiding my head and ears, trying to block out the sound.

"Margaret, what is wrong with her now?" Charles asks as he hears me moan in pain.

"I'm just peachy," I grumble in agitation.

Anger seems to lessen the pain a bit.

"Charles!" Margaret scorns. "This is why Robert asked me to come. With how close her animal is to the surface, she either has to choose from her animalistic heat or anger. Do you want to push her to that dark side?"

"She will have to learn to live with it. We all do. She will have to learn control one day. Why not today be that day?" He gives a snide smile.

I just needed a shower and some clean clothes. Maybe a little bit of bread or something to quiet my rolling stomach. At the thought of food, my stomach gave a rolling lurch. My mouth begins to water, and I taste something hot and coppery in my mouth. My mind flashes back to last night, the excitement of the kill, and how the blood tasted as it burst into my mouth.

"What was that?" I ask as I make my way over to the side, stopping and holding my stomach. I wait there, not sure what is happening.

"Stop," Natasha says quietly as she places a cool hand on the back of my neck.

I take a few deep breaths and let the coolness calm me down. I grab my hair and pull it to the side so it is out of the way and there is more access to the skin on the back of my neck.

"I think she just remembered some of her night last night," Margaret barks at Charles.

I nod my head in answer, and that stirs my stomach up once again. My mouth waters right before I empty the contents of my stomach into the ditch. I wheeze for breath as things continue to come up, not letting me catch my breath. The coolness no longer helps to cool the scorching skin as sweat rolls down my skin.

Charles walks over, and his boots enter from the side. I don't look up and just wait for him to move away. He stays there standing. "How much did you remember?" He asks in a soothing voice.

I glare at his boots but answer him since he does not seem to go away. "Not much... but enough," I pant and spit out what is left in my mouth, my stomach finally settling.

His boots disappear as I hear rustling going on behind me. I stare ahead, my face reddening as I look at the scene before me. He must think that I am weak and cannot stand me.

"Here," Charles says.

I turn to step away from Natasha's cool hand and standing on my own. Charles holds out a water bottle. I stare at him momentarily and then take it to rinse my mouth. Once done with that, I take a long hard pull and let the coolness of the water coat and cover my mouth. I chug the remaining contents of the bottle, polishing it off.

"Thanks," I say, relieved.

"No problem," Charles brushes off. "Do you need some more time, or are we good to go?"

"I think I'm okay now." I struggle to stand.

Margaret and Natasha stand close by just in case they are needed but they sense that I want to do this alone. We walk slower but arrive back at the house all too soon.

I go to take a shower right away when I get back to get everything that had happened off of me. I hurry back to my room to see the damage that was done. Blankets are strewn about on the floor, and the balcony door is still cracked open. I pull the blankets up and see the necklace there. I pick it up and place it back over my head. Glad, my animal did not try to take this with her when leaving.

The journal is lying open, and the metal box is at the top of the bed. I wrap the blanket around myself and close the journal up. My eyes are already having a hard time staying open. I set it to the side and open the metal box, searching for something else I had hidden in here. My fingers touch the rough ruby and pull it out. I feel a warmth pulling into me and flowing straight down my body.

I let out a small sigh, but nothing more than the warmth happens. Did I want to push things further to see if things would happen with this mystery guy? I bite my lip in temptation. Or there is Blaise, but things just sort of happen there as well. I don't know how to start the dreams or call him to me. The scalding fire within is burning brighter. I could try to rest. Natasha and Margaret want me to rest, but my mind can't be quiet enough to get sleep.

Trying to relax enough to fall into my dreams, I set the ruby aside. Eventually, I close my eyes and sink into my body, relaxing. I roll to my side and feel something thump against me. Even more warmth pours over my lower back.

"Minx," A very male voice growls at me.

Warmth pulls at my back and pulls me away from the growling.

"A pretty girl deserves better, doesn't she?" A hushed whisper pulls me into another lulling song.

"And you have never pushed me away." I sigh, settling into the heat.

The calm voice takes in a deep breath and forces the laugh out. "That is true, snake. Why would you ever cast her out? You should keep better track of your things." Warm fingers brush back my hair. The guy from my previous day dream sits close to mine. His warmth once again settled behind me.

"Blaise?" I ask, looking around for him. Speaking his name brings him into the light, but he is hazy.

"Yes, Minx." He comes closer. "Yes, I am here. Remember that."

The guy's face that is beside mine frowns. He nuzzles my neck, which causes me to gasp in pleasure. My fire still building with the heat that envelops me. "You have the power to send him away if you wish. Unless you want him to watch." I feel his lips twitch into a smile.

"Does she even know your name or who you are?" He hisses.

The melody from before pours out. "We do not need names, do we, darling?" He hums.

"No names," I repeat.

"There you go pet." He pulls me closer to his chest. I feel feet and pressure as he presses into me. "You deserve many praises." He tips my head back and caresses my neck. "If you need more, all you have to do is hold on to the ruby and press it where you need me. The heat and power we create make things feel like I am there."

I nudge back and stretch as I lean into him, enjoying his praises and good words. Warm arms come around and sit low on my hips as I rub against him.

"Do you like to watch snake?" He continues to sing the words.

My eyelids are heavy but they meet his from across the way. He is too far away. I needed him closer, but I couldn't go to him. The song keeps pulling at me, and I don't want to leave the warmth. I call out to him. "Blaise."

His form solidifies even more. "You don't need that hunk of rock." He walks closer to me but still is not close enough.

"You wound me, snake." His hand raises to my stomach, caressing me there. He pulls my other hand around behind me to him as I touch the warmth sitting low behind me.

Blaise wraps a hand around my other wrist and pulls me to him, kicking at the form and making him waver. I plaster myself to the front of Blaise and look up at him. "I need more," I whisper.

Blaise looks down at me. A small snake-like tongue flickers out, tasting the air. "No." He grows angry and backs up away from me. "Minx, you need to wake up."

The red ruby sits in the palm of my hand as I bring it over my sensitive skin. The mystery guy appears once again. The humming is louder as I bring the ruby down my stomach. His hand follows mine, pushing it toward my center. "I will give you what he can not." He sings closer to me. "I bet you are so slick and ready, aren't you?"

"Minx, you have to listen to me! He is not real none of this is real. He's a siren. This is what his kind does." He waves his hands in the air, trying to prove his point.

"At this point, I don't care whether things are real. I just needed the feeling of someone against me and to bring the fire in me back down to a manageable level."

The strong arms around me push my hands lower, and the ruby sits warm and pulsing low on my stomach. He inches my other hand to continue lower. "Send him away, and we can have more fun," he whispers. A low hum pours into me, lightning zinging through my veins. I cry as our fingers delve through my folds and our fingers become covered. He moves my fingers, showing me the way.

"She is mine!" Blaise bites out but does not move closer.

"Really." He turns my head the other way, arching my neck. "I don't see any marks of a claiming. I don't feel any solid ties. Come get her if you dare." The man barks back. He pulls his hands away from mine.

I whine. "Come back."

"Send him away, pet." His words strike a tone.

"Leave Blaise." My eyes turn cold and hard. "If you can't be what I need, then leave. You didn't want me around last time, anyway." Blaise's form fades from sight.

"I can explain..." His words cut off as I push him away.

The warmth comes back, and his hands are on top of mine. "Good pets deserve all the lovins. Don't they?" He chuckles.

He walks around and pushes me down onto the soft bed. "Go deeper into your subconscious, darling. I want to show you what dream we could make a reality." I push the rock further south, wanting his touch more.

"Looks like you want to be punished instead. Is that right?" His voice is stern, and the melody falls away. A chill runs up my spine at how cold things feel.

My fingers inch back up with the ruby. I hesitate, unsure of where I want to go with this.

His warmth comes down on top. He holds himself up so as not to smother me. His heat inflames and traps my hands between us. One of his big hands grips my neck and forces me gently to look at him. "I am not like your snake. I will tell you the truth even if you aren't ready for it. They have not broken me like him, so I do not expect the ones I am with to break either. I think you are strong and beautiful! But I will not be tested. I like to take charge; do you think you can handle that?"

I gaze up at him. Slight pressure presses into my neck. I force myself to speak past the block. "What's your name?" I lick my lips.

His eyes follow my tongue. "You can call me Domini."

"Domini," I test out his name.

He shivers over me and squeezes my throat a bit. "Yea, I like how you say that." His thumb caresses my throat. "Would you like to think of a name for me to call you?"

"Other than Alexia?"

The warmth of his breath caresses me as he chuckles. "Yes."

"Flower?"

"Are you asking me if that is what you want me to call you or are you telling me?" His eyebrows raise in question.

"You can call me Flower," I state in a stronger voice.

He smiles down at me. "Flower it is, oh how we will make you bloom, my deadly Flower." He rubs his heat along me, making my breath catch.

"You said to go deeper into my subconscious, where this can feel real. What did you mean by that?"

"Now you are asking the right questions." I sink into the bed. "The ruby you hold feeds off of energy. Specifically, the surrounding energy. I know a badger with plenty of energy they can share." He taps me on the nose. "This will help us converse and stay connected. So, if you need my help, I can better assist." His hips push into my legs.

"How do we go deeper?"

"We already are." His hands and body feel firmer against me. The heat of his body differed from the heat of the jewel. His hard length is pressed between us, his body strong against mine and completely naked. "Remove these." He picks at the clothes that I still wear.

"You could remove them." I tease, wrapping my legs around him, the jewel no longer with us.

His eyes dart to mine. "Flower?"

I freeze as he has. "Yes?"

"I need you to listen very carefully."

I listen to him. His voice has a deadly tone to it. The song and melody have stopped altogether.

"This is not a game. If you do not follow the rules, there will be consequences. I ask something of you. You do it. Got it."

"I was just teasing."

Something animalistic slides behind his eyes, something cold and hard. "I know, and that is why we are going slow at first. So, we both can get used to this. But do not forget what I have told you."

"Is this what sirens do?"

"Not all, but some, yes. We set boundaries and keep control of things, nothing worse than being accused we are doing something you don't want to."

"Is that what happened to the melody?"

"The melody was to tempt you to the dark side. I intend to keep you there by other means," he growls out the last part.

More heat pours into me as my legs clench around him. "Tell me more about being siren." I crave the knowledge and what he is offering with his body.

"Enough with the questions. We will have time for that later. I do not want to have to punish you."

"Punish how?"

He continues to push down on me, trapping my breath, giving a cruel smile. "You are still dressed, Flower."

"Domini?" The pressure of him digs into me more. I smile as the clothes slide from my form. "Where are you located? Your actual form?"

Warmth returns to his eyes; he stares at me as if I am a feast for his eyes. "There you are, Flower. How should I reward thee?"

My breath catches in the back of my throat as I anxiously wait. My body thrums with heat and excitement.

"Don't worry, you are far from me now, but it will not always be so. I have a feeling we will meet in the future." He pulls off my body, easing his weight off me.

"Will you let me know when we are close?" I curl into myself as his warmth leaves me.

"Don't do that." He says gruffly. "I want you to bloom for me, my Flower." One of his fingers skims down my leg, tickling me and causing a fire to burn.

I straighten back up, trying not to shiver. "What do you want, Domini?" I say in a sultry voice.

"Open up wide for me." He licks his lips as he stands over me.

I hold his eyes in mine as I contemplate. I give a wicked smile as I open my legs. Spreading them wide, I brush my hands down over my stomach towards my warm center.

"Your animal is close."

"The better to taste you, my dear." I bite my lip.

"Let's keep her at ease. This first time we will go slow, it will mostly be about learning each other and the rules to start."

"They say I am in heat. I don't know if there will be a slow." I arch myself up off the bed a bit, dipping my fingers lower just over my clit, barely touching.

"This will help in more than one way. I know it will. Listen to my voice and commands, and you will make it through my delicate but fierce Flower."

"Domini," I breathe out. "I'm listening." The talking was driving me crazy; I could feel fur once again brush up against me.

"Spread your lips so I can see straight through to your center." His eyes meet mine and then move down to my hands as they slide over my mound, opening up further.

My fingers slip through my folds, holding them open wide. "Do you like?"

"I need you to hold that position and not move until I tell you. You understand Flower?" He waits for me to nod. "I will show you how much I like it." He kneels in front of me with him on the floor while I am fully on the bed. I see his head creep up the bed and his hot breath brushes over my lower leg.

My legs shake, wanting to move or stretch, and my fingers become wetter as the anticipation grows. He hums, and I feel his cheek brush against my inner knee. My legs ease a bit as they spread wider.

"Flower, dip your fingers into the nectar that craves my touch." He kisses my inner thigh, his head not moving from watching me.

My fingers slide through my lips, rubbing against them and the juices that are pouring from me. I moan in ecstasy as I close my eyes, enjoying the feel of something there. My hips move in time with my fingers that pump into me.

A stinging bite causes my eyes to spring open. "Careful Flower, keep your legs open nice and wide." He licks the red love bite that is left on my inner thigh.

My fingers had stopped for a moment. I ease my legs back down and rub at my core. I pull my fingers away. "Do you want to taste?"

He pulls my hand closer to his mouth. "Keep touching yourself." I continue massaging my clit with my other hand.

"Domini taste me," I call out, my eyes half lidded.

He takes one of my fingers into the warm heat of his mouth, sucking it in. As he sucks on it, I dip one finger deep inside me. He hums in pleasure. Taking a second finger into his mouth. I push two fingers deep inside me. My hips buck to meet them, but I keep my knees to the side so that he can continue to see.

He slides both my fingers back out and nibbles on the pads of my fingers. "You taste so sweet. Slide your fingers slowly out and hold yourself open to me once again." He slides up closer to me.

As he sees me holding the sides of myself, he lowers his head. I feel the tip of his tongue touches my heat. I breathe out a soft groan as I melt into him. His tongue slides into my core and then up to my clit. He flicks it with barely a touch.

"Hold." He urges my fingers to move. He delves his tongue back into me, moving in and out. My breath comes in deep pants. "Do you hear me, Flower?"

It takes me a moment, but I come back from the edge enough to answer once he slows his movements. "Yes," I say breathlessly.

"She is close. She will need a release of something more than this can give."

I give a small, whining grunt in answer.

"I know. Listen very carefully, and she will get what she needs." He gives a long lick, toying with my lips for a moment.

"What do you want from me, Domini?"

"That's my Flower." He eases back. "We will come out of this, and the ruby will be close by. I need you to take it with you and find a body of water. Once you are there, keep the stone close by, and the water will take care of what is needed. You understand?" He repeats. He sucks on my clit.

"Yes—" I arch up into him. "Take the stone. Find water all better," I repeat.

"Do not let anyone distract you. Do not put this off." His full body crawls up mine, pressing me into the bed.

"But why?" I ask in confusion, the heat cooling off a bit.

"No why's, only do. Understand?" He asks.

I nod. "What about you?"

"We have time for that. I will see you next time." His body becomes less heavy, and more see-through.

"Come back," I cry out as the fire returns, but his heat does not.

The first thing I notice when I wake is that the blankets are tangled around me, and everything is hot and sweat filled. The blanket shreds as my claws easily tear through the cloth. I look down and my hands are in the shape of claws. Everything is crisp and clear around me, even though it is still dark. I calm my racing heart as I listen to the darkness around me. Nothing but normal night sounds utter. Warm heat pulses below the blankets, I slowly unfurl them, taking extra care to not rip them any further. Once free of the hot cocoon, I pull my hair up off the nape of my neck. I see the red ruby pulsing in the deep red covers and heat emitting from the stone.

"Domini?" I whisper. The pulsing strengthens as if in answer.

My head swivels around the room, and my eyes land on a door connected to mine. My room had its own bathroom. I remember what he had told me, even as something deep still clings to me and begs me to fall back into the bed. I pad over to the door and walk into the nice bathroom. I fill the bathtub with warm water when I turn on the water. The heat was almost cloying, my skin still damp from the covers. I remove my clothing, hoping to breathe easier, the claws not retracting. I glance in the mirror and notice my eyes have gone dark. My animal is the closest I have ever seen it. Nails race down my sides in answer as if my animal wants something from me. I grip the ruby closer to my body, and it throbs in time with my heartbeat. My eyes flick to the water. "Almost," I utter.

I grip my hip and feel bones slide there. Sliding my eyes back to the mirror, I notice things shift. "I will not lose myself to my animal like I did last time," I bite out.

My feet race across the tiled floor to the warm pool. It was close enough for now. Sliding one leg into the deep tub, I slowly sink in, keeping the stone close to my stomach. The pulsing heat reacts with the warm water, causing thick steam to emit. The water rises over my thighs and stomach as I lower myself slowly down. I move the stone down in slow circles, liking the heat nestled next to my core. Once the water level is slightly over my breasts, I raise to flick the knobs to the off position. I lean back, stretching out my tight muscles, them vibrating with excitement. I keep the stone in one hand but move my other down my stomach. My claws slice into my skin, leaving red lines. I pause, not wanting more pain. Firm fingers run over my clit, massaging me there. My mouth opens as I pant. I eye the water, watching it whirl around my legs, forcing me to remain wide and open. His fingers delve down south, playing with my opening.

Warmth from the stone sears into me and creates more delicious friction. The water sloshes with violence, and my head tosses back and forth in ecstasy but ultimately falls back. My hips move on their own as two fingers delve into me. The base of his palm rubs against my clit. I hiss in pleasure as I feel currents move up my lower calves. My eyes flick open. The lights are still off, but I see the water ripple. Though I can't see anything other than the water, what it is doing to me is beyond my comprehension.

"Domini, you know what I need." Something hard moves against my center as if in answer, pressing deeper still. The water becomes more solid as it moves against me, gripping in some ways and pushing in others. My claws slip on the edge of the tub as I scrabble for purchase, needing something more at my core. The ruby still sits on my stomach. I feel zings of heat as it does what it needs to. Something slides into me, thick and wanting. "Are you reading my mind, Domini?" The water moves around my breasts. It feels as if hands are all around me, ratcheting up my pleasure. I gasp as I feel the movement inside me pick up the tempo. The water continues playing with my clit as he pumps into me.

The water sloshes back and forth in time with the tempo as we build the rhythm. My body writhes in pleasure as I go over the crest. The feeling thickens and pulses deep inside me. I let out a scream as I let go. My limbs go limp as I slosh back into the water. My harsh breathing is ragged in the quiet room, and the waves slow back down. I still feel something hard at my opening teasing me. My hips roll into it, and the stone burns brightly under the water in response.

The movement begins anew and slowly stirs the waters, building me back up again. My claws melt back to fingers as I grip the tub's sides. Once I feel they are safe, I skim them over my stomach and breasts, playing with them. The water moving around, plus the light pinching of my fingers on my nipples really stirs the heat inside me. "More, Domini," I whisper. The water answers in return. It picks back up in tempo and opens me up, driving into me deeper and thicker than before. I felt it this time, just out of reach. My bottom wiggles in time to drive it deeper still. I pinch my nipple in answer, needing something more. The power from the ruby sends another bite of pain and pleasure. I grip the rock with my free hand and slide it down to my clit, waiting for it to send another spark. Once it does, the world explodes around me, and my vision darkens. White dots dance in front of my eyes. I blink them a few times, hoping to clear them, but my sight does not get better.

"Did I just have sex with water? Don't answer that question." The water cools and becomes less dense as the stone dulls down in light and heat. I catch my breath as I sit in the cooling water, it just moving around as normal with my movements. Domini is gone for now. "If he can do that from wherever he is right now, I am tempted to see what he can do in person." I give a wicked grin as I begin to wash my body just by touch. My animal is at bay for the moment. I clean up, take care of myself, and go back for a few more hours of sleep, making sure to set the stone away in a drawer for the time being. There is no risk since we satisfied my animal for now, but I am still too tired to read more of the journal. I would do that once I woke back up.

CHAPTER 9

I WAKE UP A few hours later with the journal still open to the last entry that I read last night. After I take care of things, I climb back up on the bed, crossing my legs. I don't have anything to do yet, but I would need to find Quintan or Natasha to see our next steps. Plucking the journal back up, I lean back against the plump pillows. Flipping through a couple of pages, skimming the words written there, searching for the next journal entry that might give me some insight into what I want to know.

Dear Diary,

I have got it! I have figured out a way to change everything! They will be here soon, at least by tonight. Soon this should all go my way, and I won't have to deal with this anymore. You hear that fate. I'm going to thwart you and make my path, one in which I choose.

Here is the plan between you and me, book. You are my keeper of secrets. Only those that I trust may read these words. I was looking through some of the spell books, the darker ones of course, which is why this must be kept secret, for everyone on the Light side would judge me for entertaining the dark side of the arts. I found a spell that will let me go back into the past. Now I know what you are thinking. I have heard the warnings before. You can't change my mind on this. I have to get out of here, out of this destiny of mine. These spells are supposed to be forbidden even to the dark side, but if they were so bad, why keep them then? Why not dispose of them? I have read what is needed for this, and nothing seemed out of place or horrible.

Why must these restricted tombs be locked up is beyond me? I looked over some others that were under lock and key, and some were just silly on why they are kept hidden. I am surprised that I had found the secret passageway to this hidden portal. I was doing my normal cleaning of the library when I fell into this ancient mirror. I have seen the mirror before, but when I was leaning over to clean the top of the carved wood edge, a click sounded as my fingers accidentally pushed against the wood on the side. Giving a more thorough look, multiple swirls and circles were carved into the wood where a button was hidden. After looking at the mirror and scrutinizing it, I could see the glass ripple.

I reached out and brushed my fingers across the reflective surface. It wavered. I had to know what was on the other side, so I poked my head through it. My eyes automatically closed, afraid it was like water and not wanting it to get in my eyes.

The room beyond the looking glass was dark, dusty, and dank. It smelled like old paper and vanilla. I go further into the room through the portal. Light emits from the mirror in this other room kept open like a beacon waiting and calling me back. I'm still unsure where this room is located, whether it is out of space and time, or somewhere hidden within this realm or house. I carefully navigate the crowded room, not wanting to trip over anything. There were tapers to light the candles with, which is where the vanilla smell came from.

This room didn't seem familiar at all. Many tombs strayed about the room in all kinds of manners. I looked through a couple of the books but found what I was looking for rather fast. I had heard that there were books such as these that were hidden away for the good of all people. Were these those books? If my plan goes accordingly, I will return to this mirror place once I get back from the past. When my options have changed, and the future can be bright instead of bleak. I must stop writing now. I don't want to give too much away; I must prepare the spell to change my horrible present. I don't want anyone changing or stopping this from happening.

I will write more later when the time is right, and things are not up in the air. I must remember I am not alone in this and need to remember why things must change.

Ever Hopeful,

Sera

I drop the journal to the side and think over some things. "I wonder if that mirror is still at my mother's palace or at her parent's home, wherever that may be. If I could go back in the past to figure out things, this would make all of this easier." Why am I just hearing about these spells that I could see past events? Why did Quintan need to be there to go through them with me if he had a way I could get the answer? Why not have me do it in my own time? I hadn't seen a mirror at my parent's place, but I didn't view the entire palace either. I wonder if someone would know. Perhaps it was brought here. But how to bring it up coyly? What if they knew what it housed?

"Trill or Tina, are you here?" I mumble.

"Trill went to find Margaret or Robert, but I am here?" A groggy, small voice emits. A small flame body pulls up off of my arm. She walks down with warm, tiny feet to my hand as I hold my arm up, ensuring she can balance.

"Hey Tina."

"Hi." She yawns. "So tired. I couldn't find you the other night. You weren't in bed where you were supposed to be."

"Yea, I wasn't in my normal form. You ended up finding me last night. No problem, right?"

"Yea, we have a pull to the ones we connect to. Trill was there with you when you were in animal form. So, I for sure ended up finding you, but every time I got close, you freaked out about me being a flame. I gave up after it was not fun anymore from chasing you and hunkered on one of the many candles Margaret keeps around."

"You chased me in my badger form? I don't remember that part." My jaw drops open.

She giggles. "Yea, silly, you were a lot of fun in that form. Except when you got hungry and tried to eat me."

I shudder in answer. "But that was the previous night. Why are you still tired? Did you not get sleep last night?"

"You were burning up. I keep you heated, and something else keeps you heated. This can cause you to pass away if your temperature rises too high. We had to vacate to another place while your body cooled back down. Trill said it happened to you the previous night when you changed into the other form and that you got too hot. She almost had to leave, but after changing, you could better regulate your temperature. Last night, we both stayed close to the candles."

"Oh, so you can tell when my animal is close? Does it hurt you to be in me wherever you go when you are with me? Does it hurt when I shift?"

"That is easy. We go into a trancelike state or like a deep sleep and only come out of it when we are out here like this." She hops along my hand; her hair flares out, waving in all directions. "We can't be out long without the trance until we are much older and can hold a form for longer. You shifting does not harm us at all, but we also don't want to cause damage to our host, and two flame elementals may be too much with what you are going through right now. Margaret says it happens to all women going through changes. Some are more severe than others. Will you shift more now?"

"I hope not. I think it is being held at bay for the moment. Or I think I have it under control until I can learn more."

"Can I call you badger butt if you do?"

I glare at her little form as she ignores me, looking anywhere but at me.

"Though maybe it is good for you to shift. You were so warm last night. We almost had to go get Margaret. But you got up before we could and went to the bathroom. When you got back, you were a lot cooler."

"I called you to see if you knew of any old mirrors around here or if you knew if Margaret or Robert knew of an old mirror that may have come from my parents' place. It's a long shot, but they may have it if they went through the palace like Robert explained they did." I change the subject, not wanting to go into details about last night.

"There are plenty of mirrors around here." She cocks her head and peers up at me in curious wonder.

"This would be a full-length mirror with wood carved all around it with swirls and circles that may have buttons or latches around it." I try to give an appropriate description of how my mother worded it in her journal. Going back to the journal, I skim through it and check if there are any details I may have missed.

Tina hops down off of my hand when I pick up the book. "There are a couple in the library and some others in storage. I don't think they brought over much from your folk's old place. Most of it was destroyed and burned to a crisp."

"Hmm. It was a long shot, no worries."

"I mean, there is one that looks like something charred it a bit that they keep in the way back of the library downstairs."

"Really?" My eyes lift and dance with glee. "Do you want to go on an adventure with me?"

"Adventure, why didn't you say so!" She squeals.

"Okay, let's go check this out." I place the journal safely back in its container before having her lead me to where she saw this mirror.

She zooms through the hallways, and I speed walk, trying to keep up with her. We follow the steps downstairs, and she leads me to the grand library. Tina slides under the door when we get to the room. My steps are slow, unsure if I want to bust in like last time. Perhaps there was another meeting going on. My hand shakes as I settle it on the doorknob. Slowly opening it, I peek into the room beyond. The room is dim. No lights are turned on as yet. My eyes roam from one wall to the other. I enter the room and flip the switch beside the door, turning on more lights.

"Do you want people to know we are on adventure?" Tina pipes up. She is already halfway to the stacks of books on the right of the room.

"You're right." My fingers dance over the switch and turn it back off. I let the door close silently behind me. "You said there were mirrors here. I didn't see any when I was here last time."

"They aren't in the open. Some of them are way back here, out of the way."

"Why would they put a mirror in the library, anyway?"

"For spells, I am guessing if one is needed. Why are you searching for the mirror?" she asks.

My eyes land on Tina's fading form as I walk behind her with sure steps, keeping my eyes peeled for mirrors.

"I will take you to the one that had some charring on it, since that is most likely the one you need." Tina zips up on one bookshelf, dancing around the books, not getting too hot or close to the pages.

We finally twirl around another aisle deep in the stacks of books. "Is this room bigger than it looks?" I question out loud. The mirror is cast in shadow against the corner furthest from the door and sight. The window's light does not touch back this far. If it did, I feared this corner would still be cast in shadow. My fingers sweep across the shelves, not coming away with any dust, yet the mirror is covered in it. "Does the cleaning not extend to the mirror?"

Tina brings little soot tracks across the shelves. "Maybe they are afraid to clean it. Everything else is clean around it, just not the mirror itself," she whispers.

"Perhaps it does not reveal itself all the time. Regardless of why it was not cleaned, we need to see if there is a doorway or portal to what it holds inside." I walk up to it, scrutinizing the sides of the mirror closely.

"I only know of it because I saw it with Margaret. She said you have to have a special stone or be around someone who has one of these stones to see it. You must have one, right?" She shrieks and jumps for joy.

My hand automatically goes to the gem in my throat that is hidden. "Now we just have to find a way in."

Tina launches off the bookshelf and walks up to the large mirror with her head back, peering up at it. "What do you mean? Isn't it just a mirror?"

"No, my mother talked about a hidden room inside. From the journal I was reading."

"That was your mom's. That's nice that she left you something to read." She kicks at the floor.

The mirror itself was thick and solid. My fingers brush the cold, hard surface of the reflective mirror. "There is supposed to be a button of some sort." I stand on tiptoes to reach up on the sides of the mirror. Dust covers it fully, sticking to my fingers as I brush over it. My fingers dip into the wooden swirls as it moves this way and that. "I can feel the swirls of the wood but can't see very well where a circle maybe hiding a button. Can you light some of the dust on fire to clear it?"

Tina's mouth drops open, and glances at the books surrounding her. "Do you think that would be a good idea? Margaret would be awfully upset if I burned anything like this in her home," Tina states as she comes closer to the mirror, the bottom of it right at eye level for her. Her fingers raise to the dirt-covered wood, testing a bit. She grows brighter as her flame burns bigger. Small flames ignited and burn parts of the filth away, though small embers keep burning the wood below. "No, it would not be wise." She steps away, taking the heat and flame with her.

I smudge out the rest of the embers before they can catch on the wood and turn this place into a fire pit. "I think I saw some cleaning rags when we first came into the library." Tina stands by the mirror as I dash through the aisles. I grab a cloth and race back to the antique. My feet catch on something, causing me to trip into the mirror.

My hands grasp the sides of the mirror, bracing myself before I can plummet into the glass and shatter it to pieces. I rub the cloth over the bumpy wood. The carvings are easily distinguishable through the bumps as the dirt and grime come away easily. Leaves are etched into the wood, swirling along the sides which lead to circular curves, turning on vines that lead to petals of flowers. I hum to myself as I work on clearing the dust away.

The rag as it wipes over the rough wood snags on something, tugging it free strings pull off of the cloth. It looked like a middle of a rose. I maneuver the fibers out and away; my fingers brush over the knot and press in gently but firm. "Is this it?"

The switch presses in and gives an audible click. Something whooshes from the glass, sending the rest of the dust and grime blasting away. The mirror shines and glistens as if it were just cleaned. The cloth slips from my fingers. I move closer to inspect what I have found. I poke at the glass; it moves, causing a ripple cascade out from the center to the edges.

"Amazing," I say in awe.

"This was the mirror!" Tina squeals as she hops around.

"I will go first just to make sure, but can you go around when we get in there? There should be candles left to light. Can you take care of them?"

"Yippee!" Tina dances around. "Just give me a sign."

"I will stick my hand back out when it is clear."

I slowly ease myself into the glass. It flows over me like cool liquid but does not cling to me as water would. The first thing that I notice is the chill in the room next is the stark darkness that answers. The glow from the portal only lights a small area. I notice a few candles right at the beginning. Quickly grabbing one, I rush back to the portal, pushing my hand through and motioning for Tina to come through.

"This is amazing!" Tina yells really loudly as she comes through. Her light is the brightest I have ever seen it before. She dances and hops from my candle, then to the next. "Fire!"

"Don't burn any of the books," I chide.

"Don't ruin my fun," she giggles back as she races through the books and dry parchment paper, making sure not to step on them, though she comes close a few times eyeing me to make sure I know she is kidding. "Taz would have liked to see all this and be a part of the fun. Trill would have liked the knowledge of the books and been the party pooper."

"I know Shade is taking care of Taz don't worry."

"I know. If she was in trouble or hurt, we would feel it and be more persistent about getting our sister."

I stare at her bobbing form as she catches on to another candle further away. "That's good. Can you sense anything about Shade? Or just your sister."

"Just Taz. I would have let you know if we could," she says further away.

I make my way over to the first table on the right. This place was larger than mother had written about. She made it seem small and tight. Perhaps she did something to make it bigger. My eyes scan the contents noticing maps and papers littered all around. Some maps were of my world, and others of ones I have never seen before. "It's as if they were studying other lands along with this one here," I whisper. There were scrawling of languages, some I couldn't even interpret, let alone understand, what any of it meant.

My brain scrambles to remember where Sera had said she went once she came through the looking glass. She didn't describe the scene well; some books scatter to the floor as I bump into them. Dust plumes up in a giant cloud. I cough as I fan my hand back and forth, stepping away from it and choosing a different path.

There was no reason to this place. It is so chaotic. How am I supposed to find anything I am looking for? I pulled a large tomb from a random stack, and an angry face meets mine on the cover. My fingers itch to organize the books in some fashion, one that would make sense, but most of this was of other languages that I couldn't even read.

"Oh, Lady master!" A voice chimes in.

"Not you again. Where did you come from? I thought Jazmin scared you off." A black skull floats near the portal, where some books are kept behind a glass case.

"You can't get rid of me so easily, lady. Especially when you still need your trustful servant's help." The red haze wraps around him, creating a hood and cape for his ebony skull. The red cape fades off in tatters at the ends. His bright red eyes pierce through the deep hood. His gaze beams into the glass case that holds a couple of books.

"You know, you never explained why you are here?"

"I am but a humble servant. I need not give any reason other than that, lady master."

"Well, what does your tall master or what did you call the other one mean, master? What would they think you having so many masters?"

"All of them are mean, but there is a tall and main master. The main one knows all and allows me to have so many. It also gives power to the chaos that I thrive in!" He giggles with glee. "I do all their bidding to the best of my ability."

"The main master. What is its name?" I coo.

"He has no name."

"He?" I question as I come closer to inspect the glass-covered case. He still keeps his eyes trained on what's inside. As I pass by the skull, I skim my hand over the red cape, feeling the velvet softness. My fingers bunch in its cloth to grab it. My hand slips as he loops out of reach.

"Silly." He shakes his self, ruffling the red cape, spinning around so the cloth circles around him. Only his fire-red eyes stare out between the red folds. "Master is not ready for you yet. Patience." He hisses. "You are not ready for him, either."

"I don't even know why I try. It's not like you will leave me alone till you get your way. You also won't tell me anything about why you are here. If you did, it would just become cryptic and confusing like last time."

I huff out and lean back heavily on the sturdy wooden table. My ankles cross as I stare at the case and surrounding areas full of books, papers, and dust. Tina lands on the last candle, lighting it and ensuring the place gives off a warmth now that the room is not cast in darkness.

Trix zooms around my head. "What are you doing? Go to the case," he screeches.

"Why should I do that, little skull?"

"Because what lies behind the glass is what you seek." He bobs up and down, urging me forward.

Yawning, I raise my hands over my head, giving into a full-body stretch. "I'm not so sure of that."

The tattered red cloth he wears like a scarf flop down dull and listless. The bright red fades to gray and then black as his mood plummets. "What do you mean?" He sputters. "The spell you need is right there."

An icy wind seems to emit from Trix that whips my hair around. "Why are you trying to be so helpful?" My voice lowers. "Give me a straight answer, and perhaps I will grab what is there in the glass cabinet. I am no longer just doing things because I am told without being told the answers I need."

Tina trails back quickly through the stacks, not touching anything that would cause the place to go up in flames. She jumps up and dives into my arm, settling there in case I need her.

"Why is lady master being so mean and bull headed about this?" He growls.

I keep silent.

The wind spins faster. "Fine!" He yells before he zooms off towards the glass, breaking it with his small skull. Shards of glass embed themselves into his black skull, making it glitter in the candlelight. It looks like he has a mohawk now.

I make a stand coming to attention as the little skull shakes himself loose of the glass. Some fall tinkling to the ground while others stay embedded deep in the bone. "What the — Why did you do that?"

"I am going to feel that one in the morning," Trix says as he wobbles back and forth.

"Stay still, and I will get the rest of the glass out while you tell me why you did that." I pick my way carefully through the glass that litters the floor. Walking towards the glass case, Trix inspecting if anything in the case is destroyed.

"Lady master not listen," he whispers but stops swirling around so I can get to the pieces stuck on the top of his head. "You will see. Just look. I promise it is worth it. No tricks this time. I help over all. I only play tricks sometimes."

My fingers wiggle the glass back and forth out of his skull, taking it out piece by piece. I place the glass carefully on a stack of books, making sure it wouldn't harm anyone else. Once the last piece comes free, I turn to pile the glass altogether. "You still have not answered the question." I look over my shoulder at where he had been. There is no skull anywhere in this room. It is as if he disappeared into thin air.

I check behind stacks of books and anywhere he could have hidden easily. "Typical." Why did he want me to have this spell so badly? I carefully turn my focus back to the glass shards near the glass cabinet and work my hands carefully around the books, taking care not to catch myself.

My hands were steady before picking up any of the books. Perhaps I shouldn't be doing this, especially since he wouldn't give me a straight answer. But how else am I supposed to learn the things I want to know if not through experience?

I needed to make something happen for myself instead of waiting for everything to come to me or for other people to decide it is time for me to know. These kinds of times called for action, not re-action.

I brush off the rest of the glass and pluck the book that is sitting right in front where the jagged hole was. Pulling it out, I go slow and make sure not to jerk into the shards of glass. The book itself is light but looks quite large. It is a black book with leather chords tied around it, keeping it sealed shut. It almost looked like a journal rather than a spell book.

I flip the book open to the title page. The words stare up from the cream-colored page. A guy's name is scrawled across the page.

"It is someone's journal. Or perhaps it is a spell book, but they put their name on it." I continue past the title page, scanning the pages quickly as I pass over a passage where the magic user talks about creating a spell or stumbles over a new incantation.

The writing is cluttered and messily written across the page. Many spells fill up the next couple of pages. There wasn't even an index. It all seemed random as to what spells were throughout the pages. My hands tenderly hold the book to my chest as I go back to a table where I can sit down and go over this book more in depth and actually comprehend what I am reading.

Many hours later, I yawn, growing tired with the passing time. My eyes have grown heavy, and my body is stiff from sitting in one position for so long. Tina didn't even come back out after the initial adventure. She must be dozing still. I scan the brick walls that surround this place, looking for a timepiece. There was no way to tell how much time had passed, but it felt like I had been here for a good amount of time. "One more page." I turn the page and read the passage there. "Remembrance." My face lowers as I get closer to the page, my fingers trace under the words following as I read. "Is this the spell that Trix was thinking I needed?"

My eyes light up as I take in what I am reading. This wasn't the spell that Sera had written about in her diary, but it definitely sounded like a spell that I could use to help me in my current situation. I needed to remember the rest of the memories from my past, and Quintan didn't seem too keen on helping me with those any time soon. Jade and Tom were the cause of my memories being the way they were and I deserved them, even if they weren't good.

I could at least get some answers about my past and maybe my parents another time. The spell she talked about might not even be in here. It would take me quite a while to go through all of this. I could always come back to this place and check out later. I stand up from the chair and stretch out nice and tall. My back cracks in answer.

"Oof," I say. I re-tie the journal up and stick it under my arm. Crossing the room with slow, sluggish steps has worn me out more than I thought it would. I pass through the glowing portal of the mirror. It grabs at the loose strands of my hair, pulling at them gently, as if calling me back to it.

I rub at my tired eyes and turn back to my reflection, looking for the trigger to close the portal. Nothing in the journal mention a latch that would close the portal, but there had to be one. The glow that emits from the glass is no longer there. I brush my fingers against the cool, hard surface and tap on it, ensuring there is no way in again.

"Strange, it must have an auto shut off once you come back through."

Shrugging my shoulders and shaking my head, I let go of the issue and wonder at all the other issues I have to take care of.

I walk back to the front of the room, passing by a row of windows. Before I get past them, I stop and stare as my jaw hangs down. The moon is high in the sky. It is well past sundown. Was it even the same day? Though this explained why I felt so tired. I tap my fingers on the smooth leather, reminding myself of the spell. "I can see if I can try the spell tonight and then get some rest and search for the other spell that helps me go into the past tomorrow."

CHAPTER 10

THE ROOM IS HOT and stuffy when I enter my room. The doors to my balcony are open, letting in the heat from outside. I cross over to them while waving a hand in front of my face, hoping to circulate cool air. I pull both doors closed, keeping out the humid summer heat; the lights were on when I entered the room. My eyes scan the room, seeing things have been moved and tidied up, along with food left on the desk. I set the spell book down on the plush bed and kneel down to retrieve my mother's journal from where I left it. I pick up both books and cross to where the meaty sandwich is on the desk under a cover.

I lick my lips as I dump the books on to the table. The sandwich is huge and has meats piled high on it; I grasp it in both hands as I take a huge bite. My stomach cramps at me in answer, letting me know my badger will not be happy that I ignored my body all day.

"Hey, it's not my fault that time works differently there," I complain. Hardly stopping before I shovel another bite into my mouth. My mouth waters at the taste. The sandwich does not last long as I devour it. That would suffice for the time being, though I already felt that the animal part of me wanted, no, needed more.

Before looking at the spell and opening up the books, I get up and pass by the open door. I close it before dressing down for bed. Soon I am in comfy, loose clothing. I tie up my hair in a messy bun, keeping it out of my way.

I return to the desk, unwind the ties, flip through the spell book, and find the spell of remembrance once again. I finally find it after a couple of flip throughs, I dog-ear the page it is on so that I could find it easier next time. The paper was thick, unlike the other spell books I had seen with tiny writing and thin pages. The spell itself seemed small and simple. It was just a small incantation that needed no special ingredients or preparation.

Something warm hops on to my leg. Looking down, I spot Trill. "Did you have a good day with Margaret? Or Robert?"

"Yes, both are doing well. What are you doing?"

"I found this spell that could help me remember my past. I was going to try to do a spell. They weren't looking for me, were they?"

"Shouldn't Quintan be here for that? Also, I thought you couldn't do much magic since Shade took it all. No not really. At least they weren't worried."

"Quintan is more worried about the town and getting a bat-tle-ready plan for our next steps. He isn't worried about me and what I need. Plus, it has to be a minor spell. There isn't anything to it. The previous books I read said that if there is a lot to it, it will take more power. I hope Shade left me a little power or magic and that it will work."

"What if I stand watch just in case you need some help?"

"That sounds like a plan. Then they can't say that I am not being responsible," I nod and turn to the spell and read it once more before I speak it into existence. The words do not come easy to me and I stumble over a couple of them. My eyes scan the room as I finish the last word.

The air is still, and nothing is happening.

"Did it work?" Trill asks.

"No." I shake my head. "No memories, no past flickering, noth-ing." The room is empty besides the things I brought along with me, the bed, and the other furniture here. Everything is neat and spotless.

"Maybe you need more force or emotion behind the words?" Trill shrugs. "Sometimes mother would tell us it matters how you say things."

I say the incantation once more with feeling and more gumption. I try not to speak the words too loudly in case someone heard me and tried to stop me from doing what I am doing. My fingers clench around the book's edges, holding it close to me, trying to pull the power of the words into myself. I shut my eyes and repeat the words again, pouring all of my soul into the spell, hoping it would work. Needing it to work. Begging in silence as tears run down my face to anyone that would listen for it to work.

I lift one eye as I peek out into the lit bedroom.

Trill looks around the empty room, searching for something as well.

"Nothing again," I cry out. "Perhaps he did take all of my magic with him. Why did I think that would work? Why did I even try?"

I flip to the next page, hoping I missed something, but the next page continues with a different spell. I search for something with a key, huffing I throw the book across the room. It slides over the shiny wooden floor, coming to rest with a thump against the lavender-painted wall. A breeze whips into the room right above where the book landed near the bathroom door.

I would deal with the disappointment later. "Let's just get some sleep. I'm too tired right now."

Trill gives a sad smile and dips down into my arm, her warmth covering me. I gently pick up my mother's journal and carry it to the plump bed with me, tucking it under the pillows. I would have to find other hiding spots, ones I knew were protected. Spinning back to the light switch, I flip it to turn off the lights. The moonlight helps guide me in the darkness to the bed. I settle into the covers and hunker down under them. The cool air is nice as I am covered in a fluffy warm layer. Hopefully, the spell didn't work because I am just too tired.

A light wind blows across my face. "Wasn't it just sweltering?" I mumble out. Lights twinkle behind my eyelids as I fall asleep. The little stars I follow help me go deeper into the dark void, shining my way through.

The little twinkly lights bat away the darkness. A crying wail pierces the air. I am inside a screaming and wailing baby, but my thoughts are my own and separate. Tears rush down my plump cheeks as the cold air hits my skin. Warmth enfolds me, quickly swaddling me in happiness. The bright shining light I followed into this life backs away as I settle into another's arms. I sniffle and look up at a pretty lady.

"She is precious, my dear." A man's rugged form steps up beside the woman with a hold on me. He looks familiar. My little eyes squint at him as he comes closer. *Ivan.*

My eyes roam back to the closer woman, *Sera?*

My baby eyes bounce back and forth between the two, unsure which one is more interesting. I wail at them, pleading with them to turn off the harsh lights above. This place is different from the one I am used to.

They did not move other than to rock me back and forth and make shushing noises at me. It felt nice, and soon my wails quieted down to huffs. It wasn't so bad. Maybe I could deal with the lights. My limbs kick out, and one of my legs gets free. The cold air hit me once again, reminding me that this was not right and I needed to make them listen. I scream at them, throwing a tiny fist in the air, giving them everything I had to make them hear me.

"She has a good set of pipes," Sera chuckles. Her worn-out face smiles, her brow is drenched in sweat.

Ivan takes my weight into his arms as he tucks the blanket back around me. He tucks Sera under the warm covers as well. "Rest, my love. You have been through enough today. Both of you have. She will need those good pipes for what the future holds."

He hushes me and sings to both of us until I calm down and my lungs tire. My eyes blink shut, and soon I am back in the nice calm darkness with the starlike things all around me.

"Flit, what are you doing here?"

"Do you think I would miss the birth of my grandchild?"

"You said—"

"Boy, have I taught you nothing? That was theatrics. You and Sera know how I feel. The dark side has a certain character one needs to be, and I play a part."

"This is Alexia."

"Sleep, little one, for when the night bites, remember you bite back."

No other words come into the darkness and stars where I am held.

"Was that my birth? Did that remembrance spell actually work?" I shout in joy at the dull stars that surround me. What could be next? How many memories could I get through? Was there a limit? This and many other questions flitted through my mind in a second.

The lights blur together in the background, growing hazier and duller. I hope it is not the same scene repeatedly while I sleep. Why would the spell caster not write these kinds of things down for the spell? Did they expect the user to already know the laws or rules of a spell?

Hair blows above me, and the cold wind bites into me. This scene looks familiar; one I have seen before. I watch from young eyes as the past plays out once again. Jade comes into the room and throws her wind Sera spins vines around me, and at the end, my mother leaves me to the fate of Jade once again.

After my mother's limp body falls to the floor, all that is left is the destruction of the room and Jade's hatred and anger.

"Search them out one by one and make them pay for what they thought to do," Jade yells out, raising her hand and pushing the wind out of the room, pushing her men out with it. Screams and hollers echo down the corridor.

I wail out, wanting my mother. Her calm serenity no longer soothed me. My screams match those that were causing chaos in my home. She clenches me to her and bounces me too harshly to quiet me. The blanket is smothering me. I could hardly breathe.

A shadow whisks around my head. My chubby hands try to reach for it. Jade tries to shoo it away. As I watch it flutter in the wind, this calms me for a moment. The small shadow flutters over to me and lands on my cheek. The touch is feather-light. It whisks away as Jade peers down at me, trying to discern what is happening. It flutters to the floor and goes out of sight.

What is happening? I think to; it was hard only to view what my baby's eyes perceived. My eyes kept closing and scrunching close in fear and anger.

Crashes sound all around me. The wind picks up, but the blanket continues to keep me warm. An enormous boom goes off a way off but is still loud. I am handled roughly by another pair of hands. These hands are larger and sturdier. I wail out and suck in air, hiccupping on it between cries.

"Don't hurt the child." Jade's voice rings out in a struggle. Another crash echoes around her, and she repeats the words louder this time. "Something is not right. Don't squeeze her too tight. Ack." Her voice cuts off.

The hands that held me stop their crushing weight. "I thought you said we needed to rid ourselves of the little brat!" A bellow comes from up above me, scaring me further.

"My sister tied our life force together. You can't kill her without destroying me, too," she gasps out. Her long, thin fingers come into view as she picks me out of the burly man's arms. She holds me aloft, peering up at me with a glare. She continues to hold me away from her body as the blanket unravels from my legs.

"The child must die. The council for light deemed it so. That is why they approved of this attack. If it doesn't happen, they will deny everything, and we will all be up shit's creek without a paddle." The big man bolsters out between clenched teeth.

Jade lunges away from his reach, pulling me in tow. "We will find another way. Tom! Let me find a way around the death spell first. Then you can do whatever you wish with the child."

"What is going on?" As he steps on the hard floors, Tom's boots give a low thump.

"We need to find another way." Jade rushes over to Tom's side, his face becoming clear as we move to him and away from the angry crowd that now has all three of us cornered.

"She will not let us destroy the demon spawn," The angry brute seethes.

Tom looks at Jade and I, who is held in her arms. I have quieted down, unsure of what was happening. "Why?" He raises an eyebrow. "It looks like you had no problem with your sister." His eyes roam over the room.

"The brat tied the thing to me as a curse, so if her life dips, so does mine. If she goes so, do I," Jade states vehemently.

Tom places himself in front of Jade and me, facing the group of thugs. "She helps govern the light; you can't expect to kill her! Just wait until we find a way out of this, and then we can end the little beast's life. Until then, we can siphon her power and use it as our own. That way, it is not a complete failure, and we are still using her for the light side."

Jade nods her head in agreement. "All we have to do is find a loophole to break it." Jade jostles my body as her nerves are on the edge.

"Fine... But the council will know of this; she will be your problem to watch over until another way is figured out. If she escapes once, we will do what needs to be done, no matter the consequences."

"Done," Tom says.

"I will not lose another son to these scoundrels and their war," the gruff man barks as he turns into the crowd, parting it down the middle as he leaves.

Jade bounces me up and down in slower movements. My eyes grew heavy, exhausted after all the excitement.

"We will go to the human realm and hide her there. We will then contact the council to let them know, but we must make sure she is protected from the other side or anyone else who would want to take her." Jade whispers into Tom's ear.

He nods and motions for the crowd to follow him. The lines grow blurry as my eyes shut fully.

I am soon back amongst the stars, floating around in the calm night sky. My mind whips through quick memories. Many of them were very short. I struggle to stay awake long enough to only be put under once again. They were careful not to talk around me, so I did not relive those memories. I rush past those normal, boring memories, searching for something more.

A small room with pale blue walls holds me captive when little, no people are around to play with or to hold me when I am frightened. The blue walls were my freedom, my escape from my captors. It is what I thought the sky would look like if I were ever allowed outside. Windows were boarded up, and that is when the dark shadow came.

Shade helped me grow and learn when no other would. I would be left alone for days, sometimes weeks at a time. He made sure I was fed and would sneak me things to learn. We would play, and when I was sad or upset, he would show me comfort.

I slow the memories down, looking at how Shade had helped me throughout. *Did he remember all of this? Was he upset with me that I couldn't remember this?*

My eyes skim over the little trinkets on the fireplace mantel he had brought me. We were playing hide and seek. He would hide somewhere in the room. He was a shadow, so there were lots of places he could hide, and I would try to find him. It made the dull days go by quicker than just staring off into space.

I look up and in the fireplace, first since that was his favorite place to hide.

"What are you doing?" Jade shrieks.

As I raise up, I bump my head on the underside of the fireplace. "Ouch." I rub at my head as I come out of the dirty fireplace. Soot is covering my dress. If you could call it that, it was just rags hanging off my body. My eyes land on Jade. "Playing—hide and seek—" I stutter out the words, my voice cracking from its little to no use.

"With who?" She gives a small smile.

"Shade." I lower my head, afraid of the glare that came from her glacial eyes.

"You lie. What did we tell you there is no Shade? He is a figment of your imagination. There is no one here other than me and you. You are no one special. We are trying to help you through this process, but your mind keeps making things up that just aren't true."

I gulp like a fish out of water for answers. Many times, I have tried to get her to see or understand Shade. She ignores him or Shade hides, not willing to come out and meet her.

My voice is small and fragile. "Maybe I make up Shade because you keep me here in this room all the time. Maybe if you let me out so I can be around others in the real world, I wouldn't have to invent my own." My voice waivers as I struggle to ask for what I want. I wanted to believe her, but Shade was more real than either of my parents were.

She closes her eyes and purses her lips in disgust. "Your father and I already explained why we keep you in here. This is for your own protection and for the safety and security of others. We showed you what happened last time we let you free. Don't you remember?"

I give a small nod and look to the ground, inspecting the soot-covered floor where I stand.

"So, do you want to rethink the answer you gave? Were you perhaps looking for a way out of here?" Her eyes spring open, staring at me, and my eyes duck under my bangs. "Don't we do enough for you to keep you warm and clothed? We feed you and give you a roof over your head? What more could you want?"

Tears form in the corner of my eyes as I sniffle. Rubbing my hand over my elbow, I move away from the fireplace, not wanting her to think I am trying to escape. I return to my mattress that is lying directly on the floor.

A shadow flows out of a teacup that I had drank earlier that day. He slithers onto the mantle and hides under it, deep in the shadows. Keeping out of Jade's sight.

A rogue wind comes into the room and picks up my hair as Jade yells out. "Tom!"

Why did Shade not help me? I thought he was a spell that was supposed to help fight these awful people. They made me think I was crazy, and that they were my parents.

I fast forward through the memory, not wanting to see what they do to me or how they make me forget all of this. Though I make the scene go fast, I see them continue to give me the medicine they gave to me previously that makes me sleep.

I slow it down as they talk while I am mostly out of it; the medicine is taking its hold on me, but I fight it and struggle to learn something from this and why they were doing it to me. Parents should not be like this.

I was right parents shouldn't do that because they weren't your actual parents. Thinking to my younger mind. If she only knew.

"She was trying to escape again," Jade whispers.

"What happened?"

"She was playing with her little creature again."

"Why does it stay away? Why doesn't it attack us?" Tom peers into the shadows, searching.

"Probably because we don't fully hurt her. It only lashes out when she is physically hurt otherwise, it just helps her with her emotional pain and is friendly towards her. Or is trying to help get her out? Which is what I fear. The council will have our heads if their cash cow gets out. The power that we siphon from her they feed off of to help in their war. It is the only thing keeping them at bay while we search for a way to eliminate the death curse." Jade's teeth chatter as she talks.

Tom hovers at my head, concentrating. "I can keep making her forget any magic or strange things that she sees. Shade, no matter how many times she ends up befriending him once again. No matter if I make her scared of him at first, she ends up liking him in the end. We have tried for many years. The only thing that seems to stick is that she will forget magic other than Shade, and she will remember that we are her parents. I think that just has to do with us being the only adults around her, though."

"I don't like that she is getting out more and more. Soon she will find her way out of this room and then we run the risk of her escaping. No." She shakes her head in thought.

"What do you propose?"

"Let me contact a death dealer and see our options, but we need to move her down to the basement. That way, she will not be able to get out anywhere. There are no windows or fireplaces to try to escape."

"May your will be done." He nods as he focuses on me, erasing what little memory I have.

Dark.

Caged.

Red hot pain.

Dark thoughts.

Death. Suicide—

—Nothing.

Animal-like noises come from me as the beast within takes over. She kept my body alive when my mind was too far gone. The cemented ring that kept my chain held firmly, no matter how I attacked it. Shade began to hibernate on my body and would only come out to attack Jade and Tom when they would make an appearance.

Memories faded.

Shade, who's Shade?

I am nothing.

I am emptiness.

The animal never forgot. She was hot and fiery, like her temper. Her anger would never be denied. Shadows move, time passes, and there are no more memories to witness. The last one that flits by, I grasp on hard.

Trix floats through the ceiling.

My eyes spring open as he wakes me. Anger sears deep inside me, and my animal howls with a viciousness I didn't even know I had in me. Shade also took over, both sides warring to protect.

I watch the party of strangers filling the house dance around the living room. Dancing and having a good time. I watch with intent as I take each of their lives. Jade is first. She is the only one I jump on, first taking a chunk out of her neck.

I slow the scene as I take out the people in the house one by one. Some get away, but most are caught in my claws and shadows.

I remember now!

Jade is there, yes, but Tom is not.

I scream out into the void as the lights and memories fade away. Where does Tom reside now? What sort of horror would he concoct for me when I see him next? I would find him and make him pay for the pain he caused me. The pain he and his wife caused my family.

This I vow.

CHAPTER 11

MY GROGGY EYES OPEN up, the room coming into bleary focus. A rustling noise sends shivers down my spine as I wrestle with the thick covers still wrapped around me. I force them open wide as I look around the room, struggling against the cocoon.

"What now?" I rub at the sleep in my eye, clearing them. The dark room is only slightly illuminated as the sun peeks over the tree line. The night not as dark as it was before I went to sleep. My head swivels right and left, looking for the noise that woke me up. Though I had slept, my body and mind were still so exhausted. I rest my tired head against the pillow, tempted by the softness.

I am conflicted.

Another rustle flutters across the room near the desk in the corner. I freeze and hold my breath; my eyes are wide open now as panic sets in. I slip from the bed down to the floor. Shoving my hand under the pillow, I grab the journal for safe keeping. Making my way under the bed, I wait there a moment with the journal pressed to my side. I peek under the covers partially off the bed, searching for what had made that sound.

A snick this time, along with the rustle comes from the corner. I glance over in time to see a page turn, the air cool and breezy. The glass doors are wide open to the balcony. The heat of the day has cooled during the night.

"Didn't I close those?" I look around, puzzled. Nothing else moves except the pages when the wind breezes in from the open door. I crawl out slowly with the journal and shiver at the sudden temperature drop. Walking over to the doors again, I close them shut, ensuring they seal properly this time. I sit next to the desk and look down at the open spell book, noticing that it is open to later pages, ones that I had not read over yet. "Didn't I throw you?"

"Did you have splendid dreams?"

"What the fu—" Raising the journal in my hands, I strike at something dark. Taking a deep breath, I raise my arms again, ready to defend myself. "Whose there?"

"Lady, master it is I, but your humble servant." Trix bobs and weaves around, not staying in one spot.

"Damn it, Trix. Where the hell did you come from?" I grumble under my breath, relaxing my arms and sitting back hard in the seat.

"From outside," he answers simply. His red ruby eyes start to glow red. "Did you dream?"

I look from the glass doors to him. "So, you were the culprit. To answer your question, yes, I did dream. What's it to you?"

"About your memories?" He asks with a giddy laugh.

"Yes, how did you know that?" I look at the spell book. "What did you do?"

"You can't perform magic, so main master sent me to help you with what you need. You wanted memories you could not access. I helped you achieve the spell." He dances around happily. "I did a good job, yes, master?"

"Yes, I mean no." Shaking my head, I stand up at eye level to Trix. "You mean you are why I remembered what little memories I have?"

"Yes, that was me. I good master see, I help." He bobs up and down in quick succession.

"What other spells could you help me with?" I eye the book as I set my mother's journal down next to it, concentrating on the spells within the pages. I flip to the next one, skimming over what is written, then another.

"As long as it doesn't require too much power, I can help. Main master said to help, and you are quite agreeable right now, so I help." He gives a last nod.

My eyes flick to his before they land on the page, and my mouth turns up in a bright smile. "I think I found it!"

"Found what lady, master?" He comes close to me, hovering over my shoulder, reading what is listed there.

"The spell my mother was talking about right here." I slap the spell book. The words were written in red compared to the black writing before. A few words are not ones I have seen before. I try to sound them out. "This one talks about going to the past, which is what my mother talked about.

I open the journal, scrambling to get to the right section for Trix to see. He hovers there over my shoulder, waiting all the while. "I have never heard of a spell doing something like this."

"She talked about changing the past, reliving something to change the future." I reread the passage. "Do you think I could use it to see her past, not change anything necessarily, but just witness what she goes through?" I lift my eyes up to the skull, hoping he would find a way. "I didn't have very many memories of my own."

Trix scans both pages I have laid open in front of him.

"Should I turn on the light?" I look over my shoulder at the light switch across the room.

"No, I can see perfectly well in the darkness." He floats past me closer to the pages, drinking up the pages. He mumbles under his breath but speaks louder. "Send her back to the past to witness what she rightly seeks. No matter how harsh the truth is, let her see, let her hear."

"Wait, that's not right." I squint at the words written. "Some of it is right, but you are changing things."

"Send her back until she learns what is needed to move forward," Trix cackles.

"How will I get back?" My left-hand grips the side of my chair, not wanting to move. I hold both the metal flower necklace and black stone with my other hand, needing it close. "Why are you doing this?"

The pages flutter as power, and a static charge builds in the room. Trix's ruby eyes light up in the still-dim room. The words begin to move and flicker in his gaze; it must be a trick of the light. I stare at it. A buzzing sound emits, and the light grows brighter. I bring my arms up to cover my face and protect myself from whatever is about to happen.

"Remember, lady master, you will come back when you learn all that you need to," Trix yells out above the wind whipping in my ear.

An audible pop bursts through as I am sucked out of my room and plunge into darkness. I blink my eyes rapidly, only seeing the after images of my dim room and the skull with bright red ruby eyes.

A dull blue light appears, and the room looks like it did before Trix got there. The shadows are extra-long, and the light hue that was starting to creep into the room is now not there. Storm clouds roll in. The sun is fully gone. My hands shake. "Trix! Where did you go? Did the spell not work?" My arms cross around me, hugging close. "Come out. I am getting so sleepy." I rub my eye and head back to bed. As I make my way there, my feet barely pick up off the ground.

"This is stupid," I yawn. I will find him later and demand he tells me what happened and why the spell did not work.

I get into bed and lay down, the bed sucking me in. Kicking at the blankets, I push them down since the room is a bit warm after closing the doors. I yawn once more and close my eyes.

"Why does everything mess up around me?" I mumble to myself. I twist in the soft blankets.

Blankets?

"Didn't I just push these down?"

I try to maneuver them away from me. My body settles down once again. I feel a soft warmth as the blankets glide back up my body. I raise my hands, trying to grip the edges, but my hands slash through uselessly. I call to my animal, but she does not answer. "Why will you not listen when I actually need you?" I groan out as I bring up my legs, trying to keep the covers away from my body as it pulls over my head.

The soft cloth closes around me, forcing my limbs to bunch together and compact against me. My arms and legs grow tired as the will to fight dies down and the will to breathe becomes harder with every gasping breath.

It continues to tighten around me until my legs and arms are down, and I am stiff as a board, struggling to just keep the fresh air coming into my lungs.

The darkness is claustrophobic and hot.

I am thrown from the squirming thing that continues to wrap me up, so suddenly, I don't even notice my surroundings. I fall straight down into a body of water. A loud splash crashes, and I plummet down to the bottom of the water that I land in. Hands pull at the water struggling for the surface. My mouth opens up as water flows down my throat. I cough as I fight to break free. My eyes widen, and scan my murky surroundings. My body rejects the water with the force of my coughing. Wrestling with the water, I make my way to the bank of the lake, letting my lungs breathe in what they were starving for.

Water and spittle roll down my cheeks from what I cough up. My hands slip through the mud as I maneuver on to my side. I get to my knees and struggle to the sand; the rocks and mud are slippery under foot. I wheeze through the coughs as I try to regain control of my lungs and body.

"That's it. That twerp is done for!" Under my breath, I whisper, barely containing my rage.

I wipe the tears from my over-strained face and look around to ensure no one is nearby. I cough but try to quiet it and keep the fits to a minimum as I get my bearings.

What the hell?

Why was it day time? And when did we get a lake? Streams I remembered from my walks in the woods, but not a lake.

Did I change into my animal form again and wonder away from the village and all that I knew? I didn't know which way to walk to get back.

No, this isn't possible.

"Sera!" A young boy's voice rings out at the top of a hill. I kneel at the bottom of it, where I washed up from the lake.

The boy looks down directly at me. His eyes are dark and menacing. He is tall but still looks young.

Sera? As in my mother, Sera?

I pull the rest of my body out of the freezing lake. My teeth chatter as the spring wind whips at me. My clothes pull on my body, making it that much colder and harder to move. I look down and see the dress that I wear and see it stick to me.

Dress? Why am I wearing a dress?

I struggle against the slick mud and make it over to the grass, many grunts and pained-filled noises later.

"Sera!" The boy grounds out.

"Go away," a girl's voice vibrates through me that is not my own. I make my way to a tree and sit on the opposite side so the boy would not see me as easily.

"What should I tell your father when he asks how we got to know each other today?"

"Why not tell him the truth, Ian?" I groan out. "Tell him how you thought it was so funny to get magic users to grab me and dump me in the middle of the lake all because you're big and bad and from the dark side." Under my breath, I whisper more to myself. "This is not my destiny. I will find a way out of this."

Was I in my mother's past body, reliving her memories? Witnessing what she went through? Learning her past since I had none to go off of. What did Trix say again?

I could come back when I have learned all that I need to.

Did she know I was here with her?

"I don't think that will look good for either of us. I said I was sorry. I didn't think your people knew how to have fun. At least let me help you. That way, we can at least say we are making a go of it and trying to get along." Ian kicks at a loose rock at the top, causing it to roll down the hill. He makes his way down the hill slowly.

"I don't think so," I hiss. "You have caused enough trouble today."

"Fine!" He calls out. "Do you think I want to be stuck with some bratty child? You are not my ideal mate, either." I look around the gigantic tree, noticing him running his hand through his dark hair.

"I am not a child."

"To someone such as I, you are." He puffs up his chest and places a hand on it, smirking as he looks down at me.

I flutter my dress out, needing it to dry in the sun's warmth. "You are barely two years older than me." I push off of the tree, getting to my feet. My fists ball up as I place them on my hips. "How does that make you better than I?" I jut out my chin.

"For one, if you have to ask, then you are clearly nowhere near my intelligence level; second, I am obviously more mature than you. You do not know who you are messing with."

Ian gives me a dirty look as he looks me up and down.

"Shows what you know. If I were you, I would help me instead of getting in my way if you really don't want this any more than I do."

"Unlike you, I know my place and am not just a halfling. You are just worried because you need me for your plan to work." He gives an evil grin. "My plan to torment works regardless if this goes through or not."

"You don't know that, not for sure," I grumble, bringing my arms up to cross against my chest.

He stomps his way down the rest of the hill toward me. "I am the oldest. I should have been betrothed to Jade, the more graceful and calm one, but no. I am stuck with the brat of the family all because it goes based on power." He raises a fist up as he continues quickly down the hill. "Shouldn't the oldest have the most power?"

I stare at him head-on. I unfold my arms and form them into fists, ready for the fight if he wants to start one. "Then, by all means, go be with Jade. Not like I care." I turn away from Ian, stomping my foot, causing dirt from the dry grass to poof up.

"I can't, and you know that. She would never accept me; she barely accepts Ivan. Since he is the strongest, he is the one the prophecy states will work, with her being the strongest from her side. Ivan is destined to inherit father's legacy and all when he passes on." He drops his fist before he gets to me.

I turn back to Ian. "Then help me stop all of this. I didn't know Ivan was younger than you."

"Yea, only by a year, but that has no pull on the amount of power given."

I kick at the ground.

"What is your plan exactly, anyway? The only things you could change is never being born or make sure you are the strongest so you can marry Ivan. I know you like him."

"I lived with my real father, most of my life until he passed on. I came to live with my mother, her husband, and Jade when he died. My father was mostly human, so I didn't come out with too much power."

"Drama."

"Tell me about it."

"Let me guess, you're going to go back in time and stop your father's death from happening?" He rolls his eyes.

"It can be done," I reiterate.

"Can't even articulate a full-fledged plan well." He shakes his head in disappointment. "See, you are so immature that you will not be a great asset to the dark side. You are just going to get in my way. Go ahead, though. Perhaps you will change something for the better or perhaps you will die doing so, which is okay in my book as well."

"Fine, stay out of my way then," I yell.

Ian nods once as he turns on his heal and stalks off. "Will do. I will work on a backup plan if you don't follow through."

I grumble as I kick at the ground, swinging back to face the lake instead of Ian's retreating form.

Sera! I call to her, no myself? This is confusing. I try to push her towards the water to see the reflection there but to no avail. She, we do not move. I am stuck in here, just watching and learning. How did time work? Would it take me years to get back to my body? Would everyone be worried?

My eyes flick to the lake but does not linger on the water. I shiver, remembering the water pouring down my throat. The wet soggy clothes cling to me, and no amount of shaking would get it clean again. The sun is not hot enough to dry them out. I would need to change.

I turn back the way Ian had left and stride up the hill all while stomping. "I hope he stays out of my way because if he doesn't, I will make him pay," I growl out.

I hurry the rest of the way up the slope, my lungs burning with the pressure. Coughing, I clear the rest of the gunk still in my lungs. My legs are exhausted from the miss use of everything.

The sky darkens as I continue into the woods. The surrounding trees become sinister looking. My head twists this way and that, making sure Ian was not hiding and about to attack once again.

"Sera!" A man bellows.

I rush through the foliage, tripping over the vine and weeds to get to the man. I bring up my hands and force them to my side. The tree line ends suddenly before I cross into the sunlight. I peek around, making sure the way is clear.

"Sera, come meet with Ivan and Ian. Why are you dirty? Now, I will have none of this nonsense while having company over. Go get dressed. Flit is with them." A tall, stout man with a full rusty beard barks out. His beard catches the last rays of the sun turning the red in it dark, almost brown.

"No, papa... I can't," I call out, sniffling. I call the trees closer together, hiding me deeper in the shadows. Blocking his view of me.

"Haven't I taken you in and treated you as my own through all of this when I could have cast you out as my right? You will behave tonight, Sera!" His voice booms. "I know we keep to ourselves and don't cross paths for the most part, but tonight you will do as I say."

His hands twist and rip away from one another, the trees rip apart, casting the sun into the shadows.

I stand there, mostly scared, as I back up further. "You can't ask this of me. Let Jade do what she needs to. She is ready and willing to give up her future for the two groups. She will make a great ruler. Why do you need to have me marry the other brother? This is not what I signed up for."

"You will understand when you are more grown. You asked us for protection, and this is what it requires. I know this is hard for you, and you are not used to this. But you will come to understand that this is for the best. Flit asked that we find a pair for his other son. You will be beyond protected by both sides."

"He is not my future; he will never be. He is cruel and will not keep me protected, as you think."

Shadows lengthen from the trees; His eyes shoot to the sides as he squints at them. "That is the last straw," His voice reverberates around the trees. "Guards, take her to her room and make sure she is presentable for dinner." Two shadow guards pull up from the hidden shadows a man and a woman. They stride over to me and easily capture my arms. I stand between them, cautious and unsure.

Are these like Shade or something else?

"No need to manhandle me with the shadow warriors." My eyes flick over the man, searching. One of the shadow spirits tightens its hold on me.

An icy shiver runs down my back to my toes. "These shadows were a gift, and one we would do to remember that they and the creature deserve the respect they are due." He nods.

"These soulless creatures have no spine, along with their creator. I will give him respect when he earns it," she bites out.

"Her viciousness knows no bounds. Are you sure you and Ian would not be a glorious match?" A muscular man walks up behind the more stout one. "Craig, is this your halfling?"

Craig nods. "That's right. This is your first time meeting her. Your boys have met with her on previous visits, but she was away last time you were here."

"Yes, you said she was visiting her aunt or something like that." Flit waves his hand as if the reason didn't really matter.

"And you forget the halfling is right here." I pull out of the shadows, forcing them to let go or be pulled behind. "And can speak for herself. Yes, I am sure Ian is not a match unless you want a dead son," I bite out.

"Flit, please excuse Sera here. She had a terrible upbringing by her real father and is still adjusting to reality here."

I glare at him.

"Oh, think nothing of it." He waves Craig away; his face turns to me his long dark hair falls to the middle of his back. The dark clothes and his dark eyes stare at me. "But know this, halfling. If you want to threaten the dark, make sure you can back it up." He closes his fist in front of him, and his shadows slide over the ground and pull at each of my arms, keeping me locked and standing there. He pushes his hand down, and the shadows sink into the ground, pulling me down. I bend over and then am pulled so far down that I buckle to my knees. "First lesson, if you want others to do what you want, ensure you hold the correct cards."

I stare up into his bottomless eyes. Waiting, learning, watching.

We stare at one another, neither one of us blinking.

"Jade and my wife are waiting. Sera can go change and join us all when she is decent." Craig turns from the staring match, tired of the game already.

My eyes flick to Craig as he turns away for a brief second before landing back on Flit.

Flit moves to hover over me, looking down his nose. "Precious, just precious. I think that is what I will call you. You may have some fight that will be good for this world. Perhaps people of the light are not all weaklings," he whispers. The last part is for my ears only as he turns to follow Craig. "Take her to her room for her to prepare. She will come down for dinner with us. Make sure of it." He waves his hand.

He releases the two shadow creatures as they pull out of the ground, tugging me up as well. They let go of my arms but hover near, ready to attack if Flit's words were not followed. His shadow creatures would follow me, make sure I got ready and was down for dinner. He did not say what part of the dinner I had to make it to, though.

"His mistake for underestimating me." I whisper as I wait till they are out of sight. I will be headed in the opposite direction when I reach the house anyway. That way I couldn't get in any more trouble or cause any for my mother and papa.

"Know I prefer shadow soldiers than Flit's head guy, a fox shifter. Everyone says Jeffrey is cruel and clawed his way to that spot by force alone." He brought his wife with him this time. I wonder if she is as mean as he is. "You don't talk or lash out at me as long as I do what I need to." They stand there waiting for me to make my move.

The house is grand and huge. The color is pearl and shiny when the sun hits it at the right angle. As I come closer to the grand home, my face falls, and my feet slow, stalling for time. The grand doors meet me, and two soldiers of the light side pull them open for me to enter through. "I miss my old home. This one feels open and empty. My home with my real dad was homier and more lived in."

I miss my dad; I missed our home; I missed that life. I missed everything good and right with the world then. I am still too young to live on my own; even if I was, my magic only worked half the time.

Chapter 12

THE VAST HOUSE HAS a grand staircase. When I come to the stairs, I stomp my feet up them about halfway; I quicken my step, running away from the shadow guards. Racing up to my room, I slam my door shut for privacy. "I will be out soon," I call out.

The shadows sweep under the door and slide over the wall. Their long forms hang on the walls, trying to intimidate me. "You couldn't wait?" I shake my head. "No, of course not, because I might escape your grasp and never make it to dinner."

As I look around the room, it is in disarray. There are clothes and books strewn about everywhere. Though the house did not look well lived in, this room sure does. I notice the journal lying on the bed, rushing to it. It is open to the last journal entry I wrote.

"I thought I put you away," I say as I snap it close.

The journal looks much like the one that I had read from my time, other than it has fewer creases and less dust.

"You did," a gruff voice answers behind me.

I spin around to my bathroom door and see Robert standing there. This Robert is really young and on the cusp of manhood. The journal falls from my fingers, flopping on the ground. "Robert!"

His eyebrows raise in question.

I frown in anger as I bend to retrieve the journal. Making sure none of the pages are damaged or folded as I close it. "How much of it did you read?"

"All of it." He spreads his feet into a wide stance.

"Do you not know boundaries, guard?" My eyes flick to the shadows, which remain hidden on the wall.

"Do you? You are my charge to protect. Craig ensured both Jade and you have a guard on you at all times. I can do whatever I have to, to ensure your safety. Especially after you took off that first time. You cannot run from your problems." His eyes also move to the shadows. "I watched them enter the room after you did. I know they are there, and I know who they belong to."

"But this?" She motions to her journal. "I didn't even do anything; these are just thoughts and words that I put to my frustration here." I point the book at him and shake it in his face.

"That last passage you wrote says much more than that. What is the last thing you wrote about in there?" He gives me a pointed look, grasping the billowy journal away from my hand. He holds the journal gently between his two large hands, flipping to the page he mentioned.

"Ughhh! It didn't work." I grab at the book from his hands, locking my fingers around it so he can't get at it again. "You're being such a bonehead, and a goody two shoos. Do you always do what you're told?"

Robert comes closer, looming over me. "Are you sure about that?"

My eyes never waver from his. In a low voice, I bite out, "Get out."

He stares at me for a moment, not backing down, searching for some answer only he could see.

"Now," I force out.

His eyes soften as he steps back to take his leave. "I just don't want you hurt. Is that so wrong?"

"Let me know when you actually care, because right now, I am just a job to you." My eyes snap with anger. "Look at me." I gesture. "I am fine. Other than waterlogged and a bit cold now, I am good. Now go, so I can change for my dinner with my future family and husband." I spit out.

Robert's face pales at my words. He turns to leave. I knew it bothers him as much as it bothered me. However, he would do naught to stop it. He stops as he opens the door. "If I didn't care, I would have told Craig everything you had written there. Everything I had found out, but no I keep some things hidden. I respect your privacy, but know I will use it if needed." He doesn't even turn his head to look at me, just closes the door after.

I walk swiftly to the door, locking it after him. I turn and rest my back against the door, holding the journal close to me. "As long as blood flows through my veins, I will never stop trying to find a way out of a marriage with that toad, Ian. I would not marry him; I will only ever marry for love and nothing else!" I vow at the dark, soulless creatures. "Tell your king if you must, not like it matters."

Sera said the spell didn't work? Or did she not try that spell yet? It seemed to work fine for me. Trix said words other than what was written. Maybe he changed it. Maybe it's not the spell at all.

I stride over to the bed. "I knew I shouldn't have put it under the pillow. Always hide things in a proper hiding spot. I know that. Damn guard, always too nosy for his own good. Good thing he is newer here, and I didn't write about how it was actually going." I whisper to quiet, even for the shadows to hear. I walk over to the closet with the journal in hand.

I wish I could have come back to where it all started. I hope I get to see those memories or the beginning of Ivan and Sera's relationship. Also, it is interesting hearing the thoughts that flit through her mind as she thinks them.

I shove the clothes to the side, walking past my colorful wardrobe to the back of the closet. I kneel and punch the lower panel with my fist. A board pops loose; wedging my finger nail in between the boards, I pull it aside. Sliding the book into the hidden compartment, moving the black journal aside; the spell book is further back. Wiggling and kicking at the hard floor, I reach for it with my nails and pull it forward. "You are still where you are supposed to be, though. This spell book will have the answers I need." I whisper just to myself.

I crawl out of the hole slowly, keeping my voice low. "That reminds me I'm going to have to move or hide that mirror, so Robert doesn't go looking for it. Since I wrote about that. Though I think it will keep itself hidden. But just in case, since he is known for finding things. I wonder if his finding ability is just for people or items as well." I chatter to myself, keeping myself calm.

Robert was good at reading people from what I knew. But even in my own time, he seemed genuine in his care.

Forcing the panel back into place and pushing it close with both books hidden there. It thunks close, hiding my secret away. After backing up out of the closet, I snag a plain dark green dress that matches the deep tones of my element. It also makes my eyes pop with the green flecks of color.

I eye the shadows still hanging out on the wall to ensure they had not moved through my closet excursion.

I quickly change out of the dress I am wearing and into the green one. The fabric reflects my mood. I finger comb my hair, making it lay as flat as I can manage without wasting too much time. "What do I care if they like the way I look? I just don't want my parents to say anything about my appearance. I couldn't be the reason that everything fails. If I was, they would kick me to the human realm." I shudder as I look in the mirror and see the green dress lying nicely and my hair is presentable. "No one wants to go there. Least of all a halfling like myself where magic rarely works."

As I rush out of my room, I shut the door firmly. Instead of following the hallway to the front of the house and the stairs, I follow it to the back and skip down the back stairs. They deposit me into a bustling kitchen. Even though we had a house full of staff to cook and clean, mother preferred that her children knew how to do their part if needed. Something about building character.

I dodge and weave around the cooks and waiters waiting to serve. Sliding up against a wall, I stand next to a swinging door. My fingers pull it back so I can see into the room and notice everyone has taken their seat and is talking amongst each other.

Soft murmurs can be heard from the next room. I let the door fall shut before I look to the cooks, who are watching me. The shadow guards have vanished, but I keep an eye out for them none the less.

"Marie, what are they up to? Please tell me it's dessert." I call to the head cook.

"Ha. Not even close, my child. We are not even to the main course."

I slump down on a stool and look over what is being made. "Can I help?" I lick my lips as my stomach rumbles at the sight of the delicious food.

"Normally, I would say yes, but you know they are waiting for you." Marie works while monitoring. She hovers at an open oven before shaking her head and closing it back up. Her hair is black and medium in length. It is pulled up and in a tight bun as she turns her head back to me. Her dark complexion stands out amongst the white clothes she wears.

I grab a spoon nearby and kick off the stool, going to one of the pots on the burner. I swipe a spoonful up to taste. "That's off." I point my spoon at the bubbling sauce and scrunch my face up. "Looks like you need more help here than they need me in there."

Marie waves away the young boy at the stove. He frowns and ducks to the side. She swipes a spoon of her own to taste, sticking out her own tongue. "Ugh, that is horrid. Let's scrap that, come and help since obviously I am working with incompetent people here."

I jump up and down, clapping my hands as I move and get to work on a new sauce.

"But you will be out there by the main course." She gives a pointed look.

"Deal."

"Why don't you get your hair out of your face?" She watches as I struggle with my hair.

"You know why." My eyes glare daggers at the swinging door that someone has come through, making the voices louder for a moment.

Marie frowns and nods, focusing on the pot in front of me. Her hawk eyes scan the room, making sure her other people are doing what is needed.

"Is Jade out there being her normal, charming self?" I whisper.

Marie waves her hand over at the wait staff, asking them to come closer. "How is it going out there?"

They eye me warily. Not everyone here is as comfortable with me as Marie is. One of the younger girl's steps forward. "Jade is stealing the show as normal." She waits a moment to make sure I didn't interrupt. "She is getting to know Flit, Ivan, and even Ian really well. She is keeping everything at ease and calm. She even covered for you after Ivan asked after you."

I wait to make sure there is no other news. "She was always much better at that stuff than I am. I couldn't charm anyone. I wonder why Ivan was curious about where I was. He shouldn't care, since his betrothed is right there for the taking." Could he actually have feelings for me? It's hard to remember who he is when he is so kind and always showing up when no one is around.

"Jade seems to take after Craig."

"Yea, he would explain that his genes are the better and why I am such a disappointment all the time. Since I have none of him in me."

"You have your mother's passion, though," Marie speaks up.

"Passion?" I laugh out.

"Yes, why do you think you are here? There was so much passion between your father and your mother. Your papa allowed it because he had not seen that passion for a long time."

"I have never seen this passion from her before." I give a puzzled look as I continue to stir.

"Her passion is there. You just have to find the right button," Margaret says.

An older gentleman pokes his head in the door. "We are ready for the main course." He ducks back out.

"Okay, let's get a move on, people." She claps her hands loudly. "You have helped enough, now out with you."

I grin. "What hosts would we be if I couldn't show our guests what we are capable of?"

"Don't be causing too much trouble, missy. We don't want them to look down on your family."

"Just give me the sauce, and I will enter after Ian gets his plate."

"What do you have cooking up in that head of yours?"

"You will see," I laugh.

Marie pours what is in the pot in to a gravy boat. She motions me forward to stand next to the door and has me pause after handing me the boat. She lines up the others, making sure to count them. "Flit, Craig, Daniella, Ivan, Jade, Ian, then you, and your food."

I maneuver after Ian's food but before mine. I hold my head high and make sure my dress is in place, holding the gravy boat between my hands.

"I'm ready."

The line moves slowly as the door is held open. We come out one by one; I pay attention to the food being delivered. The boy in front of me is setting Ian's food down. I move up to his left side, where he sits. I notice Flit seated there next to him. Him in between both of his boys.

A hush falls over the table as they all stare at me. Craig's mouth pulls into a frown, and Jade's mouth pinches with worry.

"Ian, I wanted to do something special for you and thank you properly for the day we spent together. It's just to die for." I look at him as I smile and pour the gravy of his potatoes and meat that is on his plate.

Ian's eyes peer around me to Craigs. He gives a generous smile. "How sweet did you make it?" He does not move to try any.

"Of course." My eyes roam to Flit's as I offer some to him.

He gives a careful look as if searching for something there.

"Oh, come now. She is a superb cook. My daughter is just playing," Daniella chimes in.

"But of course." I laugh. "But you should know I may not always." I also put some gravy on Flit's food, even though he did not motion for it. I set down the boat in the middle of the table, all eyes follow it there.

A cough emits down across from Jade. "None for me?" Ivan looks at me, giving a half smile. Where his brother and father's eyes are dark, almost black, his are blue and clear. His hair is stringy but is tied back at the nape of his neck.

"Nope, not at this time." I show my teeth.

He nods and sits back in his chair. I follow my plate to my chair across from Ian, taking a seat and making sure not to reach for the gravy for my food. However, my fingers did itch to pull it to me and have some, anyway. No, the show must go on.

The dinner is tense and stifling, with Ian and Flit looking at their dishes with distrust. I catch Ivan's eyes many times as they sparkle with laughter. Jade would deter and speak to him each time to keep his attention. As the night progresses, I find myself bored with the small talk lined with underlying emotions. I didn't seem like the only one, either. I daydream mostly, keeping one ear out for anything that may be used later. Jade is enthralled with Ivan, hanging on to every word he utters. It is weird having her play flirty when she talks about the dark side like they were evil and disgusting.

My eyes keep darting back to Ivan's as he speaks. A flutter skitters through my stomach while I continue to listen to him. He is tall and has strong shoulders. He would be good in a fight. His long shirt sleeves cover his arms, so I could not see how well-defined they are. If he is anything like his brother Ian, he would just be slight and lanky, but something in my blood told me he's different.

I shake my head to clear those kinds of thoughts. What am I doing thinking about him like that? That is Jade's destiny, not mine. As the dishes were being cleared, my leg bounces and I crave running back to my room, away from this situation. I fondle the folds of my dress, trying to keep my hands and mind busy so I don't yawn or show disrespect.

Daniella rises out of her chair, "I will get the coffee, and we can move to the seating area to continue our peace talks."

I see my exit and hop at the chance. "I will help you, mama." I all but fall out of my chair, rushing to follow.

Daniella nods once as she waits for me by the kitchen door. My father gives me a dark look as I pass him, knowing what I am trying to accomplish. "We will see you both out there." His eyes stay steady on mine.

I duck into the kitchen, not wanting to be under his or their scrutiny anymore. I help bring the cups, creamer, and sugar on the tray that mama prepares and starts. As she is busy making the coffee, I slide back, hoping to make it to the back stairs.

"Sera," Daniella says dangerously low.

I freeze and hang my head in defeat.

When neither one of us says anything for a time, Daniella chimes in. "You and Ian have barely spoken two words to each other since your fiasco at dinner."

"I know, mama, I am just not feeling like myself. Can I be excused?" I look up the stairs lovingly.

"You know this is important and that Flit wants both of his sons to be wed to make this treaty work, not just Ivan with Jade. Make this work. Do you understand?"

I turn around fully to her as I feel her fierce gaze focus on me. "I know, mama. We have gone over this already. Papa made sure I understood." I scrunch up my face in anger. "Ian is conniving and just a brute."

Daniella gives a tiny laugh. "And you're not? It seems like you are perfect for one another."

My angry eyes light up as I stare at my mother. "I have only done what I have had to, to survive."

"To get your way, you mean?" She prods. "Make sure you remember that your safety relies on this happening."

"Isn't that what you do? Get your way?" I question. "Plus, Ian and I spent a good chunk of time before dinner. We talked then. If talking is what you want to call it."

"Yes, Craig did say he found you dirty and wet coming out of the woods." She lets go of the previous argument, steering the conversation where she wants. "Looks like now someone will put you in your rightful place if you aren't careful."

"Like you don't?" I hiss.

"I have only done what I need to, to survive," She bites back, throwing my earlier words in my face. "Since you are being so disagreeable, I suspect it will be best for you not to join us for coffee. Go ahead and dive into that dusty library, but stay out of the woods after the sun goes down. At least until the dark side leaves our lands."

"Thank you, mama." I hug her, knowing this could have gone worse.

"You know I am hard on you because I am trying to prepare you for a harsh world out there. Our world is unequal, and we have to fight and scrape for everything we deserve."

"There are better ways though mama."

"I have seen none that prove effective."

I nod, letting the argument fall. There is no way to get her to comprehend she is set in her ways. It's up to me and the next generations to show them that there are other ways. Hopefully, not all would be this stuck to an idea.

I wander back to my room. The games, the sly abuse that goes into their words. I felt lighter and happier being away from the abhorrent conversation.

Why were people not just up front with their thoughts and ideas?

Before returning to my room, I head to the library with the hidden mirror. I took the long way by going up the back stairs, so I had to go down the main ones, making sure to be quiet as I head off to the right of the hallway off the main stairs. It passes close to where they sit with a coffee. I wait for my mother's murmurs in the distance and then beeline it to the library door, three doors down the hall.

Letting out a pent-up breath I am holding, I pause, hoping mama didn't take the wrath for my absence. "I know how to play with them. I just don't like to? Father was much more open and not as dark as these people. I wish he were still around." I whisper to myself.

As I am about to shut the door, I hear a low voice answer me. "Politics in times of war are never fun." His dark timber rumbles through me.

I look back over my shoulder and see Ivan standing there. "Shouldn't you be with Jade and everyone?"

His dark eyes peer into mine. "I excused myself for a moment. There was a mouse that was creeping in the hallway that caught my attention."

I let my hair move as I side step, covering half of my face. I just stare at him, unsure of what to say back to that.

His eyes roam over me and then to the interior of the room. "Your library is not very big."

"We have a portal that gives us access to the main library. This one did not need to be as big because of it." I open the door wider to make sure he could see it. My eyes flick to the mirror covered in the corner.

The mirror! Perhaps she knows more about it than I do. How do I get Sera to go there?

He nods and walks in, his boots making echoing thumps as he walks in, his presence taking up the entire room. I stand there star-struck for a moment before remembering to close the door. I shut it with a soft click.

"Jade will wonder where you have gone off to." I try to bring the conversation back so that he will go back and leave me in peace.

"Somehow, I think she will survive without me." He smiles to himself as he walks over to the covered mirror. "What's this?"

The mirror, yes, we must move forward. I feel like it will have the answers we need and I can return to my own time. Having to be quiet and just listen would make any person stir crazy. I push against Sera's body.

I stumble as I move quickly, trying to make it to the mirror before him. I over correct and fall into Ivan.

He catches me easily, helping me to find my balance.

I hold my head in my hands. "What is going on with me?"

"Maybe you're coming down with something, or did you have some of that gravy you made for Flit and Ian?" He chuckles.

Did I do that? That took a lot of my strength and energy to cause that. But what else could I do if I could cause her to stumble? Could I cause my mother permanent damage?

"That was a joke." My eyes meet his, his hands linger on my shoulders as he had helped me.

"I know."

I shake my head as I realize we are staring at one another, and I step back. "Anyway, you should get back, shouldn't you?"

"I would, but you were just about to tell me what this was for." He walks over to the hidden mirror and caresses the drape that is hanging over it.

I stomp over to the mirror. "No, I wasn't. It doesn't even matter, anyway. It doesn't seem to have what I am looking for." I tug at the cloth that is covering it.

"And what are you looking for?" He asks, letting the cloth fall from his hand.

"Salvation. An answer for a new future. But there has been nothing. It just shows me the horrors of my present." I turn my head to the side, giving a last pull-off to the side. The mirror is free of its dark cloth, and Ivan peers into it.

"It's a mirror." He takes a closer look than his eyes fall on me.

"Thank you, captain, obvious." I roll my eyes as I walk closer to it, my body coming into being on the reflective surface.

I stop, stunned at what I see there.

"Who is that?" Ivan's eyes travel from the mirror to me a*nd back.*

It's me! I get pulled to the mirror and find myself waiving at Ivan and Sera.

"Sera? Why is there someone other than your reflection there? And why is it waiving and you are not? What is going on? What is this?" He pokes at the surface.

I come closer than to touch the glass, thinking this is an illusion.

I also move closer and reach out to both of them.

I shriek and step back, dropping my hand. Shaking my hand. "That is not an illusion or what the mirror is supposed to do." My body shudders as I move away.

"Who... What are you?" Ivan asks as he backs away from the mirror.

The image fades as I move further and further from the mirror.

"Sera, wait, stop. Come back. Whatever it is, it is connected to you. You have to be in front of the mirror for it to show itself."

My steps are unsure as I come forward. I stand a way back but come into view of the mirror.

The image of a girl around our age pops back into being. Her clothes are simple, and her hair is up in a ponytail.

I come forward, tapping on the glass. "Can you see me? I'm Alexia," I call out, but my voice goes no further.

"Can you hear her? I think she is trying to say something." Ivan inspects and is a lot closer than I. He tries to cause his mirror image to grab at the imposter, but to do that, he has to get closer to me, and I keep moving away.

"No," I shake my head.

"I can't read her lips either in what she is trying to say, at least not well. She seems happy that we can see her, though." He watches as the reflection jumps around, trying to communicate.

I raise my hands in front of me. "Wait right here. I think there is a spell for something like this. We can go into the mirror world and hear and understand what is happening. I just need to show you the other secret to this mirror." I walk closer once again to the mirror. Both I and the reflection look to the side of the mirror.

"What if it is a trap?" Ivan asks.

My hands freeze in the air, hanging there for a moment. "Go to the front of the room and be ready to go get help if needed when I cast the spell, but first, we have to get a spell out of the vault."

"What vault?"

My fingers slide over the button, triggering the portal to the book vault. The girl vanishes as something slithers and moves across the glass.

"Where did she go?" Ivan moves closer to inspect. His fingers touch the surface again, and it sticks to him, this time moving with him and gripping on to his fingers.

I slip around behind him, pushing him forward into it.

He lets out a yelp as I push him through, coming through right after him. His eyes smolder at me as he comes out of a roll and crouch on the floor.

"Don't worry, Ivan, I am not the sister you have to look out for." I give a small laugh as I walk over to a stack of books in the far back corner. "Here it is. I knew I remembered seeing a book about the mirror world." I weave my way through the stacks like a second home.

He gives a distrustful look. "What do you mean by that?"

"It means don't worry, badger. You are not cruel or mean to me, so I will not be cruel or mean back. I only do what is done to me or who I call mine."

He walks up behind me slowly. Breathing down my neck. "Who says I will not be cruel or mean?" He gives a small sniff.

I turn around nose to nose with him, leaving the book in the stack. "Oh, yea?"

A glint of light hits his eye as he gives a wolfish grin, pushing me up against the books behind me.

"Intimidation is not cruel, sir." I place my hand against his chest and push him back. He moves back a bit but is firm. There were definite muscles hidden under his clothing. He is a strong one. "And also, not something that works on me." Retracting my hand, I turn back to the stack of books, distracting myself with the book I had come for. His heat towers over me.

I grab the book and slide it out between a couple of books, taking care not to knock any others off.

My eyes watch as the girl appears once again. She is standing there with her hands crossed in front of her. Her mouth and build seemed similar to Ivan's. "Are you sure she isn't related to you?"

"I have never met her before. Why do you ask?" He peers at the young girl in the mirror once more.

"Nothing. Forget it." I shake my head and study the book in my hands, flipping through to the spell letting us enter the mirror world.

Reading through the words, I whisper them and call the power I hold within. I squeeze my eyes shut, hoping. I grab Ivan's hand and push us into the mirror. This time it is thick and goopy, almost like swimming through something more substantial. We push through into a room that mirrors the one we just came from, except the girl is standing in front of us.

"Good, we made it. Glad that worked?"

"There was a chance that it wouldn't?" Ivan barks.

"Well, sometimes my magic doesn't work or glitches, so to speak," Sera squeaks out. "My earth magic always comes when called, but magic when casting, that's another story." I pull the end of my hair into my fingers and fiddle with it, giving myself something to distract away from Ivan's ire.

The muscles behind his cheeks move as if fighting to calm his anger.

I wave as I see them cross into the mirror world. "Can you hear me and see me?" I touch my clothes and hair, ensuring I am myself. That was too weird to have the ability to move my body once again.

Ivan's eyes travel over the distance to me. "Who are you?"

"Are you related to Ivan? You look like him a bit." Sera steps forward, coming closer.

"Sort of yea." I nod in excitement. "I'm Alexia."

"I don't know of any family named Alexia." Ivan hangs back, distrustful of the situation.

"Not yet," I hedge. My arms wrap around me, holding myself tight as I rub at my stiff arms. "I'm kind of from the future. If I can say that, I'm not sure of the rules. Also, how could you see me in this mirror when others you had passed did not show me before?"

"Well, you may be right about that because you sure don't look like you fit in around here." Sera circles me, checking out my clothes and scrutinizing me. "That was a regular mirror. This one is full of magic and also spelled to act differently. What spell did you use?"

"I think the past one, but Trix added stuff to it."

"Past spell. What is she talking about, Sera?"

Sera cringes in fear. "It's a spell to help you jump back into the past." She shrugs as she turns back to me. "Does that mean I know you from when you come?"

"No, not really."

"This is not your past. You are seeing it from my body. So why are you viewing the past from me? The spell is supposed to help you relive your past, not another's."

"I don't know what I can or cannot tell you." I take out my necklace and play with the flower and black jewel, zipping it across the metal chain.

Ivan stomps closer, peering at the necklace. "What is that? Let me see it," He grumbles.

I take a step back as Sera moves forward, halting him with her hand. "Easy." He glares down at the hand that stops his forward motion but doesn't push.

"Can I please see it?" He says in a calmer tone.

I pull the chain up over my head and dangle it out of reach but away from me so they can both inspect it.

"It's just a sliver, but the black obsidian is something Flit doles out to people he trusts." His eyes narrow as they meet mine. "How did you come by it?"

"My mother," I say, staying as cryptic as possible but still wanting to give them something.

"Who is your mother?"

"The past spell only allows you to relive your past—" Sera stares down at the ground. "I guess you could view someone else's, but you must be a direct descendent."

"So, you're Flit's granddaughter." Ivan nods. "Okay, that makes more sense."

Sera's eyes go wide with horror. "No, this can't be right." She looks around for a way out. "That means I don't change anything. That means my future is set." Her fingers claw at the neck of her green dress.

"Sera hold on." Ivan moves toward her slowly, not wanting to spook her.

"No, I can't." Her eyes peel wide. "I won't." Sera flips through the book that came through with her searching. "Where is the return spell?"

"You don't know for sure. Maybe something changes." He edges closer to Sera, not wanting to be left behind in the mirror dimension. She is his only ticket back. "There is no spell in there that can help you."

She throws out a hand in my direction. "She is proof that I am her mother. The stone she has is from Flit. She has your family resemblance. What more proof do you need?" She shakes her head. "I will not be stuck with your brother; I will not marry if it is not for love. I will not hate someone I have to live with day in and day out and have to watch my back constantly."

My head swivels between Ivan and Sera. They needed to stay in this world to help me. I crave communication. I want them to know me and to know them in turn. Butterflies skitter through my stomach. "You don't marry Ian," I whisper.

Her hectic eyes zero in on me. She stomps over, dropping the book. "Say more." She comes in hot and grasps my shoulders. "Explain." She shakes me a bit. "Do not go mute on me now."

My eyes skip to Ivan, begging for help. He stands behind her, settling a gentle hand on her shoulder. Her hands uncurl but still hold me in front of her.

"You don't marry Ian. Ian is not my father."

"That is preposterous. Then who?" Sera gives a questioning look, thinking.

"This stupid skull helped me back to the past but changed part of the spell, and now I am stuck living your life until I learn everything that I am supposed to, which could take years. I don't know how much time equates to a time where I am from. I don't know what is going on with my body, and I don't know how I will get back. I don't know what I can say, and I don't know if I messed everything up, and now when I go back, there will no longer be a time for me to go back to or a body." I spill out, lowering my gaze to the ground, not wanting to meet either of their eyes.

"Alexia, you said?" Ivan asks.

I nod, still not meeting their eyes.

"Are you, my child?"

I bite my lip, not wanting to say more, but also scared of how much I would blurt out if I did.

Sera's grip firms back up. "Alexia?"

I raise my eyes, first meeting Sera's and then Ivan's.

"How?" They both whisper, making eye contact with one another as Sera looks over her shoulder.

Before I can open my mouth to answer, Sera shushes me with her hand. "No, we know too much already. All we know is it happens; we don't need the why. She could change something for the worse if she tells too much."

"Or it could get better." Ivan's eyes turn dark as his thoughts spin. "You could tell us everything you know, so we know what to watch out for and how to turn things our way."

I pick at some loose skin near my cuticles. "See, that is the other thing. I don't know much or remember much, so I can't help with that. That is why I wanted to return to the past to learn more about my future. Trix tricked me and changed the spell on me, though. Why do I even put up with the talking skull?"

"Trix? Why did you not cast it yourself?" Sera lets go of my shoulders and eases back. Her eyes flick to Ivan's, checking on him.

"My magic is kind of being borrowed."

"Borrowed?" Ivan squints his eyes in confusion and tilts his head.

"Whole other story, but yes. So, no magic to help get me out of this one, plus the stipulation of me having to learn everything I need to before going back to my own time."

"How did you not see this coming? Don't you know anything about magic? Or time traveling? You hang around talking skulls and necromancers? Why, they are tricky at best and should not be trusted fully."

"Well, how was I supposed to know?" I ground out.

"You should have done your homework before trying this type of spell and not getting help from a necromancer's familiar. Though you seem old enough, you sure seem unsure of a lot. Didn't we teach you anything?"

My eyes tear up as I shuffle around, walking away.

"Great, now I sound like my mama," She growls out.

"Sera," Ivan quiets her, his voice coming forward. "We aren't there. Something happened, didn't it?" His voice is calm and low right behind me. His presence engulfs me.

I fling myself around and launch my arms around him, hugging him. "I just wanted answers," I gasp out. Tears stream down my cheeks freely as I hide my face on his shoulder.

His warm arms circle me and hold me there, rubbing my back.

"I needed the answers, and still do. I don't know enough about this world to be useful. I don't know enough about myself to do any good. I have powers I can't use, abilities that run me instead of the other way around, and a Quintan that says I have to pick up what you guys left behind."

"Quintan?" Sera's mouth opens up wide. "The mage that has a purple aura?"

"You know him already?" My eyes peek around Ivan's shoulder.

"Yea, he was the one who helped Ian."

"He didn't seem mean or cruel from my time."

"What do you mean? What happened?" Ivan asks.

"Quintan and a couple of magic users threw me into the lake on behalf of Ian." Sera shrugs. "Ivan, to speak to your earlier idea, us knowing the future won't change much. The future is more set-in-stone than most people realize. If you want to change something, you have to know the correct small things to change, and it's not always for the better." She gives a sad smile.

"Sounds like you know from experience." I smile and nod at Ivan, sidestepping away from him. "Thank you, I needed that." He gives a tight nod.

"You sound like this world, and your powers are all new to you. What do you mean by that? What happened to you? To us?" Sera asks.

A shiver goes up my spine. "It's nothing."

Her chin juts forward, urging me to answer, showing me she would not back down.

I stay silent.

"Have you already gone back to the past?" I ask my question.

Sera eyes me before answering. "Yes, but I found out that it is harder to change something than I first thought. I had to know and study the past from different angles. It would require many trips. Now you." She crosses her hands in front of her chest and taps her foot on the ground.

"Think of me as you would a human coming into this world."

"What? No," Ivan whispers.

Sera stares at Ivan. She looks like she is in pain or feels pain. She shakes herself free and walks back to the dropped book. "This is going to be harder than I thought. Everything you say, I just have more questions."

"Now you know how I feel." I chuckle as I walk up to her, looking at the book she brought. "Is there something in here that can help me not waste years learning before I get back to my time?"

"No. This book is only about mirrors and the mirror worlds, how to trap things in mirrors and what not, so be careful not to get trapped in here. I am guessing you would be trapped even longer than just years."

"Perhaps there is something in the book vault that can help her view the past events she needs to so that it is a quicker journey for her. That way we won't be tempted to avert or change our future and will only have a limited amount of time with her, which helps her from giving away too much at once." Ivan calls out.

"Hopefully, there is something in there we can use. But we also need to hide this mirror since it can show anyone who she is when she is here. Outside of here, there aren't that many magic mirrors just lying around, so you should be safe."

"It's a weird feeling and is jarring to see me from your perspective when usually I just see you. I will try to remember to hide if this happens again and we are out in public."

"Yea, then, I just have to come up with a good excuse for not having a reflection." She looks at Ivan. "You think people would believe I am a ghost?"

"How are you going to hide a mirror of this size? What will your parents think?" Ivan questions. "Careful though, they could say you are becoming a voided one." His mouth sets in a grim line.

"I will just let my parents know I am keeping this mirror up in my room instead. They won't mind. No one uses this mirror, not for what it actually is. They probably forgot what it does. It was an accident in how I found it. The books in the room were not well cared for. I don't think anyone had access to it for a good long while." Sera fights back in defense.

"We should keep it concealed, regardless. It is important," Ivan says.

"What is your idea? The only thing I can think of is some sort of blood spell, but that wouldn't help with people living in this house with my blood."

Ivan paces back and forth along the hard wooden floor. "I might have something. Well, not me, per se."

"Spit it out, Ivan," Sera berates.

"The obsidian stone. We can tie anyone who has the stones my father gives out to see and interact with the mirror. Alexia has one when she finds it, so nothing will change there."

We all nod, agreeing.

"One problem." Sera raises her pointer finger. "We will have to tell Flit he won't just tie something to things he gives out. Also how can we trust who he gives these out to?"

"Yea and he will be freaked enough when I can't marry Jade," Ivan states.

"Wait, why can't you marry Jade?" Her eyes flick to Ivan's.

He frowns and flings his arm out in my direction. "She is our daughter. Why would I marry Jade?"

Sera glares.

"All that means is that we get together, not that we are actually together or stay that way. Just because we have a child in the future does not mean you get to rule my present."

"We can worry about all that later. Right now, we just need to get this mirror hidden in your room till it can be better protected and a spell for Alexia, so she can go to the pivotal moments that she needs."

"Did I mess this up?" I whisper more to myself than either of them. They were concentrating on one another. Sera with distrust in her eyes, and Ivan angry and worried. How did they move from this to being so loving in my memory of them? She wrote about loving him in the journal. Have I changed something?

"We will be back." Sera throws out over her shoulder as she flips through the book, once again looking for the out-of-mirror spell. She waits for Ivan to hold her hand as she reads out the spell.

One moment they are there with me. The next, I see them on the other side of the looking glass. I stare at them; their hands linger but unclasp once they both notice they still held one another.

"So, this is where you ran off to," Flit's low tone booms over us.

"I can explain." Sera steps forward.

"Shh," he murmurs to her as he holds up a hand to Sera. Her eyes flicker and then fall shut she falls, but Ivan is there to lower her to the ground, making sure she is kept near the mirror.

Ivan's eyes flick to the door.

"Do not worry. They have parted ways for the evening. There is a show or something they had to go off to. Ian went off on his own, and I went looking for the boy who had excused himself and never came back." Flit moves closer and notices me in the mirror. As he cocks his head. "Who are you, my dear?"

I open my mouth to speak once again but remember that they could not hear me before coming into my world. My eyes travel to Ivan.

"Her name is Alexia." Ivan breathes in deeply and lets out a soft sigh. "She is ours." His hand's motion between himself and Sera. "She even has your stone with her."

His dark eyes deepen as he goes deathly still.

"Father. I know—"

Flit raises his hand to his son and waits for his eyes to droop and then close. A shadow bursts out from the corner, catching him before he falls.

Flit's dark eyes meet mine. He takes small steps toward the mirror. He does not stop or slow down in front of it, but comes into the mirror world without a spell to pull him in. I go as far to the side as I can, unsure what to do. This man is tall and more intimidating than anyone I have met so far. He is darkness incarnate.

He slithers into the mirror like a giant shadow without any spell. I gulp and just eye him, not sure where I could go stuck here. His eyes stare at me, keeping me in place.

"Where did you get that?" He eyes the necklace and, as he steps right in front of me, he grabs at the sliver of black stone. It tugs on my wrist as I stare at him with an open mouth. His eyes peer into mine. I had forgotten to put it back on through the whole ordeal. "Tell me."

"From my mother in a memory," I utter, almost robotic.

He looks back at Sera's form lying on the ground in front of the mirror. "Why would she have it?"

My voice comes back to me a bit. "Maybe you trust her." I shrug. "Maybe she needed your help. It did help her with a death spell she needed to perform."

His eyes slide slowly back to me. "That is too many maybes for my liking. Tell me everything."

"What, the king of darkness doesn't like adventure?" I put my hands on my hips. I didn't like people trying to intimidate me. It riled me up and made me defensive.

His shadow lengthens and covers the floor. "I could make it more fun if you wish to play a game." He gives a toothy grin.

Huffing out. Flit's fingers let go of the shard. I place it back around my neck before someone takes it from me. "Before I tell you everything. How can you do magic and other things? I thought you were just a badger shifter?"

The shadows pull back to him, leashing them for now. "There is a reason I am the king of the dark side. I have accumulated a lot of power throughout my years, and much of it has changed me. My animal is but a small percentage of myself." He is quiet as he waits.

I tell him as much as I know and have figured out so far, which is not much. I tell him about my parents and those who took me, explaining how I get away and what has happened over the last few weeks. "So, I do not have much of a past to learn from for the future Quintan wants me to run. So, I needed to learn from them." I look at Ivan and Sera, who are lying side by side.

"You are not sure they are dead, though, correct?" He asks, his fists are balled up.

"No, I might learn that from this past spell, though, if I can find some way to skip ahead."

"Sera and Ivan can help you with that." His eyes bore into mine once again. "But know I will be watching once you have the spell and are gone from this time. I will sequester both of their memories from them. That way, the information you gave them does not affect what they have in the future. They will know your name from the future, and have the urge to help you, but they can't know much more than that."

"They were really curious and could hardly keep questions at bay with what they did know," I hesitate.

"It will unlock for them when the time is right, and they will know I orchestrated it all." Flit responds with a tsk.

"Why not do this tonight and get it done?" I ask.

"Not tonight." He looks at the fatigue written on Sera's face. My yawn comes barreling out of me. "We will start on this tomorrow."

My eyes waver back to the books around the room in the mirror world. "Okay," I answer. Rubbing my hands together, trying to keep warm. "Will you not try to change things with you knowing what you have made me tell you?"

He chews on the thought before answering. "I steer into my future. I already knew of the problems between Sera and Ian and knew that would never work. Jade, though, plays a good match, is not one. Sera is the brains behind the family. Ivan needs that. But she doesn't think there can be love, so she has to find that herself. Though I think she has more than she lets on. Feelings are powerful and can move a person in a way that doesn't always make sense."

"So how does that make it that you won't change things like they would?"

"At this point, she would run away from it. As I said, I steer into things and set up things to be complex and have backup plans. Just because you do not have all the information at this current time doesn't mean someone else doesn't and hasn't planned for it."

"If you say so." My hands shake.

Flit notices my nervousness. "Calm down. Get some rest for now. We will worry about things later and will talk throughout. I will not forget about you, little one. Let's get the mirror into Sera's room and get these kids to bed."

I give him a deep, hard look.

"Stop that."

"What?"

"Stop looking at me like you expect me to kill you or do worse. I am not that terrible."

I hold my hands against my stomach, not moving. "Yea, whatever. We will see."

He fades back out of the mirror into the room. He calls his shadows back out and has one take Ivan and the other for Sera. "Take them to their rooms. I will follow Sera and get this mirror to her room."

I disappear as the shadow elegantly picks up Sera and slides away with her. Everything goes black and cold. Though I can't see, I can still hear what is happening through Sera's ears.

I hear Flit struggle with something heavy. "God damn you heavy ancient thing. Why on earth are you so awkward to carry?"

If I could, I would giggle now at him. The stairs would have been even more havoc than just the straight ways. The struggle persists for a good while more.

Once the mirror slid into place across from the bed, I appear once more. I sit down on the lower half of the bed that Sera is lying on. Flit walks back to the door, pokes his head out, and calls the second shadow that waits in the hallway. He listens to something only he can hear and nods; the shadow disappears. "Ivan is resting comfortably." He closes the door and turns the lock in place. His eyes flick to Sera's resting form and the now settled mirror. When the door is open, it hides it from view but can still be seen from where Sera rests.

Flit flicks his wrist, smoothing some stray strands of hair that have come loose. His breath did not puff out in exhaustion. The out-of-place hair is the only thing that shows he exerted himself.

"Why do you not say the spell to return to your own time or skip ahead yourself? You never explained that."

I open my mouth to speak, but remember, he could not hear me. I shake my head and look at the mirror itself.

"Oh, right, almost forgot?" He calls on his fangs and lengthens his teeth, slicing into his thumb and caressing the wood side, leaving a blood stain behind. He mumbles some words. "There, try now."

"What do you mean?" I ask tentatively.

"Yes, there we go. I can hear you, and anyone nearby will now be able to. As long as you are in the mirror with Sera nearby."

"Trix tricked me and changed the spell to where I can't leave until I learn what I am supposed to. I did not mean for this to happen, and he was helping me since I do not have my magic to call on."

"Right, a human shadow now has it. I remember." He nods.

"I am guessing you also did not read the book's warnings, and what would happen if you become stuck in the past?" He questions.

"What do you mean, what warnings?" I ask, alert, I feel an icy wind blow up my spine.

He beckons the shadow that had never left him. "You did the past spell, correct?" Once the shadow solidifies, it holds one of the books that Sera hid.

"Hey, how did you—"

"I have my ways." He holds up a hand, cutting me off. Taking the book from the shadow, it dips back down into the floor. He opens the book slowly, scanning the pages.

"There were warnings?" I look down at the bed that Sera is sleeping in. I let my hands caress the soft blankets.

He flips and lands on a page, turning the book, so I can see. "Yes, there were warnings. Is this the book you used? They are right here."

I scan the pages in front of me and see weird symbols but no words that I can make out. "Are those even words?"

"I know you said you were taken away, but they did not teach you any training?"

I shake my head and look out the window at the dark sky. "It's not my fault if I can't even understand the language. It was written to begin with. Then when Trix came in, he didn't give me much time to look at the spell before sending me here."

"I did not mean it was your fault." His eyes turn sad. "I just thought it inexcusable for them not to train you on anything."

"I wasn't meant to survive for so long."

"Yet here you are."

The smile in his voice pulls me back to him.

"The main warning you have to concern yourself with is that getting caught up in the past can cause your present to disappear, making your future obsolete. That is usually a warning dealt only when you go back to view your past. What did the little skull say exactly?"

"He said something along the lines of go back to a past to figure out the future. You will only be allowed to return once you have learned all that you can. Hearing and seeing the truth."

"What truth, though."

"My family's truth, maybe? The skull has many masters; who knows who actually carries his leash." I growl and yawn almost at the same time. I lay down on the soft bed, growing increasingly tired from the day's events.

"Don't worry. I will figure it out." He smooths the book back into place. "I will return this where I found it when done studying the language and words this book holds." He walks back towards the door.

"Ivan said you could help hide the mirror from view."

"He did?"

"Yea, using this." I hold up the necklace around my neck. "Since I wear the obsidian stone in my time, and you only give it out to those you trust, it would make the perfect thing to hide the mirror from everyone else that shouldn't see it."

"Have I taught the boy nothing?" He grumbles under his breath. "Giving away things will get him killed if he keeps up with it." His fingers pinch at the bridge of his nose. "That would work. I can get those ready by tomorrow."

I stretch out on the bed next to Sera. Groaning, I sink into the covers. The warmth envelops me. "I'm so cold." I wrap some blankets around me and sigh in bliss.

"Tomorrow, have them work on getting you to skip forward in time. Otherwise, you will grow colder and be stuck in the past." He whispers.

I barely catch his words before drifting off.

"Goodnight, Lexi." He says softly as he turns off the lights . He opens and closes the door, the room now silent.

Chapter 13

A LOUD POUNDING SOUND emits from the bedroom door. "Little witch! I know it was you."

I jolt up in bed as Sera grumbles and squirms under her covers. The door handle rattles.

"Open this door right now!" Robert's voice booms.

"Did he lock the door when leaving last night?" I hold my aching head in my hand. I look at Sera to see her still mostly hidden under the covers. "How can I wake you up when you can't hear me? Wait. He did something you should be able to do now, right?" I move around on the bed, sitting up more fully. "Since your reflection isn't here to move to get up, I will have to just do this," I whisper. "Sera."

"Go away," she calls out, throwing a pillow at the door.

Last night we were all up pretty late. The mirror world and portal to the library time move a bit differently.

"Don't make me burn down this door, youngin. You know I can." His voice vibrates through the closed door as he shakes it, testing the lock and its strength.

"Don't threaten me with a good time. You can open the door without burning it down in more than one way, and you know it," her muffled voice calls out loudly.

"You are beyond frustrating, and if you didn't cause me so much trouble, then we could have more of a civil conversation." He huffs out a pent-up breath. "I can't wait for your wedding day to finally be rid of protecting your stubborn ass. Then you are the Dark Court's problem."

That got her to perk up from under the pillow. She glances in the mirror and sees me sitting there. "It wasn't a dream," she whispers. "Wait, how are you up here?"

"What did you say, witchy?" Robert asks.

She looks around the room to see if anything else is out of place. "I said, but it is such a cute ass." She wiggles her butt under the covers for emphasis even though he couldn't see.

Smirking, I give a small laugh, trying to keep quiet. "He is rougher and a little meaner, but it is still him."

"That one will always be gruff and burley," Sera whispers back at me. Her eyes open very wide as she realizes we are communicating out of the mirror world. "Did I hear you speak? I couldn't do that yesterday." She stumbles out of bed, coming closer to the mirror. "Tell me what happened last night."

I give a shake of my head and also get out of bed.

"Open this door right now!" Robert roars.

"Our talk can wait. Just cover up the mirror for now, so he can't see me," I mutter as loud as possible, hoping that Robert can't hear me.

Sera grabs at the blanket on bed and tosses them to the floor, fumbling for the sheet instead. She snaps it out and throws it over the top of the mirror, fully covering it. Once she is not in the mirror, I am pulled back into Sera's body to see exactly what she sees.

"I'm tired of hiding things. I'm tired of being smarter than some people around here and having to play tricks and games. I'm just plain tired," she says dejectedly. "There is no point to any of this."

A low grumble emits from the closed door. The floorboards squeak near the door as someone outside takes up, pacing back and forth.

"Look at what you are doing. You are going to pace a hole in that floor out there," I call out quietly, moving near the door, and placing my ear against it to hear what he is doing.

The pacing stops suddenly. "I will take you riding," he schmoozes.

"Flying or horseback?" I perk up, finally interested in opening the door.

"You know which one."

My face falls. "Then no."

"Sera," he seethes.

I lean against the back of the door and tip my face up. My voice comes out with pain and broken up. "Listen, I started this morning; I am not feeling the best. Can you just give me twenty minutes to myself? I will be ready when you come back to get me. I promise."

"No games?" He hesitates.

"No," I say in a small voice.

"Twenty minutes. I want to know why you took the mirror also when I get back," he says. I hear his boots walk across the hallway floor as he leaves.

"That was close," I say as I breathe out harshly. I walk to the covered mirror, taking off the sheet in one smooth swipe.

"You almost gave me a heart attack!" I say sternly. "What are you doing? What if he storms back in here and sees me, sees us? What if he takes the mirror away before we get everything situated?" From the bed to the mirror, I pace back and forth.

"He won't be back. He will give me my time, even if he knows I am lying about starting my monthly." She gives a small smile. "We have an understanding. Trust me on this. Also, last I heard, I am your mother, so you have to listen to me. Stop trying to boss me around." She raises her head in the air, looking down at me.

"Could have fooled me," I harrumph. "My mother was sweet and nothing like this." I toss my hands in her direction.

"That doesn't matter now." She waives me away. "What happened? We only have twenty minutes before he is back. Did Flit make me pass out? What happened? How did the mirror get up here?" She asks rapidly.

"Flit was angry at first. Yes, he made you pass out, and then Ivan tried to stop him and made him pass out as well. I guess he is a lot stronger than his sons still."

"Yea, the magic and power don't pass to Ivan all at once. It is gradually over time so he can cope and learn as he grows into his own. Flit will be around for many years to come. That is another reason I think marriage and ties are ridiculous. They are so long-lived it won't matter much. Witches have a decent length in life, but nothing compared to what the dark side can reach if they dabble in the right magics, or wrong ones, to be franker."

"Good to know. After that, he came into the mirror world without a spell like you had to do."

"Yea, Flit is much more than a badger shifter. We don't know all that he is and what he can do, but that is why he is the king of that side and ruling them. He plays things close to the vest and has more power than anyone really has on this side. I don't know why he doesn't just take over everything."

"I am guessing he has his reasons. Or has a weakness like everyone else," I say. "Anyway, after he realized I wasn't lying or some spy. We talked a bit more like he made me tell him about myself and why I am here. I told him of your plans to help me and Ivan's plan to hide the mirror. After getting things settled here, he explained he would help but that we had to hurry. There were warnings I ignored, and he said it would be dangerous for me. So, we must work quickly on a spell to send me to the times I need so I can get back to my present self faster and not be lost in time."

"He is very convincing at getting what he wants." Serra shakes her head. "Was he mad at hearing that his plan does not happen as he designed it to, with Ivan and Jade?"

"No, he actually thought it was a good thing. He doesn't think Jade is a good match, even though she has power. He likes your drive and determination; thinks you are actually the stronger of the two."

"What, no? He hates me. Or should." She shakes her head, not believing any of it for a second. "Or he is just saying that to placate me." Sera walks back into her closet, getting clothes on. She stays in view of the mirror, so I don't get slingshot back into her.

"I don't know him very well, but he seems sincere to me."

"That's right, you don't know them or how this world really works. They are dark and are better at the harder emotions. Though they can replicate the softer emotions, most don't."

"If you think that way, then why do you build a rogue encampment in the future?"

"Rogue's? What do you mean?"

"You bring the sides closer together than some silly wedding will ever do. You mix the sides where there are none."

"Why would I do that?"

"Maybe that is why I am here to learn how and why you start this plan, even though it does not end well."

She comes out of the closet wearing a new dress. "Last night you would barely tell me anything about the future, and now you don't mind sharing things. Why is that?" She glares at me and studies my face.

"It doesn't matter what I tell you, I've decided." I shrug.

"Why is that?" She gives a suspicious look.

I stare back at her, studying her as well.

"Alexia? Why doesn't it matter?" Her voice grows very low and distant. "If you do not tell me this instant, I will not help you, and you can be lost in the past." She hisses out.

"You wouldn't do that to your child!" I scream.

"Be careful in how much you push me." Her eyelids lower. "You do not want to know what I am capable of."

I struggle internally. I want to be close to Sera to make up for when we were not together in the future, but she is making it very difficult and is nothing like the Sera I had in my memory of when I was a baby. Why is this girl so different? She is harsher, rougher, and very stubborn. She didn't trust and always thought there was some game being played. I understood what that felt like and am sad about how that is a part of both of our lives.

"Ask Flit if you must know!" I yell out.

"I'm asking you. Do you want to be stuck here forever?" She threatens.

"Flit is going to make you guys forget after it all," I grumble.

"Sera? Who was that?" Robert once again knocks on the door. "I decided we can go flying."

"Good going! You gave us away," I hiss out as she grabs the sheets on the floor again.

"Me? You are the one that yelled, not me," she hisses right back at me. Her voice grows louder. "Nobody. Hang on." Sera scrambles around the room after she settles the sheet back over the mirror. She pulls the other blankets up on the bed in a ball. "Do you mean it about flying?"

I am pulled back to her body once the sheet settles and fully covers her body from view.

I wait a moment before opening the door, catching my breath. "Ready," I say as I whip open the door. I cross through and pull the door closed behind me.

Before it can shut, a muscular arm swings out to stop the door, forcing it back open. Robert stares at me until I move out of the way. He peeks his head around the door into the room. His head slowly swivels until it lands on the sheet-covered item.

"Why is the library mirror up here in your room?"

I cock my hip and lean against the door frame. "I'm getting older now and need a full-view mirror to ensure I am presentable. I will tell mother later on today that I took it to use. She will agree and be thrilled I am working on my appearance. No one else uses it, anyway."

He sizes me up to see if I am lying. "Though you are not saying it, I know you have it for some other reason. It better not be another attempt at escaping." His eyes narrow.

"Not a way of escaping, no." I shrug my shoulders, not caring if he believes me.

"Why is there a sheet?" He takes a step into the room, growing closer to the mirror. His hand reaches for it.

I slide around the edge of the doorway out into the hall. "I don't like the way I look today." I make my way to the front stairs. If I weren't in view of the mirror, he wouldn't notice anything off with it. "I thought we were going flying?"

His voice follows me. I turn back to him as he closes the door. "I know you are hiding something."

"Look, I'm still here, ain't I? Obviously, I don't have any nefarious plans to run away and ruin this future that seems so adamant about happening right now. Go ask mother and papa. They both agree it is good for me to be growing up and acting more my age and thinking about how I look in front of others."

"You may have them fooled, but don't forget about the spell you wrote about in your journal that you are going to do, and don't forget about the one you already did." He throws back at her.

I continue down the stairs, willing him to follow and leave what is hidden behind, keeping him on the scent of another secret. I roll my eyes. "Will you drop that already? I already explained earlier that particular spell did not work? It would not do for what I need to accomplish."

"You're smart. You will find another spell or some way to tweak it to do what you want and need." He shakes his head. "No, you're not devious at all."

"Grow up, Robert, drop it," I bite out, facing back toward him.

"I am older than you by about a decade, youngin."

"Yea, you have brought that up before. Being a kitsune, you age faster than normal and stay as an adult long after." I cross my arms in front of my chest. "Can we just go, and you trust me for once that I am not trying anything right now?"

Robert's head tilts up to glance back at the second floor, wanting to go back and check under the sheet. He turns his head away and back towards me. "Fine, let's go," he growls out, turning on his boot heel, and stomping out of the room.

I push forward, following him out. "If I could trust you not to freak out, maybe I would explain things. If you could see things from my perspective, you would not be pushing my destiny with Ian," I say in a sad tone.

"Perhaps there is a way for me to witness what you have been trying to say. I can be in my spirit form and follow you around."

"With your Kitsune abilities?"

"In the spirit realm, I can witness things more clearly than if I were here in my human form. I can hide my presence from sight and witness what you want me to see so badly. If he is bad, as you say he is, I will listen and give you a chance."

My eyes raise to his in hope. "Why? You work for my parents. Why would you go against their wishes and try to understand and see things from my point?"

"I did not take this guard job just to guard the city. I took it to help people and to be able to keep them safe. Yes, I was hired to keep you safe and protected even from yourself, but I also think it should be from people who think they are helping you."

"Deal." I nod. "I need someone on my side. I am so exhausted." My fight goes out of me as I deflate.

"If we want to do this, though, we will have to skip the flying lesson today. It will take me some time to get into spirit form, and I can follow you today. Make sure Ian has his access to you to show me what you want me to see."

"Flying is my only real freedom, but I understand. We can go another time. I have some things I need to accomplish today, anyway."

"Like going to your parents and letting them know about the mirror." He raises an eyebrow. He is halfway turned to me, waiting to make sure.

"I will start by finding one of them and letting them know I have it." I give a tremendous sigh.

"Good deal. I will be around then." As he walks back towards the back of the house on the main floor, he calls back. "Don't do anything you wouldn't like to be seen doing," He reminds.

"Don't worry, I won't," I say in a low tone that he hopefully couldn't pick up on. As he gets further out of sight, I turn in place. "First things first. I need to find Ivan; he will need to search for the spell since I will be being watched all day." I walk diligently throughout the house, climbing back up the main staircase. The rich wood is carved into magnificent swirls. The hallways are bare and kept orderly. Many doors line the right and left sides of the house.

I spin off to the opposite side of where my room is kept and walk right up to the guest doors.

"Robert would need time to set up and get into his spirit form, so that gives me enough time to talk to Ivan in private."

Saddling up to Ivan's door, I knock, hoping he is awake this early. After the soft knocks, I hear a rumble and something crashing to the floor. Thumps hit the floor, and the doorknob turns a couple of times. The door cracks open as one light blue eye peeks out the door. Darkness surrounds him otherwise.

"Ivan?"

"Yes," he growls.

"Open up. I don't have much time to go over this. I will be watched for most of the day." I push against the door; he flexes for a moment, keeping it in place, then let's go. I rush in as he closes it off and leaves me in the darkness.

"Is this what you wanted?" He growls near my ear softly. Not holding me captive, but being intimidating all the same.

"You forget, dark prince, that I make sure all these rooms are full of plants." I twist my fingers, calling the vines forward. Sounds of them slithering over floors can be heard from the room's corners.

He waits until the vines surround his arms and legs, not tugging on them but making them know they are there, since they cannot be seen.

"Do you tie up many lovers, or am I the first?" His voice goes gruff.

I turn around, my hands fly out, and find his naked chest. My fingers retract almost immediately. It is hard and well-defined. "Stop that." I fling one vine at the curtains to pull it aside. "As I said, I have little time."

He hisses as the blinding early morning light cascades into the room, easily tearing the vines away from him as he steps backward. He only is wearing a pair of shorts and nothing else. His hair is messy from sleep, and his eyes are fully black.

My eyes roam over him since most of the time, he keeps hidden. My eyes meet his, and then I turn away. I feel my cheeks heat as he catches me admiring him.

"I apologize. You caught me in a good dream." He smirks as he runs a hand through his medium-tossed hair. "What can I help you with?"

I let the vines go, pushing them back to the plant, and let the curtain fall. It only leaves a sliver of light enough to see my surroundings but leaves Ivan in darkness. I felt much more comfortable not viewing what he had on display.

Before I go on, I clear my throat. "I will have a spirit walker watching me today, so I need you to work on the spell to help Alexia skip forward. I will try to hang out with Ian to keep up the pretenses. Your father has apparently agreed to help hide the mirror, but I have to let my parents know I have taken it. Robert already noticed it is missing."

"Are you saying last night was not a dream?"

Was that anger tinged in his voice or something more hopeful?

"No, Flit made you and I go to sleep as he talked with Alexia."

"How do you know all this?" He comes closer to the light.

"Alexia told me Flit enabled us to communicate outside the mirror world. As long as I am close to the mirror, she can talk with anyone outside of it that is nearby."

"So, he is going to devise a way to hide the mirror. You are going to explain why it is missing to your parents, and say I need to help our daughter skip through our past back to her present. Why not just keep her here with us where she is safe?"

"Flit explained a warning about past jumping, which I knew of. Usually, you must be careful about feeling or diving too deep into the past, otherwise, you will erase your present self. The same can happen to her if she dives too deep or stays back here too much and takes on my feelings. She can become lost and unable to find her way back to her present self."

"Why didn't you start with that?"

"Why do you care so much?"

"She is my daughter!" He barks out.

"One that doesn't exist yet, and we don't even really know."

"You do not know what makes me tick or what my dreams are. Maybe instead of questioning why I will do this, use this time to understand her and get to know her while you can."

"Why when I can fight it tooth and nail?"

"I wonder if she is as stubborn as you are." Ivan takes another step closer, almost touching. He is a full head taller than me and looks down. I stare at his chest which is so close to me before my eyes travel up.

"Anyway, the spell we need should be in that mirror portal we were in yesterday. It is not very well organized, but you should be able to use something that can push her forward to the important times she needs and then get back to her present faster."

"She is listening to us even now, I bet. I wonder what happens to her while she is in your body. Does she feel what you feel? Does she understand what is going on in your mind? Does she know what you know?" He continues his own train of thought, ignoring me.

I wish! That might have been helpful, knowing what she knew. I could catch some fleeting thoughts if they were at the forefront of her mind, but no, everything else is hidden from me. I could experience only the things she goes through.

"Okay, so you're useless." I turn away from him, walking back to the door. A cold wind brushes the back of my neck as an arm reaches past me, pushing against the door I am trying to open.

"I heard you," Ivan growls behind me, his breath right there on my neck.

I turn around slowly, facing him. Shadows have lengthened behind him, and claws are where his fingers used to be. I meet his eyes, not cowering away. "Will you then take care of finding the spell while I handle my parents and the other thing?"

"Yes." His eyes meet mine as his claws shrink back to fingers. "Yes," he barely contains a growl, he reiterates. He raises two fingers to brush through a few strands of my hair at the top, brushing over my forehead.

"Stop," I say, barely getting the words out. "You know, the more you are around and touch me, the more confusing things get."

"What if I like the chaos it brings?" Ivan brushes a thumb over the corner of my mouth. "We both have said how we feel. I am trying to find a loophole for us."

I continue meeting his gaze, not cowering back. Though Ian gave me weird vibes and could be very cruel, I did not get that from this brother. Ivan, he may outwardly show that he is on the darker side. I don't get the cruel feeling from him. Nope, can't think that way.

I look around the sparse room and notice a clock on the wall. I glance back at him, then at the clock, forcing him to see that he is keeping me. He retracts his arm, brushing mine as he takes several steps back from the door.

"We will reconvene tonight. I should find the spell needed and finish up some other things I had planned. Sound good?"

I nod. "Agreed. The mirror is in my room now. I don't think I mentioned that before. I will see you there. That way, we can talk with Alexia as well." I turn around, not wanting to wait a moment more. I close the door behind me with a soft snick. As I peer up, part of my hair falls and covers half of my face. Ian walks with his back towards me, out of his room, shutting the door. I move away from Ivan's door, so he does not know I am visiting his brother. "Ian, there you are."

He jumps a bit as if he didn't hear me. "Sera! What are you doing here?" He gives a hostile look and looks around as if searching for some ulterior motive.

"Looking for you." I smile.

"Why?"

"Can't we just try to get along since you will be a part of my future one way or another? I want to find some common ground so that we are not just at each other's throats every day till one of us ends the other."

"Though it looks like you, it sure does not sound like something you would say. Did you talk with my father?" His eyes turn distrustful.

I spun this with a bit of truth, so he would not smell any deceit. "Yes, Flit spoke with me, but I honestly thought that I could give this another try. Get to know you more before I judge you. I want to learn more about the other side of the world and see how it differs from mine. Since I may come to live there, I thought it best to learn what I am fully getting into."

"Careful, witch, my nose knows when you are not being honest."

"Damn it!" I stomp my foot and clench my fists, walking over to him so I am fully facing him. "Fine, though. Most of it is the truth. I want to know more, to hopefully find a way out of this altogether. This is not my future; you know that much is true."

He nods, his eyes turning bright gray, letting his animal closer to the surface. "Well, good news for you. I am in a good mood and have some time. Meet me in about 15 minutes near the wooded path. You know the one. The one you took to the lake yesterday." He gives a mischievous grin.

"Yes, I know the one," I bite back. "No funny business this time."

"No promises." He laughs, turning away from me, headed in the opposite direction.

Waiting till I see him turn the corner and making sure I continue to hear his footsteps recede, I step swiftly up to Ian's door, testing the handle. My hand meets the pressure of the door being locked. My eyes skim left and right, ensuring no one is watching. I whisper a few words, chanting as I call my power to myself.

"What are you doing?" Quintan pipes up from further down the hallway near the center of the house. He is taller than me and fills the hallway, more so than my slight frame.

I roll my eyes and sigh as I release the magic and drop what I thought about doing.

"Nothing, I just made plans with Ian. I am going to find mother or papa to tell them something. Have you seen them?" I wipe my hands on the front of my dress, smoothing things in place.

"Craig has already left for the morning, but Daniella can be found downstairs. Where did Ian go?" Quintan fires back.

"He is getting things ready, and we will meet in fifteen minutes. He headed down that way." His eyes snap behind me, showing his eagerness. My face falls. "Perhaps you can catch him." He nods and moves to pass me by. "You should tell him."

He freezes on the spot. His eyes cut to mine, glaring from the side and not turning to meet me. "Tell him what?"

"I mean, that is why you helped him with his plan, is it not? And why you sent me into the lake? You don't even know him, and you're not usually malicious. I hear conversations when no one thinks I am paying attention. I know what they say about you."

Wait? What? What do they say about him? Come on! Can't you give me more? Think of something so I can pick up the thought of what you are talking about?

His shrewd eyes cut me to the core. "You think you have me all figured out? You don't even know me. Do not pretend to understand me by what others say."

"If I judged you only on our interactions and what I know, I would not be as nice as I am being." I move to the side, passing him fully and making my way to the center of the house to head down to the main floor.

"Careful witch," Quintan whispers back.

I barely catch the words but do not turn back to him. He would not be someone I could trust or lean on.

Making my way down the stairs and to the main rooms, I search for her. In the main living space, the curtains are still drawn, where they are usually thrown open to let in the sun. To make up for all the darkness, there are spots of lights turned on. "Why do we have it so dark down here?" I question.

"Sera, you know our guests prefer the darkness, so we are making it more comfortable for them," Daniella utters from deep within. She sits near the back in a slit of the sunlight. Her face turned toward it.

"Just because they prefer the dark side of things does not mean they all prefer darkness. They also used to live in it perpetually. I think they have evolved since then. I was looking for you before I meet with Ian."

"Semantics. I hope you are being a lot nicer to that boy than you were yesterday." Her eyes cut toward me, but she keeps her face in the light.

"Mama, he is terrible, though."

"Yes, and what did I tell you to do about that?" This time she gets up and moves towards me, her face cast in shadow.

My hands shake, and my knees want to give out. "To get even."

"But you did it in such a way that you were caught. Never let them catch you. You should know from my failure."

"Father," I whisper.

Her mouth pinches in a frown. "He is my failure for growing too bold and thinking things were untouchable. I pay for that cost in more ways than you will ever know. This family is one way to make sure you stay safe. Learn to play a better game than I ever did." Her calm, calculating eyes caress me without touching.

I school my face and features to remain calm and stop twitching. "I will, mother." I bow my head and do a small curtsy. "You were different with father than you are here."

"I have to."

"Yes, you ingrained that into my head many times. There were not many times we were alone together since. The times we were, you were harsh to me. I know what must be done. That brings me to why I came to find you."

"There may still be a use for you yet. Now, what was it you needed me for? It is out of character for you to search for me."

"I took the mirror that was not being used in the library to work on my looks and being more." I shrug my shoulders. "Being more of what this family needs me to be."

Her eyes narrow in question. "The mirror that was old and dusty?"

"Yes, that's the one. Why? Do you know of it?" I ask, hesitant to push the manner more.

"You will not find what you are looking for in there."

I choose my next words carefully. "What do you mean?"

She faces me fully in the shadows. Her eyes meet mine. We were both about the same height. "I will allow you this only for you to get it out of your system and see that there is no other way. But know this, I will always know what is truly going on."

"Though you may know a lot, you do not see all like some omniscient being." Every time I spoke with my mother, I felt like we were on the cusp of a fight. "My life is my own, and I need to see things through."

"Comeuppance comes for all." She raises a pristine eyebrow and turns from me gracefully, her dress folding perfectly as she turns away. The silver gown scrapes across the floor as she moves. "You can report back to your guard that you have told me and approve of the mirror being in your room for the time being."

"Robert told you first. I thought he was going to allow me to mention it to you. I thought this was what all this was for."

"Though he is your guard, he works for us, darling. You must do a better job in handling the politics if you wish to survive in this family. In this world, to be more specific."

My hands clench into fists at my side. I don't turn back to her. I hold a moment before walking out of the room slowly, not showing my temper that seethes behind my mask. No one ever is straight with me in this family, and Robert proved to me that I couldn't trust him like I thought I could, either. I grumble when I am far enough away. "Should I not even do this if I can't even trust you?"

I shake my head, unsure if he is even around to hear me talk. I wouldn't know if he is around unless he moves to a plane of existence I can see.

"It's not like I can search for you to check if you were around and do what you said. Since you hide away like the coward you are." I taunt, walking through the main hallway out the front door. I smirk and look towards the forest line. I stomp my feet in the dirt, kicking up dust in my wake. I hope he can hear me. Otherwise, I just hope he would watch when Ian is doing what he does best, causing me pain. I hope he gets the full show and sees him for what he truly is.

I turn my head to the sky and take a deep breath. "I really need someone on my side and for someone to believe me." I stand still, taking in the sereneness of it all. Opening my eyes slowly, I see the trail that leads through the woods and to the lake, to my doom.

CHAPTER 14

I SPEND MOST OF the day with Ian, and though we are alone, except for the two guards, he is still on his best behavior. We only have the guards with us because we want to go to the market and see what's there. People were bustling and haggling all around us. I love this place. The crowd and people working together made me think of my home, my home before this, with my real father. I missed him. He would take me into the market every weekend, make sure we mingled and helped whoever needed our help. I pick up a necklace admiring the stonework and craftsmanship that went into it.

"That would look lovely on you," Ian purrs.

"What is with you?" I ask, not able to stand this anymore. I needed to know what kind of ploy he is playing. He tests my patience and will to even want to play politics.

Ian quirks a brow, peering at me, his hand raises with an item. He sets it back down without looking at it. The people around us quiet down to a murmur. Though it is crowded most were making their way closer to us or further away for fear of a fight and getting caught up in it. The guards glared at the ones getting closer, making them step away before drawing their weapons of choice.

"Wasn't this what you wanted? To spend more time together so we could understand and get to know one another? Be friends or, if not that, at least not enemies."

I throw the necklace back onto the table. The salesman keeps an eye on his pieces but stays out of our discussion. "But you are being nice. This is not you."

He gives me an irritated look as he looks down at me. "This is what you wanted and asked for, is it not? You wanted us to get along and not fight all the time. You wanted me to be nice." He steps back with exasperation. "Sera, I am a bit confused by your demeanor. Are you quite all right?"

My head swivels left and right, noticing the eyes boring into us. The crowd's whispers and judgments were almost audible to me. Even though he is taller than me, I raise my head and meet his eyes. I don't know why he is being so weird, but I let it go, not wanting to cause a scene. I just promised mother that I would do better in these kinds of situations and giving him more ammunition would not help the situation here. I do not want to look like the bad guy, especially in front of these people.

"Did Quintan end up finding you? He came by after we talked." I change the subject.

"He did." He smirks.

A glint in his eye tells me all I need to know: he is on to me and knows why I changed the topic. He would not make this easy for me. Well, I had news for him. I would not make this easy for him, either. "Did you two know each other before you came here?"

He shakes his head. "How would I know him? He came from the light capital with the other highly recommended officers of the council."

"You seem pretty chummy is all for just meeting one another." I shrug, throwing the ball back in his court. "He helped you play that trick on me yesterday."

Quintan was a variable I didn't know too much about. He came from the capital of the light side. He and some other members came to attend to make sure that everything with the treaty and marriages went without a hitch.

Ian remains quiet, unwilling to give me anything more about what they may have discussed.

"Flit didn't bring that many people with him, just you and Ivan and some fox shifters and his shadow goons, of course."

"It's all we needed. Also, just because you can't see them, it does not mean they are not there. We do not need our own protection. Unlike you, we know how to win our own fights," he bites out.

I was going to just have to come straight out and ask him. "What did you two talk about? Why did he need to get with you?"

We keep moving through the market as the silence lengthens. Others continue talking in the background. My eyes tangle in the bright clothing, unable to keep my eyes on Ian for any length of time. We move past the stalls and head back down the road toward my house. The guards peel off and hug the sides of the street, staying back after we leave the busy area. They only had to follow in the busy areas where people were packed, and the most trouble could happen.

"Two down," Ian mutters.

I quirk my brow at him in question. "If you will not answer my questions, just say so. You are killing each of my conversation starters, and it is getting really tiring." The road thins out. Cobblestones turn to dirt as we return.

"You can't even trust me enough not to have guards around." He zeros in on me.

I look back at the town and the bustling people. "Those? They always accompany my family and me when we are in town. Since it is busy, they like being extra cautious with so many." I look around nervously.

"Answer me, this little witch. The light capital and some other high-functioning places are more forward-thinking and tech savvy. Why does Craig keep it, please excuse me if this sounds rude, quant, and simple?" His eyes roam over me as if searching.

"Mother preferred it here. She does not like all the bustling noise. She says it makes it hard to listen to what is true. We are also elemental witches, so to be in the elements is where we are most comfortable." I keep walking but edge closer to him. "There isn't always an ulterior motive, you know."

Ian stretches out his arms and settles one over my shoulders, hugging me closer. "If there wasn't, then why are you still having us followed? Scared?" He whispers. Louder, he says. "My city is very busy and dark. I hope you will bring a nightlight."

My eyes squint in confusion. "What do you mean?"

His eyes travel to the side as if he spots something there. "It's too bad you won't see my city until you are already married into the family. I know some things would love to play with you for dinner and have a taste." He pulls me in closer and licks my cheek.

I struggle and push him away, wiping the spittle from my cheek. "Gross. You disgust me." I run for the tree line in the distance, hoping to get away from him.

"Run fast, little witch. Can you outrun your shadow?" He grins.

The sun is setting and making the shadows long from the tree's, my shadow is cast out long and running beside me. I let out a shriek as my shadow changes and morphs into spikes that come at me. Shadows from the trees whip up in a tangle as I grow closer, but I still dodge and weave towards the trees. I try to stop suddenly and lose my footing. I hiss in pain as I go down in a tumble.

"Robert!" I call, hoping he can hear me.

"Is he the little fox that was spying on us?" Ian tsks as he rushes over to me. "I got the shadow walkers dealing with him in another way. He is too busy, I am afraid." He towers over me as I push myself back. My hands scratching on the rocks and sticks on the ground. "Didn't anyone ever tell you it was bad etiquette to let your opponent see your hand?"

Purple fog billows out. My breath comes out quickly as my eyes try to find purchase in the coming fog.

"You were not the only one who prepared for this. I knew you were up to something. I, unfortunately, chose the better and stronger partner."

"Quintan," I ground out. I call my powers to me, begging them to answer. The tree line is not close enough to call the vegetation towards me. The only thing that happens is the grass grows longer and tangles around Ian's boots.

He laughs as he stomps his way through the weeds, turning his back on me. "It really is too bad you are the weaker sister. I would have had fun breaking Jade and making her mind me. You will be easy with almost no powers to speak of."

"Don't turn your back on me, Ian," I call the vines to spiral around his legs, thickening and growing in strength, locking him into place. "One day, you will all start to take me seriously."

"Seriously!" He laughs out. "For anyone to take you seriously, you would have to submit to the world you hate most. Just like your mother had to. She is where she is only because it gains her the power she requires and likes. Guess the apple didn't fall too far from the tree?" He stomps his boots once more, breaking the branches that scratch at him. They continue to grow as he stomps them out. His sly eyes cut away from me.

"I'm not like her," my voice comes out small. I turn away from him, swiftly walking into the dark woods. The branches overhead are filled with dark green leaves, cutting off the sun from view.

"Oh, but you are," I hear him call out behind me; the grin was clear in his voice. "You go back and forth about it, don't you?"

"No!" My voice comes out in a squeak.

"Yeah, you do." He flat-out laughs at this. "You want to be alone to make your own way, but you also want the power and fear that part of you craves that power, that darkness." Purple flames fly past my head toward Ian.

My head swivels to him, noticing the flames falling on the branches, making them weak and brittle. Ian easily steps away. I search the woods for where the fireball came from, knowing Quintan is hidden somewhere nearby.

"The only power I crave is the power to change the world. The power to make things happen for the better. I will not give up my freedom to achieve such things, though. I care too much about myself to do that."

"So selfish."

"Call me selfish if you must. No one in this world has my back like I do." I fling back in his direction.

He strides forward with determination, his angry eyes raking mine. "That fire is the only thing you have going for you and why you may yet survive the night and all it offers." His eyes dip to my lips.

I back up and cringe in horror.

His arms snake around me, pulling me closer. "Your little fox friend isn't here watching anymore. You are all mine for the taking."

I gasp in shock. "You knew this whole time?"

He pulls me in closer, his lips almost touching my cheek as I try to turn away. "Of course, I knew, little rabbit. We are at the top for a reason. We do not explain or tell of all that we can do, but one that is known and is surprising the little guard didn't know of is that we can see many planes of existence. Perhaps since he is new, he did not know better."

"Robert just started with us not too long ago. He might not have gotten up to speed on everyone." I bite my lip, unsure what to do with the plan now. "Last I checked, you were only badger shifters."

"There is more than one way to gain power." His teeth scrape against the sensitive skin on my neck. "Want to find out, little rabbit?"

Flames erupt around us, scattering some birds that were close by away, causing a ruckus. It encircles us and grows high around us, keeping us caged.

"What is this? Is this Quintan's doing?" I ask, scrambling backward away from Ian, putting space between us.

His hands unlatch as he lets me go. "Quintan, this was not the plan," he says sternly.

"You both must see what this path has for you and why it will not work and should be avoided," he calls out, still hidden.

"Come out and fight like a real man," I yell out at the edge of the flames, getting as close as I can.

"Enough of this," Ian growls out as his shape begins to fade and turn dark. A piercing whistle flies, cutting close to me, but lands in the dark mass. Ian's hand flies up and swats at the thing that had landed, but it is already dissolved and no more. His form flickers back to normal, and his eyes turn to surprise. "What was that?" His voice stutters, partly in shock.

"The drug will take effect soon. You will be out, and you will see a potential future that we see with this union. The light side has done extensive research, and this union can't happen. The union between Jade and Ivan must continue, but this needs to cease."

Grass surrounds me. I call my power to me as my fear spikes. I push and pull it to grow around me, pulling a shield out of the ground. It bends over me, making it so that Quintan can shoot whatever he shot at Ian. "I already know he is not my future. I don't need a spell to see that."

"Sorry, princess, you will need to see this to clarify my point." The flames close in on the circle and catch the light to my shield, burning it before it could barely form.

I continue to pull down on the trees up above, asking them for time. I search around the flames, hoping to see something. Hoping to know where his voice is coming from.

"But why?" I ask to keep him talking.

No burst comes forward from the trees, so I continue. "If I already know that combining our forces will be bad, why do you have to show me what I already know? Ian and I are not a good fit. Both of us would suffer for it, and we would focus on harming one another and trying to beat the other. We would not focus on the needs of the people, and our groups would be pulled into our game, causing them to suffer along right there with us. Ivan and Jade could be pulled in, and we could end up ruining what is to become with them as well." I pause, listening. I hear rustling and a huff of a deep breath off to the left, past the flames near an exceptionally large tree. My gaze snaps to the tree and zeros in on what I can feel through my earth magic.

Though the wheezing continues in that direction, no words come back to me. "I am not your enemy here. I agree with you that he is not my future. My family wants me to be safe, and his father wants both sons to be married. That is the only reason this coupling is happening is that Jade had a sister. Give me a way out of this, and I will gladly take it. Let's work together on this so you can try to have what you and the light side want, and this gives me my way out to decide how to live my life with how I see fit." I hold off on calling more magic into the surrounding greenery, not wanting to attack him if he is going to help me out of this problem.

Quintan steps out from behind the tree that I am eyeing. His tall stock form is clear above the flames. "Why are you so adamant and against this when your family is for both marriages?" In silent contemplation, he plays with something between his fingers at his side.

"Without really knowing me, you will have to trust me when I say I am different from them and want separate things. You heard what I said earlier about not wanting power if it negates my choice. I want the freedom of choice. I don't want to be in a relationship that makes me miserable, let alone the person I am tied to. If it is not working, I want to be able to leave or do what I want when I want."

"That seems like a tall order when it doesn't sound like you want someone in your life."

I raise my head; the warmth of the flames caresses my face as I stare at him and hope that he can see the strength and resolve I have against this. "I want to be with someone I love. I shouldn't feel caged or be afraid I can't do something I want to. That person should understand, or at least be willing to discuss, why they feel they can tell me what to do and have control over what I want to do with my body or mind." My eyes fall on Ian. "He can't provide that; he is not what I need in this life. He is not what the people need in this world, and probably why Flit chose Ivan over him." I frown as my flat shoe nudges his limp hand.

"If you value your life, I would never let him hear you say that." Quintan looks somberly over the flames at the boy lying in the dirt. He inches closer to the flames.

"If he is seeing how we ruin each other's lives and the world around us, I guess that is the least of what he is hearing from me right now. I can almost guarantee that you do not know me and how my temper can flare. I will throw it all away if there is no other choice. Believe me, on that."

He waves his hand over the flames, his eyes cutting to mine. "Fine, I will not show you this possible future, but you must get away so that it doesn't become a reality."

"Do you have a plan in mind? An idea of how we go about this?" I smooth my hands down my velvety dress and move away from Ian outside the charred circle. Quintan moves into the circle and closer to Ian. I keep my eyes trained on him as I circle around, never turning my back to either of them, keeping them in my sights in case he changes his mind.

"In fact, I have a plan. We can leave right away so no one would know."

No! I scream internally at the same time as I say. "No!"

Quintan freezes as he is about to bend down and check on Ian and stares at me, startled. "Why not?" The item in his left-hand moves through his fingers as he fiddles with it once more. Bringing it in front of him. "I thought you were ready to be done with all of this."

"I mean to say I have to pack and get some things ready and in place." I notice Quintan, about ready to interject once again. "Don't worry, it won't be anything noticeable that I take with me, and I won't tell anyone our plan. But I need time before we make this happen, or someone may come for me. Robert, for one, has found me on a couple of occasions. I am assuming you will have something for him specifically?"

"Perhaps you're right. I will need some time to come up with something. When can you be ready by then? It must be sooner rather than later. Preferably before he wakes." He looks down at Ian once again. Placing the item that was rolling around his fingers onto his chest, it dissolves into him. Making his sleep deeper and his breathing more even. "He will be out till about midnight."

"I can make that work."

"Well, it really should be before that, of course." He looks up at me and gives me a stern look.

I frown in answer and look to the sky or what should have been if there weren't so many leaves and branches in the way obstructing the view. "It is growing closer to sundown. What I need to wrap up shouldn't last too long, maybe till eleven. I can stop by your room when I am done. Does that work?"

He gives a terse nod. "That will also give me enough time to take care of Ian and some things to make this plan go without a hitch. Fooling a spirit walker will be tricky. They are sly foxes."

"That they are. I had a hard time with it the last two times. Evading him for long was not something I excelled at. Mostly, I think he just let me have my time and space before wrangling me back in, when the adults complained too much." I give a mischievous smile.

After the plan is in place, he turns his back to me and ignores me, wanting his own time alone with Ian. I bypass him quickly, making it back to the house, not thinking to ask more questions about the next steps, just trusting he had it. I could always ask more questions later. There would be time for that.

I needed to get back and ensure Alexia's spell is in place before I leave so she could skip forward and not get stuck in this past. Though I don't know much about her, she is still my responsibility, and I don't wish any ill will toward her. This would also be a way away from Flit and the spell he wants to cast on us to forget. What kind of game is he trying to pull?

I break from the trees, noticing the sun starts to decline below the horizon. Hurrying up the stairs into the house, hoping Ivan is still there. "He must have the spell ready for us to perform." The mirror would have to be left behind for the time being, and hopefully, Flit and Ivan would make sure the spell is placed on it, and I would send for it or come back and get it, eventually. I didn't want to take my chances with Robert and running in to him, knowing him he would pick up on my eagerness and know something is afoot. He also left me alone with Ian when he is supposed to be helping me with him and be on my side. Of course, he just saw Ian and the façade everyone else fell for.

Taking the main staircase two at a time, I arrive at my door quickly, with no one to stop me. I hoped I had enough time to pack a bag at least and get a few things in place to help me on my travels. I am unsure what the living situation will be, but I need to be prepared regardless. Knowing Quintan, he wouldn't be helping me all that much if it didn't help him first. He would most likely just get me out of this place and get me to a far enough destination with a charm to hide me, and that is it. The rest would most likely be up to me.

I open it slowly, bracing my body against the door, ready for anything but also not wanting to frighten Ivan if he was in the middle of something. I don't spot anyone in the room, so I toss the door fully open and make my way in. Closing the door slowly, I turn the lock. The room is eerily quiet, and the sheet is still in place over the mirror. A slight breeze moves the thin blanket, causing it to billow up.

Pulling the sheet aside, I see the mirror is blank and has a warm golden light filling the entire view. "Ivan, I hope it is you that is in there." Before plunging into the cool mirror, I hold my breath and walk straight through.

"Ivan?" I ask.

"Back here!" His voice rings out. Books cover the walkways. I make my way back through the labyrinth of books and baubles. "I think I found it, actually. Great timing," he states.

As I come around the corner, I see his dark hair has fallen in front of him, hiding his face from my view. I stop and stare. Something in me craves the caring nature that he shows by doing all of this. A part of me wants this, but I would never let that secret out, well maybe to the journal I write in, but maybe I should refrain since Robert likes to peek through it now and again.

He pulls back the strands of hair, and his eyes are on mine the second his face shows. Our eyes meet, and my mind blanks at what is even happening. What is wrong with me? I cross my hands in front of my chest for defense and cock my eyebrow. "What did you find?" I try to cover.

"I believe I found the spell Alexia needs to move through the past. First, though, Flit already made the black crystals that we need to see the mirror." He pulls out the two necklaces from his pocket.

"He already put the spell on the mirror?" I give a confused look. "How..."

"No, of course not. If he did, how would you have been able to see it to get through to here?" He gives a brief chuckle.

"Right." I also give a small chuckle; I brush a hand through my hair, unsure of myself. I walk forward, trying to see the book he had in front of him. "Will I be able to do the spell tonight? Right now?"

His eyes skim the book's page he is reading. "It seems fairly simple and should be able to be done now. We just have to be in front of the mirror to see Alexia. Of course, you will need some candles and salt and something that ties you together, which is the stone."

"Okay, let's get this going then." I turn the book around to see the spell and pull it into my waiting hands.

"Probably best to do it sooner, anyway. Are you sure you are up for it?"

"What? Because my magic might not work? Because I'm a halfling?" I glare down at him, plucking the necklace from his hand.

"No, that's not what I'm saying." He rises from his seat. My eyes follow him as he gets up. "I just wanted to ensure you weren't magically drained; I was not sure how your day was. We need to get this done quickly. I understand, but I am not the magic user here. Would it be better on a different day or night? Do you need to prepare anything else other than what is listed there? That is what I was more meaning by my question." He moves closer to read over my shoulder, almost whispering in my ear.

"Oh." I stop for a moment. My eyes are glued to the page in front of me. Holding my breath, I spin away from him, using the book as a barrier between us. "No, we shouldn't need anything else. I have the candles and salt in my room. Let's get this done now." I don't look back to see if he is following me, but I feel and hear his boots behind me.

My mind races at getting this finished and him out of the way to make plans to meet Quintan. First things first, get the spell done. The words and spell looked easy, but the craft did not work like that. It played heavily on the witch's power and with me being a halfling, which my spells didn't always have the umph they required to fully complete.

Winding our way through the stacks of books and tables, we rush through the glowing mirror. My hand reaches out of the other side and touches cloth I open my closed eyes and see the white sheet I had left on the mirror. I bat it away, pulling it off of the mirror so I would have a clear sight of Alexia as I did this. Ivan steps through the mirror, and the light dims. I am pulled into the mirror as it catches Sera's reflection.

I rub my temples as I catch myself against Sera's bed. My eyes zero in on her as she busies herself with getting the salt and candles. "

"Hey, Alexia." Ivan is looking at me and then at Sera, ensuring she stays in view of the mirror.

"Hey." I lean against the bed, the room still spinning. This didn't happen before.

"Are you unwell?"

"I'm not sure this didn't happen last time. I could just be tired, but the room doesn't want to stop spinning."

"Your vertigo is off balance. I found a book on traveling in the past. The first sign is dizziness. Sera, about how long do witches normally keep past jumps to?"

"No more than three days. Otherwise, things break down."

"What day are you on, sweetie?"

"Umm, two days, I believe."

"Shit," Sera blurts out. "And we cannot know how many days of learning you still have to go. Well, let's hope you don't go too much over the four-day mark. After that, it gets tricky if you make it back." Sera motions with her hands as she picks up multiple large candles and places them in a circle in front of the mirror. "Tell her the next warnings to look for so she knows how much time she has since she will be jumping. She won't have a good idea of how much time she has left."

Ivan nods and faces back toward me. "Coldness will settle in getting a few degrees colder no matter the amount of heat the person may be close to. Even with the mirror, you will start to not feel the heat you could before. Confusion will come next when your soul has difficulty accepting or understanding. Then there will be fatigue and wanting the darkness to shut out everyone and everything. You will shut off from the person you follow and fall into a dreamlike state. This is dangerous for you since the spell that sent you back here requires you to learn all you must before returning to your present." He reminds me once again.

"I get it focus and don't fall asleep." I shake my head and stand up, showing him my strength. "I can do this."

He places a hand on the mirror. "I know you can."

I look at Sera, who is now searching through a chest for some salt and matches. Walking up closer to the mirror, I place my hand up to his and smile. A zing shocks down my arm, making me retract my hand. "What was that?"

He looks at his hand as well. His eyes grow big as he steps back. Sera comes between us and creates a circle of salt. She quickly pours it around us and the mirror. As she dips away, I disappear back to her, then am once again looking at Ivan and Sera both.

"You need to warn a person if you will be doing that." I hold my stomach and mouth, unsure if I am going to upchuck or how I would even do that here in the mirror world.

"Stand there." Sera dictates. She flips the book back open to where her finger is holding the page. She whispers. "Burn."

Nothing happens as she looks down at the candles and stomps her foot. Shaking out a match in her hand, she lights it, catching the flame on the first wick. She moves around the circle counterclock-wise.

I gulp, unsure of what is going on. "Is that a bad sign?"

Her shrewd eyes cut to me. "No, fire does not enjoy listening to an earth elemental." Her eyes move to Ivan and pin him there. He is still standing still and shocked, looking at me. "What happened?"

He looks down at his palm and shakes his head. "Nothing, just something I had to be sure of."

"I will alter the written spell to make it more towards you." Sera moves to the center once again and stares at me with the book wide open.

"What does that mean? Isn't it a spell that is supposed to send me through the past?"

"Yes, but we usually use this to gain a lot of knowledge in a short time, but we do this in intervals. Not all at once. I am not sure what issues could arise from all of it. I will call on powers to help you through the process."

"Will this help you as well?" Ivan asks.

She gives a solemn nod. "I call upon this one's family to help push her forward in her endeavor. I call upon any ties and lines she may have to help her with her needs. Help us get her where she needs and learn all she can. Move quickly and quietly throughout time to where she needs to go, but hold her no more than necessary for, she must get back."

I look around the mirror and Sera's room, unsure if anything happened.

Sera growls in frustration.

"It didn't work?" Ivan asks.

Sera dives forward and places her hand on the mirror, and I am drawn forward. "Alexia, hear me! I call upon your ties and lines to help you through your endeavor move forward through time and space to each moment you need to understand, and stay no longer than needed." Her dark brown eyes lighten up with golden green hues as something crackles through her. "There I see it, two lines!" Sera tugs at something as if pulling it in close. Lines of cracks tear at the mirror.

The sound is deafening in here; it echoes around me. Each splinter creates a longer crack in the mirror. "You're going to break the mirror," I yell out.

"The lines. I need the power to seal it," Sera screams out. "One tether is barely there, and another is slithering and moving around to avoid me."

Ivan moves up behind Sera and places a calm hand on her shoulder. "Use some of my power to seal what is needed."

As the mirror cracks, it sends me in and out of the mirror. A shiver moves up my spine and meets where the warmth of his hand sits. I am once again looking at my parents in the blink of an eye. I am back with her. I take what is offered before he can finish the sentence.

I am thrown back into the mirror away. Wind rushes past, but I don't hear the mirror cracking or breaking anymore. I look up and see the power holding the mirror together the crack are melding back together and mending themselves. Smoke pours from the mirror, covering their forms. Golden orbs pierce the wind, and smoke fills this place.

I cough out and try to get to my knees. The wind hurls at me, pressing me down. I reach for where the golden orbs were. "Sera, I am still here. What happened?" I cough once more.

They burn brighter. "Tug on the serpent's tail if you begin to fall." The voice that pierces this area does not sound like Sera's.

"Is she gone?" I hear Ivan ask.

"I don't know. I can't see anything other than the smoke in the mirror and a wind-like sound. That is all I'm getting."

"We can ask Flit when he gets here."

"Flit is coming here?"

"Hello can you guys hear me?" I ask.

"Well, to finish the spell with the obsidian stone."

"Sera?" I ask again.

"No, not tonight. Tell him tomorrow would be better."

Weird, they can't hear me. I stand up and brace my hands against the wind; it turns to full blast as I try to push forward.

"Fine, I will tell him to come tomorrow. But continue trying the mirror and see what happened to our daughter." Ivan growls out, a hint of anger pierces his voice.

A loud boom sounds as the door is shut. "Alexia, I don't know if you can hear me or not." Her voice grows quiet. "But I can't stay here any longer. I will not be put under a forgetting spell. I can't sit around waiting and see if this spell worked. I will get where I am going to and try to send for the mirror or work on it another way. Know I care, but I have to worry about myself for once."

Rustling is heard before the fog thickens and the golden orbs disappear.

Chapter 15

M Y VISION JARS AND the surrounding air is hot and dank.

"Do you have time now to explain why you were late?" Quintan's voice seethes.

"I couldn't get rid of Ivan without setting him off. Let's just get through this now since I'm here. When I knocked on your door, you didn't seem to mind the extra time with Ian since he was still out of it." I nudge Quintan from behind.

He stumbles forward, turning around to glare. He hunches down in the small sewer system. "Quiet. We are not the only ones down here." He holds a hand up, listening. "Due to you being late, I had to give him another tonic. I will hopefully be back just in time for him to wake up and continue where we left off."

"You don't think he will be mad?" I whisper like him, keeping my voice low.

"With you, of course, he will be."

"And with you?" I give a coy smile; it slides off my face as my shoe hits something slippery. "Can we be out of here yet?"

"What did you expect? We have to run in the sewers under the city to make sure we are not seen or alert any of the guards. This is the only way out of the city." He catches my arm hard in a bruising manner and holds me upright. "Ian is different when he can be himself, that is."

"Or he is letting you believe another mask that he wears." I breathe in and out through my mouth, not wanting the stench to soak into my nose.

"Take this!" He throws a bottle at my chest.

I fumble with it, grabbing it before it falls to the stone floor. "What is this? Something to make me forget?"

"No."

"You work for Ian. Why not Flit as well?" I hiss out, still following him even though I didn't trust him.

"Look, you said you wanted a way out. I am giving you a way out. It helps that our wants align. With you out of the way, there is power up for grabs and an Ian to console. The drink is a tonic, so that little fox kitsune creature won't come looking for you." His eyes roam back over to me. "End up not taking it, and he will just bring you back to the life you don't want, and I, Flit, and Ian will make your life a living hell one way or another."

"That's all you want is power and a boy?"

"It's what many of us are looking for, isn't it?" He chuckles at that.

"Not me." I stare at the elixir tossed to me and see thick brown sludge slosh around inside. I look closer at the surrounding contents on the floor in the consistency and color it is similar. "When do I have to drink this by? And is this a trick? Did you fill it with sewer sludge instead?"

"Little princess, think she is better than everyone? No, it is not a trick. Though I helped Ian pull a joke off on you earlier, I don't hate you. I was jealous. It should be sooner rather than later unless you think the fox won't start looking for you immediately."

Uncorking the bottle, I upend the contents, shooting it straight back. I take four large gulps to get it down, then toss it on the ground. The glass breaks and crashes around in the soil. Other bottles are right there with it. "Bleh!" I lower my voice immediately after. "Sure, tastes like what I am stepping in."

"Most tonics that are super effective and that work aren't meant to taste good." His complete form takes up most of the room in the tunnel. He ducks down as we go into another smaller tunnel and has to scrunch down lower. He stops us, causing me to bump into him, as I am not watching that closely. "The next part is imperative to stay quiet no matter what. We will be below the guard's barracks and just past where the main guard station is. Once at the end of the sewer line, it dumps out on the other side of town furthest from your home. There you will find a hidden dirt passage nearby, leading to a friend of mine who will portal you to somewhere safe. I will leave you once the dirt path is found."

I nod in agreement and let him know that I have it. During this part, I have to crick my neck to the side so I don't bump my head. Quintan is hunched over, his movements slow, and his breath is labored and loud in these close corners. The straps on my bag dig into my arms as they slide down my shoulders. I hitch them back in place and hold a pillow sized sack over my right shoulder. It is all I could comfortably carry. I brought some clothes, a journal, a few witch books and tools, a small axe, and rope with matches. I felt that I would need some of these things during my journey.

Looking down at my plain brown dress and brown boots, I make sure that I can blend into the background and hide easily amongst the people. I learned that from my first trip away from here, I had stood out too much. My fingers itch to scratch at the neckline of my dress where the necklace Ivan had given me hides. It was the only bit of luxury I allowed myself to take. I would need it if I ever got access to the mirror again.

The plopping of our feet continues for a while until the water rises further up our legs. Though I fight off a shriek of terror, things bump into me and slide by me as the water gets deeper and murkier. Biting my tongue, I hold it in and try to remember to breathe through my mouth instead of my nose. Quintan quickens his pace, reaching a door. Moving as fast as I can without splashing the nasty water into my face, I slide behind him as he scrambles around the door.

A lever juts out beside the circular door. He leans on it heavily before the water starts to drain out slowly. A loud click emits through the tunnel, and the door raises almost all the way up.

He keeps his tone quiet. "Go on." He waves me to go through the door.

The water has all but sloshed out ahead. I poke my head out of the sewer to look around. This side of the wall is further away from the woods, but there are plenty of weeds and long grass to hide in. I pull back and glare at Quintan. "Won't the guards see me from up above?"

His eyes dart from left to right. He also peeks his head out and stares up at the top of the wall. "They hardly ever look straight down. They mostly keep their eyes on the edge of the woods and anything creeping up from there."

I shuffle down on my belly and hunker down in the tall grass, hoping the guards didn't choose now to look straight down. Quintan stays within the protective walls of the sewer; he points to a patch on my left. Patting the wet ground, I fumble for an opening or door. The rustling of the grass is loud in my ears. I spin and crane my head up, keeping an eye on the guards above. I spot them walking along the wall. None peer over the ledge so far.

My hand thumps against something hollow sounding, whipping my head to the change in sound. I rush through, lifting the board up, and almost fall in. After I throw my bags down into the dark hole. I slowly lower myself and grab the board overhead, dragging it back in place.

"What was that?" A loud booming voice calls out from above.

I peer up through the slats, holding my breath, trying to be as quiet as possible. Grumbles are all I hear, so I continue forward. I pat the sides of the tunnel, being careful of my steps. It is pitch black down here with no light to find. My fingers scrape the walls, hoping for a torch. I had matches in my pack, but bare dirt walls are all I find. I pick up my two bags and continue where the hallway leads.

It is not long before I bump up against something hard and wooden. I rub at my nose that had rammed into the door, feeling around searching for a door handle or lever of some sort. It is plain with no handle that I can feel. My fingers move over the bumpy wood, searching high and low. I gave up and pushed against the wood when that did not work. It gave out a groan but did not budge. I scratch and tap against the wood, hoping to call someone forward, but I want to stay discreet.

I huff at the weight of the two bags dragging me down. "It hadn't been that heavy, but I have been carrying it for almost an hour now."

"Hello?" I call out, hoping to be heard through the thick wood.

The door moves and opens up slowly. I look out at the bright room beyond and see no one nearby.

"Are you Sera?" A small voice calls from down below.

I tilt my head, my eyes gliding down, seeing a small girl with blonde hair. There were tiny antlers that protruded from her head. Her large brown eyes gaze up at me in question.

"Yes, are you Quintan's friend?" I keep back, unsure; she made me nervous.

"Is that what he called me? That one can be too kind! One day that will get him into all sorts of trouble." Her fingers twitch as she calls me forward, her head lists to the side, her long hair sliding forward. "Come now, let's hurry and get you where you need to be. We need to be quick. Someone will be here soon."

"Who?" I walk forward but take care to make sure she does not touch me or any of my things.

"None of your concern." Once I clear the doorway, she shuts the heavy door and locks it up.

Something in me tells me to be cautious. She may look like a little girl, but she didn't act or feel like one. "Is there anyone else here?" I ask to make sure.

"Those who need to be." She rushes out of the room and makes her way down the hall.

Keeping with her, I follow to a large open room that has a cauldron in the middle and an empty doorway to the side of it.

"Where to?" She scratches one of her antlers in waiting. The pot is already full and boiling.

Taking a whiff of the air. "Is that lavender and mint?" I lean over the pot. "What's all in there?" I am curious. "Also, what do you mean, where to? Weren't you supposed to have a place set out to send me where it is safe?"

"You have a good nose, yes, there is lavender and mint in there." She nods enthusiastically as she comes over next to the large cauldron with me. "Is somewhere safe a place you want to go?" Her fingers raised to touch my arm.

I back away before her fingers can land on me. "What is your name?"

"Quintan didn't tell you?" The little girl keeps her back to me, facing the boiling spell.

I wait, but it doesn't seem like she is going to answer. "I can pick where I go?" I ask instead.

She turns her head without moving and stares straight at me, waiting.

I blink a couple of times, hoping she will move. Moving further back and away, her head continues to follow me. Her huge eyes unnerve me. "If I can pick, I would like to go somewhere where sides are no longer a thing to a world where they were segregated and split between sides but have come together to be a stronger and better world."

"That is a tall order since most worlds are destroyed or have fallen to corruption before they ever reach that type of utopia you speak of. That being said, I do have a world in mind that I think you would learn a lot from. Are you ready?"

I shrug my bags into a more comfortable spot and nod back at her. She scrapes a long fingernail against her antler, leaning her head over the bubbling spell. Fog rolls out once the flecks of her antlers hit the boiling mass. It spills on to the floor and into the empty doorway. I move to the side, not wanting to get caught in it. Once it fills the doorway, the fog begins to solidify and fill the wooden barrier completely, not falling outside the beams.

"I will be safe?" Walking slowly up to the fog, I swirl my fingers, causing wisps to pull away from.

"Did you ask for safe?" She shrugs.

I hold my breath and push through the veil of fog.

Blinding lights and tall buildings greet me on the other side. The first thing I notice is color fades, and then my vision goes dark.

What is this place?

"This place is huge and wonderful. Easy for me to get lost in." Is the last thing I hear Sera say before darkness consumes me. Ice grips my outer limbs as if wanting to break me apart. The pure freezing temperature and darkness make me confused about which way is up. I try to let out a scream, but nothing echoes out of my throat. Inhaling, I realize that air is not in this place. I try to move my hands to my throat, but they are frozen in place.

My mouth gulps in, hoping for some air. In the next moment, I am thrown back into the light, and air flows freely back into me. I am panting, and everything is sore; I keep running as tall buildings pass. My head spins as I look back and notice no one chasing me. I keep running, though. I notice I am no longer in a brown dress and am now in dark leather pants and a tank top.

A ghostly fox with many tails' pops into existence in front of me. All the tails stand at attention. He growls, daring me to pass through him into his trap.

"Not today, Robert!" I skid to a stop and hang the next left, away from him. "I had one glorious year in this place. What happened? Why is Robert now after me? Did that tonic not last?" These are all questions spilling out in a huff as I keep running.

The streets are bare at this time of night. The three moons in the sky hang low and bright, and my boots splash through puddles from the previous rain we had that day. When I look back, the fox is gone. I give out a shout of laughter before turning at the next building back to the main street.

"Just because I can't see you doesn't mean you aren't around." I bring my fingers up and brush against my temple. My sight turns slightly blue as I scan around me. I see the spirits in their realm and other creatures clogging up the street. I slow down to a brisk walk; I have one eye tuned to the other layers of realities, and my left eye is trained on my current sight. I could not sustain this for long without a major migraine. At the base of my skull, I could feel the tension start. The light already digging in. The blue light pierces my eyes, causing a throbbing sensation behind my eye. "Where are you, you little nine-tailed freak?"

I saw a glimpse of white streak past me around something huge blocking up the street. I pass through easily since my body is still strictly in the main reality. His form hops around and behind, keeping in time with my steps. I spot him glaring at me; he dashes away once he realizes I can see his movements. He takes off, disappearing altogether. "You better stay gone, my friend. This is not the only thing I have learned from this new world."

Turning in the opposite direction, I head back to my flat that I share with a friend. I flick my fingers against my right temple once more, making the other realities fade from view. Shaking my head, I close my eyes for a moment, letting the reality around me settle and massage the back of my neck to release some of the tension I am holding there.

As I climb the stairs to our shared apartment, the steps creak as my weight settles upon them. The hallway is dimly lit; if you didn't know better, it looks sketchy and not a place for most people. After two flights of stairs, I come across our door with the number 215 scrawled across it.

"Home sweet home." I breathe out, placing my palm on the door before opening it up.

"We have a guest," Ophelia calls out.

"Yours?" I ask, removing my boots from the entryway before making my way down the hallway. I come around, turn into the living space, and stop dead in my tracks.

"I think this one belongs to you," Ophelia responds. She notices my face and moves to stand between us.

"Ivan." My voice breaks. "What are you doing here?" My eyes shoot to the windows and then back to the door I just entered.

He raises his hands. "Can we just talk? I'm not here to take you back, I swear."

"He can't either. He let me place him in a circle to keep him trapped. It's a good thing you have told me of him and who to watch out from your past."

"We thought it would be a good idea since we were both on the run from our own worlds," I say as I notice Ivan's confusion. "Why is Robert here, sniffing around?"

"I asked him to keep an eye on you and make sure you are safe. We found out Quintan had sent you away and made him explain what had happened. Getting a hold of his friend was a whole different story. She then put us through a whole thing to find where she sent you. Once here between Quintan and Robert, they could pinpoint you."

"Quintan should not have done that," I growl out, my mind still spinning on how to get out of this place and away.

"Robert didn't really give him a choice. It was either telling him or dying. Robert was very persistent after not being able to find you in his normal way. I was first asked if I knew anything since Ian was useless in his information. He was worried Quintan had done something to you."

"He sure didn't mind when he was watching over Ian and I the day I disappeared. Robert would have just believed everything your brother said and did, just like everyone else."

Ivan smirks and relaxes into the chair Ophelia had given him to wait. "Believe me; you are not the only one that sees him for who and what he really is."

"So, what, I'm just supposed to believe you that you only came here to talk?" My fingers twitch to have a weapon in them.

"If you could excuse us for a moment," Ophelia interjects, wrapping her arm around mine and physically forcing me towards the back rooms. She pushes me into her room and shuts the door. Her room is filled with decorations and fully lived in. Mine is still bare and not much other than what I came here with. Other than some added perks, I had added to my body to help me survive and keep hidden.

"What do you see? Did you see this happening?" I whisper vehemently to her as she lets my arm go.

"Do you think I would not have told you if I saw this? You know how my powers can be. The only thing I see clearly is my destiny and my own paths that I can take." She walks over to her table she has set up her feet light on the fluffy carpet that covers her floors. Touching a blue dome, a bubble fills the entire room with us at the center. "There we are, safe for the time being."

"Quick, do a reading."

"We have gone through this all before. All I ever get from you is a feeling of happiness and then darkness as if you are sleeping. Nothing ever changes, and nothing ever shows more than that. We have tried many times."

I pace in the small area, then kneel on the carpet in front of a trunk. Opening it, I peer into the trunk full of weapons and set some aside. Removing an enormous axe, I take the knives I had and place them back in.

"Do you think that will get you the answers you seek? You always knew you would have to go back. Eventually, you have a daughter to take care of. What if she comes back just to find out her mother will change things to ensure she is never even born?" She cocks her head. "He is cute, and he doesn't seem evil like his brother that you told me about."

"My world is not like yours, and this one, most of the men over there want to make sure their female paring has no power or lives of their own."

"Sounds barbaric. In my world, there are hardly any men left, and there are still issues with what I have told you. One of the reasons why I had to leave."

I nod in answer and stand tall with the axe in hand, ready to face my demons.

"You knew this day would come. If he is your destiny, he doesn't look so bad." Ophelia motions with her eyes to the door. She moves to block the door, her tall frame easily covering it.

The axe is heavy-ended, and swings toward the ground, dangling from my fingers. "Is it so wrong for me to want to fight this a little while longer? I like my life and what we have made of it here. The things we have seen and done together." Anguish is written across my face and in my tone. "Is it so wrong to want to live? I have explained what my future holds if I go back there."

Ophelia's dark arms cross over in front of her. "This half-life is what you call living? You know, we both are meant for more than just this." She gives a sad look of her own. "You know I would go home if I had the option to, and you should as well."

"You are stronger than I am, more fearless."

"No sweetie. I just face my fears, but that does not mean I am not afraid." She shakes her head, and the hard pieces in her hair holding the braids in click together. "It is only because I had to be tough and strong at my center, though I am scared and worried, just like you and everyone else."

"It's different. People take you serious when you speak. I am small and easily ignored." I heft the axe up into both of my hands now. "They will have to listen if I am holding something that can hurt them, though."

Ophelia moves right in front of me and places a hand on the hard wooden handle. "The point is to make them take you seriously without having to frighten them. Always be the one holding the cards, if not all, but be nice enough not to let them see what you are holding and that you have that power over them."

"Oh, they will get my point." I give a wicked smile, hefting the axe higher, catching a slice of light on the blade.

"Let's see what the nice man has to say before you slice and dice him to smithereens." Ophelia taps her boot on the wood floors. Her fingers grip mine to snatch the weapon away. Her eyes meet mine, staring until I relax my grip.

I look away first, turning away from her, stomping toward the door. "Fine, let's see what a little dark and brooding has to say about things." I yank open the door so he can hear my loud voice come down the hallway.

She laughs but stays in her room, putting the weapon away and straightening up the things I had touched, putting them back in an order that only made sense to her. I left the door open so she could still come out easily and hear what was going on.

Marching down the hallway, I slow my steps as I get closer. Coming around the corner, Ivan is facing away from me and looking out the windows that go from floor to ceiling. All three moons have turned red and give a dark blood-like hue everywhere. I am careful not to make a sound as I come up behind him in my sock covered feet. My only saving grace is that my feet are quiet. It is hard to intimidate in fluffy socks. It is the only comfort I allow myself on most days.

His eyes flick back to me, regardless of how quiet I am being. "Why is it doing that?"

"In this world, all three moons turn red for a time each month. It doesn't do harm or cause anything to happen. Just looks a little different from what we are used to. There are other times when different colors can cause harm, but we are a ways off of that time. They also would have closed off the portal, and you would not have been allowed into this world."

"Strange world." He turns back to me fully and gives me a once-over landing on my feet, giving a smile. "How are you?"

"Could be better. Why are you here?" I question immediately.

"It's been a year, Sera. You need to come home. Nothing is as you left it. Do you even know if Alexia is okay?" His face turns shrewd. "It took forever to break my brother down and explain the last day he saw you, which led me to Quintan."

Fire lit up inside me, my lips purse in anger. "Alexia is fine. The spell worked. I made sure of it when I first traveled here. I checked with multiple people to make sure. Don't act like I don't care about her. You don't know me or my agenda. So don't pretend you do.

What does it matter anyway? Aren't you and Jade figuring out things and making changes for the better?"

"You don't know?" He eases up and relaxes a bit after I explain Alexia but scrunches his face back up in confusion.

"No, I have heard no news of what is happening in our world. I was done with it and never planned to come back. I was on the run and didn't trust even finding people that had been to my world just for some news in case they knew me and that I was missing. What happened?"

He moves closer and towers over me, staring straight down into my eyes. "You can't honestly pretend that we don't end up together. Do you think I would still be with someone else when I know my future, and so do you?"

I poke my finger into his chest. "First, I am not a mind reader, so no, I do not know how or why you do the things you do. Second end up together? No, we get together, but I don't think it needs to be a set-in stone forever. We could be together outside of our world and never go back, we could change things, or it could be a one-night stand." I shake my head. My hands shake, taking my finger away. I rub my hands together, hiding the jitters.

"Sera." Ivan crosses the room and envelops me in his arms, stopping me from my retreat. "Know regardless of how it unfolds. I will be here; I am not going anywhere. I am not like others; I do not want to control you or stop you from being your own person."

I let him embrace me but do not hug him back. I can't let myself fold even if I want it, crave it. Taking a step back away from the warmth, I catch a whiff of his dark scent that wafts off of him. It makes my insides crumble a bit more. "What about Jade?"

Peering down at me. "You really do not know? Are you oblivious to everything I have said so far?" I shake my head in answer, but he places a finger under my chin, raising my head up to his. "We never married. It didn't work out. The whole thing was called off."

My eyes widen in response. "But why?"

"I couldn't do it. She wasn't you, and Flit would not push me into something I truly didn't want, not even if it was better for the whole world. No matter what you think of the dark side, he cares about what he calls his and wants me to be happy."

My tongue darts out, swiping across my bottom lip. His eyes track the motion. "Why can't we stay here, then?" I no longer want to deny my feelings if he isn't going to.

His eyes travel around the room. Raising his hands up, they rub my upper arms. "We could for a time." He brings his eyes back to mine. "But we will have to go back, eventually."

"Why would I go back? What is there that I need?"

"Family is there, though you don't like some of her decisions. You still care for your mother. Friends that you had to leave behind. Even though you ran away, don't act like you never planned to return." His ice-like eyes stare hard at me.

My face crumbles as he sees through my façade. I back up, wanting to run.

"Let me prove myself to you before you decide. As I said, we have some time. Let's just get to know each other."

"What about Robert? He was following me." My fingers itch to turn my other vision where I could see the other planes of reality. I force my hands down, making them remain by my side.

"He was following you just to make sure you stayed safe. He will be back later to see what the next steps are."

"I will give you a chance. Give us a chance. But I do not make any promises, you hear me? I will decide when or if I go back to that world, and I will not go back until I have more power to handle some people that I know will be waiting to come at me."

Though my eyes are wide, the light dims, and the color fades away. Ice grips my sides and climbs up my arms and legs. The darkness is absolute and suffocating. I try to make a noise or take a breath. All things seem to freeze in this go-between space.

Voices fade in, but no sight, colors, or anything comes to me. "Flit, what are you doing?" I hear Ivan's voice rasp out in a hiss.

"Giving the girl what she needs to feel safe enough to come home." A dark voice echoes. "She will not return any other way, and this is her ask. I respect that and understand that so should you, given how you were raised."

"I understand it, but I can protect her."

"Until you can't. Would you have accepted that if that is what I told you?"

"No," Ivan grounds out.

"If you want us not to be a part of this prophecy, then I have to be stronger than I am, or we may create a void," My voice rings out.

"Sera, that will not happen. We are going to ensure that," Flit answers.

I can hear a rustling of papers close by. "How do we do that? Without too much danger." Ivan searches through things.

"My boy, anything of worth is going to be dangerous. How do you think I came into some of the power I hold?" Flit gives out a low rumble of laughter.

"No."

"Ivan, I trust Flit. You trust Flit. We can do this together. I know I wasn't a fan at first, but he has more than made it up to me over these last few months."

"Did you hear that, my boy? I am finally growing on her! I always win them over in the end."

"This is going to take some time to accumulate enough." I grin as I interrupt. "Looks like there will be plenty of time before returning to our own world."

Ivan growls out low. "Don't think that means you're getting away from me."

My laughter pierces the silence. "Oh, I wouldn't dream of it."

The noises fade into black and I feel like I am spinning round and round. The crushing weight of love that had poured from Sera I had felt. Making me think of my own dire relationship. Falling into the deepness of despair. My throat constricts with pain and sorrow.

As I sink into the darkness, the cold surrounds me. I am so tired, and I can't concentrate on anything. Where was I? Who was I? Hissing can be heard around me as a slithering is off to my left. I yawn and just peer into the darkness beside me.

"So tired," I mumble out into nothingness.

Pull the serpent's tail.

A memory resurrects into the forefront of my mind. My hand flops to the left, my fingers crawl along the cold floor searching. They fall flat on the floor a couple of times before gaining the strength to move forward. I brush against something; I heave all my effort on, grabbing on to anything.

Tears crush out of my eyes as I scrunch my face in anticipation of a strike or pain from something. It could not be friendly, whatever was in this darkness with me.

"Minx?" A shiver runs through. "You have to send me back. I don't have time for this," Blaise's voice comes out irritated.

"Sorry," I stutter out between trembling lips.

"What is this? What happened?" He kneels down beside my cold form and raises me in his arms. "Where are you?" Anger tinges his voice.

The warmth from his body warms mine when nothing else can touch the cold. My fingers clutch around his shirt, begging him not to release me. "I... I... Don't recall. I was just so tired. I just need to sleep for a little while." I rest my head against his shoulder, happy for the warmth.

He jostles me up, away from his shoulder. "Why are you so cold? I don't think it's a good idea for you to sleep." He conjures a couch to sit down on with me in his lap.

"Am I not already dreaming?" I smile, my eyes sliding shut as I list to the side.

"You called me here. You pulled on our tie. Forced me to come here in this delicate situation."

I yawn once more, calling for a blanket and pillow to appear next to Blaise. "Then, by all means, go." I crawl out of his lap, lying on the couch. This is much nicer and more comfortable than the cold darkness. I would be fine here.

"Where is your mermaid?"

"The siren? I think he would hit you for calling him a mermaid."

"I can take it."

I lift one eye open and see the smirk that crosses his lips. He glances behind him; his leg taps in nervousness. "He is not in this timeline."

"Timeline?"

I nod and re-close my eyes, settling into the softness of the couch. Fingers caress my temple as hair is pushed out of my eyes.

"What did you get yourself into, little Minx?" Blaise states, huffing out a breath.

My head follows his fingers, wanting them to keep contact. More warmth flows down from him into me the more we kept in touch. "That's nice," I hum. "I could ask you the same question since I left you in a precarious state." As his fingers press into me, I find my voice and curiosity.

"I dislike what I do, but I am forced to do what is asked of me. I should be fine, but not for long. I must get back as soon as possible."

"No one is stopping you." I shrug away as my lips pout at the missing warmth, but I need him to know that I did not ask for any of this and would not cage him.

The surrounding room grows dim as there is more space between us. The couch flickers in and out.

"Minx." He cups my face with his warm fingers, the couch settling once again, but the lights stay dim. "Why is our connection weakening? Why are you fading?"

I am quiet for a time, unsure of the needed answer. What was I doing before this? "I don't know." I grip his hand in mine and press his hand against my face, nuzzling it. "You are so warm."

"As a snake, we do not hear that often enough." He nudges me up and over so he could sit with me leaning against him. I press into him, happy to have more contact. He raises his arm and hugs me close to his side. He takes away his other hand, resting it next to him. "I need you to remember something. What is the last thing you remember?"

I bite my lip and look up at him. Him, I need something from him to continue. "You have something I need." I shake my head. "No, that's not it."

"What do you need?" Blaise asks.

I stare into his eyes and sit up fully. It hurt to break contact with him. He is the lifeline, the essence I need to continue. Everything inside me is pushing me forward. I kneel over him, looking at his relaxing stance. "Kiss me."

He sits forward, resting his hand against my chest. A low tank top and black slacks cover my body. The warmth returns as his hand rests there. "Is that what you need?" His lips are a breath away from mine. He waits.

In answer, I lung at him, pushing him back into the couch, our lips crushing together. Fire pours into me, sparking my synapsis through my mind. A journal, a skull, Sera? I deepen the kiss, needing more answers. I would not forget this time; he seems to be the medicine I need. My fingers scratch at his clothes, needing more. His hands are light on my back, but he pushes me into him. I have a knee on each side of his legs; I feel the bulge beneath me and ground into him. He hisses out as his eyes change into that of his animal.

"What are you doing?" He breaks the kiss.

I pull on his hair, making him face me. I kiss him once more, melting our clothes like the first time we dreamed a dream. As I push down onto him, I pull his warmth into me. He gasps out at the feel, the essence he releases. I barely feel the cool black death tendrils. My mind is coming back to me.

He holds me close, his fingers digging into my hips as he controls the speed of my hips and the strength of the thrust.

Memories flick through my mind of me going into the past of Sera and Ivan. The lights rush past me all too fast to call back to me. I raise up almost off of Blaise completely and look down at him, moving his face to the side. I strike with my teeth at his throat as I thrust down on him, grinding into him. He pushes into me with everything he has as I pull his blood into me greedily.

"Little badger wants to play, don't sssssssheee?" Blaise hisses. I feel him bunch, and he is careful as his nails lengthen. He doesn't move or pry me from what I am doing. He simply picks up one of my wrists gingerly and brings it to his mouth, nuzzling it. His nose feels different, but I do not break contact to look at what he is doing.

I lap at the blood there, the warmth igniting fire through me as I begin to grind against him slowly.

"That's it, sssslow and ssssteady." A long tongue flicks at my wrist, tickling me. I try to take back my wrist, be he holds me there against his mouth. He scrapes his fangs against my skin and slowly sinks his fangs in, in time, with our movements. Which spikes our passion even more. "There is little pain if you move in time with the beat."

I retract my teeth but nibble and lick at his neck in time with our movements. I feel the energy I pull in leave me in the same pull from him, going in a never-ending circle. He doesn't pull as hard, so some of his energy stays with me. Which centers me and brings me back from the brink.

I moan out. "I needed your energy. Being in the past takes a toll on the person, and I can't come back from the past till I complete things." I swivel my hips back and forth.

His thin, slit eyes meet mine as he licks my wrist and let it go. He lets his hands rest on my hips. "Your witch side is coming out to play?" He raises an eyebrow.

"No, I wish my witch powers were stolen from me. They shoved me into the past. I guess you could say." His cock is throbbing inside me. My thoughts could not form complete thoughts. Which made my body want to twitch in the most glorious of ways.

"Is that all you require of me, then?"

My shrewd eyes bore down on him. "Stop that. I am not her."

"Who do you think you're not?" His cool eyes meet mine.

"Your master. I do not take from you and give you orders. Yes, I will admit I don't have everything under control and tied up in a neat little bow for you. I understand most of our," I look around in search of a word for what this was. "Get-togethers have been like a harsh storm, but I am trying. Did you expect a mate who would come to save you or a damsel you could save?"

He shakes his head. "I didn't expect a mate at all."

"Our story doesn't really fit well together."

"Perhaps not at all."

He is so still underneath me. "One question. Please answer honestly." I wait to make sure he is listening intently. "If you had a choice and had the freedom you needed, would you choose to have a mate? To have me?" My eyes travel away from his. Though I am courageous enough to ask the question, I no longer felt the courage to see the answer on his face.

"We don't really know each other. I can't tell you a truthful answer when I do not really know you. You are new to all of this, so I would just be guessing."

"How about we make some rules when we meet? That we have to follow to see if there is something here or if it is just sexual and the mating bond."

"What about the siren?" I feel him twitch inside me.

My breath quickens. "What about him?" I squeeze around him. "He is there when you can not be. At the moment, he is not going anywhere. He is less confusing than this is."

"That's fair. I ask for a rule, then one we both agree on." As his pupils enlarge, I clench my muscles around him. "I ask that you try to come to me first. I know I can't always come when called, but I can try. I also want to know; we are all adults, and if he is bringing something to the table, I want to know."

"Are you sure about that?" I raise an eyebrow. "That is a strange request and one that might make you angry. You are not always the easiest to be around." I give that some thought before adding. "But neither am I, I suppose. Fine, I agree."

He nods and lets out a groan as he swivels up into me.

"I ask for a rule as well, then. You don't get to lie to me. I understand if you can't talk about it now, but do not lie to me or try to shield things from me because you think I am too delicate to understand."

"I don't know if I can keep to that rule."

"I am not some damsel, and how can I help or better protect myself if I am kept in the dark?"

"Some things I am commanded not to talk about. What about those times?"

"Either find a way around the command or simply tell me that."

His hands roam up my sides. "Are we done with the talking now?"

A rumble of laughter flows up. "Far from it. I have a feeling we will have room for new rules later. There is one major rule we need to talk about, though."

"What one is that?" His thumbs brush under my breasts, lifting them up for him to gaze upon.

"This heat, if we keep this up, one of us will overtake and destroy the other, or we will both get hurt."

"So, we go slow." His tongue flicks out, swiping across one of my swollen nipples.

The pleasure swells and arks through me. "I can go slow," I pant out, my fingers scrape on his skin, pulling him closer.

"I think you are warm enough. Go finish your mission. Come back to me if you need more. I am being called away." His eyes flick back as if searching for something in the darkness.

My heart gives a heavy thump of yearning. I struggle to release him and untangle my limbs from him. The cold there waiting to take me back. "Yes, I am back to myself. I think I can take it from here."

His eyes swing back to me, pulling me in close one more time. "We are not finished here. You understand me?"

"I will find you if needed," my answer is simple.

I keep my gaze on his and feel the heat radiate from him.

He fades away but holds my gaze as he does so.

"How can a snake be so hot and cold at the same time?" I question myself as I relax on the couch, waiting for the memories to crash back over me.

Chapter 16

"**W**HAT ARE YOU DOING here, Sera?" Jade's venomous voice echoes around me.

My head comes up as I see her standing in front of me. I scan the books that surround us, looking for an immediate exit. "You're not supposed to be here."

Her eyes narrow at me. "I could say the same to you."

"I just needed to grab a book that I knew we had to help on our journey. I will be out of here soon. No need to call the guard or whoever you are about to."

Jade thinks for a moment, pressing her lips together. "So, you didn't even come here to say goodbye to Craig? Mother is beside herself, and all you can think of is how you will gain more power?"

"Papa is passing?" My hand stills on the turning of the pages as I stare at Jade. Her face crumples into sadness.

"His heart is just not strong enough for all that is going on," she wails out. "I thought you, more than anyone, would know how much this would hurt me and understand what I am going through."

Leaving the book behind, I stand and go to Jade, wrapping my arms around her. "I do." My heart clenches in sympathy and the remembrance of my past pain. "Once I gain the power needed to come back to this world. Ivan and I will take a stand against the light side and make our own way. Then, I will come back for you. I always thought of you as my sister and wanted us to be closer than we were."

Her sniffles lessen, and her body shuts down. "Ivan? That's right. You couldn't stand seeing me with him, so you had to take him for your own."

"What?" I take a step back, aghast at what she was insinuating. "Jade, what is wrong? That is not what happened and you know it."

"Your right. I didn't like him, anyway. I am glad to be rid of him. He would have just slowed me down." Jade rubs at her temple and shakes her head.

"Jade, are you sure you're okay? How is mother?"

"Now you want to know after all this time?" Her fists clench in anger, and her cheeks flush with anger. "Just forget about us. We are no longer your family."

I turn for the book, ensuring I didn't lose sight of what I came here for. "Jade, I'm not sure what you are playing at, but I promise when I get back, and things are settled, I will come back for you."

"We will see," she all but hisses.

As I sit in this in between, this time, it seems a lot longer than the first time. I continue to wait for the next scene, already feeling the tendrils of cold sneak back into my blood.

Alexia, Alexia, Alexia. I repeat to myself in my head, ensuring I remember who I am and not get confused.

Light filters in, but the ice remains as it creeps through my veins, chilling my skin once again. Cold creeps up my stomach in a circling motion.

"Twins!" I scream out, shaking a fist and finger at Ivan. "You! You did this to me." I motion to my stomach which is engorged. Tears fall down my cheeks, but I keep staring at the machine, smiling from ear to ear. Ivan grips my hand and hugs me close, staring down at my stomach.

"I know, my love. Aren't they perfect?"

"All a part of your master plan," I grumble.

"Can you give us a moment and print a couple of those pictures?" The nurse nods as she leaves the room.

My hand shakes, but I place it over my abdomen. "Wait. Alexia never told us about a sibling. What does this mean? Did we change the future, or did we mess something up royally?"

"I don't know, darling, but we will find out. Flit will need to know. It has been about two years, and we have more power. We are even stronger together. This is something we can do. We need to go back."

"Flit has helped us get that, but the powers in charge of our world will not like that we joined together," I chatter nervously.

"They don't matter," he growls out. "We will make the world our own and reshape it how we need it to be. There is a reason to go home and fight for what we want and how we want things for our future."

Lights dim, and their chatter fades out, making it impossible to listen. The world spins as I delve down into the darkness. Frost climbs higher over my body.

I have a sibling? Where are they?

Sound filters in first, a buzzing sound. The ice-like shards begin to climb up further on my torso and arms. Making it hard to inhale deeply. It makes me freeze in place and hardly able to move.

"One will be the end and the other will be the beginning. The savior and the villain. Forever at odds, even in the womb," A lyrical voice chimes through.

"Is that why Sera is so sick?" Ivan's voice rings out in the darkness. No visuals come through. The darkness is all-encompassing.

I feel fluttering around my stomach as my fingers thump my stomach in answer. "They are fighting even now?"

"They will need a tether to this world if you don't want them to become the final fate," An older voice crones from afar.

"Can you tell which one will be the savior and which will be the destroyer?" Sera's voice rings out with worry.

"That will not be able to be seen. You will know if or when they come into their powers. Even then, it is unsure you may have a void that will save the world and an all-powerful that will destroy it. That is the bad thing about prophecy reading. It is illogical and will happen regardless of how you try to stop it," She yammers on.

I yawn as I become sluggish, my ears not wanting to pick up and discern the sounds coming to me. The cold is making me sleepy. The darkness rises up and covers the sound, taking me once again. This time I am not sure of how long I pass out. Have I learned everything that I am supposed to? Is it time for me to rest again?

"Congratulations!" A loud booming voice screams through the darkness once again.

"I can't believe you pushed through two babies, a boy and a girl." Ivan chuckles.

"Did you want to give it a try?" I say in exasperation.

"What are their names?" Someone murmurs from close by.

"Should we call her Alexia? Do you think she liked her name?" Ivan's tone tinges with worry.

"Of course, we will call her Alexia!" I tease. "She didn't sound like she hated it. I hope she is doing well. We haven't seen her show up at all."

"Now that we have the mirror back, I would have thought we would have caught a glimpse of her or something." Ivan also comments. "I worry we missed our time with her to discuss such things."

"I worry as well, darling. I was hoping to have more conversation to help us through this situation and better prepare for the future. Do you remember her talking about a brother?" My voice catches in my throat.

"No, not that I remember."

"Do you think maybe she doesn't know she has one? Or does this mean things have changed, and that is why we don't see her because things were changed." My voice quivers with fear.

The question echoes around me in the darkness. The vibration shakes through me.

I have a brother? My own questions ring through my sluggish brain, trying to keep up with things.

"She lied to you. It's what she does."

I can't tell who is speaking, but it sounds as if they are very far away. Sound tunes out. Flames and heat pour in with fire every-where. Two people stand at the center of the flames, a man and a woman in the grips of battle.

"You're not even supposed to be here!" The man yells.

"You would rather hide away from the world, letting these people think you are perfect!" The woman screams right back. The fire burns higher and levels all those around them.

They burn so brightly that all I can see is the light and heat. I cough and choke as more flashes flit through my mind.

"Truth power is hard to control, let alone have."

"It will help me survive what I need to, though, correct?"

"Yes, but you may be worse for it."

"Then a deals a deal." Something chokes off my reply as the dark-ness wraps around me.

Hushed voices filter in through the darkness.

"Hush, she is sleeping. She has been in and out these last couple of days. She needs her rest before the babies come."

"Will she remember the plan?" Ivan mutters.

"All we can do is hope." An older woman answers.

"Why is she becoming confused?"

"Her power is contending with the two powers at war in her belly. We can only guess at what she is dealing with."

I screech in pain as the flames burst around me, burning me to the spot. They quickly turn to ice as I am frozen in place. The orange and red ice is clear and the only thing visible around me.

Sera's face peeks in from the side, noticing me. "Do not look for your brother." She looks away. "Or is this the time to look for him? Where are you right now?" She taps the ice. "Answer me. I should have trusted Flit and let him kill you." She gives a sad look and walks away.

"Quintan, I know we had our differences in the past, but I need you to hide one of my kids away." My voice comes through clear. No visuals once again. The darkness becoming absolute. I am completely frozen over by this point and am unsure how much I am awake. Am I just getting confused? Were things straight in the timeline?

"Both of them? When?"

"No, only the male and first thing when he is born. We need to make a plan and keep him secret. Only Flit will be privy to this information." She gives a quiet sigh. "We will be kept in the dark unless something makes that change."

In the dark, like I am. I being to feel really sad and slump into the cold and give in as I am tired of pushing everything away.

Wait. Didn't she already have the kids? Why am I out of sequence? What is going on? Did I miss something?

I want to be done!

I curl up into a ball, unsure of what is going on. I cry out silently.

A banshee scream pierces my ears. Sobbing quivers from my lips. Opening up bleary eyes, I watch as my fingers rake over my face. "My baby!" I wail. "He's gone!"

Ivan whispers encouraging noises into my ears, trying to console me.

"We couldn't resuscitate him. The girl is healthy and doing well if you want to see her," the nurse says uneasily. Her hands ring around one another in nervousness, not liking that she had to deliver such traumatic news to a new mother.

"Yes, please go get our daughter!" Ivan speaks up while I wail into his chest. His voice tickles my ear. "You are doing great. Remember the plan."

I sob and say in a loud voice. "We didn't even get to give him his name." My voice cracks as a hiccup cuts through.

"Quintan has it. He knows," Ivan whispers so the others would not hear. He climbs on the bed and hugs me close, rocking me as I continue sobbing.

Tears continue to run down my face and my thoughts race around at how I will not be able to know or raise this child. He came from me but would not really know me. A hollow ache presses into my sternum as my thoughts spiral out of control. Darkness begins to fall, and I am released back into my cold, dark frozen prison.

Pictures flick through one by one in quick succession.

"I'm sorry both babies did not make it."

The picture flickers, and Jade is standing there covered in blood. "Why did you take what was mine?"

Another flick and Ivan is standing next to Jade, her hand in his. "You were right all along. You are the better sister." His smile turns pure evil.

"No, you can't mean that," I cry out in pain. My stomach jolts as I look down from there. I see two black shadows protruding from my stomach. I stand there frozen as I truly look down and see the shadows connected to the shadow soldiers that follow Flit around everywhere he goes.

"Good job, my minions. Thank you for taking out the trash!"

Swirls of color push me as if I don't matter as my lifeblood drains from my stomach.

"Sera, wake up!" Ivan pushes on my shoulder, trying to get my attention.

"Oh, Ivan, it was horrible. I dreamed about our children being dead... and," I stutter to a stop as he interrupts me.

"That's not possible, sweetie. You can't have children." He gives a sympathetic look. "We talked about this."

"No!" I look around the room and down at my flat stomach. "But what about Flit? What about Quintan?"

"Who?" He slowly gets up from the bed and makes his way to the sink. He rattles some things there. "The doctor said to take two of these if you showed confusion. Here." He walks back with a bottle and two pills in his hand.

I reach shaky hands out for the medicine and take it without thinking. "Thanks, honey."

Darkness eats at my sight as I grow heavy and delve into another waking nightmare.

Her thoughts turn to mine as I fall into the rabbit hole that is her and my despair. I cry out and yell in my mind, flinging every part of me against the ice that keeps me trapped here. Only voices and flicks of images come through. I can no longer discern if they are real or imagined.

"Alexia and baby boy will forever be lost to me!"

Me?

No! I'm Alexia... Time goes on as if forever.

Or am I Sera... The longer I am in this place, the easier it is to let go of all thought.

Who am I? The darkness spins me in answer.

"Minx, I don't think slow is going to be a possibility for us right now if we keep meeting in these situations," a gruff voice enters the darkness.

Pain filters in as well as a mind-numbing cold. My eyes stay sealed shut, almost frozen that way. Something warm presses up against my lips, shooting warmth down my spine and my toes.

"Don't leave now. You have plenty of trouble still to cause me." His rough laughter filters over my ears. I feel the rumble of his chest up against mine. "I think you will like what comes next, little Minx." His voice quivers above me as his warm arms wrap around me, pulling me to him against the warmth he gives off. Some of the ice melts away as his skin moves against mine.

"Blaise?" My teeth chatter as I whisper his name.

"Yes, I felt our link grow cold. Why did you not come to me?" His hands rush up and down my sides, causing sweet, warm friction.

I squirm closer to the warmth he is freely giving my whole body in need of what he is offering. "Where am I? When am I?" I feel him hard against my lower region as I squirm, noticing how much he enjoys having me here with him. My eyes spring open.

"That spell is surely doing a number on you, isn't it? I followed our tether, which led me to you. Like the other time, this is a dream-like state, remember?" His eyes bore into mine, and worry flickers over his face.

My mind is still hazy, and hard to focus as I look around our dark room. "I think I forgot who I was. Where I was, it made me forget everything but what Sera felt and experienced." I say, my voice hollow. Blaise eases up off of me a bit, my arms snake around him, clutching him to me, not wanting to forget him or myself again.

"I got you now," he hushes onto the top of my head. "Tell me what you need." He holds me tighter, feeling the urgency in my scrambling fingers.

Shivers rack my body as it thaws. "I don't want to go back there." Confusing thoughts race through my mind: dreams, reality, I couldn't keep them straight. I rest my head on his bare chest, unable to look at him anymore. I couldn't stand the worry he had for me.

"Then don't."

That brought my head right up. "I have to."

"You don't have to right now." His fingers trail down my side, caressing me.

My gaze follows his hand. "Where are our clothes?" My eyes glued to the bulge that is still brushing against my leg.

He rakes his hand back up my side and tilts my head back, so my eyes meet his. "There was no time to start slow. I needed to warm you up. Your body needs mine the life power to help sustain the spell until it is finished."

"How do you know so much about magic?"

His thumb traces the bottom of my lip, which sends tendrils of heat racing through me. He moves his thumb and replaces it with his own lips. Warmth pours into me as his tongue sweeps through my mouth. I tangle my tongue with his as I clutch his body to mine.

He eases back, and his lips barely parted from mine. "Stay with me for a time. At least get warm enough to go back and make it through the rest of the memories."

The ice in my veins has turns to slush and quickly melts as we move against one another. My hands dance over his ribs and over his back, feeling the muscles ripple and dance.

"I need to feel something real that is mine." He kisses my neck down to my chest. I move my legs around him, rubbing against his cock, heightening my senses.

"I think that will have to be a discussion for another day." My nails bite into his back. "We last agreed that we go slow, correct?" His mouth moves back up to my lips, leaving little love bites as he moves.

"Slow?" I question, trying to keep up with his thoughts. Is that what we discussed last? It is hard concentrating on what his mouth and light fingers are doing to my body. Why would I have said we need to take it slow?

He chuckles and his eyes take on a green shine from his snake as his chest rumbles with mirth. "I don't think slow will be feasible right now, though perhaps this is slow for us. At least we are talking."

I still feel the pull of ice and cold against my back, warning me it is still there, begging for me to come back. There is a reason I asked for slow what was it. I racked my brain, trying to think back to our last encounter. It felt so long ago. "We didn't do much in our last dream, right?" I ask.

He shakes his head as he brushes his lips against my stiffening nipple.

My back bends, pushing my breasts up, asking for more. He takes one peak into his mouth, his hand rolling the other. My mind turns to liquid fire, cranking the heat up. He releases and blows cool air across the wet tip, which cools me back down.

I try to pull enough thoughts together to continue our conversation before we get too wrapped up in ourselves. "I think since we both didn't complete, I ran out of steam quicker this time." A look of confusion crosses his face. "Because we didn't do the deed." I roll my hips for emphasis.

"Do you know how many more memories you have left?"

I shake my head. My hands want something to grasp onto something more. I funnel both of my hands down, my fingers searching. They find what they are searching for as I grip his cock in my hands. I rub him against me, teasing him as much as he teases me. "I don't know how many more memories I can go through before I lose myself altogether." My hands shake, some from the chill and others from the excitement and the feel of him.

His molten eyes pour into me as his hips gyrate with the motions of my hands. "I will keep you tethered as many times as you need."

"You say that now, but what about before? When you didn't want me there with you, even though something called to me. You called to me."

He flips me down on the couch and lowers his lower half on top of me, pinning my hands in place against him. One hand moves over me and braces over my neck like a choker. "Don't go there. Not right now." His eyes turn dark.

"We need to be more than just this. I need more than just this." My voice comes out on a whimper as my body cools, the heat and friction not keeping the ice at bay.

Blaise nods his eyes are trained on my throat, where his hand lingers. His fingers tighten and loosen as if fighting some internal struggle. "Part of you scares me." His eyes raise to mine.

I stop moving altogether. What he just said shook me to my core. "I scare you?" I ask, unsure of how I could scare anyone, though I try to put up a tough exterior.

A partial smile tips one side of his mouth. His fingers tighten against my throat only barely. It doesn't hurt just a small pressure. They hold not releasing. I wait, unsure if he will explain why I scare him.

"I don't do this."

I bite my tongue, not wanting to break his concentration, fighting my inner self to speak and ask questions. I hope he would say more.

His eyes remain fixed on his hand around my throat. He sighs and releases the pressure around my neck, though they continue to fixate there. "I don't do feelings. I don't do relationships. I was never supposed to have a mate." He frowns.

"You are sure we are soulmates, then?" I ask. I had meant to do more research to find out for sure, but between everything that had happened, it didn't.

"Our tether tells me so and shows that it isn't anything else that it could be. Believe me; I tried reasoning it away."

"Robert said that sometimes soulmates don't go as expected and aren't healthy relationships."

He nods.

The silence crawls by and with each moment, the ice sticks to my back even more. I fight a shiver, not wanting to disturb his thoughts.

He feels the shudder easily with him plastered against me. He moves his hand away from my neck and tweaks a nipple before massaging it. The warmth pushes the ice back.

I feel like I lost a part of him at that moment. I need this to stop; I need him to listen. It is there, just under the surface. He just needs to look. "Stop," my voice is hard and something dark swims through me.

He freezes in place as he looks up into my eyes. His mouth poises over my left, breast with his lower half still pinning my hands in place.

"For now, we do what we need, but we promise each other not to hide from the other and be open and honest... as we can be." I add the last part, knowing there are some things he can't talk about. "We both are struggling through who we are separately and together. We will continue to learn about each other until we both come to a decision. Is that fair?"

"When did you become so insightful, little Minx?" He almost purrs.

"You are not the only one scared and confused. Almost everyone has had more time to figure out and work through things. I have to do it faster than everyone else, or I will let everyone down."

His eyes follow mine. "A heavy burden, for sure. Release me, and we have a deal. We will discuss this more in person."

"Deal," I respond, releasing him.

He raises his lower body off of mine. My arms move from under him, pulling his head down to mine. My lips brush against his, sealing our deal there. The fire smolders again, the cold air leaving only room for heat and steam.

His tongue slips against mine, and from there on there. There is no question about how we feel about each other at this moment.

We move slowly but with purpose instead of hot and heavy like the other times.

He eases back before sliding home nice and slow. Delectable tingles explode over my sensitive skin. He pulls me up onto his lap as he sits back. I wrap my legs around him, ensuring he is as close as possible. His tongue mashes into mine as we rock into one another. The heat searing us, together. My moans push into his mouth, filling him as he grips my sides tighter. The fire builds, and our passion fills the room as the heat grows hotter. Ice is all but a blip in my memory right now. Everything is warm and slippery, bringing pleasure to a delectable height. I feel the edge as I step off, cresting over the side. He continues to move against me as I untangle our tongues and let my head fall back as I go over. His hands were on my back, keeping me from falling back as his hard cock brushed deeper still.

"You are beautiful." His lips dance over my skin.

I have no words to respond with. My limbs would not answer me. He holds me and lays me back on the soft couch.

"Alexia, bring life to our playground, so I know you have enough power to get through the next memories."

He called me Alexia. I don't think I have heard him use it except for our first meeting, or did I? I glance around our desolate play space, only the couch here. The rest is pitch black around us. The heat covers our small space, but the cold is still there, surrounding our small bubble of fire.

"I'll need more." I take a sharp intake of breath as he rolls his hips, which causes him to hit that spot way back that sends flutters through my stomach.

"I have more to give, but I need you to create something for me."

What he is doing with his hips is sending sparks through my body straight into my mind, making it hard to concentrate on the words that he is saying. "Create? What?" I gasp out as he thrusts into me.

He slows the tempo to be measured. Which makes me burn more. My arms and legs come alive, pulling him back into me, trying to speed him up. "Naughty Minx," his voice goes lower. The timber of his voice touching something deep inside.

My lower area constricts and squeezes. "Say more."

He pushes fully back in, bringing his mouth to my ear. "Create my Minx." His voice is still low in that timber voice that is almost a growl.

"I created the mirror last time. Is that what you want again?" I ask as I struggle to find purchase on his slick muscles, wanting to keep him from drawing back out oh so slowly.

"What do you need?" His voice rumbles as his hips move again, rolling his cock into that sweet spot.

"Fuck!" I yell out, not wanting to hold back anymore. My mind locks on to a scene but skitters away, unsure. His hand moves back over my neck, giving pressure once more. I lock my eyes on his arm. The scene blurs as what I want appears on the scene. A black choker is around my neck, and connected to it is a chain. I put the end in his hand.

He smiles and slips from me. "That's a good girl." He rumbles in my ear as his fingers feel the cloth around my neck. "Flip over," he commands.

I slowly roll over and bring myself up to my knees. He holds the leash in his hand tight and tugs at the slack. He toys his head in my juices and then slams back into me. I gasp out as pleasure zings through me from head to toe. His hand does not lessen on the leash, keeping my head up. Feeling it digging into my neck works me up into a frenzy as his movements speed up. I moan and cry as the pleasure rolls around me, never letting up. He pulls harder on the chain, bringing my front half off of the bed bending me back to him. He keeps up the pounding tempo. Once he has the chain so short, he wraps his hand around the front of my neck and holds me there in his strong embrace pumping into me. I fall over the edge as his other hand slaps my clit. He rubs against me with his palm, soothing the pain and milking me on him. He pumps a few more times and then unloads with me.

He slowly lowers me down on my front and slips from me but stays close, keeping the warmth surrounding us. "Remove the collar, Minx," he whispers against my shoulder blade.

I am still in bliss. My fingers twitch, trying to do what he asks. It takes a few times, but the choker disappears.

He kisses the back of my neck, flicking his tongue over where he thought he had hurt me.

"You must go back and finish what you started. Come find me in your grandfather's court when you complete your mission. "

"You are in his court?"

"Soon I will be."

"Does he know?"

"You can ask me all the questions you can think of, and I will answer you once you get out of this spell. We can use this link for other things than this. We can talk to each other and learn from one another. But first, I need you to go back in and complete these memories.

"But you are so warm," I pout, wanting to stay here instead.

"So are you, my fiery Minx. Now go."

My mind melts back away from the warmth and into the blistering cold. At the heart, though, lives a flame that burns bright from the fire started.

CHAPTER 17

"**A**LEXIA! YOU LITTLE SCOUNDREL," I call out as I approach the crib. It is basic and can be moved from room to room with us.

"My lady, why do you not leave the child with a caregiver, so she is not in the way of these proceedings?"

I scrunch my nose at him. "We keep some of her stuffed animals and toys in here, so she does not get too fussy. The people want to see her. She brings hope for our people." I give a sweet smile. "If they want to address a baby in the room, they can let both of us know."

The man blushes and averts his eyes, lowering his head. "I am sorry no one said anything. I just thought it would be easier."

"Arnold, why don't you start seeing the people in?" I say in a crisp tone, not wanting to be too cruel but also letting him know this is no longer up for discussion.

I lean over and notice her laughing and grasping at the air. My eyes scan the empty big conference room. The only other things are the two seats at the front of the room. I glance back down, worrying if there is someone or something here with her.

That's me! Wait, this looks familiar... I watch, waiting.

My fingers slowly rise to my temple and flick something there. My vision changes, allowing me to see the other planes of existence. The colors and light dance throughout the room, many creatures going on as if I do not exist. Sounds flood my ears as I press on the top of my left earlobe, they were garbled and strange. I could only pick up sounds if I concentrate on one soul, but that doesn't necessarily mean I can understand their language.

A bright light burns close by the crib. A young girl, by the looks of it huddles and crouches behind the crib. I can clearly see her between the empty bars. The little baby's hands stretch and reach. The light looks like her hair is up and out of the way.

That is also me! I hid behind the crib when I noticed the strange woman, but Quintan said that it was just a memory.

A smile twinges on my lips. "You are here. You made it," I whisper, but only loud enough for me to hear.

A gust of wind rushes through the huge open windows, tossing the sheer curtains above and over the crib. They billow out as the baby stares at the dancing cloth above her. She smiles and kicks out, laughing in delight. I bend over her and stare at the precious thing before me. My hair tosses around in the wind. I lean down further, brushing a light touch against her cheek.

"There, there, little one. Mother is here." The light form perks up and rises from her crouched place. She leans in, as if listening intently. "Was Flit playing with you again?" I scan the room, searching, waiting, hoping she is the only one with her. My eyes track the soul that stands over the baby and ensure nothing is going on. I am sure this is also my daughter, but I should still be careful.

My eyes are glued to the light. I see her face move with animation. Though I couldn't see her features clearly, I could tell she is talking or attempting to. It takes a moment, but the sound finally reaches my ears. "Mother, that frown seems familiar."

My frown deepens before I school my features once again. I didn't know I was frowning; Arnold would be all over me if he caught that. I had to school my features to always seem pleasant or was supposed to be working on it.

I move my eyes away from her as she moves around. Keeping sights through the corner of my eye. My hands shake as I move them in the blankets, staying busy and acting as if I could not see or hear her.

The baby kicks out and giggles in play, trying to tie her legs up in the blankets more.

The bright light comes around and brushes against my side before I can move out of the way. Warmth zings me and sends tickling fingers wherever we touch, kicking out at the wheels on the crib below. I unlatch it so I can move away. I skirt past her, needing to get clear of her for fear of laughing out loud and her catching me in the act.

"Convenient." The light voice rings out, tinged with anger.

I laugh out, not able to keep it in any longer. She is so different compared to this happy, carefree baby who laughs at almost everything. She is even different from the timid girl I met in the mirror. There is some fire there, for sure.

"Can you hear me?" Her voice quivers in question.

I bite my tongue, fighting my voice. I couldn't answer her. At the front of the room, I roll the baby and crib closer to the seats. Hard wood makes my steps echo as I cross the center. Some people were trickling in. They give hushed murmurs as I roll by; they didn't want to be too loud in case it would disturb the baby. No one would want a crying child to contend with. I'm not sure when this Alexia is from or what she knew. She didn't sound like she was sure of anything or knew who I even was. Flit promised he would help things work out. He has been busy lately with the lost one. A tear slips from my eye, and my hand swipes at it, trying to keep my thoughts and feelings about it all hidden away.

"Ma'am, are you ready?" Arnold hurries in. Everything on him is in place except a few tufts of hair. They rise and catch on the wind that is coming in from the open windows still.

I nod, trying to keep my composure once again. "Of course, Arnold."

"Where is Ivan? Is he running late?"

"He is around somewhere. Why don't you go find him?"

He nods and bows as he leaves the room in a rush. Some guests laugh at this whirlwind of a man. "He means well," I jest.

I peer at the crowd pooling into the room as I sit down in one of the two chairs, rolling the crib to sit beside me. I notice the light has stopped through the room to examine the chair I sit in. They were spectacular they would take anyone's breath away.

As I see enough people have come in, I make my voice loud so all can hear. "We will begin soon, but please ensure we use our inside voices as much as possible." The baby screeches in joy as if saying watch me defy my great mother. I lower my voice so just the baby could hear. "You are just rotten. Just plain rotten."

A woman grows closer, garbed in a yellow dress. Her green skin and bulbous nose are nothing compared to the bright dress. "Children will always try to defy their parents no matter how hard we try."

"Yea, I used to do that to my own parents."

"And where are they now?" She grows closer.

"I'm sorry. I don't think I have met you before. What was your name?" As I register her growing closer to me, I bring my full attention to her. The light is walking around and taking in the sights. She sees the crowd but only a part of it. She shies away, keeping her eyes on me, the baby, and the thrones.

"Yes, I am Jill. I came in with the new goblin group. I just wanted to say hello and thank you for taking us in. You didn't have to, but you did. My own babies thank you as well." She gives a smile that reaches her eyes as she peers at the baby beside me.

"Welcome, Jill. We are happy to have you. I hope you can help us become even greater as we strive to unite our two sides."

She shrinks down and gives a brief nod. "Of course." Fear taints the air.

"Don't worry, you are safe here, and you don't have to do anything you do not wish to. You will not have to fight; all we ask is that you help, but that is up to you to decide. Your dress is beautiful."

Her nod becomes more exuberant, and her face is all smiles. "Thank you so much! I created it."

"We need more beautiful things in this town. You should open a shop or see if others would purchase your creations. You will be busy in no time if that is what you want. I myself would order something." I give her an encouraging smile.

"More than anything."

"I will send Arnold tomorrow to discuss what we would need to get a small shop up and running for you. It will create jobs and something our town is seriously lacking."

She gives a little hop and a curtsey before slipping away. I pull the crib closer and lower the bar. So that I can check on her, she is rolling around off to the side, bumping into the bars, demanding to reach something on the other side.

My long brown hair pools over the side of my shoulder as I lean down, blowing raspberries and tickling her tummy, I try to get her attention.

"What is this?" The light questions. "Why would this help?"

The light dims in answer. She sounds so dejected and alone. My heart breaks as I jerk back up from the baby. I glance from her to the baby. "All will make sense soon, won't it, my love?" I say cryptically, hoping she will hear my message.

"Sera," a stern voice emits from behind me.

I turn around, not sensing him. He is like his father's shadows, always sneaking up on people when he could. The light races away behind us. I let her go without following her, hoping I would get to see her more later.

"Ivan," I say just as sternly back to him.

"You promised." He cocks his head to the side. "They must be able to look at their new heir, my sweet." He grins as he strolls to the other seat. He sits back comfortably and tosses a hand, palm up, waiting.

I smile back at him and place my hand in his, giving it a squeeze. "They can't have her, Ivan." I keep my voice low as the crowd filters closer to our seats. "Let's leave this all together and start again. They don't need us. This is too much for someone so small." I cover her in blankets, hoping that will protect her from what is coming.

"What the fuck is this place? What are all these things?"

I laugh to myself. Exhibit A is hiding behind our seats, sneaking at the crowd.

"What is it, my sweet?" Ivan pauses, his eyebrows cast down in worry.

"Oh, nothing, you brute. I was just thinking about all these people. They will look to Alexia to lead them. What if she does not want to lead them, though?" I frown. Sadness overcomes me, unsure of the future. I twist the necklace around my neck, playing with the black stone in the middle. "What if she doesn't know how to lead them?"

Ivan's eyes pierce mine, reading the hidden question. His hawk-like eyes rove around the room. "She is strong." I push the crib closer to him, so it looks like we are just spending time with the baby and giving an excuse to keep them all at a distance. "She is the best of both of us," he states. "We will teach her and help her grow into whoever or whatever she wants to be."

"What if she does not understand? Or more so, hates us for it." The tears I had held back earlier now flow freely down. I knew she could hear what we discussed, but I didn't know if she could fit the puzzle pieces together. From what we have researched and our talk with her we knew something happens when we are not around, but that does not negate the responsibility of the precautions we put in place for when we can get into her life to help her create a future. I just wish she will understand and not be too angry with us.

My thoughts race at what I wish I had time to tell her. *Alexia, I wanted time to explain everything to you. I had hoped to see you one more time. I looked in the mirror so many times hoping for you to be there. I want you to know I am no longer that young, hurting woman you previously met in the mirror. Never think I didn't want this future or you.*

Perhaps I could tell the light or at least write it down for her to find one day, but I didn't know if she would find it. I needed time alone with her. To let her know. The tears keep running as my thoughts continue to clash with one another.

Ivan gives a low growl, not liking where my thoughts were spiraling. "We have to do it this way, you know that. The seer explained all would be lost if we did not. We must trust in things and believe they will be okay in the end. I am sorry for my part in this, but know you are the light to my darkness." He cups my cheek in his palm as his thumb brushes over my tear that drips, catching it.

I nod, trying to find my resolve. "And you are the darkness to my light." I grip his hand in mine as I meet his eyes, kissing the center of his palm. "Know this little one," our heads turn as one to look down at the baby. "We are here for you regardless of what you think and know. Though we might not physically know; we will be pushing things to guide you."

A small intake of breath gasps behind me. It takes everything in me to not turn to her.

"This is not real."

I place my hand on the baby but turn my head, looking straight into the light that is my daughter. "Oh, but it is." I go back to looking at the baby.

"Is she here?" Ivan lowers his head, keeping his voice down low.

"Yes, but not like last time. I think she used magic to see a memory of her own, not through me." My hand rubs over the little one's tummy.

"Do you think the time is close?" His eyes scan the groups of people around us, making sure to check each of the masses gathered around us. Low grumbles can be heard from the crowd, which is growing antsy as they wait for us.

"I'm not sure." I bite at my lip, worrying. "Surely not." Giving a shake of my head. "No, there is still time. There has to be."

"Be strong, my love and trust, that it will all work out. You took a chance on us, and I ask you to take a chance on Flit to finish things. He will see it out. He has helped us so far with things."

"I didn't always want this or think I didn't, but I will always choose you and them now and always. I wouldn't change things for a second."

"I know what is in your heart, my love." He places his large hand over mine and the baby. "You don't know what you were missing until you were in it."

"I am glad you fought so hard to keep me in your life until I could come around to the idea of us." The baby starts to cry and kick out, not liking the surroundings that were around her. She wants happy vibes and could feel the tension and fear surrounding us. "Ivan, sweet, she is getting fussy. We need to lay her down soon. Shall we give her the gift before anyone else visits her tonight?" She mouths to Ivan alone, *just in case.*

Ivan tsks but pushes the crib closer to me.

"Go on, be quick."

"I'll be but a moment." My eyes take in every inch of Ivan, promising things her hands could not at the moment.

Ivan growls out. "Woman, you are a danger."

I give a hoot of laughter, throwing my head back as I put the lip of the crib back and roll it around behind our seats, moving to a hidden room.

I hear Ivan call out behind me, "All right, calm yourself! She is changing the babe. Do you want a stinky infant on you?" he says gruffly.

I laugh once again but peek to ensure Alexia is following behind, taking my time just in case.

Baby Alexia gives an upset little gurgle. "Shhh…" Sera whispers. "Lexi, no giving away our secret, no crying now." Walking in, I stand back, keeping both the baby and the full-grown one in my sights. The light skitters around, unsure since this room has nothing to hide behind. Other than the glass door that led to the woods and some cabinets. "I will deliver you the greatest gift my power can bestow on you, a warrior to protect you when you may need it most." She finally settles into a corner behind me, craning my neck. I look at her, hoping she will understand why I give her this.

Turning back to the baby, I grasp at the chain around my neck. "Thank you, Flit, for all the power you helped me build." I whisper more to myself, barely audible. In a louder voice, "Your life will not be easy being of mixed blood of light and dark. We will try, regardless of where we are, to protect you as much as we can and teach you to protect yourself. Your father is of darkness, and I am of Light. Both can mix to create a most wonderful thing." My fingers tickle the feet of the baby, trying to calm her screeches down.

"Beliefs worry them, but our blood is the same. Know this to be true."

No! I try to scream out with venom. This was the last memory of her being alive! What would happen if I was stuck in her while she died? Do I just stop existing or do I go back to my time? No one ever gave me instructions on how to run this thing.

Sera! I try to yank and pull her to a stop to not continue on anymore. The scene continues to move forward as she creates the shadow creature. *Damn it! I need you to hear me. You need to stop. Stop right now. Run out of this room. They are probably already settled in taking care of Ivan. We can change this. You said you have more magic, that Flit helped you acquire. Use it to change this to change our future. I will forgive you for everything and be okay with all that happened if you do not let what is about to transpire to happen. I do not want to feel your death. I don't want to live through that sadness.* I yank and reach for anything I can. As we grow closer to Jade's supposed arrival, the terror swells through me. The ice holds me in place. The fierce blizzard is back, swatting at my small existence. I struggle to find a tether to hold on to.

Blaise! Please hear me. I need you, please. I call out, struggling to make any connection I could think of. Wind whips around, and my mouth goes dry. Bouncing back each and every time, I try to strike through. Something blocks me from even grasping the tether that bound Blaise and me. This is it; this will be the death of not only Sera but of me as well.

As I spiral out of control, looking, fighting, crying through my fear and horror. The next actions play as if in double time. All the while, my body grows colder and more numb of feeling. I couldn't calm down enough to concentrate on anything happening I just want out. I want to be free. I don't want this. *Trix, get me out of here, you imbecile. You were supposed to help me, not kill me... Maybe he sent me here to kill me. Maybe this was the intent all along. What if I had it all wrong, and he is working for the enemy? I didn't know much about him other than one of his masters was the necromancer, and I didn't even know her very well other than she came from the dark side.*

A small but clear voice rings out from me... "Always question everything," no not me.

I hear an anguished cry blurt out. "Mother? You can see me?"

"I couldn't always." I rub at my stomach, wanting to spill everything. "Look to the darkness to find your light."

"Where are you? Where can I find you?"

Did she know? How could she? No one was in the know other than Ivan, Flit, and I. This was a way I could clue her in, I would have to trust Flit with the rest. "We will meet one day again, though I doubt the way you expect."

The ice spears through my heart quickly, and cool air breezes as I feel them slice into me. Jade holds her hand up, fueling a steady stream of wind, holding me in place as she holds the air away, taking what again isn't hers. My sight is the first to fade and go. My body slowly starts to shut down one by one, but I hear Alexia's questions and crying roll through me. I want to fight for her, struggle for her, for how could I not fight for my flesh and blood? How could I walk away from her? This is the price I had to pay. If I did not, things would be so much worse. But I would be lying if I said hearing her pain and anguish is easy. Her hurt cut me in more painful ways than I can even explain.

"Trust in Shade, trust in yourself." I call out meekly before everything crumbles around me.

Trust in Shade? He took my magic; he took my power. I am in this mess because of him. Why would she say to trust him? He didn't stay to help me through things; he didn't stay to keep me safe; he left and ran off with what's mine. Forcefully took what's mine.

The coldness crushes me as everything is dark and empty. The pain we feel and the pain I felt for her loss echoes around me. I feel helpless and empty with all that I couldn't do, but I feel like I should be able to. Sera not feeling good enough or that I would be angry with her, my own angry feelings at what keeps my family apart. Rage seeps into my being so consumed, but it wasn't hot and fiery like I was used to. This is a cold, calculating rage that wants to exact revenge. It feels as if I am in an icy river, heading over the edge with no end in sight. I didn't know which way was up or if I could get out of this. I was stuck, yet very fluid all at once. It is too much to feel. Numbness set in as my thoughts go silent and all becomes quiet. A void-like state entraps me, which is even worse than when it was all coming at me at once. Thoughts creep into my mind.

You can't do this, you aren't good enough, no one will ever want you. Is this what she felt as she passed? Am I feeling what she feels, or are these my own demons? *You aren't strong enough, you will not make it through this, you are a fraud.*

The thoughts keep on attacking, spearing through my soul, cutting all the same but drawing no blood. I would give anything to go back to being able to feel something. I couldn't even feel the cold anymore that encompasses me.

No sound or thoughts from anyone other than my own were eerily quiet. I couldn't think, I couldn't speak, and I didn't even know if I could continue on existing. I lay there waiting, feeling, and doing nothing.

Something tugs at my back like I am at the end of a long rope. I ignore it, not even sure it's real. Another jolt goes through me as it pulls me back. My sluggish thoughts try to find purchase on what is happening. The void is thick, and it grips me into not wanting to do anything. The tug is harsher. I slowly push out a hand, trying to find something.

A dark shadow drops onto my wrist. I barely feel its feather-light pressure. I look at it, waiting, trying to decide what it is. It tightens around my wrist and digs in as it yanks me up. I cry in pain as my arm feels like it will be pulled out of its socket. Red hot fire races down where my skin is getting pinched by the black rope. I am being dragged in an upward motion.

"What would Blaise, your mother, Natasha, think if they saw you like this?" A low rumble rolls through my mind.

"Who, what, how?" My mouth feels as if it is full of cotton. My mind can't keep up with the turbulent thoughts.

"If you know what's good for you, let me stay lost." Is all that answers me.

Another yank at my back tugs me clear, and I am thrown from this shadow world.

"Are you back, master?" A black little skull peers at me in the low lamplight. The room is dim and dark. The curtains are drawn but I can see a slit of light between them. "You were gone so long. They became worried." He shakes his head and bobs around. "I didn't though I knew you would make it through, other master assured me you would make it through. I knew what we were doing was right."

"Trix?" I ask, my voice barely able to come out as a whisper. My body feels sore and needs a good stretch. I crawl, moving my limbs to do just that and am unsure if anything will kink up, so I continue to go slow.

"Yes, I am here." He spins around in the air and hovers next to me. "None others are here at the moment. It will not be long before they check on you again."

"How long have I been gone? Did I leave, leave or just go to sleep?" I whisper, my throat feels clogged. I need something to drink to remove the blockage.

"You have been gone for about two weeks. How did the memories go? Did you find out everything you needed? Was it a joy seeing your parents and learning everything that brought you here?" He gives a happy little loop in the air. "Your body was here physically, but your mind was gone, and no one was home. I explained to them that the spell was done with my help." He raises up as if he is proud of what he made happen. "They were upset, so I had to hide and stay hidden." He becomes uneasy. "Lady master has not been happy with me and refuses my help at every turn. They didn't interrupt the spell, though, for fear of making things worse. So, they checked on you quite often to ensure I was not corrupting you." He turns to the door as if glaring at it, angry with the people that kept him away.

My mind is sluggish. My eyes droop forward. "Why am I so tired even with being asleep this whole time?" I reach a hand out next to the dim light for a water bottle sitting on the corner of the table.

"You weren't really asleep. There was a lot of power used by you. You looked unwell a few times throughout the experience. I was unsure if you would make it back since you were not doing well just before you woke up. I almost went and got Natasha and them."

I tip the water back after uncapping the bottle. When the droplets cascaded down my throat. I intended to take it slow, but instead, I guzzle deeply. My body taking over thirsting and craving what it hadn't had in a while. I gasp out after downing the bottle completely. "How am I even alive?"

He moves up and down as if shrugging. "Magic. It's a wonderful thing."

"Where did I leave that journal?" I look around the bed, noticing I had new clothes and was tucked into new bed sheets. I shook my head, not wanting to worry about what happened while I was gone for almost two weeks.

Trix rushes around, circling the bed. "Down here." He shoots under the bed, pushing something out so I could reach down and pick it up without moving too much. I open the box and notice the ruby and journal are still there.

I look at the ruby and lick my lips, tempted. I shake my head and roll it aside, maneuvering the box. Picking up the journal, I lay the box down at my feet. Opening up, I flip through the last journal entries. Scanning them, I notice my mother's handwriting across the page. I rapidly flip to the end, where empty pages of cream paper flip by. I rush back to the last writing and scan my eyes over it. After reading the last words, I turn the page and hang my head in anguish, closing my eyes, unable to take the pain that hammers at me, unable to deal with the trauma I had gone through and witnessed.

"What is that?" Trix questions hovering over me, wondering what I am up to.

"It's blank." I call out, not opening my eyes. "It's the end of my mother's journal."

"Are you sure?" He asks.

I open my eyes and look down at the paper, and to my surprise I notice scrawling across the page as it seeps up from below. However, it is not the same penmanship as Sera. "What is this?" I quickly glare at Trix. "What did you do? Did you touch something?"

I flip to the next page and see the writing continue on.

"No, master. I wouldn't touch what is yours..." He sees my stare and corrects what he just said. "Not something like this."

"This isn't my mother's handwriting. Whose is it?" There were just two pages filled up, and nothing else came through.

"What does it say? Maybe they say in the writing." Trix pushes at my shoulder, wanting me to read. "What if it disappears?"

"I hadn't considered that." My eyes roam the page, scanning for a name. They slow down to actually read what is on the page.

Dear Alexia,

By now you have unlocked the secrets of your parent's past. Maybe you do not have answers to your own past, but you do have something. With that, I want to offer you condolences for what you must have witnessed and assure you they both are okay in a roundabout way. I can't explain everything in order for you to gain that understanding. You will have to come to my domain to see what you want to know. Sera lives, and you have a brother. If I write more than that, I fear others will find out what they are not supposed to. Keep this journal well hidden. There is a spell on it, but even a great one like this can be broken. I have watched over you and made sure to push things into place to gain this future. I will not state my name here, for I feel you already know it, and if you don't, you will be headed my way soon enough.

I will warn you that not everything is as it appears and to take care when dealing with the darker side. Not all are misunderstood. There are truly some horrific things in this world, but in our long lives we have learned there are things worth fighting for that are just as beautiful. Come see for yourself to know what wonderful things can be. Do not fret, she is alive. Quintan will help you gather your forces.

Always watching

"Always watching? Why didn't they keep me safe like they wanted if she is alive? Why was I stuck with Jade for so long? If someone was watching, then that means they let this happen to me!" I screech out, my fingers bend the edges of the book, gripping the paper and scrunching it up.

The skull floats to the door, then races over to the bathroom door, sliding into the darkness there. "Alexia, are you awake?" I hear Natasha call out.

I don't hear anything but know she must be on her way. "Coward," I hiss as I scramble to get the journal back into the box. Looking around, I am unsure where to stash it. Under the bed would take too long, and I'm sure my legs could hold me. My whole body feels weak with disuse. I shove it under the pillows and lean back as the bedroom door creaks open.

"Oh, good, you are awake." Natasha rushes in on socked feet. "Are you okay? How do you feel?" She glances around the room, taking notice. She notices the empty water bottle thrown on the bed. "Do you need some more water? Quintan will be glad that you have made it through this trial."

"Quintan..." I zero in on her as I lean against the pillow with the metal box the corner digs into my back. "Where is he?" I ask.

"He is down below. Do you need more rest?"

"I think I have rested enough, don't you?"

"What's wrong? You don't seem yourself," she asks hesitantly. She slows down before getting to the bed fully.

"Why would I be myself? I have been gone for a couple of weeks, and you expect me to still be myself?" Anger rises in me. "Take me to Quintan."

"Trix was here, wasn't he?" Her eyes zero in on the bathroom. "Don't get huffy with me. Did you learn what you needed to?" I give a tight nod and try to remember that Natasha has been the only one that has helped me through this entire ordeal.

"I'm..." I let the words hang there.

"At least you're learning." She rolls her eyes. "Don't forget who has had your back this whole time and is still here for you."

"What has happened?"

"While you were on your own adventure, we have people reporting of hearing of a man named Shade that is stirring up information. The other front is your uncle has been all quiet, a little too quiet if you ask me. Quintan has been focusing on Shade since you two are connected, and he was worried you may have gotten stuck in any spell that Trix had helped you with and couldn't get yourself free due to not having any magic."

That name grates on my ears. Quintan, he seemed so horrible in Sera's younger years. He could not be the same person. Obviously, he has grown, but is he here for his own nefarious plans? He craved power. Maybe he still does.

"Take me to him," is all I say.

"To Quintan?"

I nod, ending the discussion.

CHAPTER 18

WE BOTH FIND QUINTAN in the library with Robert, Robert's wife, and the necromancer.

"Alexia!" Margret calls out. "Are you okay? The fire sisters have been staying with me while you were away." She says immediately.

Natasha helps me through the doorway, holding most of my weight up. My legs are full of pins and needles, but I am determined to talk to Quintan. I hadn't even felt the fire sisters or worried about them upon waking. I nod my thanks but feel horrible that they were not a priority.

Margret moves forward to my other side, wanting to help. I let her. "It seems like that spell was used at a great time; you slept through most of your heat cycle. I wouldn't count on that for the next one, though. Those types of spells are dangerous and hard to come out of. We were worried there were a few times when you didn't look like you were going to make it."

"You shouldn't be up in this condition." Quintan gives a disapproving stare but does not move to help.

"Why are you worried?" I throw back at him. We would have this out now.

He looks stunned as Margret and Natasha lower me into a chair across from Quintan. "No, As Margret stated, we were worried about you and after being who knows where for two weeks because someone couldn't control their minion." His eyes cut to Jazmin.

"Didn't that minion tell you exactly where I was and what spell was cast?" I ask, waiting to see where he would go with this.

"Yes, that is why we were searching for Shade. He had your powers and thought that would be the best start in helping you get out of wherever you were."

Jazmin's cool eyes hide everything. She does not react to Quintan's outrage or comments. Just now, she sits back and lets the events unfold around her.

"I let her know our plan," Natasha pipes in.

Quintan nods. "You should rest more. That must have taken a lot of energy from you. I don't know how you are still alive after all this time."

"Were you hoping that I would waste away? It doesn't seem like you searched for any way to get me out faster."

Quintan's eyes scrunch in confusion. "Why would we want you to waste away?"

Natasha's voice is small and unsure when she speaks. "Trix told us to have faith that things would turn out like they should. Something about his master knowing how things would shake out."

"Which is why she is here." Quintan points to Jazmin, zeroing in on her once again. "She has dominion over her little skull. She controls him, and yet she claims to know nothing about the subject or what Trix is talking about."

I cock my head to the side as I sit up straight in the chair, giving him my full attention. "So, I don't have a brother?"

Looking him straight in the eyes, I see the emotions dance over his face. First astonishment, then confusion, and at last fear.

"What is that there? Fear?" I sniff at the air. It smells more delicious than when I first smelled it with the rat shifter. My face turns cold and calculating as I watch him.

His face turns red with fury. "Where did you learn about that?"

I give a smile. "You know."

He looks around the room, his eyes bouncing to each of us as if looking for a scapegoat or an exit to get free.

"What is she talking about, Quintan?" Natasha grows angry, standing strong at my side.

"Alexia is confused. She does not know what she talks of."

"Oh, but I think I do. Or did you betray my mother so long ago that you forgot about it? It was just like yesterday for me. I didn't forget. Not a bit. Tell them how you treated her to just get with Ian."

He runs his sweaty palms down the sides of his rotund stomach. "That was when we were younger. That was water under the bridge. I have been there for both of your parents through it all."

"Okay then, where were you the day Sera died?" I sit forward at the edge of the seat. "Where did you hide, my brother?" I stand up, the anger bringing me the strength I did not have before. "And where is my mother now? Because I know for a fact that you know exactly."

He presses out his palms, trying to calm me down. "Wait a minute, just let me think through things."

"I think you had your time to shine and had a go at things. It's time for you to be done." I step forward, gripping the chair hard to remain upright. Natasha is right there with me, just in case I need her help.

"How could you? Is this all true? You were supposed to help us; all you wanted was more power." Natasha is stung by everything. There is dejection all over her face.

"What I would give for a bowl of popcorn right now." Jazmin comments as she sits back, getting comfortable.

"You could be helpful, you know." Quintan seethes.

"After you were about to throw me under the bus. I think not." She lifts an eyebrow and gives a shake of her head. "Also, being helpful is not really in my character."

I ask her directly to confirm some things. "You are from Flit's land?"

She nods, giving me a curious look.

"You were going to show us how to navigate the dark side of this world. Is that still on the table?"

"It is," she says simply.

"Good." My eyes see Natasha's anger and feel the cold temperature off of her as she stares at Quintan. "Quintan, we will no longer need your services unless you can help, but I don't think we will need the kind of help you can offer."

"Listen here!" Quintan bellows.

"Go on," I say in a deadly, calm voice. All eyes zero in on me. My head is straight after I set my shoulders back. I would not show any weakness and would no longer be viewed that way. No one else would take advantage of my family or me. I am done being nice and confused. It's time for action and pain.

Quintan backs down, unsure. "I helped Flit with everything. We knew what was coming and had gone too many seers. We had to do what we had to do. No one is to know of his existence. It took me off guard that you knew. It wasn't supposed to be written anywhere for anyone to find. It's why I have been so close to you so that I knew the knowledge you were gaining and which to steer you away from. Flit orchestrated this whole thing. If you want to find your brother, you will have to go to him to find out. All I know is he is with the voided ones who Flit also deals with."

Gasps run around the room from everyone except Quintan and Jazmin. Somehow, I knew she was in on, if not all, of Flit's dealings, most of them.

"No one should work with the voided ones." Robert steps in, wrapping an arm around Margret, pulling her to his side, and tucking her in there as if to protect her.

"Flit works with everyone. It is why he is in the position he is in," Quintan states.

"Fine, we have to go that way anyway, but tell me this and answer truthfully, and maybe, just maybe, I will allow you to stick around."

"What?"

"What happened to Ian?"

Hurt crosses his face, and old pain resides there. His lips scrunch in thought, and he looks up at the ceiling as if resigning himself to answering. "I truly don't know."

"But you know who does." I see it there in a glint of his eye or the way he holds himself. Something is off, something he is holding back.

"Flit it all starts and comes back to him. After I helped your mother go into hiding."

"Was forced to help her go into hiding," I interrupt.

He nods, not correcting what I said, knowing it was fact. "After that, Ian was furious. He was so angry at her. Looked for her and went through everything she had done that day. He remembers me and the lost time, so it didn't take him too long to figure it out. I thought it would be sweet, and he would like what I had done so we could give ourselves a chance." He frowns.

"I am guessing it didn't." Though my voice and face stay firm, a part of me feels for him all he wanted was someone to love, like we all do.

"No," is all he states, not wanting to continue.

"You haven't seen Ian in all this time."

"I have not, and Flit will not explain what happened to him. It's as if he was shipped off never to be spoken of again."

My eyes stay trained on Quintan for quite a long time. I wasn't sure if I could trust him or not still. "You will stay here, behind in case. It will be Robert, Natasha, and Jazmin traveling with me through the dark side. That is if you guys will be okay with that."

Robert looks at Margret and kisses the top of her head, hugging her close. She envelops him in a hug and closes her eyes, enjoying the time she has now. "I will go, Zeek will also want to be going." His eyes zero in on Natasha.

She rolls her eyes at the inconvenience. "Of course, he will want to." Her eyes shoot at me. "We will talk later about that, not now." Her eyes stop me dead in my tracks from pursuing that line of questioning.

"Jazmin, I am guessing Trix will come with us."

"He will be around." She gives a sly smile. "Though knowing him, he will keep hidden most of the time. He causes trouble wherever he goes."

"I am starting to see that."

"Now hold on, you can't just kick me out of things. People look to me."

"And they can look to you here. Keep things going here while we are gone. I am not banning you entirely just away from me for a bit. Until we get some perspective and answers on a couple of things." I couldn't trust him; I was already going into unknown territory. I need to have people around me I can trust and know I could count on.

"I could be helpful; I can be useful."

"What do you know about the voided ones, then?" I question as I sit back down. All my energy flows out of me. I need to rest. Natasha helps me get back to the seat and stands beside me, watching over me.

"Just what is in the history books?"

I motion for him to continue.

"There was a union between our sides before which created voided ones. Magics did not affect them. Because of this and how they were treated, fights erupted, and deaths occured. Love made deals and betrayal destroyed walls. They were cast away to the edges of the world, or the edge of what we knew. We were never accepted, but they were by the mountain range. Many have searched for answers and the voided ones, but no one ever comes back with any tales to tell." He looks around, making sure he has everyone's attention. "There are some whispered stories of some that have dealt with them, but they are not forthcoming and scary creatures that no one wants to mess with. Flit is one of those creatures."

"He didn't seem so scary."

"You do not know him as he truly is." Quintan frowns. "It is why I haven't been open with all the information. You are still very naïve and do not know what is going on with the forged politics and deals. No one is as they appear. Most are a lot darker and scarier than you can even imagine."

Jazmin comes forward. "I can attest he can be very scary." Her eyes look down her nose at Quintan. "But not everyone gets to see all sides of a person. Only those willing to understand and stand with them, regardless, may see what is actually there."

"Margret, will you be able to watch the fire sisters while we are gone?" I ask, hoping to put them in a safe place since I did not think of them when I first came back. I was going to feel bad about that one for a while.

"That's the thing you will need them with you." Margret comments.

Robert speaks up. "We found out through them how to find Shade. Since Shade has the other fire triplet, they can zone in on him. I think it will be best to find him before we get to the Dark Court."

"I agree. We will have more cards to play with that way and potent forces. With you not having your magic, you may be seen as weak if we can get Shade on the same side. At least we won't have to worry about that part of the politics," Jazmin says.

"We will plan for that," Natasha bites out.

"When do we want to head out?" I ask.

"Once you are back to full strength, we can get going, though it should be soon." Robert nods. "Let's shoot for two days to get things and supplies together. Zeek should be back within that time and be able to go with us."

"I will let him know the plan," Natasha says calmly.

I raise my head up, surprised by that. Last, I had heard from them; she had barely wanted to be around him. What had changed?

She sees my eyes and gives a shake of her head. At that moment, my stomach makes itself known, no longer wanting to be ignored. "With that, let's get you some food and shower, then back to bed so you can rest and recharge."

"Oh, Flower, how you have bloomed. You are starting to come too all on your own." A warm, thick voice rumbles through the ruby as

I sink into the tub even more. The warmth of the water coating me fully. I just finished eating, and now I want to enjoy this time and get clean then I would rest.

"Did you miss me, Domini?" I ask.

"You know the answer to that." Ripples rush out from the ruby into the water surrounding me. "Do you want to talk about it?"

I shrug. "Blaise and I talked through some things."

"He didn't mention it."

"No, I suppose he wouldn't have." I frown.

The warm waters envelop me and feel solid around me as if he is holding me there. "If you two talked, why am I here? I would have thought he banned you from talking to me."

"Are you two being held by the same person?" I change the subject.

He raises an eyebrow in my mind's eye, as if waiting.

"He did not ban me from seeing you, just that if I needed something, I come to him first, he said he would not run me off again." I fiddle with the ruby, running my fingers over the edges and points, trying to calm myself. I close my eyes and can see him so clearly. "He confuses me at the best of times. I don't think he knows what he wants, let alone what I want. You're easier to talk to right now."

"By the end of this, I don't think you will say it is easier, little Flower." His voice rumbles around me, which causes more ripples in the water. "To answer your question, the same person holds our chains, but one of us more so."

"She must be powerful," I gulp.

"She has her ways," he sneers.

"We are going to be headed that way. Well, to the Dark Court, I think you two will be close by somewhere. We have to deal with something else beforehand, but then we will make our way there."

"Sadly, we are not kept near the Dark Court, far away, in fact, as far as possible. Though a party of sorts will be happening in the Dark Court, she takes some of us with her as her entourage. I will make sure our paths meet."

"When is the party?" I light up, happy that he would be there.

"In about three weeks' time, but guests arrive sooner sometimes."

"I will bring you what is yours." I hold the stone closer to my center, holding it there.

"That's a good girl." The water caresses me, enticing me. "If you keep the ruby with you the whole time, I will show you something spectacular when we meet."

"I have a necklace I can attach it to with other trinkets. But I can't have you distracting me the whole time," I give a husky laugh.

"Nothing we don't agree upon first," he whispers into my ear, which sends tendrils down my sides.

I lean back in the tub but almost feel him as if he is behind me. "Tell me about sirens and how you were caught."

"Sirens are close to mermaids, except we are born to the darkness, the underbellies of the sea. As youngins, we are put in dangerous waters, and if we survive, we win the chance to continue to live. My kind also lives by many rules because of this. One's that must be followed, or the chance of survival diminishes. Sirens are not at the top of the food chains in the water, but we are given powerful advantages. Our voice, for one, can help lure people and creatures as we see fit."

"I remember your voice called to me when I first picked up the ruby... but you haven't done it too much other than when we are doing something sexual."

He chuckles, and water droplets fall onto the back of my neck. "It is also used to heighten things or pull a lot of power. It helps connect me to my siren heritage to pull more power."

"So not to make me do something?"

"I'd rather get you to do things willingly and reward you for them." He gives a sly smile. I nestle between his powerful thighs and lay mine open against his. Water fingers circle my thigh, keeping it there. "You have not been in this world that long, and taking advantage of you would be too easy. I am not a villain here though my species and the side I was born to make me out to be one."

"Okay, I get it. You're basically like sexy sharks."

Laughter erupts behind me as the water is choppy. His hands slide to the inside of my knee.

"Girl, what kind of kinks are we going to uncover in you? No, not like a sexy shark."

I wave my hand at him, wanting him to bypass the dumb analogy. "What about the next question?"

"How I was trapped where I am now. It was stupid, mostly on my part. I came to her by making a deal that I thought I could win. At the time, I had already been parted from my siren skin. When we part, from our true form for too long... we... become... vicious. You having this stone pulled something from me that I had thought died long ago? The game was rigged from the start. She claimed I would not be able to get my siren form back, and if I couldn't, then I would become her warrior."

His left hand travels up between my breasts to fiddle with the necklace. "Keep these hidden wherever you go. For they may cause more trouble than help, especially mine." His right is still massaging and keeping my leg pinned to his. "I will help you as much as I am able, but remember the rules."

"Do as you say when we are together." My legs relax against his. "I remember Domini."

"We must have something in place, a word or a phrase. Even if other people hear it, we will know what it means." His hand moves down my leg as his other one tightens and pulls up on my chest toward my neck more.

"What about weather?"

"What about it?" He cocks his head to the side and holds steady, not moving, waiting for me to finish my thought.

"If you worry something is too much, ask me how the weather is. If it is bad weather, I will state so, or if it is sunny, then that is a good sign to continue. It will hide what we are trying to communicate to one another."

"You are a brilliant little Flower." His hands dip down and tease my lips.

Melting into him, I purr. "What if you don't stop when I want to stop?"

His hand travels up and tightens around my throat ever so lightly, but with a firm grasp. "That is not an option for me. I follow the rules just as much as you do. You will see. That is how trust is gained, and respect is earned." My nipples grow hard in answer to his hand around my throat. "Oh, you like that, do you?"

I try to nod, but his hand stops me.

"Yes or no, delicious Flower."

"Yes," I whisper.

Domini helps me see myself and knows what I want. Blaise leaves me with more questions to which I couldn't find answers. I would need to make a decision eventually, but I didn't want to.

"Do you want more, my Flower? Or do you want this to be a training session?" I feel his breath at my ear as his hand tightens on my throat.

"Blaise wants me to come to him for things like this." I answer as my breath comes out choppy. My nipples harden in the cool air as the warm water stirs below.

"What do you want?" He all but growls. "Bring me to the games next time with you and him to have more fun. Make things fair for you." He chuckles. His fingertips brush up from my leg all the way to my breast as he flicks his finger over the sensitive nub.

I suck in a breath as the sensation burns through me.

"I want something more real," I huff out. My body feels hot and needy, as if it hasn't really gotten what it has been craving the whole time. I squeeze my legs together, unsure if I could handle any more sensation. His hand on my breast pinches and squeezes at the tender flesh.

"I understand what you need, my Flower. You have been ever so patient when you haven't wanted to. You are such a good girl. If you promise to wear the ruby against your skin while you travel, I will ease your pain. It will take much of my power, but I want you to have something more solid and real."

"Like you here? In body." I bite at my lip as he tightens his hold on me as he does. I feel him more solidly behind my back, something warm and throbbing against me.

"Yes." He gives a throaty growl, turning my head to his. He kisses me deeply, stealing my voice and air from me. "I will be the water, but more solid, this time more real. We will be able to feel each other. For this to work, you need to keep the ruby in hand." He states as he himself comes up for air.

My fingers clamp down on the ruby, keeping it in my left hand, safe and secure. "Do it."

"When I do this, there is no going back. We will see this out to completion. Are you sure my Flower?"

I look up at him. "I'm sure." I feel the power thrum through the stone and sizzle its way up my arm.

"What's my name?"

"Domini," I respond.

"I want you gasping my voice by the end of this. You hear me?" He rasps in my ear, keeping me pinned to him. "Remember the weather if you need it."

I nod but don't say much more. I feel him solidify even more, and his arms wrap around me. His hand is heavy and warm against my neck.

"I will talk with him; don't you fret, my dear. If he gives you grief, think of me while wearing the stone, and I will come talk things out."

I whimper.

"How do you respond?" His hands draw down my body, only the tips of his fingers caressing me.

"Yes, Domini."

"That's a good girl. Are you ready for me?" He rubs himself against my lower back for emphasis, making me know he is.

I pant out. "Yes, Domini. Please show me what I am missing."

He pats his hand across my pussy, rubbing down to the smooth the hurt. "Rise a bit, little one, and I will show you just what you have been wanting."

I do what he asks; he halts me midway. Rubbing himself over my folds, he slides between my legs sitting me back.

"Lean back onto me." He takes my legs and moves them over his, so mine lay outside of each of his.

Part of me doesn't relax. I sit there fully engaged in his lap.

He massages my legs as they begin to loosen and relax. He takes a few fingers and dips them into the water, moving it in time with his motions.

"What else plagues you?" He rubs his cock against my folds but does not enter me, massaging my clit with his hand as he goes nice and slow.

The water and his attention have brought me down. I begin to get nervous. Something still holds me, though I can't put my finger on it. His were doing quite well, though. My hips move with his motions, wanting more than just the rubbing sensation.

My eyes roll back into my head, and a moan utters from my throat.

His fingers stop exploring, but he continues to rub his cock against me in time with the water.

I hiss out.

He grips my lower jaw in his large hand and forces me to meet his dark eyes. My eyes flutter open as he holds me there. "You do not go until I say you can. Do you understand?"

I nod, my body not wanting to listen to me, only to what he says.

"Tell me what holds you back. If you do, I will give you what you truly desire." He smiles as he nips at my lips.

My body leans into his, trying to kiss him, but he holds my jaw firm, keeping us barely touching. He hums a tune that is the beginning of his siren song, trying to call me forward.

"That," I sputter out, my breath shaky. "That is what bothers me."

He quirks his head. He relaxes his hand against my jaw and lets me lean back onto his full and hard chest. "My siren song bothers you?"

"Not always. Just when I am unsure if you are trying to make me do something."

"I only used it at the beginning to ensure you took the ruby and then only to relax you when you need it. While I am parted with my soul, I can't do the full force of the song."

Turning my head, I reach down, not just wanting the small bumps of his cock as the waves were batting against me. I want him fully against me. I slide my fingers down the underside of his shaft and rub myself along the top of him. He feels so good, so delicious.

"My Flower wants to bloom, doesn't she?" He forces my chin back up so we look at one another. His pupils have dilated as I continue to touch him. "I will only use the song in teasing or if needed. A request for it would also work." He gives a wicked smile.

"I accept those conditions," I whisper after a long pause. He needed something to confirm I was okay with what was about to happen. His lips crush into mine, sealing the deal. His tongue mixes with mine as his arms wrap around me. He brings one across my stomach and holds one of my breasts in his hand, brushing against the side delicately.

His other hand slides south over mine. Moving my hand aside, he taps against me a few more times before pressing himself further into my folds and juices. I am slick enough as he enters me and makes small movements with his hips, pressing himself further into me. I groan out as I feel him inch by delicious inch.

"Yes," I breathe out as I rock with him, enjoying how he stretches me to him. His kisses grow fierce as his body demands more. I roll my hips with him, wanting the same thing. His tempo increases as he goes deeper inside me, crushing me to him, and forcing me down onto his cock harder.

I brush my hands over my nipples softly. They are hard little nubs with how turned on I am. The soft brush almost causes me to come undone. Groaning out, my hips take over all on their own, dancing to their own tune.

He grips me tighter against him as he slows himself. "You better not," he threatens, looking down at me. He nips at my mouth and then at my chin as I stare at him, trying to catch my breath.

My body fights to move all on its own, not wanting to stop. He freezes inside me mid-stroke. I swivel my hips, wanting to inch down all the way. Needing the feel of him.

His arm is tight against me. He circles my throat with his free hand and holds me against him. The pressure is firm but not deadly so.

"Cease your motions." My head is directly under his chin, near his throat. I feel the vibrations up the center of my spine. The water also stops its motion. All things turn calm. Other than him, he is hard and strung oh so tight.

I cry out, needing more, wanting more. Feeling my teeth descend, my canines poke out of my mouth. I open my mouth open wide, biting at the air, frustrated. His hand tightens on my throat. Swallowing is difficult, but breathing is still okay. I concentrate and try to force my body into what he wants.

"Yes, Domini," I pant, my tooth catches on my bottom lip.

"You are so beautiful and perfect in my element." He lets his hand hold my breast up a little so he can get a better handle on my nipple. He squeezes it tight.

Screaming out, I lean against him fully, my bones liquid and giving him complete control. His hand on my throat clenches harder as he drives into me with a ferociousness that he did not have a second before. My body rolls with his as he slams into me repeatedly. My sighs become choppy and uneven. I try to quell my hips from moving in rhythm with his, but again, they start their own dance without me even realizing it. The water sloshes once again, and he pulls the warmth up high as it falls onto my breasts, their hard nubs loving the warm water as it crashes on my chest. The hand tightens more, not giving me room to breathe. As he slams into my body, my voice chokes off, and no pleasuring sounds can be uttered.

"When I lift my hand up, breathe deeply and then hold all of it in as long as you can. You will see stars from under the water once I am done with you." His low growl rumbles into me as his hips still shoot into me. My legs are as wide as they can get, letting him fully into me. "When I cut off your air supply again, hold until I take my hand off your throat, then find your release. Let me know you understand and are ready for what I am about to do to you."

My hand follows his where he is still pinching my nipple and rubs the nub in between his pinch. I throw back my head as the intense pleasure of that, plus his movements, are almost killing me.

"There you are."

His hand releases my neck. I take in a deep breath, expecting to hold it. He takes the time to widen my legs and pile into me. Which causes me to gasp out a throaty moan.

"Domini." Cutting it off, I take what little breath I can before he pushes me under the water and chokes off my air supply. He holds me tight against him as his hips move and jackknife into me. Since he had released my nipple to move my legs, the blood has rushed back into them and they are extra sensitive to the heat of the water. I brush my own hands over them as he has me locked against him, making the friction even better. His fingers are on the pulse in my neck, keeping track to ensure I am there with him. My body is strung tight as the sensations build. My body struggles against him, wanting air. He is relentless and doesn't give in and release me. I feel the waves begin to turn and brush against me in other sensitive areas. It all is almost too much. My undoing is right there at the edge. My heart slows even with his quickening movements.

The dark begins to take on colors as they flash behind my lids. I try to keep my eyes open, but dark colors surround me. My hands die down and not move against my breasts, which built things further. His hips rotate, finding a sweet spot that rubs me just the right way. He swivels that way a couple of times as he shoves me from behind up into the air, loosening his hand. I gasped as his last few pumps slammed into me and rocks me over the edge.

"Domini!" I scream. My whole-body tenses around him as he rocks against me. I feel warmth fill me, which brings tiny bursts of pleasure coursing through me. I slump back into his arms, losing all thought and the ability to control any of my body parts.

"Look at you, my dark Flower, your passion knows no bounds." He growls into my ear as he takes my weight. Slipping out of me, he tucks my legs back into the tub and lets the warm water cascade over me, keeping me warm. The water dies down from our adventure. "How are you feeling?"

Words would not come to me at first. My lids want to remain close as I nap in this man's arms. I focus on my mouth and force them to form the proper response. "Well loved," I breathe out.

"It will be better even in person. This is but a taste." His form is becoming less solid by the second. My weight is sinking to the bottom of the huge tub. "I must depart now. I wanted to make sure you were in a good place before I did, though."

My fingers continue to clutch the ruby. "Until next time," I say in parting. His body fully fades, and my limbs are not ready to catch myself. I plunge into the water and go all the way under. Causing me to sputter and flop. I do not let go of the ruby, though. Spinning around, I bring my knees up and push up, coming out of the deep water and taking a gasping breath.

"Alexia, are you okay?" Margret is in the bathroom staring at me. I didn't see any others standing behind her, but I crouched down behind the back lid of the tub, the back higher than the rest. I quickly brush my hair out of my face to better see her and try to wipe my face with water.

"Yea, I am fine!" I say in a high-pitched voice. "I just lost my footing is all."

She looks around the room, surveying everything, and notices something. "Why is there water everywhere? It looks like there is more out here than on the inside? What happened?" She rushes to the towels I have set out and gets one over to me.

I shiver. My extremities are sluggish and slow to move. I just want to sit down and fall asleep after all I endured. Hiding my hand in the water between the tub and my body to cover the ruby, I make sure it can't be seen while wrapping the towel around my body.

Looking down, I blush as I see the damage we had caused, or mostly that I had caused. "I lost my footing a couple of times..." I sputter out. "My balance is not great since getting back." I mumble some lame excuse, trying to think of something to put her at ease so she would leave and I could clean up the mess.

"All right, dear. If you say so. I will get some more towels and leave them in your room if you like." She stands close to the door, not intruding. Giving a small sniff, she freezes, backing out slowly. "Never worry, dear, we will get this cleaned up and everything situated. Once you get some more food in you, your footing will return. Just give it a few days."

I nod as she leaves. I hear her close the door in her rush. Sighing, I unwrap the towel and sink back into the warm water. It had never grown cold and still held a bite of heat to it. I wonder if Domini made sure the water would keep warm, heightening our pleasure. Sinking down, I let the water cover me, not worrying about cleaning. I worried about the next time I would see Blaise, but Domini said he would handle him.

Shaking my head, I close my eyes and focus inwardly. I want to be the one to address it and I want him to know that I am home safe, so he didn't have to worry. It is going to be a hard conversation, but one that had to be done.

"He said I could willingly call to him, but I have only done this when in dire need." I scrunch my nose, unsure of how to proceed.

Thinking of a rope or tether, I grasp it in my metaphysical hands and pull myself along the line. Hoping it would take me to where I need to go. It is flimsy and seems slippery at best; the string is rough in my hand and not nice to the touch. As I follow it forward, I soon come to a door that blocks me. The rope goes into it. Pressing a hand against the door, it is very solid and heavy.

"This must be a block that is between us, but who put it here? Was it him? Does he want me to stay out?"

I raise my fist up to knock on the door, quiet at first but more obnoxious after nothing happens from the first few knocks.

The door opens up a crack, but I can see no one through it. I try to push it, thinking it is open so I can go in. It sticks in the position. A yellow eye glows from the darkness. "Yes." A snake-like hiss echoes around me.

"Blaise?" I ask. The darkness and anger coming off of him is not something I had felt before. Could Domini have told him already, which is why he is blocking me out?

"Yesss." Something shakes behind him in a rattling noise. I look past his yellow eye, but nothing can be seen.

"What's wrong?"

"Do you need something, Minx?" The coldness dissipates as warmth flows into his throat.

He sounded less angry, but I still wasn't sure. "I wanted to let you know I am back in my own timeline."

His eye bobs in time with his nod. "That is good."

I let the rope fall from my hands, unsure what to do and not wanting to tell him about the siren if he was already in this kind of mood.

"Is that all?" He waits patiently.

"I wanted to let you know before Domini told you, but I was with him." I lose the nerve to keep quiet, so I rush to explain. "What we have is complicated on the best of days and not even something I am sure either of us wants. Domini is my choice right now and someone that I like. I know you wanted me to come to you if I needed something, but it wasn't a need. It was a craving. Something I don't think you could help me through. He could with his power," I gesture with my hands, unable to stay still through this. "Somehow, he made himself corporeal enough for us to come together."

His eye never flickers or wavers from me, but that is all I could see of him.

"I see," Is all he states.

"I still want to see where this leads, but I also need to know I have other options. I am naïve when it comes to this, and I want to make sure I am making the correct decision and not just listening to someone else because they view it as the right thing to do." Kicking my shoe, I toe the ground.

"We only agreed that you would come to me if you needed me and that if you did end up going to someone else, you would not hide that and let me know what transpired. You did everything we agreed upon. We never said that we would just be with each other." His voice is low, in a calculating tone.

"Yes. I wanted you to hear it from me before Domini talked to you. He let me know you belong to the same person. I also wanted to tell you I will head to the Dark Court soon in case you are there or can be. But if you do not want to be there, I understand that as well." I take a step back away from the door, no longer keeping it open.

"We will see, but believe me, if I am not there, it is not because you are there." A long tongue flicks out. It is forked and snake-like. He backs up further from the door, his eye almost being hidden by the shadows.

"Are you sure you are okay, Blaise?"

"I am fine enough. We will talk again another time, all right, Minx?" He is not mean, but I feel he does not want to continue talking here.

"Thank you for not pushing me out completely or not answering me at all." I say. He doesn't answer, but the door remains open. "Another night then." With that, the door closes and again is solid and in place. I press against it, testing, but it doesn't budge.

Whispering to the door. "My journey will lead to you eventually, and you will not be able to hide behind a closed door. What are you so scared of me seeing?" Giving a final tap, I dissolve out of our mental space and prepare for the coming weeks of our journey to the dark side and, eventually, the Dark Court.

Acknowledgments

I would like to thank Sarra Cannon. Her class was a big reason why I was able to get my books up and going. There is a wealth of knowledge you need to start a business, let alone write and get a book ready for publishing. She showed me the steps to take to get there, as well as the small steps needed to get up the mountain. Everything looked like it was too much and would be too hard, but she broke it out in little bite size manageable pieces and we kept at it till we were at the top! Her class is excellent for many things and one I plan retaking soon to get more in depth with the marketing. Every time I go through her videos, I feel like I learn something new. She will never realize all the people she touches and help! She is a light to this world and one that is very much needed.

Sarah Sutton is a fellow author and one I have been watching on YouTube. She shows how things have been going for her and gives tips and tricks that she does for her own career. I follow many fellow authors on Youtube, but she is one that has stuck with me for about a year and a half. She is an inspiration for me and helps me hope for my career. She again has a vast amount of wisdom mostly by trial and fire, but she does not hide them away she lets people, know so perhaps they can learn as well. I am glad I get to chat with her now and then.

Allen, I feel like I will always thank him in each of my books. He is always loving and excited about the next book. His excitement helps me and pushes me to the next level it is amazing. I have never met another person like him. This book and this series wouldn't be here today if he didn't believe in me as much as he does. My stubbornness and his belief were enough to combat the problems that this book gave me, along with the many years it took for me to figure away around the issue. We made it! Stubbornness, along with dedication to figure out the problem, is an amazing power. One I will never doubt again as I continue down this road of authorship.

As always, I thank you the reader. You all are wonderful and live in these fantastical worlds. Every once in a while we are given a special person who takes the knowledge and thoughts from a world and brings it into reality and shares it with the rest of the world. I feel like stories bring us closer together and know there are others out there that feel the same. It helps us to live in another's shoes and understand them like we couldn't ever before.

About Author

Raquel Gabrielle resides in Oklahoma with her husband, dogs and cat. She grew up loving stories so much that she even made up her own tales. Writing has helped her in many ways and continues to do so. Writing has always been there for her and something she will always fall back to when things get tough.

If she isn't writing or telling stories, you can find her hanging out with friends or traveling. She loves to see the world and all its wonders.

She mostly dabbles in Urban Fantasy but has been known to go outside the box from time to time. For more information about her book and writing journey, you can join her newsletter at www.RaquelGabrielle.com or on her Facebook author page Raquel Gabrielle

Coming Soon...
Available 2023

Don't miss the next novel in Raquel Gabrielle's A Soul Saga. Keep reading for a blurb of what book three will bring:

The picture is becoming more clear for Alexia. She now has an idea of where she comes from. But did she remember everything accurately, or was it tinged by who she was viewing things from? With what she learned, she now has a more solid idea of what her next steps will be. Her mother is alive! She also has a brother. Flit holds these answers on where she can find her family. She is headed to the Dark Court to find what she needs. What she doesn't expect is all the games and sabotage that she clearly is not ready for.
She is not alone though, along her travels with Natasha, Zeek, Robert, and Jazmin. She stumbles across a plot that her men are caught in. Domini is new and exciting, where Blaise comes with a lot of trust issues and hides behind walls. Though she has an automatic pull with Blaise, they do not fit easily together. She is realizing they both have a lot of growing to do apart and together. Domini knows how strong she is and trusts her, unlike anyone else has. Domini is her choice. They all are learning and growing together like they never knew they needed.
She will learn what secrets the Dark Court and Flit hold through it all. Or will she learn something that she never should have started down this road all along?

www.ingramcontent.com/pod-product-compliance
Lightning Source LLC
Chambersburg PA
CBHW030800210726
48290CB00002B/348